Wolf & Eagle

A Historical Novel

About Ancient Rome & Germania

By

SEAN KRUG

This is dedicated to all who have never given up on me. Especially my wife, daughters, parents, brothers, and dear friends.

Reading to children, even before they can understand words, teaches them to associate books with love and affection.

-Unknown

For rights and permissions, please contact:

Sean Krug

snl2krug@gmail.com

ABSTRACT

This story is a work of historical fiction. Although the overall major events and a few major historical persons are inserted into this story, their personalities, characters and external relationships, their actions and thoughts are all largely made up by my own imagination. All of the main characters are fictional, their acts and relationships are not intended to perfectly represent or depict an actual record of events. This book is about the lead up to the Cimbrian vs. Roman War.

Historical Reference

The Roman Republic, would grow from the city of Rome and expand through conquest across the Mediterranean. It would later become a massive empire. The Roman Empire was the largest empire of the ancient world. The Roman civilization would survive roughly a thousand years from beginning to end, the Easten half would survive another thousand years. Rome's cultural impact would survive to the modern era. This story starts 47 years prior to the birth of Gaius Julius Caesar. It is during the middle part of the Roman Republic after Rome's 2nd Punic war against Carthage. Roman territorial gains would continue to expand in territory for over the next two hundred fifty odd years.

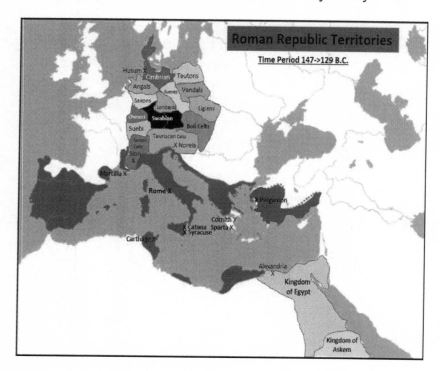

Table of Contents

Chapter I Pris

147 BC

JOTLAND GERMANIA: Modern Day's Northern Germany/Denmark

My mother's people were strong, she told me how they had survived in a place where the environment was at times harsh. A determined people, warlike against outsiders and neighboring tribes. My mother's journey, undesired as it was, would change the tribe forever.

Pris walked down a dirt road from their village towards the forest with her friend. Her friend asked "Do you think your dad will be upset that you didn't take your spear?"

Pris shrugged, "Well Lena we are just out for squirrels or rabbits, I don't want to carry too much."

Lena nodded feeling the same. "Wait!" Pris and Lena turned around and saw Jürgen and Karl, two boys about the same age, running to them from their village.

Jürgen caught up first, "Where are you two going?"

Pris responded "Hunting rabbits and mushrooms."

Jürgen said "Let's go together, more people means a better chance."

Pris looked back at the village "Will your uncle Ubel get upset?"

Jürgen shrugged, "He hits me no matter what I do. If I bring home some dinner, maybe he won't."

Pris looked at them, "You two have to stay quiet, your endless jokes will scare away the animals."

Jürgen and Karl shrugged "Of course, no worries."

They walked through the forest for a while, the boys kept talking and laughing, drawing Pris' ire. "Could you two shut up?"

Karl, who was red faced from laughing over a joke, responded "Sorry! I'm sorry…. Jurgen is just too funny!"

Pris sighed, "You promised to be quiet…." The boys nodded.

It started to rain, Pris held her hand up, "Well I guess we won't catch anything but getting wet and cold out here, at least we got some mushrooms. Let's go back."

Lena asked "Do you think our parents will be upset since we didn't catch anything?"

Pris shrugged, "We can try again tomorrow."

Lena said, "If they'll let us, they might think we cannot catch anything since we are girls."

Pris frowned, "We are just as good as any boy."

Jürgen laughed, "Pris you and Lena are tough girls but you are still girls, boys are tougher."

Pris laughed, "You think so, but the reason we didn't catch anything is due to you two laughing endlessly."

Jurgen and Karl crossed their arms, Jurgen shook his head "Not true, we haven't been THAT noisy."

Pris and Lena gave annoyed looks, Pris said "Ok if you're such great hunters you lead and catch something"

Lena agreed, "Yeah, anything."

Jurgen and Karl, started to walk ahead back towards their village and shouted backwards, "Fine! We will find something on the way home, you'll see our bravery and hunting skills!"

Pris laughed, "Great, show us your great skills!"

The boys walked ahead down the forest covered road, the girls a short distance behind the boys to keep them from hearing what they were talking about. Jurgen looked at Karl, the rain beginning to fall a little lighter. "We are almost out of the forest, if we don't find something those girls will laugh at us!"

Karl agreed "We are 13, a whole year older than they are. We have to find something!" Jurgen nodded his head seriously as Karl continued "...there has to be.... Oh my, look at these tracks! They followed the tracks that had crossed the road. Near the tree line where the fields of wheat of their village were visible, the boys spotted a huge brown bear attacking a beehive that was on a lower part of a tree trunk on the side of a connecting road. The distance from the boys to the bear was an approximate distance of about six adult men away from them.

The bear seemed intent on the hive.

Jurgen pulled out his sling, "There, if we kill that bear, we will be legends, even our parents would be impressed!"

Karl had concern on his face "I don't know, those bears are hard to kill even with spears or so my dad told me...."

Too late Jurgen had a rock in his sling and was spinning it. Karl was backing up, his face turning white.

Pris and Lena had just caught up and looked to where Jurgen was aiming.

Pris loudly hissed "Jurgen, don't shoot at that...."

Too late, Jurgen pitched the rock as he had at squirrels and rabbits many times, the rock flew fast and hard, it struck the bear on the back of his ear. The bear growled in pain and turned to see the four kids, it roared loudly as it started to charge at them.

"RUN!" Pris screamed, the four of them ran as fast as they could towards their village screaming.

In a cool dark forest Krull sharpened his arrows listening for an ominous growl he thought might announce the fearsome bear they had been hunting. As he did this, he thought about his daughter Pris. He had not slept all night, the danger his daughter had encountered still played over and over in his mind.

The sounds of the forest woke up the others in his party. Mist covered the ground, it was still fairly dark under the many layers of tree branches, making a natural umbrella blocking out most of the dawn's light, the sunlight appeared here and there in hazy beams through a thick fog... Their small camp fire brought a small amount of illumination to them. The hunters checked their gear, their arrows, swords, spears and knives, all ready. They were wearing dark leather armor as it was lighter to travel in than chainmail and it makes less sound. Their capes and other garments kept them warm in this damp environment. They had tracked the brown bear since it had rampaged near their village yesterday until it got too dark to follow.

Drenor came over to Krull and offered him water and smoked dried deer meat, his normally booming voice hushed and concerned, "Cousin, I meant to ask how Pris is?"

Krull Haas

Krull pat Drenor on the shoulder, who took a bite of deer jerky. Krull put his sharpened arrows back into his quiver, his husky voice balanced, "She had quite a scare, some bruises, but she is ok." He glanced at his other equipment double checking things and looked back at Drenor "Why did she not bring her spear as I had told her to? She can be incredibly stubborn at times not listening to me, and look what happened this time!"

Drenor let out a sigh of relief, "Well perhaps in time. What did she say happened? I was so busy fighting it, and then when we chased after it, I didn't have time to ask."

Krull motioned to the trees, "Pris and her friends went hunting for rabbits and mushrooms in the woods that morning with a few of her friends. She told me that on their way back when they were within sight of the village, they came across the brown bear as it was devouring a beehive."

Drenor shook his head as Krull continued "One of the boys apparently used his sling to propel a rock striking the bear, which enraged the bear... Pris and her friends ran for the village, going through the high crops in the fields."

Drenor concurred, "I was just collecting some water at my well when I saw the roaring bear as it chased after the screaming children."

Krull acknowledged "I was working in my garden when I first heard their screams."

"I saw you grab your spear charge at the bear solo." Drenor gave a half grin "That was brave of you cousin."

Krull raised an eyebrow "I wish I had been faster... It jumped Ubel's nephew, what was his name?" "Jurgen?"

Krull continued sighing "Yes, Jurgen he was the one who hit it with his slingshot. I don't think he will make it."

Drenor shook his head, "I saw Pris, when Jurgen was mauled and in trouble, she threw a stone at the bear."

Krull acknowledged, "Yes, I saw that too, I guess she did that to distract it. Thereupon the bear charged at her, knocking her down."

Drenor nodded, "Yeah, lucky for her, those three farmers working in the field attacked the bear with their farm tools…"

Krull grimaced "Those poor men, I saw all of it as I charged over trying to get to it. All that's left of them are mangled bodies." He sighed again. "We cannot lose any more friends to that beast; it is not afraid of attacking humans."

Drenor nodded "True. That bear would have been feasting on you or me too had Sveinn and the other warriors not arrived."

Krull closed his eyes wearily "We fought off the bear together, and together we will kill it."

Drenor nodded "Absolutely."

Krull rubbed his face, "I couldn't sleep, just kept thinking of how close I had come to losing Pris".

Drenor nodded, "I know, you treasure her more than your own life, just be careful."

Krull nodded "Pris is so strong willed and independent. When will she start to listen to me?" Krull looked at Drenor rubbing a cloth over his unique looking bow, "What a strangely shaped bow you've got?"

Drenor smiled, it's a prototype, I traded for this, the owner called it a composite bow, I will try it on this beast if I have a chance."

Krull smiled, "Ok, with this fog, be very careful what you shoot at."

Drenor gave it to him a smile "I'll just make sure to shoot at you intentionally."

Krull started laughing, "I've suspected that for years." Drenor suppressed a laugh.

Karl said "Seriously, I look forward to seeing it in action. If it works well, I want a copy of it."

Drenor nodded, smiling "I plan to make copies."

Krull looked to his men, his voice husky "Everyone ready?" The party with a collection of half-awake nods affirmed. Krull looked at each of them as he said "Ok stay vigilant, all we did yesterday was scare it away."

A young hunter asked "Why would it attack people like that?"

Krull looked at him, "Good question Rob... when bears get old, some will attack people as they know we don't run as fast as a deer."

Krull continued, "Three dead farmers, one child possibly dead or dying and then one of us in the woods last night... no more charging after it solo. Understood?"

The hunters all grunted agreement. Krull hit his right fist in his left palm saying "We must work as a team, that way we'll kill it, eat it and turn its skin into a blanket." He looked at each of them, "Alright, let's kill this beast, fan out!"

They nodded, and each somberly paid respects to their fallen friend's body as Sveinn extinguished their small fire.

Alger was the last warrior to leave with the group, his spear in hand and ax holsted on his back.

Soon the party of six headed into the woods following the paw markings that went slightly downhill. The misty fog obstructed the view to just a few yards. It was not long before they heard the sound of the bear attacking an animal, probably a deer, the terrified scream of the deer suddenly went silent. All was blinded by the misty forest, their prey awaited them somewhere out there in the mist, and they headed in its direction.

They spread out as they went towards where they thought the bear could be eating. Trees, rhododendron bushes and haziness obscured their view of the deer's body. Sounds of roaring water in the distance announced a river, those sounds echoed as they came upon what was left of the dead deer. The hunters looked around and then back at the deer.

Drenor walked up to the animal, "The blood is still warm. These bite and claw markings..." Krull nodded "Bear".

Drenor nodded "it went for the kill, but... but most of the deer's flesh is still here." He looked to Sveinn "Have you seen this before?"

Krull, Drenor and Sveinn examined the body and the paw markings in the area. As they were talking a hunter started to look at the paw tracks that led into some bushes. The mist obscured everything beyond the leaves, he followed the tracks.

Krull glazed up and yelled "Luther don't..." suddenly, a deafening roar erupted as the enormous bear leaped out from the bush and mist, landing on top of Luther, he screamed in terror swinging his ax as the bear knocked him down and bit on his shoulder. The sounds of bones crunching under its jaws caused Luther to scream.

Dietrich and Zetkin rushed at the bear with their spears ready, the bear violently swatted the closest one with both paws, the left paw pushed the advancing spearhead away as the right paw scratched across the attacking hunters' face. Zetkin fell down screaming clutching his bloody face.

Alger, his way now clear, stabbed at the bear but missed as the bear deflected his spear away with another swipe of his left claw, the right claw followed at Alger hitting him so hard that he was thrown a few feet onto the ground, after a moment Alger rose pulling out his ax.

Dietrich pulled the spear in and stabbed at the bear's mouth, it avoided the thrust, catching the side of the spear pole in its mouth, biting the spearhead off and spitting it out. At the same time an arrow flew from Drenor but the bear's movement caused him to miss.

The bear stood on its hind feet roaring triumphantly looking at which hunter to attack next. Dietrich dove, dodging another swipe by the bear, he picked up the spear that the slashed face hunter had dropped, he charged towards the bear making it back up, thus providing protection for his injured friends.

The bear swung and hit Dietrich, sending him flying, knocking his head on a tree and he didn't move. The bear growled in victory, but was suddenly hit by an arrow in the neck fired by Drenor.

Krull and Sveinn came forward adding protection to the injured, their spears at ready. The huge growling bear rushed at them, its roar deafening in its furious attack.

The men poked at the bear with their spears as Drenor rapidly shot it with three more arrows hitting the bear with each.

Alger ran in from behind shouting a yell with his brandished ax, the bear hearing him coming turned and scratched at him, the claws landed on his leather armored chest, knocking him down.

Drenor. Krull and Sveinn attacked the bear at the same time, stabbing it and Drenor shot another arrow into it. The bear, having received dozens of wounds from their spears and arrows, howled in pain from its many wounds.

The bear turned to run between multiple trees knocking away smaller bushes, howling as it went towards a rocky river that was down the side of a ridge,

Sveinn stayed with the wounded as Krull, Drenor and Rob chased after it. The bear found and went onto a massive fallen log that stretched across the narrow river, the mist obscured sight about halfway across the log. Krull, the fastest runner, could see the bear climb onto the log and go across.

Krull climbed onto the log to follow it and yelled "Come here!" The bear suddenly roared and Krull felt the log vibrate as the bear had turned to attack him, the roar was deafening as suddenly Krull saw a dark spot in the mist rapidly leaping at him.

Krull reacted without thinking, putting his spear end in the base of a tree branch aiming his spear tip at the center of the now fully visible and airborne bear, the spear stabbed right through the bear's heart as it crashed into Krull, it died instantly as the spear snapped and they both fell into the river below.

Drenor and Rob arrived just as they saw the impaled bear crash into Krull, from this angle they saw that the bear's path had been blocked by dead branches that stuck out like spikes.

Drenor and Rob pulled Krull out of the river, with their help he crawled onto the bank of the river, not knowing if his bones were shattered, he looked at them and they all started laughing.

Drenor and Rob retrieved the bear's dead body out of the river. After this Rob and Sveinn helped the two wounded party members, while Krull and Drenor returned to their village to fetch horses, wagons and more people to harvest and haul the bear's meat and useful body parts.

That night Krull and the group celebrated being alive with their families and village.

Chapter II Krull

147 BC

My mother and her father loved each other, and yet they had a complicated relationship.

A rooster crowed as it always did at sunrise, it was answered by other roosters in the distance from other small farms. Krull Haas opened his eyes and felt pain throughout his body. It took a long time for him to sit up, he suppressed the urge to groan.

Finally sitting up, he saw the top of Rúna, still asleep, her head on her pillow, her long arms positioned comfortably on top of their blanket. Krull leaned over feeling more pain as he kissed her head he whispered "Good morning love" her rhythmic breathing so pure and peaceful. Krull happily thought about how wonderful the night before had been. His body ached from the encounter with the bear, but the grog and mead had helped the many new scratches and bruises that he wore.

Krull turned and rose quietly out of bed. Totally naked, he walked past their clothing that was placed offhandedly on the wooden floor, he looked at his thatched roof, thinking he would need to work on it within this season. Krull's long red hair and beard made for quite a sight.

Krull went toward his daughters' room, he put on some clothes as he went, next he pushed the door's curtain over and looked in. A wave of contentment went through him, seeing them both asleep under the straw ceiling; Pris' blonde hair was laying neatly on her pillow, Tuli's red hair was underneath her. The world was right. I live to keep you safe. That bear will never get either of you, he thought. Krull next went down the wooden stairs, grabbed a metal bucket and went outside to relieve himself in an outhouse by a tree.

Finished, he next went to their chicken house in their garden. Seeing 6 new eggs, Krull grabbed them and put them into his bucket. He next went over to the well, lowered another bucket that was at the well and retrieved it full of water. Krull poured the water into the metal bucket that contained the eggs returned inside and started a fire in the cooking place. While the fire was growing, he placed the metal bucket on the metal cooking surface. Placing the bucket on the metal slab that was being heated by the fire, Krull soon had the eggs in boiling water.

Soon an appetizing smell invigorated him as he cooked. He pulled out a cloth wrapped bag of smoked bacon that he had traded for from his neighbor and placed the bacon on a second smaller pan, after that was cooked, he placed the food on plates as Pris, his eldest 12-year-old daughter, came downstairs in her plain nightgown.

Pris and Krull saw each other, Krull saw some bruises that had happened when the bear had hit her and sent her flying.... Krull smiled at her, feeling proud of her bravery and relieved that she was alive.

Pris returned his smile, *Papa at least still loves me*. She thought her blonde hair jumbled as she went outside to

24

their backyard to relieve herself. As she opened the wooden door to go out, she saw his hunting gear, a leather backpack, his bow and a quiver of arrows that were all placed by the door.

After she returned from outside, Pris came over to her dad with a quizzical look on her face, her silvery voice questioning "Papa, are you going today?"

Krull looked over, "I have a meeting with the town elders this morning, later I will go hunting with Drenor."

Pris raised an eyebrow, "I thought we were supposed to all go to the beach to find oysters and seaweed for grandma Fiona not you go back out with your cousin!"

Krull nodded, "You and Tuli will do that. Mamma and I have to speak with the elders, there is a disagreement about whether we need to build a longer fishing dock or extend the village wall to give more room for new houses. Mamma will drop you and Tuli at Grandma Fiona's. It might take a while, so Grandma will take you both to the beach. Mamma will later meet you there."

Pris put her hands on her hips "And what about you?"

Krull shrugged, "Our village needs more meat, so after the meeting with the elders, I need to go hunting."

Pris crossed her arms as she shook her head ``No, there are other warriors who can hunt. You just got back and promised that we would spend more time together!"

Krull acknowledged, raising his brow as he glanced at the ceiling, next he looked back at her "We are, and we will." Pris gave him a sideways look, Krull continued "Our village needs more food. That one bear is not enough, not for everyone, and I am the best hunter, you know that."

Pris frowned, her arms still folded "Papa you're great, so everyone says, but you're hurt I can tell just by how you are staggering like an old man."

Krull became angry "You should not have gone hunting yesterday for rabbits without bringing at least a spear like I had told you! Jurgen might still be alive and now the village thinks you are acting out of place!"

Pris frowned. "It's not my fault Jurgen attacked the bear, he wanted to show that he was brave."

Krull was annoyed, "You are a girl, you must know your place like all in our village. Girls should not go hunting unless they have a male escort."

Pris' face became pink "We did have a male escort, that is what got us into trouble!" Krull looked shocked; but Pris continued "You cannot go hunting in this condition."

Krull said nothing, *"she's right",* he thought.

Pris continued her voice becoming softer "Papa, Drenor said that we almost lost you to that bear, I don't want you to die."

Krull turned to her, "Pris, I won't die, but if I do not hunt, others might take twice as long and maybe still come back with nothing." Pris was about to argue, Krull continued "My place is as a hunter and leader. Aside from potatoes and wheat, Meat and fish are the only things we can be sure are out there... You are still a child; you will stay here where it is safe."

Pris waved her finger at him "But you promised to teach me horse riding after the beach."

Krull stopped and lowered his head thinking through his hazy hangover about the family dinner last night and his conversation he had with Pris while he had drunk mead to kill his pains. He said "Ah shoot, I did make that promise... Tell you what, we are low on meat... but a promise is a promise, we can do horse riding together tomorrow."

Pris shook her head "No, I want to go with you papa, I...."

Krull shook his head "No, first I need to give my condolences and apologies to Ubel about Jurgen. I will not take you hunting until I am sure you will listen to me."

Pris stamped her foot and yelled loudly "Why am I not surprised? It's not my fault! Arrrrrww! Stonehead!"

Pris went upstairs before Krull could finish his statement.

Krull's face showed a flash of anger, but he sighed and shrugged, hearing her shout "You are the worst papa ever!" *Was it this challenging for my parents with me and my brothers? Pris must learn to listen to me, it's her place, it is the natural way of things. Jurgen might not have been killed by her, but he would still be alive if they had not been out there. If I take her out and we run into another bear, a pack of wolves or a cougar and she's not ready or worse argues with me out there....*

Krull could hear the floorboards squeak announcing his wife Rúna's rise from bed. Rúna whispered to Pris just quietly enough that he could not hear it easily. He imagined Pris saying that he was being unforgiving and overprotective. Krull looked upstairs, *Rúna is probably telling her to cheer up, or that men are hard headed, or that I am stubborn as an ox. All true he thought with a grunt, but that is the world we live in.*

Tuli, his younger 7-year-old daughter, had come downstairs. Tuli, had curly bright red hair, and unusual for most people she had one blue eye and one brown like her grandmother.

Tuli's normally singsong voice was full of concern "Papa, are you angry at Pris?"

Krull knelt down "No, I love her like I love you and Mommy, but I don't think that she is ready to come along with me, it's dangerous out there and I don't want her getting hurt. There are things beyond our walls that would hurt you and Pris, I must protect you. You and Pris must stay with Mommy today."

Tuli started to look sad whispering "But you told us...."

Krull opened his arms "Do you know what the best part of my day is?" Tuli shook her head, "It is when I am able to return to hug you or Pris or mommy. I am the luckiest man alive because I have all three of you in my life. Throughout the day or night, whether you are awake or asleep, I know how lucky I am. Believe me I do not enjoy leaving any of you for an instant, but these hugs will protect me so give me a strong one."

Tuli hugged her father tightly. "Can you do me a favor?" Tuli widened her blue and brown eyes waiting "Please go and tell Pris that I love her?"

Tuli smiled, nodding as she went upstairs. Tuli found Pris sitting at the top of the stairs with her arms folded around her knees, her head resting on her knees.

Krull could hear from the floorboards that Rúna had returned to her bedroom and was probably looking at her clothing options.

Tuli came over and whispered into Pris' ear "Papa says he loves you."

Pris raised her head looking at Tuli and smiled a little, "I know."

Pris thought *"How can I get papa to trust me? It wasn't my fault Jurgen died, I wanted adventure, to show I can be as helpful, as useful as a boy…. But then this happened"*.

Tuli smiled as she whispered "It is ok Pris, Papa will come home."

Meanwhile, Krull had placed the boiled eggs and smoked bacon on his girls' plates. He next covered them with another plate and called upstairs announcing breakfast was ready.

Krull devoured a couple eggs with some bacon and bread, washed it down with water before he walked to the door to grab his gear.

Pris came downstairs with Tuli behind her. Opening the door, he looked back and saw Pris and Tuli back at the stairs with unhappy expressions on their faces. Krull then saw Rúna come down as well, he blew them kisses and waved goodbye, they waved back.

Krull had been raised in a family of all brothers, no sisters, so raising girls was a new experience for him in dealing with the intricacies of girl relationships. As Pris grew from a young girl into a preteen seemingly overnight, Rúna and Krull noticed that her independent nature was increasing. Pris often surprised Rúna and Krull with her daring, resilient, resourceful, ambitious and adventurous nature, who in her headstrong ways occasionally and unintentionally caused her parents anxiety.

Wild or calm, whether fishing or on land, the people of Husum village had been crafted by the ocean's presence. The cold wind, waves and weather that blew inland. It was situated near a bay on a hill from which one could see several large islands that made lovely formations at sunset. Their village population was around 2,000 people all living in wooden homes with thatched straw roofs. Husum was surrounded by a thick wooden wall made from cut timber which was wide enough for men to walk along the top's catwalk space. There was a gravel road that went from the backside of Husum down a well-traveled stone path to a fishing hut and small dock in a small bay. Another road from the front gate connected to the forests encompassing the North-South gravel road.

After dropping their girls at her mother's, Rúna caught up with Krull at the Elder's meeting. After hearing everyone's viewpoint she gave a few suggestions and her thoughts on each, which seemed to make everyone happy. Krull and Rúna mounted his horse soon after, he then took her to the beach followed by two of his guards.

As soon as they arrived, they kissed, then Rúna walked to the beach. Krull stopped by Ubel's home with his warriors to pay his condolences about Jurgen. Approaching the door, he could hear Ubel and his wife Saxa shouting with each other, some furniture being thrown about. Krull pounded on the house's door and the commotion ceased.

A few moments later, Ubel opened the door, his voice deep and sonorous "Yes?"

Krull covered his concern "Ubel, I have come to pay condolences about Jurgen, I understand he passed last night." Ubel nodded but said nothing.

Krull asked, "I heard some shouting, is everything ok?"

Ubel took a breath, "Saxa is upset about Jurgen, I told her that he was old enough to decide his own fate. He was stupid like his mother."

Krull looked at him sideways, "He was a brave boy, who tried to impress you, I gather."

Ubel snorted; "The boy was a fool. Is there anything else you want to ask? I am dealing with my wife's swinging emotions."

Krull looked at the house, "I shall leave, you have my condolences." Ubel went back inside, his door slammed shut. Krull rode off feeling concerned about what was going on. "*I will have to look into what's going on there.*"

Back at the beach, Rúna saw her girls building a sandcastle. with her mother, their grandma Fiona laughing with them. Fiona, Rúna's mother, was their town's healer, shaman and soothsayer. Whenever she needed ingredients for her medicines, they would hunt for what was needed. This typically meant seaweed, oysters and sea salt at the beach or often mushrooms, and herbs at the nearby hills.

Fiona would always make encouraging remarks in her kind croaky voice such as "Rúna, Pris' blond hair is so lovely" or "Pris' dark blue eyes match her clothing well." and "Oh Tuli has shiny mixed colored eyes like mine!" Fiona used these chats with the girls to mix in information about which flowers are medicinal or which mushrooms are edible or poisonous.

32

Pris and Tuli loved these excursions as it gave them opportunities to explore and ask questions of their grandma. Today they enjoyed the beach, the waves that came in washing their feet, the familiar sounds of crashing and spreading water mixed with the sounds of seagulls echoing across the landscape.

The Summer weather had a nice blue sky, gentle wind and the ocean made for a perfect day. By the time Rúna arrived, Pris and Tuli were getting ready to seek oysters with Fiona.

Fiona smiled at Rúna when she arrived, "I love seeing them playing in the sand with their blonde and red hair blowing in the wind." Rúna smiled, "Yes, they're my treasures."

Fiona continued "They are turning into such lovely ladies.I love spending time with them, and since your dad passed seeing them gives me happiness".

Rúna smiled, "Thanks mom for sharing your time and knowledge with them and with me." The old woman shook her head smiling. "Rúna I taught you the healing arts just as my mother had taught me. It has always been that way."

Rúna smiled, "Yes, and thank you for teaching Pris" Rúna looked back at Pris "This morning Pris and Krull had an argument, I could hear them from my bedroom. Pris was so upset, how has she been with you?"

Fiona smiled, "Just fine."

Fiona looked back at the girls and nodded, "Yes, she is a strong willed one. The boy Jurgen died in the bear attack, much the pity. We should encourage her towards less dangerous pursuits."

Rúna hesitated, "I have told her so a few times, but Pris has ambition and determination."

Fiona agreed, "True." The ladies were all dressed in colorful cloth dresses that Fiona had weaved for them which came down to their ankles. Each had cloaks that could protect from the wind or rain if needed, Fiona had brought a basket, hand shovels and a sack into which they put oysters. They dug oysters out of the wet sand together. When they had enough, they decided it was time to take a break and eat some lunch. They walked over to where Pris and Tuli had made a sandcastle.

Seeing them approach, Pris walked over and they began to help her mother lay out a large cloth to sit on.

Rúna opened her basket of fruits, boiled eggs and a canteen of water. The wind started to pick up a little, so Fiona helped her with the blanket by sitting on it.

Runa called "Pris, Tulli, come eat!"

The girls joined them. Runa wiped sand off their hands with a wet hand cloth.

Pris looked at her mother "Can you tell me more about our family? Why has father not told me much?" Rúna didn't quickly respond so Pris asked "Mother, why does father have so much authority outside of the house?"

Rúna looked at her, understanding "We are a noble family because of your father. Krull's family has been in charge of our village for a couple generations. His grandfather was a brave warrior who helped win a war against a tribe to the South. Since that time Krull's family has ruled our village"

Pris listened then asked "How did you come to marry papa?" Rúna smiled, "My father was an advisor to our King Urix, I also worked for the King before I married. After my father died, the King arranged my marriage to Krull. I had no choice about it, but I quickly fell in love with him."

Tuli finished eating and ran over to pick up a stick and started drawing in the sand.

Pris looked back at her mother "Does that mean that papa can do whatever he wants?"

Rúna laughed, "Your papa, Krull Haas, is our village chief, but our village is but one of many of our King's tribe, he has limits."

Tuli called to Pris to show her the sand drawing so Pris ran over to her.

Rúna was silent for a while as she and Fiona ate, while occasionally watching her two girls. Fiona asked "Rúna, what are you thinking about?"

Rúna said "My life with Krull"

Fiona touched Rúna's arm "Everything good?" Rúna smiled "I sometimes think about my marriage. Krull is younger than me, by a few Summers" Fiona smiled "True, but it all worked out. He loves you, you soon were pregnant with Pris and then again a few years later you gave Krull Tuli." Rúna agreed "Krull is a happy man. Krull surprised me early in that when time allows Krull enjoys wood working to help the people of the village.".Fiona nodded, "His father knew that our village needed everyone to work together. I have long watched Krull use carpentry when he was not making big decisions or hunting."

Rúna smiled, "Since we married, carpentry always makes him happy, it is a way for him to connect with all the people of our village and stay busy." Fiona smiled "That might be true Rúna, but his main happiness is you, his family, then hunting or enjoying food. You got lucky marrying him."

Rúna blushed a little nodded. Fiona smiled "Well then…" she stood slowly up, "I feel recharged, shall we collect some seaweed while the tide is still low?"

Rúna smiled nodding and got up, they collected seaweed in the surf.

As Fiona and Rúna collected seaweed, they also watched the girls while they worked. Fiona looked over and saw her daughter's face, "What's wrong Rúna?"

Rúna looked to be in deep thought, she looked at her mom "I am torn between the desire to let my daughters be the person they desire to become and the roles the world has expectations for them to play."

Fiona looked at Rúna, "Such were my concerns as well, but you and soon your daughters will become the women they are meant to be regardless of what the world thinks."

Rúna nodded "Krull really treasures the time he has with his daughters." Rúna thought *It is a simple but more or less happy life which I treasure.* "Yet, I notice that Krull's absence has caused Pris to act as though I am the only parent to listen to seriously. I'm the only one who is always around and the one who normally feeds the children. I need to get Pris and Krull together more. Pris loves nature, and we love how Pris enjoys exploring along the ocean's shoreline or in the forest to find things."

Fiona sighed, "Well perhaps you should speak with Krull about your concerns?" Rúna nodded. After they had collected enough oysters and seaweed, they returned home to the village to prepare dinner.

Early the next morning Fiona awoke before dawn with shock, *What an awful vision*! It was so vivid. Hurrying outside she entered a misty fog as she hurried down to the bay next to the wooden fisherman's dock and started putting her hands in the water, she next put her wet hands on the dock, all the while men in fishing boats stared at her blankly. Fiona looked at her handprints for a moment, seeing it she gasped, Fiona hurried to Krull and Rúna's home. The dawn was rising as Fiona arrived at Krull and Rúna's home to knock loudly on their door.

A sleepy looking Rúna came to the door "Yes mother, what is it?"

Fiona said panting "Daughter, I.... I had a vision of Pris, she was surrounded by shadowy figures. Something may happen to her in which she will need survival & fighting skills. Have your husband Krull teach her his arts of hunting and battle."

Rúna was alert "Is this something she will need soon" Fiona responded "I cannot say dear, Pris will be in great peril in her life, I saw a blur of visions of suffering and death all revolving around her. I can only say for sure that hunting and fighting skills will be vitally important for her survival."

Rúna agreed, normally for girls such skills were optional. "Thank you, mother, I will make sure Krull teaches her." Rúna shuddered wondering what it was that her mother saw. "It must have been a terrifying vision for you to rush here so early to tell me that."

Fiona nodded, "I woke up before the dream ended covered in sweat, so I cannot be sure about the ending. I must return to the forest for some mushrooms and special herbs, I wanted to let you know before I left"

Fiona gave Rúna a kiss on her cheek before she hobbled away, staff in hand towards the gate.

Rúna watched her leave before she returned inside her home, putting a new log in their home's fireplace. She went outside, fetched water from the well, before she returned to make some tea.

Krull's familiar comforting husky voice called to her, "Good morning dear" Rúna smiled, turning around "Good morning

Krull". Krull looked slightly down into her eyes, Rúna my wife, you are one tall woman." Krull thought *You're almost as tall as me, my lovely wife, your intelligence and wit, your blonde hair, I feel in a lovely trance with you love. I hope we can have another child.* Krull smiled a moment but sensing his wife's concern Krull asked "What's wrong?"

Rúna told him about her chat with Fiona.

Krull quietly listened, occasionally scratching his bearded chin. When Rúna finished he said "Very well, I will start training Pris daily".

Rúna asked "Do you think Pris is ready?"

Krull nodded, "Pris is a strong one, she is starting to become a woman, time for her to grow up." He looked up then refocused on Rúna's face. "Darling there is something else I must speak with you about."

Rúna focused on her husband who said. "I went to Ubel's home the other day to pay condolences to Ubel about Jurgen's loss. it seemed odd at the time when I would think Saxa would be consoling Ubel, I overheard a loud argument and sounds of a possible fight going on."

Rúna's face became concerned. "Have you seen Saxa at the market or in the village recently?" Rúna shook her head. "Ok next time you see her give her a look over and ask her how things are going." Rúna nodded her head.

When their children had come down for breakfast, Rúna looked at Pris "You are to go train under your father in how to use a sword and how to use a bow. Eventually he will take you hunting to teach you survival skills. Learn what he shares with you, and it will be a way for you both to connect."

Pris raised an eyebrow "What? I want to meet my friend Lena. For how long will we be out?"

Krull said "A typical hunt takes 1 to 3 days. Better if Lena stays home."

Pris stammered "Why not?" as she played with her breakfast of soup. "Why can't I bring a friend?" Krull shook his head, "I will need to focus on teaching you, if you have a friend with us, it will be harder to teach you." Pris was going to object but Rúna looked at her and so she just nodded her head. After she finished her breakfast Pris went upstairs with Tuli following her.

Krull looked at Rúna "Pris is perhaps the most creative, opinionated, headstrong and independent girl I've ever known." Rúna smiled, "But she loves you." Krull nodded "Tuli is perhaps the sweetest." Krull asked "Rúna, I was raised in a firm disciplinarian style to raise children to respect their parents." Rúna asked "Did that work?" Krull shrugged "I do not believe that harshness, fear and intimidation is the best way to raise a child. I think that they should be like you Rúna, a strong woman. Rúna blushed as Krull continued, "I have been thinking of the recent bear attack and with Pris' independent tendencies I wonder if I should be a little firmer." Rúna touched his arm, "You are a good father, continue doing what you have been doing. Fair but tough on things that matter."

From that morning going forward, after breakfast each morning Krull trained Pris in the way of hunting, tracking, survival techniques and swordplay. They would practice swordplay with wooden swords and archery. Over these days Rúna saw Saxa from a distance a couple times across the market, but each time Saxa would disappear into the crowd.

Krull was at this time focused on teaching Pris how to do archery with Rúna's bow, and how to throw a knife. Krull was happily surprised by how naturally Pris took to the sword and bow. Pris learned how to track animals and practiced her archery skills by shooting rabbits and squirrels with her bow. Krull taught Pris ways of predicting where one's sword should be striking in a series of practice maneuvers

Krull would say "If you panic in battle, you have already lost. The first rule of battle is to never panic."

Krull practiced with Pris using wooden swords in their yard. "First strike to the opponent's head's left side while sidestepping right. Good. Next, the opposite side, good. Alright, now strike to the left while stepping to your right, now the opposite. Good. Now stab to the center, followed by a circle overhead and come down on the opponent's head. Good."

Krull handed her wooden swords and practiced with her in which they would counter each other in attacks and blocks.

Before long they were able to do the practice while circling each other, their wooden swords cracking as their blades connected.

Krull next had Pris practice her sword skills against him while mounted on a horse, finally he took Pris to a hill top to show her how to fight effectively facing uphill and effectively facing downhill.

They sparred and Krull knew Pris was now sufficiently skillful with her sword that she could protect herself in a fight.

Before returning home, they sat at the edge of a cliff watching the sunset going into the sea, Krull turned his gaze from the Sunset to look at her "This is a dangerous world, but you have learned well." Krull pulled out his real sword, and held it showing her the metal blade, "Always remember: When we cannot trust men or women or beasts, this…" he pointed to the blade "…This we can trust."

Chapter III Rúna
147 BC

My Grandfather had trained my mother to be ready for the wild, little could he have known the cost of these actions.

Krull's pride for Pris' dedication and desire to excel in these skills was immense. He felt that she was ready watching Pris fire arrows in target practice as her arrows all hit inside the small center ring. Rúna and Tuli watched and clapped at each shot.

Krull scratched his beard, "Very good Pris. It is time to prepare for our hunting trip and get you a proper bow." Rúna smiled, "Great, I need to buy some yarn to make a quilt, so let's all go to the market together."

Tuli cheered as Pris excitedly jumped in the air knowing she had impressed her parents. Enjoying the sunny day, they walked from their home towards the market. Tuli walked closely behind Pris, which Pris waved her away, finding the company a little annoying.

Arriving at the market gate, Alger and Rob stood casually at the entrance. They nodded to Krull as the family entered the market. It was located in a large open grassy space that was in the center of the town used for big gatherings, musical events and celebrations. Today the area was full of small tents that were all selling privately made goods; everything from handmade clothing, beddings, candles, wood work, crafted soaps, elixirs, food venders, yarns, blankets, clothing and fortune tellers. Knowing that Drenor,

Krull's cousin, made and sold great bows, Krull and Pris first went to his tent first while Rúna and Tuli shopped for yarn.

Drenor had several bows laid out on his table at his tent. Drenor saw them coming his voice boomed, "Ah our fearless bear killer! Hello cousin!" They shared a quick handshake and half hug, "Great to see you all! What can I do for you?"

Krull described how they wanted to buy Pris a new bow. Drenor waved his finger in the air, "I have just what you need. I made copies of my own!"

Krull smiled "Great, I remember your powerful bow!"

Drenor smiled, waving to his bows, "All of these bows are from Oak trees. the design is a little different, something I came across and have been experimenting with." These bows are made with a fusion of materials that have significant reflex, sort of a composite style of bow.

Krull picked one up, "These are like yours from the hunt; really different! Where did you come by this design?"

Drenor smiled "The guards of that Thracian trade caravan that came through had them; do you remember?"

Krull smiled, "Of course."

Drenor continued "One of the guards loved our mead and I admired their Egyptian made bows, so I traded 5 barrels of mead for one of their bows. I next spent weeks analyzing it and have created these copies. As you saw, they are much more powerful than our local bows."

Krull looked at one that had a black colored rod, "So tell me more about how they're made."

Drenor pointed his finger in the air, "They are made of the three layers: horn, oak wood, and deer sinew; on the inside of the bow is bone from deer, the middle is wood and the face is made from sinew skin of the deer. Like mine, these bows have a double recurved shape. I guarantee they will fire arrows with about twice the power of a normal bow."

Krull's eyes lit up as he rubbed his hands, "Incredible as they are a little smaller in size than our normal longbows."

Drenor put his hands on the table, "Yes, they are easier to handle on a horse too."

Krull's eyes darted to Drenor and again back to the bows "I will have to buy two, one for Pris and another for me." Drenor smiled, "Excellent!"

Rúna and Tuli returned from buying yarn.

As Drenor smiled at Krull and Pris as he pointed with his hand, "Let me introduce you to your new bows. I want to teach you about the types of woods used, and how to handle and maintain them."

Tuli suddenly saw Fiona in the market and waved to her grandmother who came over for a hug, she turned to Rúna

"Buying your girls things? You and Krull are so good to them. I see you're buying her a bow, that's great."

Rúna nodded, "Can you tell me more of your vision?"

Fiona shook her head, "There is not much more, the dream has reoccurred, but each time it has Pris in danger, in the woods with shadowy figures as they chase her…. Krull is good to teach her his skills."

Rúna agreed "I just hope Pris will listen to him and his hard headed way of speaking…" Fiona grinned at that, seeing Krull was busy talking to Drenor about the arrow selection.

Rúna continued, "Pris often teases her dad about things. She instantly reminds him saying "" Papa, aren't you supposed to…."""

Fiona raised an eyebrow, "Krull doesn't get upset?"

Rúna shook her head, "No, Krull usually just nods, responding "Ah yes, thank you love".

Fiona laughed, "Such a kind father and husband, you are truly lucky Rúna." She confessed, "Krull is a wonderful father and husband. As to Pris, she seems to love to order Krull around, and she is full of endless questions."

Rúna gazed at her children, "Tuli is loving like me, Pris is more like Krull, adventurous, strongly opinionated and talkative. Tuli is patient, quiet and dependent on us. Pris carries a desire to learn as much as she can about the world."

Just then Saxa, Rúna's friend, appeared out of the crowd walking towards Rúna, Fiona and Tuli.

Drenor saw Saxa in the corner of his eye and felt longing as he gazed at her. Saxa was wearing a cloak over her head which he assumed was to protect her fair skin from the sun. Saxa was a beautiful 25-year-old redhead, she was fairly tall and always carried a happy disposition.

Drenor smiled broadly at her thinking he saw through her cloaked head that she smiled back to him. Suddenly he looked up at the sky, his face blushed. *What are you doing? She is married, he thought.*

Saxa had been Rúna's friend since childhood; she had married Ubel Trauben through arrangement. Ubel, her husband, was a warrior in the village, or so Drenor had heard. Damn, if only our stars had aligned differently! Krull saw his cousin's gaze and thought Sad that you had not asked her first cousin, Ubel's parents had arranged that union when they were children....

Krull pointed to two quivers of arrows "We will take those bundles too" Drenor nodded, "Absolutely." composing himself, the presence of Saxa still on his mind.

Seeing Saxa approach, Fiona asked Tuli if she wanted to see the puppies at the next tent, so Fiona took her there.

Saxa greeted Rúna, "Hi Rúna, it's good to see you." Rúna turned to her and on seeing her was immediately concerned. There was a bruise around her right eye which she had been trying to cover with her long hair. "Saxa it is

47

good to see you too, we are..." Rúna looked at her intensely, "Are you alright? What has happened?"

Saxa looked away, turning the faded bruise away from Rúna's view. Saxa spoke looking away from Rúna "I was sleeping next to Ubel... he had a bad dream in his sleep he struck out for no reason."

Rúna looked at Saxa hard, gently holding Saxa's shoulders and looked over her friend "Saxa, are you being truthful with me?"

Saxa had put her hand on Drenor's tent table, Rúna glanced down at her hand and found another mark the shape of a hand "What is that mark on your forearm?"

Saxa looked away, "It was my fault... You know me, I am always very opinionated about where I like things. Well, I knew Jurgen liked Pris, I had encouraged him to spend more time with her, he had liked her a lot. Ubel thought that I was partly to blame for Jurgen's death. Ubel was drinking last night, he started complaining that if I hadn't encouraged Jurgen he would still have someone to play drinking games with. I told him that wasn't fair, that he was being a rude drunk and he snapped."

Rúna, horrified, confirmed "He beat you?" Saxa nodded, "First with his hands, then after throwing me down whipped my back with his...." Saxa looked at her embarrassed, "with his belt." Saxa started shaking, a few tears ran down her face "I... I should not have enraged him."

48

Rúna was in shock, before she could say anything, Saxa turned and hurried away into the crowd, Rúna called after her, "Saxa don't go, we need to talk about this!"

Saxa shook her head, she darted her hand inside her cloak, Saxa turned and hastily hurried off. A look of anguish passed across Rúna's face, *did I act too directly? Should I have avoided the issue?*

Fiona hobbled over to Rúna with her staff. She had seen Saxa rush away, she saw Rúna bring her hands up covering her mouth. As Drenor was helping another customer, Fiona asked Tuli to go to Krull, when Tuli had run over to them Fiona asked Rúna "What was that about?"

Rúna looked at her mother "Saxa has a bruise on her eye, she admitted that Ubel hit her and I noticed another bruise on her arm. When I started to ask about it, she became evasive and fled."

Shaking her head Fiona said "I immediately suspected that something was wrong." Fiona looked in the direction that Saxa had run, then she looked back to Rúna "We have to tell Krull. Saxa was lucky this time, next time could be worse."

Rúna accepted this advice, "Could you take our girls to your home, I will come for them after I have spoken with Krull."

Fiona nodded and they turned to Krull and their girls. Krull looked so content, he smiled as he gazed at his daughters. It was always the same, they were his treasures. Rúna knew Krull was ready to do whatever needed to be done to protect them. Pris was always full of questions for her and Krull about how to do things. As independent as Pris was, she occasionally showed her powerful love for her dad through unexpected hugs. Rúna thought about how Pris loved to ask how to do things and a constant battle of the wits.

Common conversations between them were "Papa, I want to see the world, and try new things!" to which Krull would reply "Sure someday, not now." or "Papa what kind of food do people eat down South?" to which Krull would reply "Nasty things." or "Are there any lands across the seas?" to which Krull would reply "Probably, someday we may know" or "Papa, can ships sail anywhere?" to which Krull would reply "Only if sea monsters don't swallow them" or "How can ships navigate across water or people find their way across land" to which Krull would reply "There are ways, but you're not ready yet." or "Do animals speak to each other?" Sometimes Krull would get focused on something else, listen and ask her to ask him again later or only grunt.

Pris contained so much zest and pizzazz for life. Rúna smiled seeing Pris showing Tuli how to properly pull her bow's string, as Tuli protested saying "I can do it! I can do it!". Fiona smiled too, remembering her own past.

Rúna turned to her "I am so lucky my husband adores our daughters and is kind to me. I cannot imagine what Saxa must be going through." They thanked Drenor and began walking to the area where the food texts always were.

Fiona nodded, "Yes, good men are like a diamond in a pile of stones." They giggled as they saw Tuli get a hold of and try to keep Pris' new bow, Pris tried to get it back from Tuli's hands. Normally Krull tried to keep out of their arguments as his handling of girls lacked finesse and he knew it, so pretty much all the girl argument management went to Rúna. This time however, Krull got down on one knee, said something in Tuli's ear and Tuli immediately gave Krull a hug and gave Pris back her bow. They waited while Rúna bought them sweetbread, thereupon they walked Fiona and their daughters to the exit. She next waved to them as they happily went home with Fiona.

Rúna turned to Krull "Honey, Saxa unintentionally revealed that her husband Ubel beats her."

Krull looked at her "You're sure?"

Rúna looked at him in a way that concurred. Shock passed across Krull's face before it started turning red. Krull shut his eyes, nodded, took a deep breath and looked up exhaling slowly before looking at Rúna. "Thank you Rúna, I will speak with Ubel about this before I leave."

Rúna touched his arm, "Krull if you speak with him and then leave, she will be at his mercy while you are gone if he blames her for telling you."

Krull acknowledged, "very well, I will bring him along our hunt and have a serious talk with him."

Rúna ran her hand through her hair brushing it behind her ear, "Thank you love."

Krull nodded "Let us return to Drenor's tent". They walked back to Drenor's place who looked at them in surprise seeing Krull's face.

Krull said "I will need you to join our hunt tomorrow, to show us these bows and also in case Ubel does anything stupid." Drenor widened his eyes a little.

Next, wanting to be sure that they could handle any issue in the wilds, in addition to Drenor, Krull sent Rúna to go to Fiona's home, he went and invited Sveinn, Bryn and Saad to attend. Last he ordered Ubel to join the hunt.

The next morning, the group was ready outside his home. Krull's smile went wide, "Everyone ready?" Drenor pointed toward the forest "Here we go!!"

Chapter IV Krull
147 BC

The Hunt begins…

They had ridden for an hour, and it began to rain. They dismounted at the edge of the woods, leaving two young warriors with their horses. As they walked through the woods following Drenor, Krull quietly spoke to Pris about his beliefs of hunting. "When hunting it is important to think like the animals, think like the wolf, listen like the rabbit or see like the eagle."

Pris looked at Krull inquisitively "What do you mean father?"

Stepping over a small log that lay across the path Krull said "Well any wolf can track its prey but for larger animals, it must know when to attack or flee, when it attacks larger prey, they will do so in packs." He turned and as he helped Pris over the log saw the others of their party behind them.

Krull continued to speak quietly "Any eagle can spot its prey, but it must attack skillfully, without sound swooping down and snatching a fish or squirrel without crashing and killing itself. A rabbit must know when it's safe to eat and when it must flee. In war, we must use our brains first to beat enemies because occasionally your opponent will be stronger than you or have more energy. Always try to gain an advantage of terrain or having the sun in your back or a better use of weaponry. Do you understand?" Pris smiled and nodded. The rain stopped and the forest was again full of sounds of birds and other little animals surrounding them.

After traveling by foot to where they knew there was a small rapid river, its many rocks and boulders in it caused the water's noise to be loud as it ran through the land. Krull turned to Pris "This is a good place. The sound of the river covers the sound of our footsteps. The rocky landscapes are covered by trees on either side of the river. We often find animals coming to the river for a drink of water. Due to the sound of water rushing over the rocks, we might get lucky to sneak up on an unsuspecting deer or rabbit for a kill shot. In other parts of the forest the animal's hearing could alert them to the approach of us." Pris nodded understanding.

They walked deeper, Krull pointed out important things as well as occasionally putting his finger to his mouth. Pris nodded understanding the importance of silence and of respecting nature. They were careful not to break dry bush branches or leave any signs of their passing.

Krull quietly hummed a song, "Hhhhhmmmm, hmmmmm hmmmm hmmmm, hm hm hm hm, hm hm hm hm hm hm....." Krull kept humming for a while. Pris had heard him hum this song many times throughout her life but had never asked him about the words or why he did it.

This time Pris wanted to know, so she asked him "What's that tune father?"

Krull looked over and touching her shoulder he said, "It is the song of the warrior at hunt, Krull sang in a low voice.

"We are one with nature, we hunt to feed our families taking only what we need, oh nature give us the prize and a safe trip home oh please."

Suddenly Krull motioned all to stop, he pointed down at the mud. Looking at Pris, he said "Deer tracks! Deer tracks have two big toes with a couple small toes on each foot. These are definitely deer tracks."

Pris smiled, then asked "Father, how do we know those deer tracks are new or that they are not very old?"

Krull looked at her and smiled, "The plants around the tracks have been smashed from the deer's landing in muddy ground and yet there is not much rain water in them. This tells us that the deer passed through here after the last rainfall. The front feet made a deeper print, meaning more weight up front; these are absolutely deer tracks, probably a stag."

Krull whistled to his cousin Drenor and signaled the others behind him to spread out with men on either side of the tracks and they continued to ride until the tracks became closer, showing that the stag had stopped running. Krull smiled to Pris, "The stag stopped running here, and over there had a meal." he pointed to a tree that had some bark shaved off. The stag must have sharpened its horns there. The tracks go on to the river ahead." Pris nodded.

They walked along following, Pris was right behind Krull, she froze when he stopped humming, stopped moving and also motioned at her to be silent. They grabbed arrows for their bows, Krull signaled that they needed to stay quiet.

Pris didn't understand the signals, but she understood through the basic body language.

The trail continued past several bush varieties and hundreds of trees, where at a small waterfall in the river they could see a large horned stag drinking.

Krull breathed a prayer to the lady of the forest "Thankfully, we ask of thee". It was still a good distance away, Krull looked at the trees to judge the strength of the wind, smelling the forest air. Pulling his arrow in his new composite bow into a torqued firing position, rolling his lips kissing the air a couple times. After a moment Krull smiled as the arrow fired out, it flew with great power and force striking the stag in the neck near the head, going through and sticking out the far side. With a loud cry, the stag wobbled for a moment and all at once fell over.

"Wow father, did you kill it with one shot?" Pris exclaimed.

Krull looked surprised and smiled bittersweetly, "It seems so, with my older bow I've often had to shoot and chase a stag for great distances and reshoot it a few more times." Looking at Drenor, "This bow is incredible."

Drenor was excited too, "I did it, this copy works as good as the original! The arrow must have severed the Stag's neck bone, what a lucky shot."

Krull grunted, "No luck." He smiled pleased, looking at Pris "This will provide enough meat to feed many families." Krull signaled to two of their companions, they nodded and went back to fetch their horses while the rest of the party approached their prize.

Arriving at the stag they said a prayer of thanks to the stag and to the Goddess of the forest for providing them with this gift of food. The other hunters spent the better part of that day cutting the stag, preparing the pieces of it for transport on their horses. While this was being done, Krull taught Pris the importance of savoring every scrap of meat, the fur covered skin, the bones. Krull saw Pris throw a stick in the river and then use her sling to shoot rocks at it.

Seeing that Pris could do this well Krull smiled "Dear, rocks are effective at medium range, how about we practice more with your new bow. Come here."

Krull pulled an arrow from his quiver looking from the river into the woods, finding a large tree in a direction away from where they had come from. Krull turned around again towards the big tree. "See that over there? I will hit an open space of it away from the limbs for you to aim at" Releasing the arrow, it flew powerfully striking the middle of the trunk of the tree, not far off the ground. Krull looked at Pris ``Try to hit my arrow, your turn".

Pris took her bow and inserted an arrow, pulling back she began to aim, Krull began to say "A little lo…."

"Sssssss" Pris hissed, as she relaxed the arrow giving him an annoyed look. Krull shrugged and motioned for her to retry for the tree.

Pris pulled back on the arrow, aimed and released it, the arrow flew striking the tree about a fist length higher than where Krull's had hit.

"Good shot" Krull said,

Pris leaned her head to the side as she looked at the two arrows in the tree. Pris fired a few more times, her shots all hit the tree near the proximity to Krull's shot, her fourth shot finally split Krull's arrow straight down the middle.

Krull clapped "Good Pris, you're getting better! With a little more training you will be great." Pris went to retrieve the arrows.

While she did this, Krull pulled out his round metal shield from his back and scooped it full of water from the river. Pulling out a needle, Krull began to sharpen it with his knife at one end. Pris returned with the arrows and stood next to him watching. Looking at her he said "Pris, grab me a big leaf off a tree."

Pris was curious, "What's this Papa?"

Krull smiled, "Please do it now."

Pris walked over to an oak tree and cut off a leaf, afterwards she returned to Krull, gave it to him.

Krull smiled "Good pick. Someday you might be on a long hunt and need to find your way home. This is a method my grandfather taught me to give guidance at such times." Krull put the leaf on the water and placed the metal needle he had been scraping onto the leaf. It turned and stopped in a certain direction. Krull pointed at it, this will always point towards where the land becomes colder quickly and Winters are longer. Home is that way" He said pointing "This is a way you can use to guide your way home."

Pris' eyes lit up, "Wow that is neat!"

Krull smiled. "Tomorrow I will start teaching you more advanced single and double swordplay."

Pris looked at him "But why Papa, I don't plan to get into battles?"

Krull looked at her "We live in a dangerous world dear; it is best for you to know how to defend yourself. The better I am at teaching you, the better you will be if the need ever happens." Pris gave him another look.

Krull continued "This world is never easy or fair. Anyone who says so is selling something. Sometimes one must do things to survive, rather than things we want to do." Pris looked at the needle again then back to Krull, "Is that true for everyone, for you, for Tuli, for mama, and for me?"

Krull shrugged "Yes. life can be challenging, but we must never give up, if we use our heads we will survive and thrive." Seeing that the companions were done harvesting the stag's meat Krull looked back to her. "Pris, I have some important business to deal with." He pointed "Go over there near the river where there are those wild red and purple flowers, collect them for mother and Tuli." Pris nodded and walked off down to the river.

Krull turned and returned to where the stag had fallen, looking at Ubel, who was tall, muscular and had a tattooed body, his shaved bald head quickly identifiable. "Ubel, we need to speak."

Ubel Trauben

Ubel looked at Krull, his sonorous voice had an uneasy depth "Yes, my liege?"

Krull looked at Ubel hard as Ubel approached. Drenor, Bryn and Saad approached behind Ubel, his eyes darted left & right showing an awareness of them. Krull's face was serious, "Ubel I saw your wife in our market the other day, her right eye was bruised. I have heard rumors about her being hurt before. Did you beat your wife?"

Ubel frowned, "That is none of your affair." Krull's face turned red his husky voice barked "I am the leader of our village; I am making this my affair now! Do you deny that you beat your wife?"

Ubel's knuckles turned white as he clenched his hands into a fist, Ubel's voice sounded like the rumble of thunder "She is mine, my property, you have no right"

Krull's voice became enraged "Do you know who you are speaking to?"

Ubel yelled "I…." Krull interrupted him, "Silence!! My responsibility is the safety of all who dwell in our village, that includes Saxa."

Ubel moved his hand to his sword hilt as Krull yelled, "Stop! Do you know what you are doing?" His sword shot out his blade at Ubel's neck.

Ubel stopped, knowing he was beaten, lowered his head, "I mean to give you, my sword." Ubel scoffed, "Don't, my father had once saved you from drowning" Krull's blade did not move "And Jurgen's death is on your daughter, the Gods will not favor you if you kill a defenseless man."

Krull held the blade pointed at his throat, finally saying "Slowly put your sword on the ground." Ubel did this, doing so he glanced to Krull's right, where he saw Pris at the river; *that pretty thing, how Krull would be crushed if I had her, but she is too far away.*

Krull nodded seeing that Ubel was not attempting to fight, "Since you have chosen peace I will not kill or banish you, but you and Saxa are henceforth divorced. Saxa will move back into her brother's home, you may not take revenge against her, if any bump or bruise happens to her you will be banished. If she is killed you will share her fate. Now back away from your sword."

Ubel sat motionless and backed off barely able to contain his rage. *You will pay for this Krull. I swear it. But killing you alone is not enough. You and your family must all pay.*

Krull picked up Ubel's sheathed sword. The group mounted their horses and brought their stag meat back to the tribe. Arriving at the village, Krull told Pris to go home, then he and his warriors escorted Ubel to Ubel's sister's house. Krull told him that Ubel had to stay in the house until the festival. Krull left eight warriors there to keep Ubel under house arrest; he then went to Saxa and Ubel's home with six warriors. Krull knocked on the door.

Saxa came to the door, Krull looked over her face, "Show me your arms, Saxa did. Krull asked "Saxa do you enjoy being Ubel's wife? Do you want to divorce him and move temporarily in with your brother Dietrich?"

Saxa nodded.

Krull put his hand on her upper arm "I am truly sorry, I did not know that he had abused you so, and that it took me so long to find out. You are a single woman now."

Saxa blinked and smiled as a tear rolled down her cheek, beginning to understand that she was free.

Krull gave her the six warriors to help her move her stuff out of her old house.

Saxa looked relieved, Krull said, "You must leave by tonight, take your things to your brothers; then come see Rúna at the feast, she will want to know you are ok." Saxa nodded and hugged Krull.

Later at the feast, Rúna saw Saxa arrive with Dietrich who was a guard. Rúna came over and gave her a hug, "Come have some Glogg with me, we will drink to a happier life ahead."

The village had a great celebratory feast, there were a few cooking fires made in the middle of the village that evening starting with prayers to their gods. Another hunting party had killed another deer, the food stores were good with plenty of stored wheat and corn in their supply house, the vegetables that had been grown the last season.

Pris and her friend Lena happily danced with Tuli and the other children as flute and drum music played.

Drenor smiling with a cup of Glogg in his hand, his face slightly pink. He came over and whispered in Saxa's ear, Saxa's face brightened, she nodded smiling, placed his

Glogg on the table and they began to dance among the many other villagers who were dancing and the elders talked at length.

Krull and Rúna saw Drenor and Saxa dancing and cheered. They were eating their meal of deer meat, carrots, potatoes and drinking mugs of beer with Stefan the town druid across the table. Fiona joined at the table eating happily looking at one of the older men. He waved at her, so she waved back and soon he came over to sit with her. All were happy except Ubel who sat at the end of a far table with a simple-minded man.

Dietrich, Saxa's brother and one of the guards, eyed Ubel continuously from afar. *If that bald creep even talks ill to my sister again, I will use this ax and have his hands as knockers for my door!*

Chapter V King Urix

147 BC

Mother and her family would be impacted in their journey ahead.

A familiar horn's cry bellowed out, with the sounds of horses, Their clan leader's horn signal. The town's gates were opened promptly as Krull, most of the warriors, and the entire town went to the front gate, where they bowed their heads. Sure enough, old Urix, a large yet healthy 55-year-old, arrived at the head of 60 warriors, all on horses. Urix rode into the town, he looked at Krull and laughed jovially. "Krull, so good to see you again," Urix said.

Krull bowed his head, then looked up to see that his king's hair had started to show gray and he looked as though he had gained weight "This is an unexpected delight to see you my King, what has brought you so far South?"

Urix smiling as he embraced Krull said "Lets go grab refreshments, then we talk" Krull led Urix to the festival tents. After receiving beers, Urix looked at Krull, "I have a special task for you. As you know our tribe has been trading goods with our friends the Angles and Teutoni..."

Krull nodded, saying "They were just a few days' ride South of here."

Urix continued "We have had a great year for catching fish and our stores of smoked fish and woven cloth are plentiful, so I want you to lead a trade mission to the Saxons. They are a strong tribe to the South of the Angles. I need a solid dependable leader to head this mission for our tribe. You are exactly who I need, a wise, dependable and great warrior. I remember that your wife Rúna is also a great negotiator, so I want her to speak on our behalf, you both must go."

A look of surprise washed across Krull's face as Urix continued "I have already received agreement from our trade partners the Angles for you all to pass safely through their lands, I am confident that this is a great opportunity to establish trade."

Krull looked at his wife then back to Urix "You do us a great honor my liege, however my wife is raising our daughters."

Urix took a big mouthful of beer, "I understand, but I need her to lead this expedition. Is there no relative or friend your children could stay with?"

Krull hesitated a moment running his hand through his red hair, Urix raised his hand a little, "This is all sudden, but we have been contacted by the Saxons, apparently the Angles traded some of our goods to them and they want more of our stuff. Trade with these neighbors should ensure peaceful relations and it will mean prosperity".

Krull wanted to refuse, he thought *our life is here, yet there is not any way that I can refuse the responsibility and honor, we are a Cimbri noble family, I am loyal to Urix and our people.* "I will do as you wish, my King."

Urix laughed "Excellent! I know this is not easy, but there is no one I trust as much as you Krull. Please leave within 3 days. Now we feast!"

They celebrated over the bear and stag meat, and the upcoming trade mission.

Krull had not noticed that Ubel had been listening to Urix saying where and when they would be traveling. Urix had a bottomless appetite for food, grog and women, Urix took Krull aside, "I need to piss, come with me"

Krull took a deep breath and followed him.

As soon as Urix and Krull had walked out of sight, Ubel came over to Rúna. "My lady, I want to complain, your husband pushed me into divorce without my agreement."

Rúna looked at him "You treated Saxa worse than one treats a dog, you do not deserve her."

Ubel painted a smile over his face as he talked "Do you think what I did was unjust? She did not tell you the whole story, Saxa likes rough sex. When I got tired, she got angry, we had been drinking and I accidentally hit her. But this claim that it was a beating is false, you should see the nail marks on my back...."

Rúna rolled her eyes, "I do not wish to hear your filthy lies."

Ubel moved closer, "I could do you like this; I would give you such pleasure, things that Krull would never do."

Rúna signaled her guards, Dietrich was the first one to reach Ubel, grabbing Ubel violently, Dietrich pushed Ubel away.

Rúna shouted "Stay away from me and get out of my sight."

Ubel batted away Dietrich's hands, holding his hands in the air, chuckling with apparent insincerity "Apologies my lady, I'm leaving now." Ubel flapped his tongue at her in a suggestive way as he walked out.

Dietrich was about to pull his ax, Saxa shouted "Don't kill him Dietrich, he agreed to the divorce."

Rúna looked at Saxa, "Yes, he did…. Dietrich let him leave, killing him would leave a foul omen on this festival."

Dietrich, Drenor and four other guards escorted Ubel from the festival just as Krull and Urix returned from their walk.

Krull and Ubel looked at each other crossly, but Urix was talking to Krull about what the great opportunity trading with the Saxons was and Krull kept his attention mostly on his king.

As they reentered the festival, Urix saw a female servant who was working at the event, he asked "Is that woman taken?"

Krull shook his head "No liege, I believe she is single, her husband died last Winter."

Urix smiled, "Perfect" he signaled, beckoning the woman.

The woman walked over, Urix whispered in her ear and she nodded, they left the feast together.

Krull waved to Pris who had been sitting on the other side of the table, so she came over. Krull smiled, "You did great during the hunt today, since it was your first hunt, I have this necklace for you as a gift."

Krull gave Pris a medallion that had the symbol of her people. "Thank you, papa,"

Krull held out his hands, "You are now a warrior of our people."

Pris gave Krull a big hug and looked at it intently, liking it very much. "I will hold it while I sleep tonight."

Ubel watched them from a distance before he departed the village alone on his horse before the feast had hardly begun.

Ubel told the gate guards he had forgotten something in the woods during the hunt in order to slip out.

Ubel looked back, his eyes wide, his face looking demonic. He angrily whipped his horse and galloped into the night Southward.

A few days later, Krull led 50 of Urix's 60 warriors along with several of his own best warriors to go as part of a caravans of a few wagons of sample goods to go as emissaries to meet with the Saxons, a Germanic tribe in the South to establish trade.

Krull was packing his things as Rúna prepared eggs for breakfast, Pris and Tuli sat at their table. Krull came over, "Pris, Tuli, you two will stay with your grandmother Fiona while your mother and I travel on this trade mission. We will be gone for a couple of weeks."

Tuli began nodding her head but Pris shook hers, "No I will go with you."

Krull frowned "Pris, it is too dangerous, you must stay home and protect Tuli and grandma Fiona."

Pris shook her head, "All the warriors of our town will do that, who is going to protect you, Papa?"

Krull gave her a surprised look "I will protect mys..."

Pris interrupted him, "No, you need me to be there with you just in case."

Krull looked at her, *I cannot get angry, she wants to protect me and her mother.* He smiled "You have the heart of a warrior my dear, but you are not ready for what is beyond our borders, not yet. My decision is final, you and Tuli will stay with grandma Fiona until we return."

Pris started to shake her head "No father I...."

Krull's fist slammed on the table "Know your place girl, I have a duty which could take me to danger, maybe even death, this is NOT your duty, you must stay here where it's safe, protect the village, my decision is FINAL."

Pris was about to shout back when Rúna came over "We must go Pris…"

Pris turned to Rúna, "But why you too mama?"

Rúna smiled "Your father is going because he is a great warrior, I am going because the King needs someone who is good at diplomatic negotiating." She gave Pris and Tuli hugs and kisses.

They all walked outside, the girls saw Fiona approaching, Rúna pointed, "Go to grandma now."

Krull packed their wagon and then mounted the wagon's driver seat in the lead wagon. Fiona walked over with Pris and Tuli to give kisses and bid farewell to Krull and Rúna.

After the girls kissed and embraced their parents, Fiona saw the girls cry as they ran off towards her home. Concern went over Rúna's face.

Fiona said "Don't worry Rúna, I will make them something special for dinner tonight…" she reached into her bag "Dear, here is a pouch of smoked deer meat, please be careful and don't worry…." Neither Rúna nor Fiona saw Pris and Tuli run to the other side of the wagon, but as they did Pris noticed that the driver of the following wagon was not in his seat yet.

Pris told Tuli "Go to Grandma's home I need to tell Grandma something" Pris watched Tuli start off, she instead climbed into her parent's covered wagon. Pris didn't see Tuli stop, turn around, then drop her doll and come running back to her wagon.

Fiona gave hugs and a kiss to Rúna and Krull, then waved goodbye to them as they climbed onto the wagon.

Pris looked around from behind the furs that were in the cart, her heart racing. *I cannot let my parents leave without me, this is a grand adventure, and my dad might get into trouble with his temper.* Pris heard Krull shake the reins as she looked, she saw that Fiona had walked away towards the market as she felt the wagon start to roll. Pris overheard her mother talking to Krull about how proud she was about herself and Tuli. Pris felt a shake on her arm, turning she saw her sister Tuli had climbed aboard too and Pris had not even noticed her.

Pris hissed "Tuli, you need to climb out of this wagon when we stop at the gate and run home."

Tuli shook her head "No, I can't do that! I just had a vision now. Someone scary will attack us."

Pris shook her head, "You're just scared, I can help Momma and Papa"

Tuli shook her head "I will go too" she whispered.

Pris wanted to argue with Tuli, but it was no use. If I argue too much with her Tuli will scream. Pris was depressed. Mom and Dad will kill me for sure.

Rúna held Krull close as they drove the wagon, "I once worried that I have not given you any sons, shall we try again?"

Krull smiled "I would love that, our girls make me so happy that sons or no sons, it doesn't matter to me. My brothers already have sons and can worry about carrying on our family name. I love you and our daughters more than anything, you all are my treasures."

The group journeyed for two days from their home before their mother discovered their girls. Too far to turn around, Rúna was furious at first, but figured at 12 and 7 it was time for their girls to grow up. The group made good time, and within several days traveling they arrived in Saxon lands.

The land was mostly covered with tall fir trees, the Saxon's town stood at the edge of a forest to one side, it was fortified, surrounded by a wall made of logs, their village had over 500 buildings and were all made of wood. The town had plowed farmland that stretched across an expanse of flat land towards its East. There most of the trees were cut, beyond the farmland was more forest as far as the eye could see. Behind the Saxon town in the forest there was a fast-flowing river, which their caravan passed over on a bridge on the only North-South dirt road. Inside the town, Smoke billowed from multiple smoke stacks on house tops though the roofs were made of straw.

The convoy was allowed into the town without issue. Rúna and Krull hopped off their wagon and greeted the King of the Saxons.

Rúna said "Mighty King of the Saxons, we are on a diplomatic trade mission from the Cimbri. We have arrived per your invitation to establish trade."

Chapter VI Prince Volker

147 BC

Trade negotiations with the Saxons were the reason for the journey, but the price to be paid would be crushing.

King Lanzo Ragnarr had 50 warriors standing with him; they were lined up in two lines. Krull and twenty of his warriors assembled behind Rúna, the rest staying with the wagons.

The Saxon King welcomed them inside his large wooden house. Krull motioned to Rúna, "We are from the Cimbrian nation. Our King Urix has sent his trade advisor, Rúna Haas to conduct trade negotiations."

Ragnarr smiled, "Very well, follow me inside." Although the Saxons spoke a slightly different accent of German as the Cimbri, they could understand each other nonetheless.

They followed Ragnarr and ten of his warriors inside, where they were led through a narrow passage into a large hall that had a fire in a fireplace at the opposite end. There was a round table at which stood five people all wearing rings, necklaces and capes on top of their otherwise mixture of dark and light brown clothing.

Ragnarr motioned to the people standing at the table "These are my advisors, please be seated."

Each side had ten warriors seated on either side of the table. The trade negotiations lasted for a few hours, Rúna was very effective at identifying what the Cimbri were offering, and what they wanted. Negotiations covered the amounts and frequency of trade, King Ragnarr and his advisors spoke with each other and Krull smiled seeing the heads nodding. The two sides proposed terms back and forth giving and receiving, Rúna was concise about what the Cimbri could offer and at how much, per her own instructions from Urix. The negotiations arrived at a price both sides felt was fair. The Saxons desired to trade for fish, furs, weaved fabric cloths and desired a trade route to the North. The Cimbri negotiated for sources of iron, various kinds of furs, grains and meat.

While Pris and Tuli were waiting, they saw a kind looking Saxons woman who was delivering beer, water and bread coming and going to the King's building. As she returned, Pris grabbed her hand, "Is there anyone we could play with."

The servant said, "You might find prince Volker and his companion Konrad in the stables."

Pris smiled "And where are the stables?" The lady pointed and the girls headed off in that direction with two Cimbrian warriors following them.

They arrived in the stables where they saw two boys cleaning a black horse, Pris thought one, perhaps both of the boys might be servants, Pris said politely to them "I am Pris of the Cimbrian tribe, I am looking for prince Volker Ragnarr of the Saxons".

Volker laughed, "Well you found me! I like your accent, where are you from?"

Pris blushed with surprise, she glanced at the horse and back to Volker " You enjoy horses?"

Volker nodded "I love them". He smiled "It stinks in here; would you like to go somewhere more enjoyable?"

Pris and Tuli clapped excitedly, smiling, so Volker looked at Konrad, "Fetch a few friends and meet us at the river."

Konrad nodded and hurried off.

An excited voice asked "Oh, can we come too?"

Volker turned around and looked at his 10-year-old sister Christina and 8-year-old brother Gisbert standing there, hands together in a begging gesture. Volker said "Only if you promise to take care of Tuli. She and her sister are new here, and don't fight over anything."

They both breathlessly jumped up and down "We promise!"

Volker smiled, "Alright then."

They all spent the next hour walking around the town, Volker pointed out various things enjoying Pris and Tuli's company, while largely ignoring his younger siblings. Volker's uncle saw Volker, Pris and Tuli and his siblings heading to the river, he ordered an escort of 6 men to go with them to the river; there they met Konrad and a few of his friends. Heidi, Gisbert and Tuli went down to the river where they had a grand time throwing rocks in the river.

The guard's captain smiled at Volker and Pris "I will blow my horn when it's time to leave." They walked downstream,

Volker and Pris could be heard talking and laughing in the distance. Volker could not take his eyes off Pris, her presence captivating him; they walked along the river away from his friends.

They found a location where there was a grassy bank clear of trees, there they talked for a couple hours enjoying the sights of the forest, the water going down around the rocks of the river, the sights of occasional birds, they laughed and enjoyed each other's presence.

They saw a stag in the distance on the other side of the river, Pris quietly whispered "Oh that deer's so pretty."

Volker blurted out, "You are far prettier, you are the prettiest girl I have ever seen."

Pris smiled looking at him, they both felt a magnet energy, she liked him very much. With hardly a thought, they came close for a kiss, Volker hugged Pris as a gentle breeze blew, the world seemed right.

Cedric, Volker's older 17-year-old brother, rode up to the river with a few guards, he yelled out, "Volker, everyone, time to return home, we shall feast!"

Volker and Pris held hands for a few steps as they walked back to where the others were, before long they let go, not wanting the others to see them in an embrace.

The Cimbrian group was welcomed in the Saxon town for a week, the plan was to travel to the Treverii tribe to the West before returning to their homelands. After a week of feasting, the caravan departed and traveled a day with a Saxon guide along a dirt road through the woods until they reached a steady river.

They found a bridge that went over a fast-moving river, it was getting close to dark, and a scout found a large meadow surrounded by forest off the main dirt road upstream on the river. A few charred stumps showed that a forest fire had once occurred in this area. There was a small hill at the far end of the meadow, this is where they parked their wagons, at the top of a hill in the far side of the meadow, as Krull wanted to take the most defensible position in the area.

Chapter VII Attack of the Swabians

147 BC

The Attack of the Swabians and the traitor, may they forever live in infamy. The next morning a light fog made visibility low, yet Krull's warriors saw a wild boar crossing the wooden bridge, so Krull and several warriors grabbed their weapons, mounted their horses and taking their two dogs with them chased after it in a sudden hunt.

Drenor had not gone on the hunt; Krull had left him in charge of defense of the camp. Looking around the trees that were partly obscured by the fog, Drenor chatted with four of his men, after they had covered the perimeter once their conversation topics went from logistics to hunting.

Drenor's men Alger, Bryn, Rob and Saad could not resist asking Drenor about Saxa. Bryn laughed saying "Drenor, there is an important matter to discuss, we've seen you with Saxa almost continually, and I've known you since we were kids. I've never seen you *uh and ah* as you have around her." Bryn laughed as he said that.

Rob chimed in "I think we have a love puppy …."

Drenor grinned and shrugged, "Have I been that obvious?"

Saad laughed, "I saw you picking flowers last night. Did you give them to her?"

Drenor shook his head, "She had already gone to sleep…"

Bryn laughed "Truly Drenor, don't overthink it. Ladies want to be wanted, why else do they make themselves look pretty?"

Saad picked a small grass flower and held it for Drenor, "Will you two become one?" Drenor chuckled, feeling too happy by a happy envisioned future, "You all… I cannot speak for her, but…. Alright, alright yes Gods know I love her. I hope she loves me…"

Alger grinned "Better get her before someone else does."

Rob gave Alger a friendly elbow to the ribs smiling "Saxa is stunning, you'd be damn lucky to have her Drenor!"

Bryn clasped Drenor's shoulder "I saw the way she looks at you, I know where I would bet."

Drenor smiled, his excitement oozing "I want to marry her, I just need to tell her the right words! How do you think this sounds?" Drenor got on one knee "Saxa, I.... "

He looked up but then their attention was pulled towards a horn's sound from the forest.

The bellowing noise of a horn from behind the trees followed immediately by a terrifying roar of war cries as hundreds roared their attack, suddenly a horde of blackened Swabian raiders came out of the tree line. They saw that most had long hair, straight, braided or shaved heads. Their shields colored black and white made them unmistakable. They had their battle axes or swords brandished with shields, some had spears. Immediately a few Cimbri guards who happened to be closer to the attacking horde were overwhelmed by the charging attackers, overwhelmed and killed. Drenor, Bryn and Saad pulled their bows out as they saw a flood of Swabian blackened raiders rushing at them, they fired a round of arrows, next Bryn and Saad switched to their swords.

Drenor immediately sounded the alarm using his horn, he then aimed his bow, firing rapidly his arrows killing many as the horde attacked his position, the camped wagons were behind Drenor.

Rob, Alger, Bryn and Saad stood defensively, their swords ready as Drenor fired a few last shots with his bow; he immediately dropped his bow, as he pulled his two swords. Together they engaged as the Swabians reached them. An advantage they had was their ground was slightly inclined in their favor.

Drenor fought valiantly, almost dancing around as his two swords parrying multiple opponents and one by one finding openings which he exploited to kill left and right as he moved around. Yet, there were too many Swabians, he was doing all he could to defend from attackers all around him, as Drenor occasionally found an opening to kill an attacker.

Meantime as Bryn got locked sword to sword against an attacker, another attacker was about to stab Bryn in the back, seeing this, Saad stuck his sword into the ground and threw his dagger striking the attacker in the neck, but by doing so took his attention off the next opponent attacking him, he pulled his sword out of the ground, but too late, the attacker stabbed him in the heart, Saad howled in pain as he fell.

Alger had been swinging his spear around stabbing his spear head when he found openings, after a while a strong Swabian slashed his spear in half, Alger dodged backwards as he pulled out his ax from his back. A master at ax fighting, he killed many opponents with it as it broke through shields and knocked off hands that held swords by stepping in close in their mid-swing.

Rob had become separated fighting with a two-handed battle ax, he slashed and destroyed many attackers that came at him. Many Cimbrian warriors were not so lucky; of the 40 warriors left to guard the camp, half were soon killed or were dying as their blood turned the ground red.

Rúna gasped, she saw these things of the battle unfold, knowing their warriors were vastly outnumbered and that they could all die, she screamed "Swabians! Quickly children run to the hiding place we played at by the river, go there now!"

While exclaiming that Rúna grabbed a small axe and short sword to defend her children. Rúna motioned them towards the river, she began running with them, but she saw four Swabians charging at them. One of the attackers yelled "Fang sei ein!" Rúna quickly turned to attack the enemy.

Pris led Tuli, they rushed away to go down the side of the ravine to the steady river; they had not gone far when they came to a fallen tree that was half sticking into the river. Still hearing the metal banging sounds of battle, men's screams of agony and her mother's battle-cry, Pris could not control herself, she grabbed Tuli and hugged her, holding Tuli's arms hard she screamed "Tuli wait here, papa taught me how to fight!"

Tuli shook her head, eyes flooded with tears, her face pale and body shaking, "No!! Something bad will happen! Don't leave me Pris!!"

Pris ignored Tulli's cries as she ran back towards where they had come from, towards the battle.

Fear gripped Tuli, terrified her hands shook, she was unable to follow.

Pris climbed through the trees up the ravine following her own footsteps to return to help her mother. Fear for her mother overpowered fear for herself. Pris thought *Papa taught me well, I will help them.* Pris thought that continually, in her young mind she replayed her father's lessons, she imagined visions of all her people triumphantly beating back the attackers, she imagined none of her people hurt and the evil attackers cowering against their sure defeat. Pris thought that her side, the good guys, would not have many injured or killed, they were the good people, they would be fine she hoped. About this time, Pris heard her father's hunting horn, "Papa's back!" she said breathlessly as she arrived at the base of the ascent.

Pris ascended the river's ravine, she passed a few trees before arriving at the clearing there she overlooked the meadow, now a bloody battlefield full of warriors killing and being killed. At the far end she saw her father and his seven remaining hunting companions were attacking the backside of the Swabians. At the other end of the field the Cimbrian wagons, Drenor, Saxa, Alger, Bryn, Rob and 16 odd Cimbrian warriors, her mother and some servants were all either defending against a horde of Swabian attackers.

Pris saw her mother about where she had been before, wielding a battle ax and a short sword in her two hands, Rúna was covered in her enemies' blood while still fighting against several warriors. Pris saw that all the attacking Swabians warriors were all wearing black pants, their bodies were blackened with ash, their faces painted white. Most of them were armed with swords or axes and their shields were the shape of elongated hexagons and

Octagons all which were painted black with white images of bulls, boars, and other animals.

Across the battlefield's opposite side at the treeline Pris saw the Swabian chieftain, he was surrounded by guards, he had tattoos all over, similar to how Ubel had, his sword's blade looked big. The Chieftain laughed as his men attacked the Cimbrians, he had long brown braided hair, he wore black armor and a black cape, he stood with another huge fearsome looking warrior who was taking the Chieftain's directions and shouting out orders to their warriors. A larger warrior wore a bear skull as his helmet, his shoulders had human skulls on them, his black armor had a black cape attached that blew in the wind.

Pris gasped, she saw Ubel standing next to the Swabian's chieftain, his muscular tattooed body bare from the waist up, his bald head shiny from the sun. Pris saw Ubel point at Krull and at her mother. She could not hear anything due to the distance and sounds of battle, but the chieftain nodded, they shook hands, the Swabian chieftain then blew his horn pointing. The Swabians not already fighting joined the attack towards Krull while others kept attacking Rúna and her companions. Pris saw Ubel return to the woods beyond the tree line where he disappeared from view. *Wait until I tell papa about that traitor!* Pris thought.

Around Rúna there were the bodies of several dead Swabians warriors. Rúna spun around fighting several warriors at once as though she was in a dance, her vision was endlessly spinning as attackers would miss her or be blocked and then fail to block her counter slash and would be the next to fall.

Pris looked on, feeling some fear about engaging. This was not a choice about whether to train or not against her dad, this was for real, she saw all manner of violence, dismemberment, horrific injuries and death in this battle. Krull had not told her so much about how limbs get cut off in battles, how the dying sometimes lay screaming on the ground, the blood and agony everywhere. The ground had turned red as the combatants continued to fight, struggle, kill or be killed.

Pris saw that Saxa was standing on the driver seat of a wagon shooting Swabians with one of Drenor's bows, Drenor, Alger, Bryn, Rob were all surrounded and each fighting attackers. Pris saw that the Swabians were not taking prisoners, all the Cimbri who had been washing clothing or eating without their weapons close were quickly killed without mercy.

At that moment Pris saw Alger try to get to Rúna, but he was killed. Rúna was fighting well against many opponents, having killed many, the Swabians warriors held back defensively, Rúna laughed at them.

Pris gasped as she watched the fearsome looking warrior with the skull cap charge from his leader, to attack Rúna, yelling something foul in their language as their blades clashed. Rúna seemed to be in trouble against his powerful attacks. I have to do something Pris thought desperately.

This newest attacker was unusually tall and looked very strong. As they started fighting, at first, they each parried each other's sword strikes, but Pris saw that Rúna was breathing deeply, her shoulders were rising and falling quickly, Rúna appeared to tire as this Swabian champion swung his blade at her fiercely.

Swabian Champion

Suddenly the warrior deflected her short sword hard and it went flying, the blade of her ax got locked next with his sword and they stood there trying to out maneuver each other, though he laughed as Rúna appeared to weaken. Pris saw another warrior sneaking up from behind Rúna as her ax was locked with the large champion. *I must help Mom!* Pris thought she pulled out her sling and used it to pitch a stone as hard as she could, something she had done thousands of times when hunting squirrels and rabbits.

The stone hit the warrior who was behind her mom in the back of the head, he stopped, took a last staggered step before he fell down.

Two of his fellow warriors turned and saw Pris at the tree line, enraged, they shouted in rage and went for her instead.

The champion kicked Rúna, and laughed as he watched his men attacking Pris.

Rúna, having been knocked down, saw them rushing at Pris and screamed at her to flee.

Pris tried to run in the direction towards Krull, whom she knew was in another direction from Tuli at the other end of the battlefield, a few of his warriors still alive and fighting Swabians. Pris ran towards her father but the Swabian warriors caught up and abducted her.

Rob had been separated from Drenor; he was somewhat close to where Pris was. Rob saw Pris get abducted by a Swabian warrior. Rob tried to run to her, but he could not reach her as he was suddenly surrounded by enemy warriors.

Pris was carried by the Swabian warriors towards from where they had come, Southeast towards the massive Alps mountains. At that moment when Pris was carried off, she saw her mother, Rúna distracted by Pris' abduction, had started to run after Pris, but in that moment, Rúna was killed by the champion.

Not far away, Drenor, who also had seen Pris scooped up, killed his latest opponent, and had started to run to chase after Pris. A fearsome Swabian warrior Drenor intercepted him.

They clashed, the Swabian warrior spoke in bad Cimbrian "You killed my brother!" Drenor had begun to tire, having already fought and killed so many; while his opponent was fresh to the battle. They fought briefly, but rapidly the Swabian's blade connected to Drenor's face along the right eye and across his nose. Drenor spun around howling in pain as he fell to the ground. extreme pain erupted he could not see from his right eye. His whole face was covered in blood, blood covered his hand, he knew this was the end.

The warrior stood above him laughing "You die now!" He readied his sword overhead to cut off Drenor's head, suddenly an arrow went through the warrior's right eye and poked out the backside of his head. The warrior spun and fell, the arrow shot by Saxa.

Saxa rushed over picking up Drenor's sword, checking Drenor she realized he was out cold but was alive, she stood up and killed another Swabian attacker. As she did this she called out for help, in the chaos a handmaiden rushed over to Drenor and wrapped a bandage cloth around his head. Another Swabian warrior rushed at them,

Saxa parried three quick strikes and saw his fourth was a little off-balanced which she blocked with a quick counter slash that went across her opponent's belly, blood erupted as he fell. Saxa continued to defend from more Swabians attackers.

Rob killed the last opponent who had kept him from chasing after Pris, he saw Rúna killed and started chasing after her killer, but noticed that Saxa was close and in trouble, so he fought his way to Saxa and helped her defend off Swabian attackers from her and injured Drenor. The champion blew a horn and yelled directions at his warriors to focus their attacks at certain skillful Cimbrian warriors.

Krull had been fighting at a distance, seeing Pris' abduction and his wife Rúna killed, Krull screamed with rage and horror. Distracted; he was wounded in his leg by the enemy he was fighting. Krull turned and sidestepped, avoiding a follow-up slash, he countered with a stab and saw his blade go through his opponent's gut.

Dietrich who had gone hunting with Krull yelled "Krull they have Pris and have killed Rúna! Go save Pris, we'll hold them back!" Krull nodded, then fought through the many combatants, parrying as he went, killing or wounding and continually moving towards where Pris had been taken, but there were so many of them. By doing this, he, the best Cimbrian warrior of the group, left Dietrich and the other four warriors who were still alive who had arrived with him. With Krull gone and outnumbered, Dietrich and the others fought valiantly for a time, keeping many Swabians occupied, but were eventually all killed.

The battle's result looked grim for the Cimbrians, The Swabian champion was briskly walking downhill now towards Saxa and Rob, but a horn's sound suddenly erupted across the field followed by a hail of arrows as a large hunting party of Saxons appeared on horseback led by King Lanzo Ragnarr out of the woods. Saxon arrows rained down on Swabians from behind killing many as they charged at the Swabians joining the battle to aid the diminished Cimbrians, Ragnarr was charging from the front his sword brandished as he yelled "No mercy!" The Saxons charged their horses into the Swabian horde, knocking down many and slicing down many more as their horses slowed.

The Swabian chieftain cursed, realizing that his remaining Swabians were now losing, pressed between Cimbri and Saxons blades. The chieftain blew his horn, his champion with the skull helmet who had just started fighting against Rob yelled. The champion beat his sword powerfully against Robs, they locked in place and he headbutt Rob, who staggered a moment. The champion's thrust would have killed Rob, but Saxa's sword shot out, blocking the thrusted blade.

The champion kicked Saxa in the stomach, sending her backwards. The champion turned and fled as both Rob nor Saxa were on the ground and neither could attack him.

Rapidly the champion and the other Swabian warriors all started running for the tree line, a few attackers continued to fight.

Saxa looked around and found her bow under a dead Swabian. Most of the Swabians fled towards and then into the dark forest from where they had come, those who continued to fight to hold back the Saxon and Cimbrian counter attack were rapidly killed one by one.

The Swabian leader stopped at the tree line to watch his warriors retreat past him, he yelled at the Champion grinning who passed by him. The leader started to turn intending to leave as well. Yet his taking time to stop and look back allowed Krull to catch up to him, Krull charged his tall long haired muscular opponent, his arms and neck were covered in tattoos like Ubel's body had, his sword had a wicked looking skull engraved on the hilt.

Krull, slightly wounded, summoned all his energy as their blades clashed at the tree line where Pris and her captives had disappeared moments before. Krull, a great swordsman, was tired having run uphill and being wounded. The enemy's leader was able to parry Krull's attacks, Krull was growing weak due to loss of blood.

The enemy leader kicked Krull in the stomach knocking him down and was about to go for the kill when he was suddenly hit by an arrow in his shoulder armor. The enemy leader howled as he looked up and saw it was from Saxa who had hit him from a great distance with her arrow shot. He saw many Saxon and a few Cimbrian warriors charging towards him. believing he could not win, he broke the arrow, blood spurted out as he howled in pain again. He turned and ran into the woods behind him.

Rob, one of the few surviving Cimbrian warriors, arrived at Krull moments later, "Krull, you need to be seen by Stefan." Rob turned and yelled "Druid, help here!!"

During the battle, many on both sides had been killed, Krull stared at his wife's body from this distance, he also saw that Drenor was injured, being tended by Saxa, Saad, Alger, Dietrich and many others were dead or wounded.

Bryn was weeping at his friend's bodies. Rob and others were trying to help those injured to stay alive.

At this point a Cimbri woman brought Tuli back from the river.

Tuli was crying at all that had happened, she ran to her father who was now being attended by Stefan, their druid. In a shocked voice Tuli cried "Papa, I, I…. I screamed at Pris not to go, but she wouldn't listen, Pris said she knew how to fight. I'm s-sorry". Tuli wept bitterly as Krull hugged her tight, now feeling very weak due to his loss of blood. At that moment Tuli saw her dead mother and screamed.

Krull held Tuli tight, his face shaking as tears flowed from his eyes like hard rain, his wife dead, his eldest daughter gone; Tuli's presence was the only thing that he could hold onto. Krull held Tuli, "It was all my fault, I encouraged and taught Pris how to fight and defend herself." Krull thought *Those lessons made Pris believe she could help, emboldened her to return to the battle to help her mother. What have I done?* He thought miserably.

Looking at Tuli who was crying he tried to give her some hope, he managed to say "Darling, we all did the best we could, Pris may yet survive, if they had killed her, her body would be here. I will try to get her back."

Krull tried to get up but was stopped by Stefan, who had a woman assisting him with Krull's leg. Stefan said "Krull, we must stitch you and you must stay off your leg while it heals, otherwise you could lose your life if not your leg."

Krull began to try to get up anyway, but Stefan told Krull to smoke some herbs to kill the pain, he then gave Krull some water. After drinking this Krull started to feel drowsy.

Rob told Krull that he requested the Saxons to track where the Swabians had come from. Krull nodded as he fell into a deep sleep.

Rob helped Stefan to carry Krull to their wagon with Tuli following.

Krull awoke a few hours later very groggy, Tuli was sitting next to him still weeping as she held her mother's lifeless hand.

Drenor sat next to Tuli, his injured eye bandaged. Tuli realized Krull was awake and gave him a hug sobbing. "Drenor", Krull asked "What happened?"

Drenor grimaced, "With the number of wounded and dead, most of our remaining able members have decided for us to return home with Saxon escort."

Krull asked "Anyone follow the raiders?" Drenor nodded "10 members of the Saxon hunting party, Bryn, Rob and 4 Cimbri warriors stayed behind to try to track down the Swabians raiding party." Krull closed his eyes.

Chapter VIII Krull's Revenge

147 BC

My grandfather was eager for revenge…

Krull Haas

A few weeks later, as soon as his wounds had healed enough, Krull used information provided by his scouts to find the Swabians fortified village. It was about a seven day's journey South of the Saxon lands. Krull was joined by his three brothers, two cousins and dozens of warriors from his tribe; they raided the Swabians village in the night. Their scouts had stayed in hiding to locate which house was the chieftain's, it was the largest house in the village, after the large hall and it was the only one that had guards at the front doors.

They were wearing all black & brown clothing; their faces and hands were blackened by ash. They dug a hole under and between a section of wall, when Krull arrived his scout told him which building to go to. Krull patted his shoulder "Good work. Any sign of Pris?"

Bryn shook his head "We arrived two days after the raid, we have not seen her." Krull nodded and signaled his men to go forward. Silently and like blackened shadowy ghosts, one by one they silently killed all the guards as they went around the nearby streets of the village.

They came into the house and suddenly a couple dogs began barking. Krull's men went inside, the dogs attacked them but were cut down. They rushed upstairs and burst into the large room. The tattooed chieftain had been having sex with two of his women. He jumped off his bed and grabbed his skull handled sword.

Krull recognized him from the battle, the same tattoos on his arms also covered his muscular body, and he had the same long hair. Krull charged at his opponent who was completely nude, he held his sword high. Krull charged holding his own sword, their swords clashed ringing with each blow parried by the other. In this fight Krull was completely rested and ready, the chieftain was obviously intoxicated as his speech and movements were a bit sloppy; he called for help, but his calls fell on dead ears.

Seeing his opponent adjusting his stance, Krull saw an opening, as their swords clashed again high he kicked the inner side of the chieftain's left knee with his right foot. The sudden kick made the intoxicated chieftain lose his balance, Krull kicked him again in the stomach and swiftly batted away the chieftain's sword.

Immediately Drenor, Bryn, Rob and two of Krull's warriors came in and grabbed the chieftain holding him down. They wrapped him up in ropes, gagged him and then took him out of the village without further incident. They went about 30 paces past the tree line from the village to where they were sure they wouldn't be seen. There they promptly interrogated the chieftain trying to learn Pris' fate.

Krull grabbed the Swabian leader "Where is my daughter?!"

The chieftain looked at him and laughed, his foul statement making his accent all the uglier "I used your daughter for sexual purposes and then killed her and had her body tossed into a river."

Krull felt like his world had shattered again, his love, his wife and now probably his elder daughter dead. He wanted to kill this merciless man,

Drenor stood there, his patched eye hiding his recent wound. "He is lying."

Krull looked at Drenor "Think so?" Drenor pointed back to the village, "Why bring her all this way just to kill her?"

Krull thought while pacing. Rob, seeing Krull silent, suggested "Shall we kill him?"

Krull shook his head "A blade is too good, too quick for this creep. We shall haul him back to our town, he is responsible for the deaths of many of our people and there we shall burn him alive."

A week later, after that was done, teary eyed Krull and Tuli held each other in their town praying to their gods that somehow Pris might yet live. They watched the fire, looking at her father, Tuli saw that tears were falling from Krull's eyes, Tuli tugged on Krull's sleeve, "Papa, I had a vision… Pris may be alive!"

Krull nodded thinking even if she is alive, daughter, it is doubtful we will ever see her again.

Chapter IX Helga

147 BC

My mother had been captured and was unaware as to whether she would live or die as she was being taken South from one owner to the next.

Wador's Slave Cart

Pris was treated like a dog, she could not stop shaking in fear. She remembered her father's words that she needed to be brave and to never give up. It was one thing to hear those words at a campfire with mother holding you, when one can believe the world's violence is somewhere between scary stories her dad had said; something that happens to other people and could never happen to her.

This nightmare was real. Pris had been tied up, carried with a bag on her head, she was put into a cage and traded a few hours after arriving. Pris was brought out of her cage without being fed anything, she saw the Swabians eagerly receiving blocks of salt from a bearded Germanic looking man who had a receding hairline. A rope was tied around Pris and a few other captured ladies' wrists and they were taken South to another tribe, whom one of the other women said were known as the Boii.

The Boii gave them some water after they arrived and put them in a caged pit for a few days. Pris and the other ladies cried for food, begged for nourishment. On the second morning their guards brought them cold soup. It was a short-lived happy moment. A few hours later Pris and the other slaves were brought to a caged wagon, they saw an ugly looking man shaking hands with the village chieftain whose warriors were rolling away received wine goods from this new buyer.

This buyer had a guard who he spoke with in a language Pris did not understand, one of the other slaves said to another "These men are Tauriscian buyers".

Pris asked "What does that mean?"

The slave turned to her saying "They are from even further to the South."

Pris felt ever more depressed with each passing moment being pulled farther away from home. Their buyer was an ugly bald overweight man with a patch on one eye, though he was strong. He grabbed Pris from the seller, opened her mouth, felt her body all over and next smiling said something in Tauriscican to his partner, another Taurisician slightly younger who was completely bald, had tattoos and a ring in his nose. Pris did not understand what was said, but after they selected the other healthy slaves, they were taken away by her new buyers. They walked a short distance and Pris saw the caged wagon that she would be riding in.

Pris started to resist, she did not want to ride in another caged wagon. Feeling a sense of urgency and dread, she started to flail trying to run away though she was cuffed and chained, the ugly buyer laughed as Pris screamed "No, don't take me away in that! Let me go!"

The ugly man pulled her as she resisted with all her might, but it was no use, he was too strong and she was dragged a short distance. In her frantic state Pris thought I've got to get loose somehow, instead of pulling away from the ugly man Pris switched and charged at him, jumping on the captor's arm she meant to bite his ear, but he evaded and she could only scratch his cheek a little.

The ugly man yelled angrily at her as he hit Pris in the eye hard, Pris was knocked unconscious. The ugly man tied her up to the side of the wagon, then after loading the other slaves into the wagon, he took a whip off his belt, unraveled it and began whipping her.

Wador the Slaver

Pris awoke at the first lash, screamed and cried hearing the crack followed by intense pain. The ugly man laughed and said something to his younger bald partner who laughed as his whip lashed her again.

A female slave from inside the caged wagon yelled out loudly her singsong voice full of concern in Tauriscian, "She will be valued less if you lash her too much!" The ugly man stopped, began rubbing his shoulder, on which he unchained Pris and dragged her into the wagon. The female slave took Pris and laid her on her stomach. The woman applied an ointment from a capsule on her necklace, she then ripped part of her own dress and applied the ripped cloth to Pris' wounds.

Pris drifted in and out of consciousness over the next few days while the Taurisci slave traders hauled the group to the Taurisci's fortified town of Noreia which was situated at the edge of tall mountains far to the South. The woman who had cared for her in the wagon was with her when she woke up sitting next to her. They traveled through mostly forested lands; the land gradually became hillier to mountainous. A few days later, the wagon cleared forested land and entered into a farmed area, they crossed a bridge over a wide river and saw a large walled town at the foot of a mountain.

Pris tried to rise to see where they were going, but the young woman stopped her, the woman's singsong voice comforting, "Don't get up, you are still too weak." Pris rolled to her side. "I am Helga, I have wrapped your wounds with a shirt from one of the men." Pris looked grateful at the 20 something year old woman. "Who should I thank?" Helga's face turned sad as the wind blew her brown hair in her face.

"The man was killed the morning after your beating, so I took the shirt from his body." Pris was silent, Helga continued "He tried to escape when Wador had stopped the wagon to pee. The man had somehow picked his lock and the wagon's gate lock during the night. I wish I knew how he did it, but he did. Unfortunately for him Raez, the other Taurisician with the tattoos, seems to be good with a bow and the man did not make it 10 paces before catching an arrow in the neck."

Pris cringed in pain, "Who's Wador?"

Helga reached into her dress, there was a pouch that she opened a little and moved her finger around, "Wador is the ugly man who whipped you." Helga had a yellowish cream on her finger, "This is Arnica ointment cream, it will help with your wounds."

Pris let her apply the cream to her back. The wound immediately felt a little better, "Thank you!" Pris looked at the small city they were approaching, "I wonder what that place is called?"

Helga said "Noriea, it is Taurisci's capital, a Celtic stronghold."

It was the largest city that Pris had seen in her life. Noriea had a stone wall that surrounded it with a large central building sitting on a hill in the middle of the city. There were hundreds of straw roofed houses and smaller two-story buildings inside the town. Pris imagined that there must be at least several thousand people living here, the town seemed enormous compared to her town. The wagon rolled into a wide street where it stopped. Pris and her companions were taken out of the barred wagon they had been riding in and were put into a large fenced area. Pris was lying on a small pile of rags that the other four slaves had laid together for her to lay on. Pris started to get up but felt a dizziness and a searing pain from her back.

Helga could see that Pris was shaking a little as a tear ran down her cheek "Why am I here?"

Helga touched her gently, her long brown hair blowing gently with the breeze in heavily accented Germanic she said "We are slaves now girl."

Pris asked "Do you know why they took us here?"

Helga shrugged "I have some suspicions. My father used to come here on trade missions. He told me that the Tauriscians are allies of Rome, they have long supplied the Romans with lucrative trade materials for slaves, salt and iron ore. They trade for Roman wine, consumer goods and protection. My guess is we are ultimately heading to Roman lands."

The door's lock made a loud mechanical sound as Wador, brought in a large barrel of watery soup with a large spoon, spat next to the barrel and left. The slaves each took a turn drinking the soup which had a little bit of chicken cooked in the broth. Foul as their situation was, the soup was at least tolerable. Pris had not eaten anything in days and her self-control over her hunger was ravenous, she slurped down the remaining amount of soup after the others had eaten. Helga had only taken a few sips knowing Pris, the last person, would need as much as possible.

After her meal, Pris smiled at Helga "Thank you so much for taking care of me. How do you know the names of our captors?"

Helga motioned to Raez and Wador who were carrying sacks of something from a store to their wagon. "I can understand their language and it's what they have called each other."

Pris grimaced, trying to reach around to touch her back.

Helga stopped her "The stinging pain may last a while as it heals, I've cleaned the wounds with water, and my arnica ointment will work, don't scratch or it might get infected."

Pris stopped and tried to ignore the ache and itchiness, "Where are you from Helga?"

She brushed her hair away from her face, "I am from a tribe called the Boii, I was a common servant. Not long ago the king's son who was already married, tried to rape me, I fought the brute off. As I fought him my nails left a slash on his face. The King was furious that his son had been hurt, he was going to have me burnt at the stake the next morning."

Pris cringed as Helga put more arnica on her wounds. "Your wounds are healing, courage. My father snuck into where I was tied up that night and broke me out. We were fleeing, but the guards found us. My father fought the guards while he shouted at me to escape. I ran, as I climbed over the wall, I looked back in time to see my father had killed one guard, but was then killed by another guard, so I ran from that place. I ran and ran, but a Swabian hunting party caught me."

Pris looked at Helga, "I am sorry, did you have any other family there?"

Helga shook her head, "No, my mother died of fever a few years ago, I had a brother who died young. I am an only child."

A Tauriscan woman and her children passed by the slave cage on their way somewhere, the boy that was with them stuck his tongue out at the slaves. Pris frowned at him as they disappeared into the crowded street.

Pris looked at Helga "Why do they treat us so poorly?"

Helga touched her wrist, "We are slaves now girl, as valueless or worse than animals to them."

Raez and Wador put the last bags into their wagon. Next, they opened the wagon's back door and at that moment came over to open the cage, "Nasedněte do vagónu!" they shouted.

As the slaves lined up, a slave man who had cut his ropes ran out of the cage and went down the street. Raez chased after him, a Tauriscan warrior grabbed the man and handed him to Raez. Raez brought the man back to the wagon where he whipped him for several minutes.

Then Raez and Wador, having put all the slaves back into the wagon, took the wagon South again. They traveled a great distance across mountainous regions followed by wide spaces of farmland, a few days later they traveled through more mountains and arrived at the Northern Roman city of Bononia. There they met a buyer from the Roman republic, they traded all the slaves and bags of salt for wine goods.

Their buyer was a fat Roman; he spoke in a weird language to a man that Pris guessed was his guard. Neither Pris nor Helga understood anything they said, though he did not say anything to the slaves, they led the group of slaves to their wagon. The wagon had two big horses harnessed to it. This wagon had metal, not wooden bars, her buyer pointed and she climbed aboard, her companions Helga, and the other Germanic slaves, a mixture of young children and adults, males and females. Pris did not have to be whipped to get in, she did not want to experience a whipping again. Pris and the other slaves were immediately put into chains and before long they departed There was a constant jingle of metal chains as the wagon moved South. Pris and Helga hugged, not knowing what was next.

At first the roads were all dirt, however going South from the city there was an audible sound difference now. Suddenly the cart's wheels were rolling over stone, which Pris did not think much about beyond it being strange to her as she had never walked on anything but grass or dirt.

Pris occasionally wept. Helga comforted her each time. Eventually she asked, Pris told her about her remembering her mother dying, her father and sister's fates being unknown. If only I had just stayed in Jutland, she told herself again and again. Helga asked "How did you come to this?" Pris told her about her circumstances.

Helga nodded as she rubbed Pris' shoulder in a half hug sitting next to her. "We must never give up hope girl, your father and sister may yet live and perhaps someday you will escape back to them."

Pris began to sadly hum the song Krull had taught her "We are one with nature, we leave to feed our families taking only what we need, oh nature please give us the prize and a safe trip home."

Helga smiled, "I like that tune, it gives hope."

Pris looked at her, "What does it matter, I fall asleep crying, in my dreams I see my mother, her father and sister, of home and in every dream."

Helga gave her a half hug as Pris continued "Then it changes midway, the weather turns foul, like the world is ending or that some terrible force has captured me. In some dreams I am hunted by a Swabian champion with a skull helmet, in other dreams my sister screams at me blaming me for my mother's death and for my leaving her."

Helga comforted her "That explains why you jolt awake, your body sweaty."

Pris nodded "Yes, I have no family here, and it's back to living this horror as a slave and prisoner."

Helga shrugged "True, we are no better than caged animals with these horrific odors and confinement; a living nightmare, but we have each other." The wagon stopped as it had periodically along this journey.

The driver let them all exit the wagon, he gave them food and water, then urinated by a tree motioning them all to do the same. The slaves were all chained together, one by one they took their turn by the tree. Pris began to have a distant look about her, a tear appeared in her eye.

Helga touched her face "Don't cry, you have a family to return to, until then I am your family."

Pris smiled, "You're an angel, thank you for caring for me."

Helga nodded as they watched the scenery change from flat wood lands to steadily become smaller woods with cultivated farms and vineyards.

Chapter X Cyprian Treneca

147 BC

Mother was brought to Rome like a cage animal, hungry, unable to understand what Romans were speaking, Rome would be the place for her to grow and achieve redemption. This is where she would eventually meet my masters. Arriving near Rome, there were endless farm carts and bustling traffic the closer they got to the city. Pris was at first surprised by how the surrounding lands had all been devoid of trees. The land was hilly in places, there were farms worked by a variety of ethnic slaves that she could see planting crops in the distance. At every farm she saw a few men on horses who wore armor, a cape and had whips.

They finally arrived outside Rome late one morning, Pris was in complete awe, the city was unlike anything she had ever seen. There were a few massive bridge-like structures that led off towards the mountains. Like the other smaller Roman cities, they had traveled past, there were massive stone walls surrounding the city with towers. Along the side of the road, there was a line of wooden crosses. Most were empty and only had blood stains on them near the ends of the boards, however as they got close to the city, Pris saw bodies nailed to the crosses, on some the nailed persons cried out in agony, being a recent occupant. Seeing these punished, only added to the feeling of dread for the wagon's occupants.

The wagon stopped for a moment at the gates, Pris saw these Roman warriors wearing all red clothing with chainmail armor stood guard. Yet it was more than the identical clothing and weapons, they marched in unison, in an organized way that her tribe's warriors never did. One guard with a sideways fan over his helmet that went from one ear crested over his head and to his other ear spoke with the driver, read a scroll the driver gave him and then waved the wagon inside.

Rome

Entering Rome past the large stone walls, their awe only increased. The city was alive and busy, there were fountains and massive stone buildings that made Pris and all her fellow captives look on in awe and concern, most of the women and small children had begun to hug each other not knowing what would happen to them next.

Roman warriors all wearing red marched in long disciplined lines singing a loud impressive cadence. They all wore the same styled red clothing, shiny helmets, shiny armor and shields. Whereas in her tribe, only the chieftain and his bodyguard wore metal armor, and none of the warriors in her tribe wore the same exact clothing. Of the people who were not marching around, they all wore white clothing that looked like bed sheets. They were walking around speaking that weird language she couldn't understand.

Rome was full of impressive buildings made seemingly of white marble with pillars that held up the roofs, constructed in a way that she had never seen. There was a great amount of traffic, horse or oxen pulled wagons, there were men on horses, and some in chariots. Frightened beyond belief, hungry for not having been fed for a couple of days, the younger children cried ceaselessly. The cart went down a wide avenue that had buildings lined up one after the other.

The wagon turned a corner to go slightly downhill. Through their caged wagon, they saw before them in the distance Rome's market, it was inside a walled area, the outer shape of this was a heptagon that had a long exterior wall lined with marble pillars. The wagon pulled up next to the walls and stopped without any announcement.

The cart's doors opened, men came in to grab them, the slaves were unloaded, their legs all chained at the ankle, while several other men stood ready with whips. They were all led away from the cart and lined up then the ring of guards started shouting, motioning them to start walking.

Central Rome

1

The group was led into an entrance of the heptagon wall, inside there was a wide area, in this space where thousands of Romans who were shopping in a large market full of kiosk tents, this market was lively, sellers and buyers all speaking in that same language which Pris didn't understand, bartering over prices and goods.

Pris shuddered at the sounds of strange voices shouting at her and the others. They were led to an area that had a wide fenced open space, there was a small stage in the middle where a single fat man shouted towards the crowd. One by one the slaves were taken off the chain and

116

brought up to the stage when the fat man would point at each displayed slave, his hands raised and the man continued to shout rapidly pointing at the displayed slave and waving his hands around. Then one by one the slaves of her group were then led off to some buyer.

Helga had many men bidding for her, her long brown hair blew gently with the breeze. Her rags of clothing were removed and she was made to stand on a platform, she tried to cover her private body parts. The bidding went on for several minutes as the crowd of men roared eagerly. Eventually she was sold, given a toga to cover herself, then brought to a tall older muscular Roman who smiled upon receiving her. Pris was the next to be sold. The bidding also went on for a few minutes, next Pris was sold. Pris was happy when she realized that she was sold to the same buyer who had bought Helga earlier.

Her owner, who received Pris at that moment pointed to himself saying "I am Cyprian Treneca",

Pris and Helga looked at him, he pointed at himself again, "Cyprian"

They nodded. He opened a bag, confirmed the contents and then tossed it to the seller, the coins rang when they were caught.

Pris and Helga were unchained, then they were tied up to a rope by their wrists which he had brought with him.

Cyprian gave them sandals to wear, then he said something to them in his weird language and at that time led them into the city. Cyprian smiled, *these two are truly alluring, they will be great slaves for me and my home.*

Cyrian led them across Rome hardly caring that they were wide eyed looking at all the ongoings of the big city.

Pris saw some children walking with their mothers or handmaidens here and there; she pointed to some saying "If they're kind to their own children, perhaps they will be kind to us?"

Helga looked at them and said "We are wearing chains, don't forget that."

Chapter XI Aelianus and Decimus

147 BC

My mother and Helga were forced into a new life, there would be challenges and dangers yet to come.

Cyprian brought Pris and Helga to his inn which had a tavern on the 1st floor, guest rooms on the second and his home was behind an atrium garden on the first and second floors behind the tavern and inn. On arriving at the inn & villa, Pris walked through his large tavern which had a rectangular layout, there were eight tables, a bar at the far end and stairs leading upstairs to the right. Cyprian gave them to his elder female slave before he stayed in the tavern as he waved Ingrid, Pris and Helga away.

Ingrid led them to the back of the tavern saying in accented German, "Welcome to our house. That is Cyprian our master."

Pris and Helga were brought through a doorway into the entrance of the villa's courtyard. Pris saw a line of Roman style pillars lining the courtyard, which held up the visible 2nd floor via the open atrium. In the courtyard there was an open middle circular gravel covered area where marble benches were situated to watch the activities of the circular space. Rose bushes were in the four corners, separated by dirt and gravel walking paths just wide enough for two people to walk. On the side of the villa an open door revealed a weapon storage room to the right of the entrance, next to that was the guard's room, at the far end was the entrance to the stables, with an exit behind the house for the horses.

Hastati Roman Infantry

Pris and Helga saw two Roman men practicing swordplay with wooden swords. One was fit and muscular, the other was overweight. Ingrid motioned to them, they wore their Roman uniforms, armor and shields. "These are Decimus and his younger brother Aelianus, they are Cyprian's sons. They joined the legion a few months ago, and are home on leave until they return."

There were two older slave women with pitchers of water awaiting in attendance as the two men practiced with wooden swords and shields. Two mercenary guards stood at the entrance and Pris noticed another slave man in the stables attending the horses. Pris and Helga stood there, the other two slaves nodded at them.

Decimus said something and Ingrid turned to her, she said something in Latin. Pris, not understanding Latin, did not know what to do. So, Ingrid took her to the water well, where she said 'aqua' is the word for water,"

Pris said this word in Latin several times as Pris brought water to the young men. The elder woman followed Pris and apologized to the young men as they drank their water, but they shrugged then continued their conversation.

Cyprian came from the tavern entrance to the courtyard where he proudly greeted and patted the muscular elder young man affectionately. Pris noticed that he all but ignored the bulky younger fat one.

Cyprian held his elder son and said smiling "Decimus...." and continued in Latin as Pris and Helga looked on. Decimus was a stunningly handsome man, his muscular body was obviously strong with a powerful gaze. Decimus walked with a purpose of authority and had sharp looks.

Cyprian spoke for a long time to Decimus and Pris assumed that he was lavishing praise on Decimus for some reason. Pris had a hard time not staring at Decimus, seeing the new young slave girl Decimus smiled at her a little to which Pris blushed.

Cyprian didn't give much attention to his other son Aelianus.

Pris and Helga were taken to their common quarters where they were washed and dressed by other female slaves in plain toga garments that were already prepared for them to wear.

Helga

Cyprian came to the room just as the ladies finished dressing, he said something to the old woman in Latin and motioned her to leave, she grabbed Pris and they walked out of the room, as Pris left the room she looked back at Cyprian who was grabbing Helga's breasts and removing her clothing.

Pris was brought to the kitchen and made to help prepare the dinner for the family. While preparing the meal she overheard moaning coming from the room that Cyprian and Helga were in.

Later Cyprian emerged looking quite satisfied, Helga did not come out. After a few minutes, Pris finished cutting some carrots and went to the room, Helga had put her clothing back on, sitting motionless. Pris did not know what to say, "Are you alright?"

Helga looked at her, her face looked tortured, "He did not say anything to me, he just tore my clothing off like I was a statue and raped me." Helga began to shake,

Pris hugged her, "We must survive, that is all that matters. You helped me survive the whipping, we will survive this and someday we will escape this place." Helga acknowledged while tears ran down her face.

After Pris held weeping Helga for a while they heard two sharp claps from the room's doorway. They turned to see Ingrid, the old slave woman.

Ingrid looked to be Germanic, Celtic, or Gaelic. "Ladies, master Cyprian and his sons need dinner, feed them well and live, or do not and risk a whipping, branding or worse."

Helga looked at her and shrieked, "He just raped me!"

Ingrid looked quizzical as she came in, "My dear, this is something you must get used to, we slaves have no rights here in Rome, we are property of our master; that is Cyprian in our case. I was raped hundreds of times by Cyprian's father and then by him when he was just old enough and I not yet too old."

Ingrid touched Helga's face, "You are alive, survive and eventually it won't pain you so. The other choice is to try to escape, to do so would mean branding or whipping if they catch you. To kill our master would mean crucifixion for you and all of us." Ingrid helped Helga get dressed, "The best thing you can do is try to get Cyprian to like you, at that point he will be gentler and your life will be tolerable."

As they exited the room, Ingrid led them across the garden, there Pris saw that Cyprian was yelling at his younger son Aelianus. When they got to the other side Pris asked "Why is Cyprian mad at his son?"

The old woman shrugged, "Aelianus, his younger son, had an unhappy start in life as his mother had died in his childbirth, and his father Cyprian, blames him for his wife's death." Ingrid continued as they walked upstairs to the 2nd floor, "Cyprian has always been harsh to Aelianus, but became even harsher from age 6 or 7 when Cyprian realized that his son is gay by nature and perhaps also due to Aelianus' fat physique." Ingrid brought them into the kitchen "Cyprian is a veteran of Rome's legions, he had fought in the 3rd Macedonian war long ago, of which he boasts about when drunk. I think his experiences are a part of the reason why he became a hard, harsh man."

Pris walked out the kitchen door and looked down past the atrium's marble handrail at Cyprian, yelling at Aelianus Pris whispered "Kill that rapist Aelianus." Pris saw Decimus standing near Cyprian and Aelianus, trying to negotiate.

Ingrid continued "Often Cyprian berates Aelianus as one the Carthaginians would have sacrificed or that he was a fat lazy excuse for a Roman."

Helga, hearing the shouting, came over, "He is cruel even to his own blood. Scum." They returned to the kitchen, Ingrid turned to them both, "Are you hungry?"

The ladies nodded. Ingrid smiled, "Good, here is tomato sausage bean noodle soup and bread to warm you up". As the ladies ate, Ingrid knitted socks. After they had finished, they brought the prepared food to the dining room.

Pris asked "Has Aelianus tried to do anything to impress his father?"

The old woman said "Aelianus studied everything Roman boys are expected to without complaining, his education consisted of rhetoric, martial skills, horse riding and Greek epics. Aelianus can quote the Iliad, speak in Latin or Greek flawlessly, he often knows about effective business strategy and he can recite the wars of Alexander or Hannibal by memory. Still, Cyprian has never given Aelianus any warmth,"

Helga was amazed, "What is the problem of him being gay or that his mother died in his birth, it happens everywhere, doesn't it?" The old woman shrugged, placing food on the table and she shook her head, "I suggested once that Aelianus tried to make himself act less gay, to be more like his brother Decimus, Cyprian has never opened his small heart to his younger son."

Pris was confused, "Why has Cyprian kept Aelianus if he is so uncaring?"

The old woman looked at her "The only reason Aelianus has not been cast out of his family is his grandparents would not allow it, they love him." Ingrid looked down at Cyprian yelling at Aelianus and began to translate "...You should quit Aelianus, although you both will serve in the legion as Hastati infantry. I only expect Decimusto to survive, he is everything you are not, clever, decisive and masculine. A perfect Roman."

Aelianus said "Perhaps father that is because you taught Decimus all your old sword fighting techniques."

Cyprian yelled "Using my techniques Decimus could perhaps be the reason a battle is victorious! Although you Aelianus managed to survive through your basic training drills, if you go to a battle, I bet you will be the first to panic, drop your weapon and be killed. You are too lazy and weak. You will shame our family!"

Cyprian stopped yelling at Aelianus when Decimus told Cyprian something. Cyprian threw his hands in the air, yelled at Aelianus again then left the hallway and went downstairs to the tavern. Aelianus and Decimus entered the dining room. Aelianus was almost as tall as Decimus, however he was built like a house, he had thick bones with a thick neck, jaw, arms and legs. Decimus's body had an athletic, sleek toned muscular strength.

Decimus looked over towards the kitchen calling "Ingrid? Is our meal ready? It smells wonderful."

Ingrid came to the atrium where she responded "Yes master, it is." The men came upstairs to the dining room chatting as they walked. They sat couches that were positioned around a low table, food was brought out and they began their meal.

Decimus looked at Aelianus, "Areli, don't worry about father, he is strict, but you will always have my support, not to mention grandpa's."

Aelianus looked back at him, "You and grandpa are my only supporters, how many times have you stopped father from giving me beatings simply for looking too gay? He will not change."

Decimus swallowed a mouthful of wine, "Surely he will come to respect you for joining the legion, give him time."

Aelianus looked at him, "When we both joined the legions, father was sure that I would be kicked out or that I would be killed somehow along the way. You know how when drunk; father makes it clear about how much prouder of you he is."

Decimus watched Aelianus, "Your face looks like father's, grandma always told me I resemble mother's. That may be why father is hard on you."

Aelianus looked at him, "You are always supportive, I treasure you brother."

Decimus smiled, "I've known since you were young that you were different, it never has mattered to me that you are gay."

Aelianus stared at him then drank more wine, he looked back at Decimus "Do you think father will ever forgive me for mother's death?"

Decimus shrugged, "Let us hope. Question is whether any Roman woman would want to marry him?"

Aelianus suppressed a laugh and whispered, "I doubt any Roman woman would want to be connected to him."

Decimus nodded, "Father doesn't need to, what with his mistress and how he often enjoys himself with our slaves, you saw how quickly he went to that new one"

Decimus motioned towards Helga, "She was here hardly a few minutes when he started to remove her clothing."

Aelianus shook his head, "I feel pity for them you know, there is little difference between a slave and a master."

Decimus said "They wear chains"

Aelianus raised his eyebrow as he reached for his wine, "Not all chains are made of metal. I am surprised our father did not give me away at birth."

Decimus responded "He couldn't, grandpa would kick him out of the family."

Aelianus whispered "Grandpa, thank the Gods." as they savored the wine and food.

Aelianus and Decimus gave the ladies a passing greeting of thanks as they left the room. The ladies cleaned up the dirty dishes.

Ingrid looked at them and smiled "Helga, Pris, come here girls." They came over. "One thing Cyprian loves more than anything is my cooking. I will die someday not long from now, so I will teach you both how to cook. It will increase your value in his eyes."

Pris and Helga whispered in bed that night and often every night planning how they might escape.

The following day Decimus and Aelianus departed for their legion. Cyprian became very emotional for Decimus, while he ignored Aelianus altogether.

BOOK 1 Chapter XI

146 BC

In order to understand my master better, one needs to understand his background. Aelianus, the boy Cyprian called "The fat one" would, counter to his heartless father's predictions, excel in the legions and become a great legionnaire of Rome.

A year passed. Their father only wrote letters to Decimus and only inquired about Decimus' fate, he never inquired about Aelianus.

Cyprian was right about Decimus, he was always a very athletic alpha male, Decimus became very strong, a reliable and efficient weapon of war, however Cyprian could not have been more mistaken about Aelianus. Having a quick wit and sharp sense of humor Aelianus enjoyed the work outs with his brother Decimus. They pushed each other to be better at everything. Soon "the fat one" lost a lot of weight, became quite the muscular man.

Aelianus' ability to get the men of his manipular and Decimus laughing in any tense situation made Aelianus a delight to them all. Decimus and Aelianus worked well with their manipular as a battle-ready team.

Decimus was the man's man, he could do the most pushups, sit-ups, he was able to march long distances without tiring, he was masterful with a sword and shield. Through his training, Aelianus became strong and well liked. Both were great Hastati soldiers serving together in the same cohort of their legion.

Meanwhile back in Rome, Cyprian discovered that Pris was very intelligent, as within a few months Pris had begun to understand and speak basic daily Latin. Pris impressed Cyprian so much that he began to teach Pris without thinking much about it.

One day Cyprian entered the dining hall and saw Pris cleaning the dishes. Remarking on how skinny she looked he told her to eat more. Pris, not knowing what to do hesitated, "Thank you master, I will eat this in the kitchen".

Cyprian shook his head "No I would like to see you eat; you must not have eaten all day". Pris sat down at the table and started to eat the food. Cyprian looked out the window at the vast city then looked at Pris. "Do you know how big Rome is, girl? "

Pris shook her head, Cyprian looked back at the city. "Rome has roughly 500,000 people, it has aqueducts, temples, marble buildings and a sewer system that keeps the streets clean and people healthy. Rome is the finest power that has ever been".

Pris, with her limited Latin, only understood about 85% of this saying "Rome big, and is strong".

Cyprian raised an eyebrow, "You are learning Latin swiftly, I am impressed. I want to see how smart you are. From tomorrow I will have tutors teach you to read, write and do basic math. Perhaps one day you will be even more useful to me. Eat your fill, clean up and go to bed".

Cyprian left the room and went to his office. After Pris finished eating, she started to clean up as Helga entered the room and began to help her collect dirty dishes.

Cyprian returned to the room "Ah Helga, just the one I've been searching for, it is time for more fun."

Cyprian walked over and took her by her hand. Helga walked along with him having endured almost nightly rapings, she was somehow surviving through it.

Pris felt great pity knowing Helga had no love for Cyprian as she went to bed, how can he be kind to me and treat Helga like furniture?

A few years went by with no sign of word from Decimus or Aelianus. Cyprian had Pris taught by tutors to learn basic skills, and he continued to use Helga for his needs from time to time. Cyprian never allowed her to sleep in his bed, he was outwardly non romantic with her.

Pris was now 15 years old and was developing a beautiful young lady's figure. Pris worried that sooner or later Cyprian would use her body as he had been using Helga's.

Chapter XII Vicidius

146 BC

While my mother was surviving as a slave in Rome, my master learned to survive in the legions, to become a great Roman soldier.

During this time Decimus and Aelianus served in their legion in Southern Italy, not knowing when they would be sent into action. As always, Decimus was confident in their mission and purpose, he always woke up early, polished his armor, searched through his clothing for any thread that might be sticking up.

Aelianus wanted to make him feel supported, so Aelianus also would wake up and make his own uniform, armor and sword shine. Decimus told Aelianus that he had a destiny to serve, that he truly believed Rome was to be the great power of the world.

Their manipular's lead centurion died in a chariot racing accident, and they were given a new lead centurion; a man named Vicidius Marcellus Paullus. Vicidius set out harsh training in order to weed out any weak legionnaire candidates. The men quickly learned that Vicidius was a man to dread.

One morning Vicidius awoke early and during his rounds found a guard who looked sleepy. Vicidius beat the man with his wooden stick before he tied the laggard soldier to a fence. At that moment Vicidius banged his stick against his shield to awaken his manipular. After his 660 half-awake

soldiers had lined into formation Vicidius loudly barked
"This man put the whole legion at risk," Pointing to two
whips on a weapon rack, "Each of you must punish him. 2
lashes each, and we have 660 men...."

Roman Centurion

Vicidius smiled as he motioned towards the rack as the
man began to beg for mercy. The first line of 33 men took
turns whipping the prisoner twice each. Aelianus was the
first in line of the 2nd row, Decimus was next to him, they

grabbed their whips and lined up on opposite sides of the tied bloody man who looked to be on the edge of death.

Aelianus looked at Decimus, but slowly shook his head. Decimus stood there surprised as Aelianus turned to Vicidius, "Centurion, we should stop this whipping, he has already received 66 lashes, he could die."

Vicidius walked over to Aelianus, "Why is that a problem? He endangered the whole group?"

Aelianus looked at him questioningly "Do you not know? This is Cassius Carbo, he is a younger cousin of Gaius Papirius Carbo, an influential senator. Wouldn't Cassius's death at your command be risky to you?"

Vicidius turned and looked like he was going to yell for a long moment, next he barked at Aelianus and Decimus "Release Cassius and give him medical treatment."

As Aelianus began untying the ropes Vicidius asked him, "Why did you not tell me about Cassius before this?"

Aelianus shrugged then smiled slightly as he said, "It just occurred to me, good thing I remembered."

Vicidius looked angry, his hands shaking behind his back as he yelled to his unit, "Dismissed!"

Aelianus and Decimus began to carry Cassius who said in agony "Thank you...." and then passed out.

Vicidius drilled his men harshly, he would at that time lead the group into daily calisthenic drills, followed by long group marches, Sword & Shield drills, next more calisthenic drills and endless face to face yelling throughout. "You twits are all equally worthless, you must be descendants of Samnites or Etruscans!"

Vicidius would yell referring to kingdoms of Italy that had been conquered by Rome 150 years earlier. Decimus was already naturally fit and a strong man, for him, Vicidius was just another strongly placed loudmouth. Decimus's arms became bigger, stomach abs fitter, the other men of the group would nod their heads when he worked out. Everyone, but Decimus, thought Aelianus would fall out.

Vicidius called him "Fat boy" or "Fatty" or "The Fat one". Vicidius was eager to try to break Aelianus every day. I will make him drop today, Vicidius would think excitedly. Weeks went by, Vicidius never gave up, but his taunts backfired, they only reminded Aelianus of his father Cyprian and he wanted to prove them all wrong.

Aelianus never faltered, sweat poured off him as he grew stronger, he lost 45 lbs. of fat and gained 30lbs of muscle. During this time a few other men did fall, Vicidius would sneer and laugh as they were told to return home.

Decimus and Aelianus had become perfect Roman soldiers, everything was done properly to the point that Vicidius had begun to point at them as the example of how he wanted the rest of the manipular to emulate. Vicidius even started to brag to other manipular leaders that his policies made his manipular the perfect legionnaires.

One day as the men were dismissed from a long day's work out, Vicidius approached Decimus with a scroll, "Looks like you've got mail champ."

Decimus took the scroll and read it silently, his face turned from a happy expression to one of shock.

Aelianus sensing that something was wrong grabbed his shoulder, "What news?"

Decimus looked up, "News from my lover Tatiana, she has been pushed into an arranged marriage with a senator's son by her parents."

Decimus was quiet for a long time, the naturally strong man sat on his rack, dropped the scroll and held a long stare to the distance.

Aelianus watched him, he read the scroll then after a few moments said "Decimus, I know you well enough to say I think you're hurt in a way that you're not ready for... but remember this.every other woman in Rome save that one is happy now" and "You are a liberated man, no matter where we go you can go hunting for the perfect smile."

Decimus nodded, laughing a little from the joke and feeling some relief. Decimus said "In front of all the world I show a face...."

Aelianus nodded "I know, one full of confidence and a quick intellect"

Decimus nodded "True, but with you brother, I can just relax, knowing there will be another dawn and another laugh."

Aelianus grinned, "That's what I'm for."

Decimus smiled "Thanks brother, you're the best."

Aelianus shrugged "Just remember that next time we spar, your hits on my sword make my hand numb after a while. Now for some wine!" Decimus laughed, feeling better.

Cassius arrived at their tent, "It is great to see you both. I have to thank you for sparing me the other morning."

Aelianus nodded, offering him some wine "I know that you were working out hard that day, be sure to drink plenty of water before a watch, it will help."

Cassius got on his knees, "I owe you, my life."

Together, helping each other, they never gave up, they survived Vicidius' drills when many had not, and had transformed into model legionnaires. Aelianus had become like Decimus, a very intimidating fighting machine, in his own right. Now Aelianus was like a muscular giant, his muscles blown up and toned.

Through working out together Cassius also became toned and strong. The legion had to adjust Aelianus' set of armor as his original set no longer fit him correctly. Decimus felt pride when Aelianus had his new set, "Brother you are now a force to be reckoned with!"

The brothers would often duel with wooden practice swords with a combination of shields. They were simply gifted at fighting, no one in the legion was ever able to beat either of them in a one-to-one bout, they would often spar each other for several minutes, always unable to know which would be the winner. Against anyone else the bouts ended fairly rapidly with the brothers always the winner.

Their manipular centurion Vicidius Marcellus Paullus had his own goals, he would tell his men daily "I am here because I am a winner. I will gain my personal victories, honor and glory will be mine."

One night Vicidius was drinking wine with centurions of other cohorts. Decimus and Cassius were guarding his tent and heard from inside Vicidius boast to his guests "My manipular's men are the finest in the legion, perhaps of all of Rome's armies!"

Another voice said "They are impressive, Vicidius, you have certainly done well in training them."

Vicidius said "Believe me, my cohort will bring me victory; and victory will bring me power. That is what I Vicidius must have. The future of Rome rests in my hands, there is no difference."

The men laughed, "I think he's serious! One of them said as they laughed."

Decimus told Aelianus about this, and a few days later, Aelianus was ordered to get 3 dozen new sandals. While at the manipular's supply office, he learned Vicidius' history.

On his return he shared it with Decimus. "Vicidius is the grandson of Lucius Aemilius Paullus who had been a Consul twice. Lucius had attained some glory for Rome in battle as a general when he once defeated the Greek King Demetrius in the Second Illyrian war. Power and greed had grabbed Lucius and he was charged for unfairly dividing war spoils though he was later acquitted. Lucius' political connections redeemed his name."

Decimus nodded "Ah that makes sense why he said what he said the other night."

Aelianus continued, "Meantime Hannibal and the Carthaginians had been invading through Italy and defeating Roman armies. After those defeats, the Roman senate realized they needed a great general to achieve victory. Lucius' victorious war record was more attractive than his grab at war spoils and so the Senate recruited him to be one of three generals to lead Roman armies at the battle of Cannae."

Decimus shook his head, "His grandfather led our forces at Cannae, the slaughter?"

Aelianus acknowledged, making a half smile, "Vicidius seems to have a desire to redeem his status through achieving glorious aggressive attacks."

Decimus nodded his head "That makes sense…." Aelianus grinned.

Cassius asked "I haven't read about how that battle unfolded…"

Aelianus nodded "At Cannae, Lucius led his legions in an aggressive attack which at first appeared to have the Carthaginians on the run, but it was a massive trap. As the Carthaginian center had retreated, the Carthaginian cavalry had swept around the army, they defeated the Roman cavalry, all at once the Carthaginian infantry on the sides charged around and inward towards the sides of the Roman advance. The Carthaginian center turned around and their army encircled the Romans."

Decimus acknowledged, "I remember the history, they annihilated our forces."

Aelianus continued "Yes, and Vicidius' grandfather Lucius was killed in the battle."

Decimus nodded his head understanding, "So Vicidius is eager to restore his family's honor?"

Aelianus agreed, "It seems so. Vicidius' family has been rich since before Lucius, but they experienced the dishonor of his defeat plus his grandfather's scandal. Vicidius seems to feel the need to prove himself as the better man than his late grandfather and drunkard father."

Decimus and Cassius listened, Aelianus looked at them both, "We must be careful of Vicidius."

One morning Vicidius formed up his men, "Last night, our Legatus's Beneficiarii, who worked as a scribe, fallen ill and died. Does anyone among you know how to read and write? If so, step forward."

Aelianus and Decimus stepped forward. Vicidius smirked, pulling out a scroll, "Aelianus, read this."

Aelianus opened the scroll and read the latest supply orders of food and arms that their manipular would be provided for this month.

Vicidius acknowledged, "Alright, that's fine. we will need those skills, since you have already become a great fighter, you will be bumped up to Beneficiarii to which you will perform administrative tasks for whatever our Legatus needs, in battle you will join us. Lucky you survived my training, screw up and you'll be back among us. Now fall out."

Decimus smiled, knowing this was a promotion for Aelianus. Vicidius cared not either way, for him it just meant he could focus on constantly drilling his other men and would get a new recruit, he enjoyed getting rid of weaker men and Aelianus had survived.

Like any Roman commander he was quick and severe in his punishments to any in his manipular who got caught doing anything out of line. Vicidius truly enjoyed exacting harsh punishments on his subordinates when they made a mistake. The men under his command were powerless to stop Vicidius should he beat on one of their fellow legionaries. Vicidius would beat a man senseless for yawning at his post.

Chapter XIII Cassius

146 BC

On to war with the Greeks, a campaign which would have great costs.

A few weeks later Aelianus came to Decimus' tent and showed him a scroll. "What is it?" Decimus asked.

Aelianus read the scroll, "From grandpa, he says that his friend in the Senate told him that the Senate is unsatisfied with the diplomatic efforts with the Greeks in the Achaean League, which they claim would push them into an unfavorable peace, and the Achaean leaders may have deliberately provoked Rome into war. Grandpa goes on to wonder if it is possible that they simply miscalculated the Senate's patience for diplomacy."

Decimus looked at Aelianus, "These developments are probably unknown to most people."

Aelianus said "Grandpa wrote that Rome may go to war."

Decimus looked confident, "We are ready, we have the best armies, we have been training for this."

Aelianus nodded, "This is war, not training brother, we must be careful and support each other."

Decimus nodded "Always."

Just then Cassius arrived at their tent "What news?"

Aelianus looked at him, his face serious, "If this is right, we will be leaving Southern Italy soon, for war against the Greeks."

Cassius stopped "You think they'll send us? We have not seen action."

Aelianus, "Our legion is a newer one, we have been in reserve during the 3rd Punic war and the Macedonian wars were ongoing, see here."

Aelianus drew a map of the Mediterranean in the sand with a staff, "Here is Roman Italy, there is Carthage…."

Pointing at the map Decimus interjected "Carthage, soon to be ours."

Aelianus nodded, "Here's Macedon…"

Cassius interjected "Was Macedon, now ours" Decimus chuckled.

Aelianus shook his head smiling, holding up his hands as the others chuckled, "If I may finish… Yes, once they both are conquered and under Roman control, our legion has been held back in reserve, in case somehow Carthage or Macedon managed to somehow defeat our legions in those territories. We were here roughly in the middle, ready to be sent in as reinforcements to either theater."

Decimus clapped, "My brother, you should be a general."

Aelianus smiled, "Perhaps brother, but war will come soon. Decimus, Cassius, be ready."

Decimus nodded "We are."

Cassius gave a Roman salute. As a whistle sounded the signal for chow.

In 146 BC, their legion had learned of the fall of Carthage. While many of the legionnaires cheered the sack and destruction of Rome's once great enemy,

Decimus and Aelianus took no happiness out of the news. After supper they both had some wine, and remembered that their wet nurse and woman who had largely raised them had been a Carthaginian slave in their home, it just did not feel right. There was a great celebration among the men in the camp the night they learned of Carthage's defeat.

Vicidius had walked to the supply tent to grab a jug of wine, on the way back he noticed Decimus and Aelianus were not joyful. Walking over he inquired about it "Decimus and Aelianus, you two do not rejoice, why not?"

Decimus and Aelianus looked at him, Decimus answered "Carthage has long been a weak power, we did not need to sack that city."

Aelianus nodded, "How many Roman soldiers were wounded or died because our leaders were unwilling to be merciful?"

Vicidius stood stunned and said nothing. Aelianus followed Decimus "Ever since the end of the 2nd Punic war and

Hannibal, Carthage has not been a real threat to Rome, this war was unnecessary."

Vicidius shook his head, his voice rang out with fury "Attention"

Decimus and Aelianus snapped up standing at attention as Vicidius paced in front of them. His voice was introspective and at first rose like a storm "My grandfather was general Lucius Aemilius Paullus. Hannibal and his horde killed my grandfather and annihilated our forces at Cannae, as if that were not bad enough. Do you forget that Hannibal won a string of victories over our Roman troops at Ticinus, Lake Trebia and Tarentum?"

Vicidius looked them in their eyes "Have you two ignorant pansies read the histories about how many of our men died due to them? You two will celebrate this moment as Rome's finest hour for we have finally given them what they would have done to us, no mercy. They are finally annihilated, they were our enemy, and ever-present threat. Rome is superior to Carthage, the survivors and their children will be our slaves, no mercy, or no pity. Is that clear?"

Decimus and Aelianus said together, "Crystal clear."

Vicidius felt the handle of his whip, "I could lash you for less, but we are about to fight the Greeks, you both had better excel while we fight them or,"

A gruff voice spoke loudly from behind, "Vicidius are you busy?"

Vicidius turned around, his face showing annoyance and suspicion of who dared to interrupt, then a smile broke across his face as he embraced another centurion "Cousin Titus, you've come over?"

Titus clasped Vicidius ' shoulder, "I have been transferred here just in time to learn the news, the Carthaginians are finished, our family has been avenged, let's celebrate!"

Vicidius smiled, "Absolutely, shall we have some wine?"

Titus nodded, "Bring it. In my tent I have two female slaves awaiting us in chains, I acquired them from the local town, shall we have some fun?"

Vicidius smiled, then said "Absolutely." They went away with a jug of wine, forgetting about Decimus and Aelianus.

That evening after Aelianus returned to his tent, General Mummius called for him to go over the supply inventory lists. Mummius sat drinking wine listening to Aelianus read off the various items. Aelianus stopped midway and took a deep breath. "Aelianus, what is it?" Mummius asked.

Aelianus looked up from the list, "My general, my brother Decimus is a member of my old unit. The centurion there is an unforgiving man who has a personal reason for hating Carthaginians."

Mummius sat impassively listening. "Go on."

Aelianus knew he was on thin ice. "My brother and I had been raised by a Carthaginian slave woman since our birth.

147

She even taught us a few words of their language. When we learned of Carthage's destruction, we chose not to celebrate the end of worthy foes out of respect to her. Vicidius became enraged and probably would have made life Hell had he not become distracted by his cousin. Now after the wine has worn off, I fear that my brother, who is still under his command, he could be in peril."

Mummius nodded "Actually I want to handpick a couple guards for my tent. Anyone else you would recommend to be my tent?"

Aelianus grinded, "Decimus and Cassius."

Mummius nodded, and a few days later, Decimus and Cassius were promoted to be their Legatus General Lucius Mummius' tent guards. With Aelianus in their Legatus' tent daily, thus the brothers were together again.

A Senator arrived with a message from Rome. Decimus and Cassius stood guard outside their Legatus's tent, they overheard the Senator speaking with their Legatus "Mummius, the alliance between Rome and the Greek Achaea League had begun to fracture. Spy reports state that the Achaeans are threatening our ally Sparta."

Their general paced inside his tent, "Senator Quintus, tensions between our Roman and the Greek Achaea league's political leaders have been building up for a long time, I suspect due to the growth in Roman territorial and economic power?"

Quintus stammered, "Yes to the victor go the spoils."

Mummius agreed "Our republic has been in a state of quasi-perpetual war since its founding. It has been the main way that we have grown."

Senator Quintus spread his hands as he said "There are some who wonder if the population will accept another war. Do you think with Carthage and Macedon now conquered; our military can handle yet another war against the Greek Achaea league's forces?"

Legatus called out, "Decimus, Cassius enter and stand at attention."

Mummius looked at Aelianus and signaled to him "Stand at attention with them."

When the men were at attention, Mummius asked "Senator Quintus Maximus wishes to know if you men are ready for a war?"

The men saluted, shouting "Roman Victor!"

The general smiled looking at Maximus, "I suspect that our Roman leaders are looking East and desire to check any equivalent Greek Achaean ambitions of uniting Central and southern Greece against our growing Roman power in the Mediterranean. Our successes must have caused Greek resentment at being reduced to a lesser trade, military and diplomatic position given their once equal Roman status."

Quintus nodded looking back at him, "Give me your word, are our men ready for war?"

Mummius smiled "Absolutely." Mummius pulled out a scroll, "Our spies report that the Achaea are attempting to fully bring, or if necessary, assimilate Sparta into the league. If this were to happen, Rome would face a united Greece which could be a powerful counterbalance under the right general to Roman aims."

Quintus was quiet for a moment, thoughtful. "Is that possible? We've beaten the Macedonians 4 times, and Epirus before that."

Mummius gave Quintus a glass of wine. "If the Greek scrolls I've read are correct, under Alexander, Greek and Macedonian armies conquered the entire Persian Empire, and the old kingdom of Egypt, they went all the way to the faraway Maurya Empire."

Quintus raised an eyebrow, but our Roman armies conquered the Carthaginians as well."

Mummius finished his first glass, acknowledging while he poured more wine into his and Quintus' goblets as he stated flatly "Only after we had lost four major battles against them and Scipio Africanus used Hannibal's tactics against him. Besides that was a generation ago. Never forget, anything is possible in war."

Quintus drank another mouthful, "We sent two diplomats to Corinth, their Achaean capital. Each one tried to persuade the Greeks into a peace deal which the Achaeans rejected. This is a complete failure of diplomacy."

Mummius chuckled, "Perhaps they think they have another Alexander. Based off what my spies say, I think that they do not."

Quintus said, "There is little doubt the Roman senate will decide on war against the Greek league, be ready."

Mummius smiled, "Just give us the order."

A week later Decimus and Aelianus' legion and four others were ordered to join in the upcoming Greek invasion against the Achaean league. Their legion was fully supplied, trained and ready for battle. They departed from Taranto in Southern Italy on a large fleet of trireme ships. When their fleet was about halfway bound for Epirus Greece, a sudden storm hit them.

A Trireme Ship

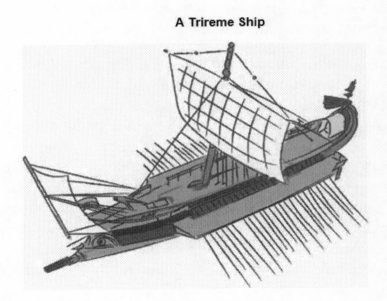

All of the men were sea sick, their trireme rocked, howling winds and rain ripped across them, the sky became dark and the sea got steadily worse, massive waves crashed over their ship. The fleet's other triremes disappeared from sight by the high waves. Aelianus and Decimus had gone top to throw up and escape the stench of the vomit below. Someone had handed them a bucket and yelled at them to help bail water, already there were 60 crewmen fighting to keep the ship from going under. About 20 other legionnaires were already doing the same thing, all of them clung tightly to rails, ropes, anything to stay on board as the ship lurched about, then almost as though by Poseidon's own hand the ship was slammed by a huge wave on its broadside, already tilting far to starboard the ship capsized. The scene inside the ship went from non-stop rocking, men throwing up, to suddenly the floor becoming the ceiling as water blasted inside the ship. When it rolled, all the topside was thrown into the violent sea. A few men from below managed to get out, but most drowned.

Aelianus and Decimus had the luck of knowing how to swim as they had often swam at a lake near their grandfather's vineyard as children. Aelianus found a floating wooden oar from their ship and grabbed onto it. Decimus was close enough for Aelianus to grab him. For hours during the terrifying storm, they survived being tossed about. By dawn the next day the storm had dissipated and soon after disappeared although the seas remained a little rough. They were in the sea for two days when Aelianus saw an oared merchant ship sailing by. They called out to it and felt surprised relief when the ship turned towards them.

The ship rowed over to them, two ropes were thrown down to them and they were pulled aboard. Aelianus had been brought up first, he was grabbed by a large strong black man, his skin as black as night, his voice boomed "Welcome to Seawitch friends, Poseidon has spared you."

Aelianus smiled, "Great Gods, thank you for saving us."

As Decimius was being brought onboard, the captain asked Aelianus about their identities.

Aelianus took a chance and told him the truth. "We are Aelianus and Decimus Treneca, legionaries of Rome." This is how Aelianus first met Daminian, the young black African captain who welcomed them onboard. Daminian gave the survivors warm blankets and freshwater, he spoke to them all in highly Aksum accented Latin stating "Welcome to my ship, we are a merchant vessel bound for Alexandria, my crew and I are originally from Aksum and Egypt, though on this trip from Taranto."

Decimus asked, "Where is Aksum?"

Daminian smiled, "It is South of Egypt my pale friend."

Daminian's ship searched for a few hours finding Vicidius and 30 other Romans floating in the sea. Vicidius had been too weak to speak, so Decimus and Aelianus thanked Daminian. Aelianus saw Vicidius and thought. "How much better had he drowned."

Daminian looked at Aelianus, "So here's our situation. I can take you survivors to Eprus, but it is out of my way and I would need payment on arrival. Can you promise that I will be paid for delivering you there safely?"

Aelianus nodded, Rome always takes care of her friends."

Daminian clapped, "Good, otherwise I would have to take you with me to Alexandria. Meantime, I have lost a few seamen due to the storm, we could use some extra rowers below, would you all mind helping out by rowing for us?"

The Romans agreed. They were given plenty of water and the oarsmen rotated out every 30 minutes so that they were not overworked. Within an hour, they roared like a seasoned team. During the trip Daminian spoke with Aelianus at length, learning about them. Aelianus mentioned that he and Decimus were originally from Rome.

Daminian smiled, "It just so happens that I am interested in selling ivory and buying wine in Rome to sell around the Mediterranean, do you know of any wine sellers in Rome?"

Aelianus smiled "Our grandfather owns a wine vineyard and our father manages the wine selling business from our family's inn in Rome. When you come to Rome, come to the Happy Moon inn not far from Isola Tiberina Island in the Campus Martius section of the city."

Daminian smiled, writing down the inn's name on a scroll, "The Happy Moon…"

Aelianus waved his hand in the air, "Our family has some of the best wines in Rome, it is the way we produce and store it that is better than most."

Daminian smiled "Well then, I must certainly try this wine. I will look into finding you and your family when I am in Rome.

The seas were still a little rough as their ship made its way to the Roman colony of Epirus. Aelianus, Decimus and the other Roman survivors deboarded. Aelianus made arrangements with the local governor to pay Daminian, who wished them all good luck.

As only a third of their legion had been saved, their unit was short of men. Vicidius, Aelianus, Decimus, Cassius and the other survivors were reformed into a manipular of Roman veterans from the Macedonian war who had need of reinforcements and they immediately began training to be ready for the upcoming action, they were now a part of the 9th legion's Lion manipular. Reformed into the army, Vicidius was given command of their newly formed manipular.

Vicidius called their group to attention. "Men of the 9th manipular, we are to be seeing action soon. I demand you all give your best efforts and I shall lead you all to victory!"

Aelianus, Decimus, Cassius and a few others from their old unit cringed as they knew all too well that Vicidius had no mercy for his men, and would be pushing them into extreme danger for his own glory. Something was afoot, Aelianus could see that all the units of the army were being called to attention. Soon general Quintus Metellus came out of his tent.

Praetor General Quintus Metellus Macedonicus gave a speech to the assembled army. "In Achaea, the Greek city states have become hostile to the power of Rome, they have foolishly declared war against us."

Quintus Metellus started walking along the rows of the assembled army. "Perhaps they've forgotten how our Roman armies once defeated and conquered all the former Greek city states in Southern Italy?" The army roared.

Quintus Metellus continued "Perhaps they've forgotten how Rome defeated the once mighty Epirus here in Northwestern Greece. Perhaps those lunatics ignore that we conquered Syracuse and mighty Carthage, the Hellenic-Greek Selucids, and we have had 4 victorious wars and then conquered Macedon to the North!"

The army cheered throughout this speech whenever Quintus Metellus paused. Metellus continued "Those cowardly Greeks have been led by fools to think they stand a chance against us. I bet their king is cowering in his toga!" The army roared in response.

Metellus continued "Rome has always won in the end; we will now take Corinth and the other states of their league have foolishly declared war against us, they have chosen doom, they will soon become part of our Roman colonies!"

Another deafening cheer arose from the legions Metellus yelled "Now our spies inform us that King Critolaos of Corinth has led a combined Greek phalanx army of the League in an attack against Sparta to try to intimidate, punish or persuade the Spartans to join their cause. Let it be known that our ally Sparta has stayed true to her word, they have openly stated their honor to our alliance. We are duty bound to them and must go to their aid!"

More thundering cheer erupted. The general motioned for silence as he continued his speech, "Our Roman Senate has selected me, Quintus Metellus Macedonicus, to lead this army South at all speed. We cannot wait for General Lucius Mummius, most of his forces have not arrived from the sea, we have only gained some reinforcements from his vanguard. We will attack the League before they can be ready for us! We must move now against the Achaean League before King Critolaos can complete his siege of Sparta, to do less would endanger our allies and our honor!"

The general motioned to the Southeast "Our spies report that Critolaos have defeated a smaller Spartan army before they put the city of Sparta under siege; we must get to Sparta before they sack it."

Metellus mounted his horse as he yelled, "Now let us move with all speed to save our allies, let's save Sparta!" The legion roared in support of this declaration.

An aid handed a scrolled message to Metellus who read it and said, tell Sabonis of the fifth equite cavalry to pick 20 dependable men to stay behind and communicate our destination to the local governor, his eyes only." Turning to his army "Alright strike camp, we will leave immediately, on to Sparta and to victory!"

Aelianus, Decimus and Cassius' newly retrained manipular traveled along with their legion into Greece's interior lands, Vicidius marched alongside the first row. They stopped and camped at the battle site of Thermopylae.

They were eating food in camp as a legionnaire played a flute. When he finished Aelianus called him over, "Come eat with us!" The man came over, "That was wonderfully played, what is your name?"

The lower ranking man said "I'm Septimus, attached to da 9th legion centurion."

Aelianus nodded "Ah, you are one of the 9th, who served in the Macedon war?"

Septimus nodded, "Yes, but what I enjoy is dis flute and how it makes women swoon!"

Aelianus laughed, "Well when you've finished eating play some more for the men it will keep our spirits up on this hallowed ground." Septimus did so.

Decimus and Aelianus took a moment before going to bed to pay their respects to the dead. Aelianus told Decimus "In this place 336 years before, 7,000 Spartan & Greeks made a defensive stand against 200,000 Persians."

Decius whistled as Aelianus continued "Then 46 years ago consul Manius Acilius Glabrio had led Roman forces to defeat the Seleucids at the same battle site."

The next morning the Roman's Macedonian companion cavalry scouts returned, informing them that Critolaos' Achaean League army had lifted the siege of Sparta and was approaching from the South, Metellus ordered his army to march immediately to intercept them. The Roman army was able to pass close by Athens without a fight as most of their soldiers were assembled in Critolaos' army. The Romans arrived in Southern Greece catching Critolaos' stratagem completely off-guard as he had believed the Romans would first strike Athens, which the Romans had bypassed. As the scouts reported, Critolaos had led his forces North, but they ran into Metellus' army on a foggy morning on slanted rocky terrain near to the town of Scarphe.

Chapter XIV Scarpheia and Corinth

146 BC

The battles of Scarpheia and Siege of Corinth forever changed my master.

The battle near the small town of Scarpheia took place on a foggy morning. Critolaos' army was still laying siege to Sparta, suddenly appearing out of the fog, A contingent of Macedonian cavalry appeared, mistaken as enemy scouts. Critolaos ordered them to be chased off, but as his own calvary started pursuing, a long line of Roman chort's in battle formation, starting with Aelianus and Decimus's unit in the vanguard appeared with others one by one appearing in an all-army wedge-shaped formation, the weight of their armor clanking in unison, their shields all held together to make a collective blocking tortoise formation.

The Romans caught the Greek phalanx formations of hoplites on rough lower rocky ground between the Romans and the still hostile city of Sparta to their backs and the sea to their right flank. A wave of collective panic overtook the Greeks as this ground was terrible for the Greek style phalanx, which needed units to be on flat ground or higher ground for their best effect.

The Roman legions pressed rapidly into battle. Led by the experienced praetor general Quintus Metellus Macedonicus the veteran legions were ready to fight against this phalanx army of the Achaean League. As panic increased, several Greek mid-level commanders called for order while King Critolaos sat on his horse unsure of what to do and steadily lost control of his ability to lead.

The battle of Scarpheia[2] erupted with the Romans closing the distance of the field at the center of the Greek line as the Greek phalanx line tried to line up, the phalanx formations formed into a tight defensive line facing towards the Romans, however the unit commanders of the different city states could not agree whose unit should be on what side and were arguing violently against each other. King Critolaos saw the commanders arguing and came out of his daze, he tried desperately to get them all to face the Romans in a unified manner, but it was too little too late.

A Greek phalanx formation

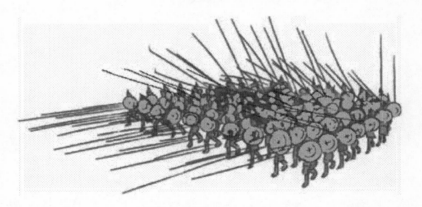

The Roman Velite skirmishers first threw their volleys of javelins that landed on the Greek Phalanx shields rendering many of them useless. Six Roman catapults shot

---

[2] While the defeat of the Greek army at Scarpheia by the Romans was a complete route, I was unable to find any actual information about the battle, and so the battle as it is described is this author's imagination.

fiery iron balls that landed and exploded up, down, in front and behind the Greek lines, each iron ball that hit took out a small group of men.

Roman Velite Skirmisher

The Roman Velite skirmishers ran out of javelins to throw just as the front line of Hastati, Principe and Triarii heavy infantry advanced past them. The lines got within javelin range and all at once stopped to throw their own two paella javelins that they carried, the javelins brought down many more shields, although many were also deflected off shields and long 45-degree angled spears, a great many impacted through, pinning arms to shields and inflicting terrible injuries and deaths. The unit commanders of the

Phalanx shouted out orders to hold steady as their men's morale began to wane.

By this point, the fog began to clear. The Phalanx commanders saw some group commanders and the King in a heated argument which led to the King pulling his sword and pointing it at the commander from Athens, causing the unit of Athens to pay more attention to what was going on with their commander than with the enemy.

Roman Triarii Heavy Infantry

The King's waving his arms around caused a few phalanx unit and cavalry commanders who were out of hearing range to think their unit was supposed to attack and they began to advance their units independently. This was done at an inopportune moment as the Romans were able to isolate and annihilate those units by attacking the rogue Greek units from two and three sides. The commanders, knowing unit cohesion and morale were critical, with the Roman manipulars just out of spear range, independently started ordering their unit to face the Romans and defend in Phalanx shield formation.

Aelianus and Decimus' manipular was closing in at the vanguard, suddenly the Greek Hoplites turned to face a wall of shields with spears sticking towards them. The Roman manipular continued forward in testudo formation, from behind his scutum shield Vicidius blew his whistle and yelled "On now men of Fox for Roman glory!"

They began hearing a deafening clatter from hundreds of Greek spear pike heads hitting their Roman scutum shields. The five ranks of spears got through in some places claiming a few legionnaire lives, but as a man was killed the man behind took his place. Decimus and Aelianus in lined formation fighting shoulder to shoulder, suddenly looking at each other Decimus said "Let's go!"

On que both used their scutum shields to suddenly knock the spear heads with their gladius swords overhead, with their way clear they instantly charged forward under the spear pikes to get in close to the Greek Hoplite spearman where under the spears they quickly used their gladius swords before the enemy hoplites could react. The two began to strike at the open necks, chests and slashed wildly around their enemy's shields instantly killing several.

Roman Principe Heavy Infantry

When the Greek phalanx's center was impacted the whole tightly packed cohesion began to collapse causing a panic among this phalanx as more of the legionnaires followed flooding into this opening in the enemy unit. They could not now use their long spears as they would have to kill their own men to do so, thus all of the phalanx dropped their spears resorting to swords, however by then the whole of Fox manipular was upon them from the front and internally where Aelianus and Decimus were killing with wild abandon.

A neighboring Phalanx to the left, seeing that one of their units' integrity was destroyed and the men were in danger of routing, turned and began advancing hurriedly on this deteriorating group of panicked hoplites. Another Phalanx to the right, was blocked by rocky terrain and a sloping hill covered by rugged rocks and that phalanx had to back up and circle around in order to get to where they could join the action, which would take too much time.

Roman Testuto Formation

As the left Phalanx advanced towards their manipular's position, another Roman manipular advanced towards the Phalanx's right side to which that Phalanx suddenly turned its spears down as that manipular switched to a testudo formation deflecting the spears.

Vicidius yelled "Reform" and Aelianus, Decimus and their group reformed to a solid block of men, pointing his sword Vicidius blew his whistle and barked "Fox forward left face brisk march!"

Their manipular next advanced on the Greek Phalanx that was striking the legionnaires who were in Testudo formation. Seeing that the spears had pierced through the shields and killed several legionnaires, the Roman unit was wavering. Aelianus heard Vicidius yell, "That is my cousin's unit, let's kill them all! Charge!""

Their manipular broke and all the men charged slamming into the left side of the Greek Phalanx. Attacked from two angles the Phalanx spears were dropped and their hoplites broke formation in order to fight man to man, but being attacked from two directions caused disorientation and panic among the Greeks as the manipular in testudo opened into charging at the hoplites once the phalanx spears went down.

Soon the whole center of the Greek line was engulfed in battle with the center having been pushed back as the Roman front line was pushing inward causing a wedge line battle.

During this massive mix of men fighting Cassius had been fighting near Aelianus and Decimus, he was fighting one on one against a Greek hoplite, but made an extended stab which was avoided and the Greek managed to deflect the attack on his shield before the Greek stabbed Cassius in the throat.

Aelianus saw and ran to Cassius, arriving too late. The Greek turned towards Aelianus, their swords clashed in three quick secessions before Aelianus found an opening and cut off his opponent's head. Aelianus went to Cassius, but saw that he was dead, a fellow hastati legionnaire grabbed him yelling "He's gone, kill the enemy!"

The overall Phalanx unit tactics of the Greeks had a major flaw. The classic Greek military training was that their line of spears would cut down the enemy, they did not have training for what to do if the enemy got under and past their spearheads. The Romans had four backup heavy infantry Principe manipular units behind the front line of Hastati.

In a few places where a Greek Phalanx unit defeated a Hastasi cohort, the second line's veteran Principe manipular would fill the gap and engage. The sounds of screaming dying men, metal hitting metal, filled the battlefield's air. One by one the Roman manipulars attacked the Greek Phalanx formations.

In some places the Phalanx's attacked, where the Roman units would separate and then attack their enemy unit from all sides, a big advantage the Romans had was flexibility by counter attacking from two or more sides as well as the ability to move over rough ground without breaking formation. The Greek Phalanx would become disorganized over rocky grounds, these combinations of Greek formation weaknesses gave the Romans a superior edge, enabling them to win the day.

After a few hours of intense fighting, the remnants of the Greek army panicked and were routed from the field. King Critolaos appeared directing two reserve Phalanx to advance towards his collapsing center, when hundreds of Roman equite cavalry, which had fought and defeated the Greek cavalry some distance beyond the ends of the battle line appeared from behind the Greek lines. They charged towards the Greek Phalanx's rear. King Critolaos, knowing he did not have enough body guards to counter the Roman equite cavalry, ordered a retreat from the battle. As the Greeks retreated, the Romans with their Eprus and Macedonian vassal units and Spartan allied units swept over the fleeing Greeks. The result of the battle was a wild and chaotic route, with the Greek Achaean Leagues forces fleeing in all directions away from the Roman army, the Macedonian-Roman cavalry continued to sweep through, killing or capturing fleeing Greeks.

When the action of battle had passed, Aelianus and Decimus looked at each other and hugged, happy to be alive. Aelianus and Decimus walked by the thousands of dead, dying and badly wounded Greeks and hundreds of killed or wounded Romans littering the field as they searched for their friend Cassius' body, eventually recalling the hill, they found him as ravens flew overhead eagerly seeking their meals. The injured on both sides screamed in pain due to a lost arm or leg that had been struck by an arrow or stabbed by a sword. Here and there a comrade was shaking as he called for his mother in his last breath.

They would learn later that it was a resounding Roman victory in the unit's first major battle, the speed of attack had surprised, crippled and destroyed the main Achaean force at the outbreak of the war.

Aelianus and Decimus were both celebrated by their unit as being instrumental in getting past the enemy spear heads and causing the first of many phalanx units to collapse. Decimus felt that Roman power was on full display whereas Aelianus had mixed feelings now that he saw the many thousands dead or dying, especially with the death of their friend Cassius.

Their army had lost about 10% of its men, so they were able to reform and proceeded to Corinth where they laid siege to the city. Shortly after General Lucius Mummius arrived with his additional legions and assumed command as Mettelus had sustained a minor leg injury in the first battle.

The night prior to the next battle Lucius Mummius had Decimus and Aelianus posted as his tent's guards trusting them. Lucius greatly respected Decimus' ability in 1-1 sword fighting and grappling, he also knew that Aelianus was another great warrior who also had a great sense of situational humor and Lucius often laughed at Aelianus' jokes.

The next morning the order was given to muster as whistles blew. "Decimus, are you ready?" Decimus had just come from behind the tent, "I went to relieve myself, and somehow felt ill, and threw up."

Aelianus nodded, "We will be fine, have some water, then we have to go, muster is sounding."

They formed at the back of their manipular just as Vicidius took muster; following this he sounded off to the army, "All present!"

Mummius rode up on his brown horse, "My fellow Romans, those cowering men beyond those stone walls are the overly proud Greeks, they think they are strong, our equals, but they can die like any other men. There are not so many lefts, you killed most of them. I think they must be sticking hay in spare armor. Our men are proud to serve Rome, but to add some incentive, I pledge that the first men to get beyond the walls will have some of my finest wines, and will have their picks of the females for their slaves."

Arriving at the end of the assembled line, Mummius turned his horse and slowly rode back along the line as he continued speaking loudly "Now, remember we have already destroyed their main army, some of the warriors they have left may be made up of old men, boys and the cowards that ran off the field, but you all must fight with vigor. A cornered animal is a fierce one!"

Mummius overlooked his men to his right. "Remember, this is their main city and a cornered rat is sure to bite. Remember your training and your gladius will do the rest! Now forward to victory!"

The legions formed up, as several catapults began to shoot flaming bolts. The legion's units began marching behind the several rolling tower structures that had been recently built. It was not long before volleys of flaming arrows shot out from positions on the walls.

Aelianus and Decimus marched with their manipulars' testudo formation, their armor all rattled in unison with their fellow legionnaires, they could see the walls and city of Corinth ahead, arrows were clinking off their shields and sticking into the tower they marched behind. The walls had a few archers along their battlements as well as in their towers, but with very few hoplites on the walls. The Roman and allied Spartans rolled up their towers and stormed the walls. A hastily assembled and poorly equipped town of old men put up a weak opposition on the walls.

After their unit emerged from the tower, they expeditiously engaged and killed the unit town watch. Aelianus felt pity as his blade turned red. These men were not front-line troops, old men and boys…. he took a moment to overlook the besieged city, Aelianus estimated that they may have at most less than a quarter of the strength they had at the battle of Scarpheia, he saw only four phalanx groups in the city's core streets below.

Vicidius saw where he was looking, "We shall attack and kill them, soon after we will be the first to raid their palace!" Their men roared in approval as he continued "Now let us form down below so we may go do our bloody business!" After forming up, Vicidius roared his orders "Forward March at the quick step!"

They quickly moved forward from the walls to march down the street that led towards the palace. Their unit went down the street, their armor clanking in unison, the buildings on either side had shut doors and windows, they entered an intersection.

They saw a few hoplites retreating in between the poor cement looking buildings. One of the hoplites was limping and his fellows were helping him escape. Vicidius yelled "Velites, rush ahead and kill them!"

The lightly armored young men ran ahead and threw their javelins at the hoplites, one was killed. The others kept running towards the back of the building, the Velites in pursuit. Suddenly a crowd of hoplites came around from the back side of the two buildings forming into a Phalanx and blocking the far end.

Their men looked determined, these men were fearsome looking as they switched to a defensive stance, their battle worn shields emitted a loud collective clank as they came together forming the familiar shield wall with their spears sticking forward towards the approaching Romans. Vicidius yelled "Velites attack! Hastati, Principes and Triarii, Testeto!"

The Roman unit immediately closed together becoming a solid unit of men, their shields protecting them above them and around their front and sides. They marched slowly forward towards the phalanx, Vicidius watched as his Velites, who had already thrown all their javelins, brandished their swords then bravely attacked the Phalanx, they never got past the spears, most of them were killed before the last 10 Velites retreated, as they did so Greek archers in the near building windows shot at them. None made back alive.

Vicidius clanked his sword against his shield in a march beat. At another whistle signal, the back row of legionaries pulled out and threw their two pilla javelins into the engaged phalanx unit which had become engaged in attacking them with their spears. A few javelins found their marks killing the several men, many more javelins went through shields and pinned the carrier's arm to the shield.

Suddenly a whistle blew from behind the phalanx and the windows on the two neighboring buildings opened up and Greek archers appeared in each window. The Roman testudo was immediately hit by several waves of arrows, though most either stuck into or bounced off their shields.

Vicidius blew his whistle three times. Their unit of Hastati, Principe and Triarii pressed ahead. Now the spearheads of the phalanx began to jab at their shields as well. "Steady!" Vicidius yelled, he blew his whistle again.

The line of hastati engaged the Greek Phalanx Aelianus and Decimus engaged again going under the spears as they had done in the battle before, this broke the formation and it became a massive sword battle with their hastati and veteran principes attacking behind them.

Vicidius barked out orders to his mid row of Principes to throw javelins at the archers in the windows, this killed several archers who were within short range. Vicidius signaled to his lines of triarii to stay in the back in reserve.

The Corinth commander blew his whistle and the hoplite warriors of the phalanx dropped their spears that were not penetrating the Roman shields and pulling their swords, they attacked the Roman formation.

At that moment a few dozen hoplites who had been hiding in the two buildings rushed out to attack the Roman units' backside while it was engaged with the hoplites of the phalanx. The veteran Triarii turned to engage them and a massive melee ensued in front and in back of the Romans this ambush had caught Vicidius off guard.

Vicidius whistled as Greek hoplites attacked their unit "break formation!"

The Romans fought both in front and behind now, but now they were vulnerable to the archers in the windows who were still shooting at them at close range while also reacting to the attackers behind.

At that moment three more Roman manipular units arrived and began attacking the two buildings and the Macedonian Companion Cavalry slammed into the hoplites who had come from the buildings. another Roman manipular charged into one phalanx's from behind. A mass mix of individual fighting erupted as the hoplites in the road received a few hundred reinforcements. Aelianus killed many Greek hoplite soldiers, as did Decimus, the two never left each other's side.

Towards the end of this part of the battle Decimus was locked sword to sword against a hoplite. As they were locked another Greek hoplite stabbed Decimus through the side of his chest under his arm with a xiphos sword.

Aelianus, having just killed another opponent, happened to see Decimus as he was stabbed, seeing red he jumped over a dead body from where he had been to land close to the two hoplite's kill zone spaces, his blade clashed with the two other blades, he immediately killed one and then smacking Aelianus' shield into the other's sword, sent it flying; as he swung his sword back powerfully sending the hoplite's head flying in the same direction.

A Greek Hoplite

Aelianus turned to see his brother Decimus on the ground bleeding out in a pool of blood. "NO!" Aelianus wailed and rushed to him, he pulled off Decimus' helmet and tried to cover the spraying blood wound with his cape, "No Decimus, stay with me, you're going to live, you…"

Coughing up blood clinging to Aelianus, Decimus shuddered saying "I cannot…. see…. St…. ayy safe….. bro…ther…." his eyes rolled to the back of his head, his bloodied body shook before his head fell and his body went limp as death took him.

Vicidius had been finishing a hoplite who he had injured, he approached and yelled at Aelianus for going to his brother during the fight.

Aelianus had been in such shock he did not hear, so Vicidius grabbed Aelianus yelling at him to get back into formation. In almost stunned shock, Aelianus turned around instantly and grabbed Vicidius so forcibly and pushed him backward causing him to fall over into the mud.

Vicidius muddied, got up, pulled his sword and was about to kill Aelianus. Aelianus knew he should die, only then realizing what he had done.

General Lucius Mummius rode up on his horse. "Centurion, hold there! I saw what transpired, Aelianus was not at fault."

Vicidius yelled, "He struck me, his superior, by rights and honor I can take his life!"

Mummies shook his head, "You were out of line, his brother was killed, and had you not charged off disobeying my orders these Roman dead might still be alive. You need to obey orders and not attack unless so ordered!"

Vicidius was now stunned as Mummius continued. "Your zealousness put this manipular at unnecessary risk which would have been your deaths had I not sent these other three manipulators after yours, now fall in."

Vicidius wanted to say something, but knew that any more protest and his general could have him demoted or worse killed for disobeying during action.

Mummius yelled again "Your unit has lost roughly half in that callous attack. You will lead your unit towards the square outside the palace behind these three other units to act as support."

Mummius looked at Aelianus "Legionnaire Aelianus, you are hereby promoted to command Stallion manipular as its centurion as their centurion has been killed."

Aelianus looked at his brother's body, a wash of memories passing across his thoughts.

Mummius said "Do not worry, I will have our support units take your brother's body to the hospital tent."

Aelianus breathed and stood up, he pounded his chest in Roman salute. Vicidius stammered, "But Aelianus just dishonored me! I demand justice!"

Mummius bellowed "Centurion Vicidius, you will stand down and lead your men as I order or you will join the dead!" Vicidius pounded his chest in salute.

Mummius yelled "All units attack down the main avenue, head for the square outside the palace! We capture that and the royal family will surrender!"

Mummius watched Aelianus hurry over to his new unit and next ordered them forward. After Aelianus had left for the other unit, Vicidius shouted with zeal for his unit to move out.

Aelianus looked back at them feeling pity for his former teammates, he absent mindedly muttered "Vicidius will get them all killed, he is too aggressive and stupid in his eagerness for glory." He looked at his new unit, "Men of Rome, we move to secure the square and next to the palace. Move out!"

Without Decimus or Aelianus, his manipular's former best fighters, Vicidius led his manipular towards Corinth's palace behind the other three manipular units. Ahead there were 6 hoplites who had survived the fight at the crossroads running ahead and they went towards the palace.

Vicidius' unit was followed by the three other Manipular units, the last one of which was being led by Aelianus. They entered into a huge open square that had a massive water fountain of Zeus in the middle.

Vicidius saw around 6 hoplites retreat into their palace and pointing to the palace yelled "Onward Fox for greater glory!" There was a barricade that was abandoned in front of the palace. Their remaining manipular force of roughly 300 men raced up the palace steps. At the top of the steps they were engaged by an ambush of hoplites who attacked them from three sides, the men of Fox had limited room to maneuver the fighting was intense as the hoplites fought back before they slowly retreated.

Vicidius urged his men forward, the hoplites retreated in the middle as their men held their ground on the left and right wings. Vicidius waved his sword in the air, his glee at killing hoplites noticed above the sounds of battle. He pushed his manipular to the top step, past a pile of hoplite and legionnaire bodies.

Aelianus saw that the other two manipular units had secured the square, that many Roman and Spartan units were approaching the square from the walls, there were no Greek units in sight, so he turned his manipular from securing the square and ordered his unit to head towards the palace ordering a quick march.

At this moment, Vicidius' manipular was engaged on three sides, Vicidius knew that in this situation Roman tactical doctrine was to order a defensive stance to fight in place until help arrived. Vicidius, looked at the palace, I shall be the first to raid the palace, I shall have glory no matter what! Instead of ordering a defensive stance, Vicidius ordered an attack.

The Roman manipular, engaged on three sides, was held back, the formation broke as the majority of the defending hoplites and many Romans were killed in the massive melee. Vicidius saw that the last few hoplites were defending the front door, as their leader banged on the door to escape the battle, the door opened, and Vicidius led the other Romans to attack the last few hoplites. The bodies of killed, dying and horribly wounded Greek hoplites evenly mixed with killed, dying, and horribly wounded Roman velites, hastati, principes, and triarii legionnaires.

As the door swung rapidly to be closed, Vicidius threw a spear into the closing opening stopping it from closing. Vicidius and the last 200 of his men of Fox pushed their way inside through the door. They killed the slaves who had been trying to keep the doors closed and then rushed down an opulent hallway to a large darkened room that had two upward stairways on either end, a fireplace was at one end, there was a throne at the far central back wall with hallways that led further into the building. Vicidius led his men upstairs where his unit encountered a group of 20 hoplite warriors who fought them on the stairs. These hoplites wore black and gold armor, they were part of the Greek King's elite fighters.

The King of Corinth arrived in the back of his hoplite guards, the Romans fought up the steps, both sides lost men. The Greek King yelled at one of his men who ran back into the room behind them, the Romans that went upstairs with Vicidius were down to their last 16 men. Vicidius attacked against the King of Corinth in 1-1 fighting.

At this moment Aelianus and his manipular unit of roughly 600 men entered into the building.

Vicidius had been running and fighting aggressively for a few hours by this point. His sword, shield and armor weighed down with every slash and movement he made. The Corinth King, suited in hoplite armor was also breathing heavily and his movements began to slow a little, but he fought on with abandon, Vicidius was impressed by this warrior King's bravery. Vicidius used multiple attacks and parties against this King but his attacks were blocked each time, his skills were so great that Vicidius imagined that this is what Achilles himself would have been like, fighting to the very end.

Their swords clashed against each other's shields and blades. At one point the Greek slammed his shield into Vicidius as Vicidius had been swinging for his opponent's head. Vicidius' sword instead hit a pillar, and he counterattacked with an upward slash that cut Vicidius' left cheek and eyebrow. Blood started pouring out of the deep gash, the Greek king laughed as he yelled in accented Latin "Your helmets don't protect your ugly faces!" but he miscalculated his next blow which Vicidius ducked then seizing the opening Vicidius stabbed his sword's blade into his opponent's throat.

The man dropped his blade as Vicidius pulled his sword's blade out, his opponent grabbed his throat as blood sprayed out as he tried to scream but the sound came out as a bloody gargle, he collapsed.

Vicidius, bleeding badly from his slashed cheek and eyebrow seeing his opponent curling in pain, finished his opponent by stabbing his gladius blade deep into the King's chest.

Vicidius was still burning with rage from Aelianus' from earlier slight. The push was bad enough, the fact that Aelianus was not by his side, putting him into combat with this hoplite made him feel as though Aelianus was not dependable and that he would not have been injured, he indirectly blamed Aelianus for his injury and he vowed he would have his vengeance someday.

He and 10 of his men from Fox charged into the bedroom quarters, the others were checking other rooms as the final two hoplite guards attacked but were quickly killed. Behind them Vicidius saw the queen holding a xiphos sword, behind her, three young children. She attacked Vicidius and he deflected her blade, and pushed her onto the bed as he yelled "put her children in chains they will be slaves!"

As two legionaries grabbed the children another asked "Will you need time?" Vicidius smiled as he began taking off his armor.

An older female slave came out of a closet with a knife attacking Vicidius, he saw her coming and his blade's slash caught the slaves throat and she died.

Aelianus had just arrived outside the room as he saw the legionnaires leading the crying royal children out in chains. He could hear screams and thrashing from inside the room. Aelianus ordered "Take those children to General Mummies' tent, he wants them alive!"

Aelianus pointed towards the exit to those men, men who had been his comrades in Fox until today, men who Aelianus had worked daily with. The men nodded and saluted.

As soon as they had left Aelianus went into the room, he saw that Vicidius had torn off most of the queen's clothing, her face and body showed bruises, they had fallen off the bed and Vicidius was choking her neck. The queen scratched his face and chest ferociously.

Vicidius howled in pain as her nails scratched across his wounded face "Bitch I will make you feel me!" Vicidius was half undressed, his armor and helmet scattered near the bed, his manly parts bulging through his underclothes. Vicidius let go with one hand from her throat to slap the queen again as he yelled "damn it!" Without looking at Aelianus he yelled "Legionnaire, this queen is not giving up, I shall have to be extra rough, come hold her down!"

Aelianus nimbly walked up grabbing a flower vase and smashed it over Vicidius' head. Vicidius was knocked unconscious as Aelianus went to the Queen who was puzzled and in shock. In fluent Latin she asked "Why?"

Aelianus motioned to the dead female slave, speaking in fluent Greek "No time, get changed into your servants' clothing, I'll take you out of here and to your children."

Aelianus tied a rope around the queen's hands passing hundreds of Roman legionnaires, Aelianus saw that many of the legionnaires had begun looting the palace, men were carrying armfuls of treasure.

As he came to the stairs Aelianus saw the two legionnaires who had the royal children down below.

Aelianus yelled to the legionnaires, "Men of Fox, stop!" Aelianus brought his captive down the stairs, passed the many bodies that lay where they fell. "You two should grab some treasure while you can, I will take the captives." Aelianus received the children from the two guards as they hurried off to look for loot.

Aelianus led his captives to the front entrance, when he arrived there General Mummius walked to the top of the stairs near the entrance with dozens of legionnaires, outside several manipular units had arrived, using horns Equite cavalry units could be seen calling to civilians to come out of their homes and gather at the square.

Aelianus saluted "Ave General."

Mummius saluted to him, "What is the status of the palace?"

Aelianus motioned backwards "Centurion Vicidius Paullus led Fox into the palace with all haste, Fox took heavy losses, I brought Stallion to the palace as reinforcements, I last saw Vicidius upstairs. I am taking this servant woman and those children as captives."

Mummius took a quick glance at the woman, "Aelianus, I didn't know you had a taste for women. Oh, very well, use my tent and then do with her as you wish."

Turning to his men Mummius yelled "Find the royal family, I want them alive. Let us bring all the treasure to our wagons, and have our troops bring all civilians to the square."

Aelianus saluted following this he led the queen and her children away from the palace. Aelianus led his captives out of the city. The field outside the city had many Roman auxiliaries checking the fallen for those who might still be alive, one tower had been hit by a number of flaming arrows and had burnt to the ground.

Aelianus led his captives towards where the Roman camp was, on the way the children looked back and started crying. Aelianus glanced backwards, followed their vision to the city and saw that some buildings were burning. They had to pass near a cluster of trees, walking around this, Aelianus told his captives "Hide here in these trees, tonight when it becomes dark, I will direct this area to be unguarded, try to escape after dusk."

The woman looked at him "Why?"

Aelianus looked at her, "We do not need to make war on women. Go live a farmer's life."

The woman thanked him, afterwards Aelianus left them there; he returned to the camp to check for his brother's body, he passed several medical tents where medics were hard at work. Wounded men were laying with their wounds wrapped, while the dead were all being laid in a separate field. Unable to find his brother among the many others, Aelianus said a prayer for his brother.

Aelianus returned to the city square and saw on the way that many more of the buildings were burning now; he reformed with his Stallion manipular.

By this time, he saw that Vicidius was in a meeting with General Mummius in the square. There were Romans leaving buildings with boxes and newly captured civilians whom he knew would all become slaves.

Mummius looked furious "Centurion Vicidius Paullus, you're disobeying my orders to stay as support in the square needlessly sacrificed the lives of your men. Once you got inside, somehow the queen and her children disappeared."

Vicidius looked up in the air and down to the ground, "My men wished to gain treasure and glory, they had sacrificed so much coming over the walls, I couldn't deny them, so we went through their surviving men, we fought through their defenses and following this we looted the building, we killed any who resisted."

Mummius scratched his face, "So why then did the royals escape?"

Vicidius stammered, "I was in the bedroom searching for the royals and someone hit me over the head with a clay vase, I was out for a long time until our men awoke me."

Mummius nodded, "Do you know who did it?"

Vicidius shook his head, "I took my helmet off for a moment to drink some water"

Vicidius' face showed his fury. "Must have been a slave, anyone else would have killed you. Very well, I will be transferring you to be in charge of our supply chain's inventory control."

Vicidius stammered, "But I am brave, I want a field command, that is where glory is!"

Mummius shook his head "You callously attacked the palace when your orders had been to just secure the square. We have a need for a good supply manager and tax collector, besides there are no units now that need a centurion."

Vicidius interrupted, "Give me Stallion!"

Mummius shook his head "And how would you get them killed? No, Aelianus follows orders. The Supply unit is back in the camp, go there and assist with conducting an audit on how much ammunition, medical supplies and food we have. I want a report in two days. Dismissed."

Vicidius' face turned red, but he said nothing and saluted before walking off.

Mummius watched Vicidius walk off before turning to Aelianus "Aelianus, Vicidius claimed that he gave custody of the royal family's children to two of his guards, they said that you had taken custody of them. I remember you leaving the palace with a female servant and two children. Was Vicidius right?"

Aelianus shrugged, "I found the female servant in a room and grabbed her, then I found the two children being escorted out. I did not know their identities, whoever they were… but I did not want to have them killed. I escorted them outside the city and released them."

Mummius walked over to Aelianus "You released them? They could have been the heirs to this city, they might come back in 20 years to try to reclaim their throne…"

Aelianus shook his head "Perhaps my general, but there won't be much of a city left and they were terrified, our nation will not be strong by killing the innocent and mercy, like hate, is never forgotten."

Mummius paused, taking a deep breath "Alright centurion, next time ask me before you do something like this. I'll assume your instincts are right. Take your manipular back to the camp, have them perform guard duty tonight."

Aelianus saluted and left the city that was now being looted and many of its citizens had been gathered at the square.

Aelianus led his men out of the city and they arrived back at the camp. He ordered his men to be hourly rotational guards for the night. After the unit had been dismissed and he sat in his tent, the tent he had shared with Decimus since becoming a legionnaire, sitting there, remembering his brother, his one lifelong friend, he wept as never before, more than he had from one of his father's beatings.

One of Aelianus' men arrived with Aelianus' new helmet, the crest situated from ear to ear, he saluted and exited without Aelianus saying anything, tears fell freely and the man thought that it looked as though someone had ripped out Aelianus' heart.

The Roman forces would over the next few weeks pillage the city and raze it to the ground, all the Greeks who did not resist became slaves, those who did got the sword. General Lucius Mummius had been very fond of Aelianus and Decimus as well, how many times had Aelianus entertained him with humor such that his belly ached. Decimus too had been a great loyal soldier, Mummius had felt of them as sons and his anger was such that he commanded his army to sack Corinth in order to quell any remaining Greek resistance, the Romans razed and plundered the city and took all the greatest symbols of Corinthian wealth.

Vicidius knew he could not have his vengeance against Aelianus now. Furious at the affront that had happened, suspicious of being knocked out, jealous of Aelianus' promotions, and his carefree nature. Yet for now, Aelianus was protected by Mummius, revenge would have to wait.

Chapter XV Justus

146 BC

My master was crushed by his brother's death. From there he had to restart anew trying somehow to carry on finding strength in loss by focusing on keeping his men alive. Meantime my mother learned at what cost her position as a slave would be changing her life forever.

Aelianus returned to Rome with his legion. At Decimus' funeral his father hardly acknowledged him. Cyprian embraced Decimus' lifeless body, next he turned to Aelianus stone faced "I must have done something to anger the Gods, it should have been you."

Lucius Mummius spoke up, "Cyprian, Aelianus fought well, Decimus too, these things happen in war." Cyprian shook his head. He was about to say something but Aelianus' elderly grandfather, Justus, gave Cyprian an annoyed look so he walked out of the tomb.

Mummius turned to Aelianus who asked "General, what is next for you?" Mummius said "I am assuming a post in the Senate."

Aelianus smiled, "Rome will be in good hands General"

Mummius nodded, "I will have to visit your tavern and have some of that great wine I've heard of. Take care of yourself Aelianus, I will always be a friend to you. May the Gods grant you glory and protection."

Aelianus and Mummius saluted each other, embraced, then Mummius looked at Justus and saluted,"You look good Senator."

Justus waved him away, "If only, retirement has been tough, now this…."

Mummius nodded, "Decius was one of our best. He died a hero of Rome. " Mummius turned and gave a last prayer to Decimus before departing.

After Mummius left, Justus embraced Aelianus, he turned looking at his half Greek half Jewish servant "David, go fetch Cyprian"

When Cyprian arrived, Justus looking down on Decimus, spoke, "Cyprian, you have never been kind to Aelianus, I know it was due to the loss of Quintia, but it is far past time you let that go and forgive him."

Cyprian shook his head "Never, that freak killed my wife and there is no future for the family with him. Aelianus is gay and has no intention of marrying."

Justus turned to Aelianus, "Aelianus, you will inherit ownership of our family inn and all of my properties as I am dying."

Cyprian stammered "I am to inherit everything!"

Justus shook his head "My daughter, was your wife, I was going to give everything to Decimus. You have always just managed things, I never told you that you would inherit anything."

Cyprian's face turned red, his hands became white fists, but he said nothing. Justus looked to Aelianus "One condition, you will either marry a woman of your choice within the next few days, or I will have you marry my friend's granddaughter, I saved him from death in battle long ago. They are a poor family, but they're Italian."

Aelianus thought for a long time, "You are sure your friend will agree?"

Justus smiled, "I already have his agreement and offer."

Aelianus nodded, the truth was that he had never thought of any woman romantically. "Very well grandfather, I will accept to have this arranged wife."

Justus signaled to David his scribe, "See that it is done. On my death, Aelianus shall inherit our winery, the tavern and house, also our house at the beach. Once I am gone, I shall have David there to take care of things, he is loyal to our family." Aelianus nodded.

Cyprian stood there, still in shock at what had been said, still red in the face he blurted out "Does this really mean that this oddball will inherit everything?"

Justus looked at him "Did I stutter before? Yes, you will remain as a manager, you are not my son except by marriage, Aelianus will own everything."

Cyprian cursed and appeared to threaten Justus physically had Aelianus not stepped in between them, his muscular body towering over his father. "Do your job well and if you cannot bear to see your son, I will give you that new land and villa I purchased up North near Arretium."

Cyprian cursed Mars and Hades bitterly as he stormed out.

Justus sighed, "If only his father had not saved me and been such a friend of mine…"

Aelianus looked back after Cyprian with sorrow, a tear went down his face "Until Decimus' death I tried earnestly to make him proud of me grandpa." Aelianus turned to Justus "I even risked death by serving in the legions, all in order to make him proud of me."

Justus looked at him "I am well aware that you have done all you can to cover up your gayness to your father and act more "manly", but at this point he is right that you must marry and have children. You can sleep with men for fun, but it is your duty to the family to have at least two children. For that reason, at least, you must have a wife."

Aelianus touched his grandpa's shoulder, "Whatever you say, I no longer care about trying to make father happy. Only you are all I care about."

Justus weakly smiled as he put his hand on Aelianus' forearm "Then marry soon. I will contact Sabonus and let him know that you accept. She is pretty, her name is Sabina, she is in her early 20s."

Sabina

  The arranged wedding's ceremony happened two weeks later. It pleased Cyprian a little, knowing how uncomfortable it would make Aelianus both in matters of bed activities and that just having a wife could annoy him made Cyprian smile. At their wedding, Cyprian came over to Aelianus shortly before they pledged their vows, whispering to Aelianus' ear "If you are not up to the task of producing a son, perhaps I should step in tonight and speed up the process."

Aelianus looked at him, his face showing annoyance, but Cyprian only smiled.

They had the ceremony at the temple of Aphrodite, following which they returned home without any party. Sabina arrived, looked at the slaves, "I'll have that one be my attendant" She said pointing to Helga.

Aelianus shrugged and motioned Helga to follow Sabina as Sabina walked to her bedroom. From the start of their marriage, Aelianus never received any affection from his wife Sabina.

Aelianus

One evening when David brought a wine delivery to the tavern, Helga asked him why Cyprian had been drinking night and day at the bar. David shrugged "Could be Decimus or perhaps because Aelianus received control over the family farm and inn that has caused his father's chagrin?"

A few days after his wedding, Aelianus received news from the legions, recalling him for duty within a week. Aelianus tried to fulfill his duty as a husband, but Sabina resisted. Aelianus suffered from terrifying dreams, he would wake up screaming almost nightly. Sabina became annoyed by it thinking, why cannot he handle his stress from battle like a man, he is such a weakling. Sabina decided to sleep separately from him in a guest room, which she thought. This will also give me more freedom during the night. Occasionally after such dreams Aelianus would not be able to return to sleep, so he walked down to the courtyard and sit on a marble bench sipping wine.

On one such night Pris awoke to use the bathroom, seeing him there sat next to and comforted him asking "Master, are you ok?" Aelianus smiled "Thank you Pris, Sabina has never been so kind." Pris sat next to him listening to him speak about fighting in Greece, the loss of his brother Decimus and his hopes to become valued in his father and wife's eyes, of his belief of achieving that through business success. Pris just listened and nodded.

The next day, wanting to give Justus purpose in life, he arranged to have Justus come to stay at the inn while he was away. A few days after Justus arrived, Aelianus prepared his things, he went to their room, and knocked on the metal door. Sabina yelled at him to get out.

Aelianus' mouth dropped, he said "Sabina, I promise to come back to you." Sabina got up and walked over to him, "Get out."

Aelianus' eyes went wide.

"Go." She said as Sabina pushed him out, Aelianus' mouth dropped, he nodded then bid all in his house a farewell and brought his legionary gear to his horse.

The next day Sabina came to Aelianus at breakfast, saying "I want my own bedroom from now on, you wake me up with your snoring and bad dreams. Sadly Aelianus agreed.

Chapter XVI Pris & Quintus

143 BC

Two weeks after Aelianus' legion was stationed in Southern Italy for training, Justus decided to travel to his beach villa at Tarquinii, a town northwest of Rome on the coast.

While he was away Cyprian began to make risky business decisions with some of their wheat suppliers. In 143 a drought happened, it was the year Pris turned 16, the drought impacted their wheat supply, a problem for Cyprian.

Cyprian had made an investment of an advanced purchase for a large amount of wheat from northern Italy; however, as rainfall had been sparse, the crop size had not been abundant, then to make matters worse, a bandit raid had killed the driver and stolen the wheat wagon that had been sent, in short Cyprian was at a loss. Cyprian needed to pay for some debts but he was short and did not want to report this to Justus.

Cyprian did not take long to figure out a way to add coins to his pocket. A few nights later a couple of rich Roman aristocrats patronized his tavern, they feasted on his food, drank lots of wine and stayed the night. Cyprian made sure to have Pris and Helga serve them, one was an older man, the other was handsome and had a youthful look to him.

As Pris served them, they rapidly became entranced animals, as they called on Pris to refill their wine goblets many times. At the end of the night one requested Cyprian to have Pris stay with him for the night. Cyprian told him a high price, and the agreement was immediate. Cyprian then had Helga do the same with his friend, he didn't think twice to have Pris and Helga sleep with his buyers.

Slaves in the Roman world had the same value as a dog or a horse, what a slave felt or thought internally did not matter. Slaves were something to be used by the master when and how the master deemed fit. The aristocrats didn't seem to care about the money, so they paid obscenely high prices for the ladies and Cyprian pimped them out. The ladies were indicated to go with the men with a snap signal.

Pris and Helga came over to the buyers after they had paid and finished their wine. Immediately the men groped the women at their table. The buyers got up to go to their two guest rooms. The younger one was with Pris, he smiled at her as they went upstairs. Pris felt panic as she knew what it meant.

Cyprian saw her reluctance to go and yelled, "Make them happy, do whatever they want or you'll regret it!" Cyprian watched the two couples go up the stairs from the bar, there was nothing that either of them could do.

The man brought Pris into their room. Pris had hoped that perhaps he was so drunk that he would just fall asleep on the bed, no such luck, he started holding her breasts from behind and he began removing her clothing. Pris hid her fear, she turned and thought for the second time, at least he is not old and he is handsome. The buyer raised his hands, showing he didn't want to hurt her, Pris forced a slight smile as he ran his hands through her hair caressing the back of her head. He kissed her cheek and neck, his hands massaged her back as they moved slowly to take her clothing off. Pris knew there was no way out, save an earthquake or act of the Gods, yet there was no sign of supernatural disturbance.

The man began kissing her neck as his hands touched her rump, waist and rubbed her back. Pris felt a warmth in his hands and while she had not planned on any of this, affection, this sexual advance was the closest thing to affection and happiness that she had experienced. Pris' body needed love, she closed her eyes needing these kisses and then a feeling that gave her a freedom and moment that took her out of slavery. Pris wanted more than anything to have a life, to have love, to wake up and walk along a beach with a child the way her mother once walked with her.

It was a choice between possible death or momentary love, momentary happiness and a glimpse of what it would be like to have safety, freedom and love. What a normal life could have been like.

Pris gave in, "What's your name?"

The man stopped kissing her neck "Quintus" He returned to kissing her.

Pris opened her toga as they joined a man and a woman with deep kisses. He turned her around, then stood behind her. He gently felt her sides as his hands slid down, he moved his tool against her special place, it was wet and warm, she gasped as he gently pushed it inside, he also breathed wholly, slowly inserting into her.

Their bodies slowly moved together, feeling, sharing, enjoying and their bodies reacting to each other in the most natural of acts. This was the first time Pris had experienced a man in this way, it hurt a little, it started with slight ache expansion of her part around his tool, but became an exhilaration of pleasure. She gently chirped at first as he started probing with incredible gentleness at first. They switched positions from being vertical to where he was on top of her. Her body reactions caused her to breathe deeply, they both felt pure joy as their bodies came to rhythm with each other and the speed of his tool increased, their bodies both fully engaged. Pris felt the pleasure become increasingly intense and invigorating, Pris felt incredible pleasure surging through her body with every stroke of his tool as she moaned loudly with pleasure, as he also breathed heavily and moaned with pleasure. The feeling of ultimate pleasure exploded within her body, she grabbed tightly to him as he also neared his climax, he had one hand interlocked with hers as his other held her shoulder at that moment as his body also exploded massively, he gasped in shouts of joy, suddenly Pris experienced a 2nd explosion of pleasure as well, their bodies had moved in unison with such perfection.

It was the most incredible physical action she had ever experienced. Their bodies suddenly rested, sweet sweat covered them, the man still inside her, he kissed her neck gently, saying words of love in Latin before he rolled off her body, they fell asleep laying next to each other. Pris had also felt such pleasure that her body gently shook, she awoke and smiled having felt a cluster of supreme sensations that eclipsed any other physical pleasurable experience she had enjoyed.

Pris looked at him a while, watching him breathe, she fell back asleep next to him, her leg over his. It was not long before her young adult body was so full of energy and craving for more pleasure that even before she woke up, she was rubbing her special parts while half in dream. Pris opened her eyes and looked at him again, he was handsome, she looked at his tool, amazed that such an odd-looking thing could give her such pleasure, it was hard again. Pris started to gently rub her hand on his chest, he woke up, seeing her naked body on his, her pretty breasts against his chest's right side, after a time of rubbing and kisses they began making love a second time, soon after that a 3rd time.

Finally morning light came in through a small window. The man awoke, he kissed Pris touching her gently, he said thank you to her and rose from bed, picked up his rich toga clothing that had been laid carelessly across the floor, and put his clothes on. This done, he blew a kiss to Pris who had sat up in bed watching him leave. He then went to his friend's room and shortly after they left the tavern.

Helga came to her room, her face full of concern, "Are you ok?"

It was at this point that Pris felt a tear run down her face, understanding that he would probably not return to her, and that her first experience with such a physical supreme joy had been with someone she did not know and would probably never come to know. "He used me and before long left like nothing had happened at all."

Helga gave her a hug, "I'm sorry my dear.... I could not protect you from this."

Pris looked at Helga, another tear fell, "Will I ever see him again?" Helga went to her and gave her a hug. Pris said "I do not know if I love him or feel used by him. I am so confused."

Helga kissed the side of her head while she gave her friend a half hug, "It is like you said once to me, all we can do is try to survive." Pris buried her face on Helga's shoulder, she didn't want to show anyone her confusion and a mix of emotions that caused her to silently weep.

Pris weeped, "I just don't understand, in one moment, I felt more physically, completely satisfied beyond anything that I've ever known, but it was not for love with him... I was just like an apple to him. Now I am a slave again."

Helga nodded, "Yes we are slaves, we have no rights"

Pris said "I had only hoped somehow to not be violated sexually."

Helga sighed, "You and I are survivors Pris, we have to support each other."

Ingrid and the other slave servants empathized with her, Ingrid gave her a big hug when they came to the kitchen. Cyprian had her back to work the next day.

A few weeks went by and Pris began to feel sick each morning. A couple months later Pris knew without a doubt that she was pregnant as her belly began to show. Pris was perhaps lucky in that Cyprian seeing that Pris was pregnant, did at least give her easier duties during her pregnancy. Nine months later Sarth and Luciana were born.

Pris was amazed to see that her twins both had one blue eye and one brown eye, the whole household was amazed. It was only then that Pris remembered that her grandma Fiona had had mixed colored eyes. Cyprian allowed Pris to rest for several days after she gave birth before she was sent back to work in the tavern.

Even Traaz, the slave in the stables, who people who laugh at due to his high-pitched unmistakable voice, remarked to himself on how uncommon mixed colored eyes were.

Due to the babies needing mother's milk, Pris would try to sneak off and take care of her babies. Yet sometimes Cyprian had her waitressing for hours on end. The babies needed changing and feedings. Cyprian had Helga working in the kitchen, to hide her away from male customer's gazes, which allowed Helga to take care of the twins much more frequently while they were still infants, as they did not always have cow milk available, Helga started breastfeeding the babies feeling that she had to take care of them in Pris' absence.

There were a couple other slaves working at Cyprian's tavern, all of them older. Yuria an elderly Iberian woman and Teana an older ethnic Carthaginian woman who both cooked, and Ingrid the 50-year-old Eprian Greek descended woman who cleaned the house above the tavern. While they all helped care for the babies while Pris worked, it was Helga who did the most when Pris was unable. Sarth had brownish hair with amber highlights and his sister had dirty blond hair.

Pris made a point to speak to them only in Cimbri saying "I love you" every morning when they woke up and the other slaves spoke to them in their common language of Latin. Pris would sing in Cimbri lullabies and stories her grandmother Fiona once sang to her. The years rolled by, as young children, they were made to be kitchen, laundry and bedding servants as soon as they turned six years old. They helped each other and were very close in all their activities.

Occasionally about once a week or so when the tavern was slow Cyprian would take Helga to the beach to visit Justus. When they were gone on those days Pris would let her children play in the courtyard, pool and garden. It was not a huge place, but the children were able to spend many hours imagining themselves in various hero and princess type games.

Traaz was an Italian slave of Aelianus' family who had been born a bastard and abandoned as a baby. Life for Traaz had been one of hardship. Born to a poor Roman tavern woman and a father who had been killed in Greece fighting Macedonians, his mother abandoned her baby and it was collected by a slave seller as an infant.

Traaz grew up a slave on a farm and had been resold at age 8 to Aelianus' grandparents and sent to the fields to work as a farmhand. Traaz had a high-pitched voice that was unmistakable, he grew up on the farm herding cattle and harvesting grapes for their wine presses. Eventually Traaz grew strong and was good at handling animals. One night Cyprian became enraged when the previous stable hand he had working at the inn was caught affectionately flirting with Helga. Cyprian whipped the stable hand for an hour, then he sold the slave to the gladiator ring. Cyprian had Traaz brought to the tavern to do the old stable hand's job. Traaz carried an annoyed look, whenever he spoke with the other slaves it seemed that they were always on guard.

When Traaz was 9 years old he had saved Aelianus from a wild boar that had been sleeping in their vineyard. Traaz had been following Aelianus, helping him pick grapes when they came upon the boar. Traaz jumped, tackling Aelianus to get them both out of the way, the boar for whatever reason did not come back but kept on running, leaving the vineyard. Aelianus had told his father about this, but Cyprian had looked more disappointed that Aelianus was still breathing than the act of a slave saving his son. Traaz was annoyed by that and years later as a teenager Traaz tried to escape, Cyprian had caught him and whipped him for a long time. Angry at the world for his situation, at Cyprian, and at Aelianus for not doing more.

Helga once went to the stables to fetch some tools, she saw Traaz angrily squeezing some cloth "Cyprian, Aelianus, I shall have my vengeance…." She rattled the door a while before making an announced entry. "Traaz, I'm here for some gardening tools." She walked inside hearing some rustling behind the first wall. Seeing what she needed, she grabbed the tools. "Traaz, why are you hiding? I know you're in here." Helga waited a few minutes, "Traaz, are you ok?" she shrugged, and left. What a strange man.

Traaz stood there on the other side of the wall a while after she left, a knife in his hand, his breathing hard. So easy it would be, but how to hide the body? He touched the horse. They are such noble creatures, they are the only ones that I love, they are divine.

Aelianus and his legion were sent down to Sicily to help subdue a major rebellion that occurred. Then as if hardly any time had passed, one morning Aelianus arrived back at the tavern, home in Rome again. Aelianus' shield and helmet had a few new dents in them, his gear all had a well-worn look to it. That day Justus told Aelianus that he would return to the vineyard, "I do not necessarily like living in this busy noisy city."

Aelianus agreed. That night after dinner Justus departed for the vineyard with his bodyguard David. Late at night,

Pris overheard Aelianus tell Sabina that his legion had encountered major action, "We did things that are horrifying".

Sabina responded in her usual flippant manner "Your gloominess is annoying and the sign of a weak man!" Sabina grabbed a bottle of wine leaving the room without waiting for his response, Sabina went to a vacant guest room in their tavern. Pris watched Sabina pass through as she was still cleaning the dining table. Aelianus later came into the dinning room and called for wine, Price could see that his face showed shock and frustration.

One night as Aelianus was pouring wine for customers Cyprian and Helga arrived in the tavern after returning from the beach. Cyprians' face was red as he yelled slurring his words. "You good for nothing bastard, you stole my inheritance!"

Aelianus went over to him, trying to intervene, as their slaves did not know what to do. Cyprian continued "Why have the Gods done this to me, Decimus was supposed to be the next in line, not you!"

Aelianus tried to calm Cyprian down, "Father you've had too much wine, let me take you to your room…."

"Lay your hands off of me!" Cyprian shouted, "I am the head of this family you burly moron, I am the one who has kept profits coming into this place. What Justus did is not right!"

Aelianus nodded, he motioned Cyprian to leave the tavern through their home's entrance. Aelianus said "Yes, we need not discuss that now, it is time...."

Cyprian roared, "It is time for me to take what is mine you freak!" He grabbed a knife off a customer's table and tried to stab Aelianus.

The customers at the tavern all ran for the door as Cyprian tried to stab Aelianus again and again.

After backing up with his back to the wall, at the fourth strike Aelianus swung his arms together one hand hit Cyprian's knife hand at the wrist, the other hit his elbow and he grabbed them hard and twisted them, he had the knife now pointed to Cyprian's throat and pushed down using his body weight, Cyprian dropped the knife not wanting to impale himself.

"Let us talk now father!" Aelianus pleaded, kicking away the knife and subsequently letting go of Cyprian."

Cyprian yelled "Arrrrgh!" as he tried to grab Aelianus, twisting his hand and pushing him down to his knees, "Why don't you just die thief?" He shouted as he kicked Aelianus in the gut hard, who fell backwards.

Cyprian grabbed Aelianus by the head and pulled his fist back, Aelianus saw this and blocked his punch. Aelianus grabbed Cyprian by the throat, picked him up and threw him onto a table which collapsed under Cyprian's weight.

Cyprian charged Aelianus, they grabbed each other as fists flew, their bodies crashed into walls and surfaces, both men soon landed punches on the other though to no advantage. They crashed through the garden entrance and onto a stone bench.

Cyprian tried to smash Aelianus' face onto the bench, but Aelianus stopped him by elbowing Cyprian in the gut. Cyprian kicked Aelianus in the gut, then he ran to the weapons room that was nearby and came out holding a gladius sword as Aelianus was standing up a little dazed, Aelianus yelled "Father stop!" Cyprian lunged a stab at Aelianus. Cyprian was breathing heavily as he stabbed at Aelianus.

A seasoned sober veteran and 37 years younger than his older drunken dad, Aelianus nimbly dodged his father's strike, grabbing the attacker's sword arm, he threw Cyprian over his back making him land hard on his back on the stone covered ground, Aelianus now held the sword in his hand the blade pointed at Cyprian's head, "Father this is over, if you resist, I will finish you".

Cyprian, rose to his knees slowly, shook his head. He tried to get up, but moaned in pain as he came up holding his back in agony. If he wanted to continue, he didn't. He couldn't stand up straight, apparently his old body was too damaged.

Aelianus looked at his dad with pity, "Why do you hate me so much; all I've ever wanted was your love?" Cyprian sneered without responding. Aelianus shook his head and took a big breath before saying "I cannot allow you to stay here further. I forgive you, but you are too dangerous." Aelianus stepped back a few paces then said, "You are banished, if I see you again, I will kill you. I will give you a bag of gold so that you will not be homeless. That will be enough to keep you alive for a while"

Cyprian looked at Aelianus, now he could see that Cyprian's face was bruised, "I want to take Helga, too, she is mine".

Aelianus looked at Helga who was watching from the atrium's second floor, she shook her head. Aelianus shook his head, "You used her like a horse, you may not have her."

Cyprian's face twisted in rage at Aelianus, "You would steal all of my property?"

Aelianus wagged his finger, "She is not your property, you lost all rights to anything associated with this place when you attacked me. Helga is mine. You leave now or I will use this blade on you."

Cyprian, defeated, spit on the dirt of the garden, he grabbed the bag of gold and limped away from the tavern. Aelianus signaled his guards "Make sure he leaves out the front door and never allow him back."

Aelianus took over managing the tavern, regularly visiting his vineyard over the next few days to get to know his staff, the slaves and products. Aelianus appointed Ingrid to run the tavern whenever he was away visiting Justus and inspecting the vineyard. When Aelianus went to the vineyards he would visit with Justus and he always took Pris and her children too. While he was away, Sabina would go to the market daily with Helga for her shopping desires. They never saw or heard from Cyprian again.

Chapter XVII Aelianus & Rufus

133 BC

Ten years went by, my master continued to serve occasionally in reserve duty with the legions stationed outside Rome. During this time, Aelianus stayed in the tavern or managed his winery; meanwhile my mother brought us up in the world. Without warning, one night Justus died in his sleep, life became bittersweet for Aelianus as his grandfather had set him up only to pass away. Partly to avoid his grief, Aelianus stayed busy managing his tavern. When he had to visit his winery and vineyard, he would leave management of his tavern to Ingrid. Aelianus went to his vineyard weekly that was run by David, his vineyard enforcer and servants to sample the wines that were being made. After visiting the winery and vineyard, Aelianus always made a point to visit his grandparents', brother's & mother's tombs.

Pris had been purchased by his father some 15 years earlier. Aelianus told Pris that he was not his father and would never pimp her as his father had, to which Pris was grateful. Aelianus, when needing some companionship, he would occasionally take Pris, her children to go fishing, to hunt squirrels with his military sling and stones, or to go swimming in the ocean.

Though he enjoyed sampling wines, most of his time was running his tavern and interacting with Rome's political elite. Owning and socializing with the customers of his tavern, the Happy Moon. Aelianus met Senator Rufus Sextus who had come to his tavern during this time. Soon he and Rufus were infrequently sleeping together and occasionally other gay men.

One day after purchasing food at the market, Aelianus was returning home when he walked past Tiberius' home. There he saw many homeless veterans camped out. Aelianus saw an old comrade. Septimus, one of the veterans he knew from serving in Greece. Septimus had been camped outside, a homeless man playing music for coins.

Aelianus approached him "I know you, are you not from the 9th legion?"

Septimus looked up as though confused, so Aelianus pointed his finger at Septimus saying "I ordered you to play for our men. Don't you remember me?"

Septimus gasped, "Centurion"

Aelianus smiled, "Are you happy here? Would you like to work for me?"

Septimus looked at his hands "I don't ave many skills, just make tunes and make meals."

Aelianus nodded, "I could use a good musician for my tavern. Would you play there each night?" Septimus nodded.

Aelianus grinded, "And, you can cook?"

Septimus nodded. Aelianus tapped Septimus on the shoulder "Good, I will help you get back on your feet." With Septimus soon playing music, and he would occasionally help Ingrid and Helga in the kitchen, the Happy Moon's great food, wine and ambiance had spread as the inn was making profits like never before. Through Senator Rufus, his owning one of Rome's most popular taverns, and supplying Rome's best wines to the highest paying customers, our master became connected with many members of the Roman Senate.

Aelianus decided that in addition to his practicing with his two guards and having a couple dogs at home, it made sense to train Pris and Sarth swordplay and he wanted to share his knowledge about the art of war. Aelianus began to train them after lunch every day in swordplay during this time and shared his martial strategies. Sarth expressed interest in swordplay after watching Aelianus practice each day with Pris, so Aelianus began to also teach Sarth the basics of swordplay in their large courtyard or he taught Sarth of Rome's strong place in the world.

Aelianus was pleased to see that Sarth like Pris was another natural with the sword. Aelianus taught both how to use one with a shield and without a shield, how to use a sling, and a dagger as well as defensive moves for these in the garden atrium of their home. They used small tomatoes to sling at targets on the wall, used wooden swords and wooden daggers for 1-1 practice.

Aelianus taught them how to do open handed fighting, use of pressure points on a person's body, where to aim her blade, how to switch eyes to different targets just before striking making it harder for an opponent to block, where to cause immeasurable pain without killing and also how to kill quickly. Aelianus taught them how to be at one in the mind to control panic when fighting with or without a sword, to anticipate where a strike might be coming from and how to avoid or rush or escape from a blade wielder when swordless and then to grab or grapple the opponent in order to turn the weapon against the attacker. He taught them open handed combat, punches, blocks, grappling, throws, holds, as well as how to disarm an armed attacker, etc. Pris remembered how her father Krull had once said that swordplay was almost like a lover's dance. Aelianus had learned so many of these skills from his time in the legions practicing with Decimus, and skills that he had continued to perfect on his own.

Aelianus taught both how to use psychological warfare to weaken an enemy even before the battle begins. He taught them these quoting Greek philosophy and he taught army and fighting commands in Latin as well. Aelianus taught more and more without holding back. Pris had become like the daughter or sister he never had, he realized that he had begun to care for her more than any female since his late grandmother. Weeks went by, using wooden swords Pris and Sarth trained nightly with Aelianus giving him much pride in their progress.

Aelianus asked if Luciana would want to practice swordplay as well, but Luciana shook her head, she said she loved music and wanted to learn to play the cithara, so Aelianus made arrangements with Septimus to make that happen.

Chapter XVIII Tiberius Gracchus

133 BC

The world of Rome was changing, though most did not realize it. Whether through peace or war it was a very tumultuous time for the Roman Republic. The many victories in wars that Rome had been involved in since the Punic wars, Rome's power and area of control had grown from just the Italian peninsula to also control over Sicily, Iberia (Spain), Greece and Carthage. Long gone were the days when Roman farmers would just fight in wars for one season, since the Punic wars, the legions were gone for years at a time.

While they had conquered all of Rome's original neighboring rivals, Rome's larger farm owning class who had not gone off to fight had been busy buying slaves from these conquered countries. They had also been busy buying the small farms from these Roman soldiers who were now bankrupt due to not being around to harvest any crops. Rome's internal political situation was increasingly volatile. In the last hundred years, there had been several wars. Since legionaries were required to serve in a complete campaign, no matter how long the war was, soldiers often left their farms in the hands of wives and their children.

Aelianus was aware of this situation as many of his friends were former legionnaires who had owned or came from families that had owned small farms. Aelianus met with many of them in his tavern. Aelianus gathered many of these veterans to speak with his lover Senator Rufus Sextus at his tavern to indirectly make their voices known to the Senate.

Rufus listened to them and their stories, they asked Rufus ``What can be done?"

Rufus shook his head "Sadly, small farms are going bankrupt and are being bought up by the wealthy."

Aelianus agreed "Yes, my neighbor paid his sons to not have to join the legions due to his family's connections. Meanwhile he has formed a huge private estate run by the slaves we've gained from our victorious wars."

Rufus acknowledged, "Yes, the rich sent the people to war, and after the war is over, much of the newly conquered land is sold to or rented to various members of the elite of our populace. While our common veterans get nothing."

A tall veteran said, "The new land we've conquered is being purchased by those who are already in a financially profitable situation, meanwhile the veterans of our legions on retiring find their old farms desolate, with a mountain of debt that needs to be paid." Rufus agreed, "Yes, and then they must sell their land and go to Rome looking for work."

Aelianus took a sip of wine sadly. "This situation of the rich buying up most of the farmland and using slave labor is creating a land crisis that is creating more and more homeless veterans in Rome who cannot find low wage work because the slaves are cheaper."

The tall veteran asked "What will we do? They will become steadily angry and our politicians will not make any real change because most of them are in some form connected to the rich land-owning class."

Aelianus agreed, as his friend continued, "Many of the veterans cannot find work and have formed gangs and we all have seen how crime has increased."

Rufus agreed "That's true, it is causing a diminishing sense of loyalty to the Republic; something must be done or we will be in big trouble. Aelianus, I know a senator who feels deeply about these issues, I would like you to meet him, his name is Tiberius."

A few days later Senators Tiberius Gracchus, Linus Scippio and Lucius Mummius arrived at the Happy Moon with Senator Rufus Sextus, Tiberius was weary from his long travels. Tiberius was a 30-year-old man who looked perhaps 10 years younger than he was. They came in and sat at the bar, they ordered some wine.

Seeing them and knowing who they were, Aelianus immediately came over, "Senators, welcome! It is perfect to have you both here, men who have also served in our legions. Thank you for your service!" Lucius Mummius gave Aelianus a friendly hug, "Good to see you again Aelianus" Aelianus smiled "Good to see you as well general, ahem senator."

Lucius smiled "Good to see you again Aelianus, thank you for your service as well."

Tiberius acknowledged, "It was a hard duty for me, I saw action in Carthage, but it had to be done. It was necessary. Sadly the action in Iberia was dreadful". Enjoying the wine, Tiberius, Lucius and Aelianus talked about their time in the legions. Tiberius and Linus of fighting in Carthage during the 3rd Punic war, while Aelianus and Lucius compared those experiences with their own fighting in Greece while Rufus mostly listened.

Aelianus nodded, "I just finished my time with the legions as well. I fully understand. If a general is not the brightest commander disaster will strike. But you, I understand Tiberius, that you saved some 20,000 legionnaires through peace negotiations. You saved them from captivity, to that I salute you".

Tiberius shook his head, "The victories we racked up feel hollow if Rome's victories in wars are causing internal strife."

Aelianus was nodding his head agreeing. "While my farm has survived in my family for generations, most of our neighbors have had to sell their farms."

Lucius shook his head, "It isn't right that the people of Rome should lose their properties for defending our republic. Aelianus signaled to Pris to pour them all another round of wine.

Tiberius agreed saying "When I returned from Numantia on passing through Etruria and I found the country almost depopulated, the Roman husbandmen and shepherds who were there before have been replaced by imported barbarian slaves."

Tiberius looked intently at each of them, "That is when I first conceived of a needed policy which shall be to reward the veteran soldiers on returning home with either state assistance to forgive their debt while they were away or to offer them new lands in the areas they helped conquer."

Lucius cheered, banging his fist on their table "Bravo!"

Linus yelled toasting his wine "I will support that in the Senate."

Rufus looked concerned "Such a policy would make you many enemies among the rich in the Senate, such enemies who will be a threat to yourself."

Tiberius shook his head, "My mother was the daughter of Scipio Africanus, the general who saved Rome from Hannibal and the Carthaginians. The people are behind me, the Senate will be shown that they need to support my cause for the good of Rome."

Linus smiled "I will support you cousin!"

Rufus cautioned "That might not be enough…"

Tiberius shook his head, "I have men who are all veterans ready to protect me and once the Senate sees me approach them with hundreds of Romans at my side, they will not try to stop us".

Aelianus stuck his lips out like he was kissing air "Tiberius, my advice is at least you wear a gladius and have a few bodyguards, until this honorable law you propose is enacted".

Tiberius acknowledged, "Perhaps you are right friend, I will take some precautions, but I took an oath to serve Rome. I still serve it, and this festering problem has existed since the Punic wars and it is getting worse. If I do not, all that we fought for is greed, ambition and vanity."

Lucius had just finished another mouthful of wine, "I have been concerned about this since returning from Greece. When our soldiers return from the legions, many have nowhere to go, the injured often die, the ones still whole go to Rome looking for work."

Aelianus waved his hand towards the door "Many do not find work and instead join thousands of unemployed who roam the city. My musician Septimus was one of them, his family lost their farm and his elderly parents died in shock from bankruptcy."

Licius nodded, "Yes, as only men who own property are allowed to enroll in the army, the number of men eligible for army duty has therefore been shrinking; and hence the military power of Rome."

Aelianus rolled the wine in his glass, in thought.

Rufus said "We must do more for the veterans, it is shameful what's happening to them."

Tiberius nodded, "So in summary, many of the poor, who were land owners of small farms have been ejected from their land, due to serving in the legions and then they return to nothing. Then because of their bankruptcy they no longer quality for military service, and they neglect or are incapable of bringing up their children, right?"

Rufus nodded "If this continues all Italy will suffer from a lack of free workmen, full of gangs of homeless and foreign slaves.

Tiberius acknowledged, "Yes, those who's labor will aid the rich cultivate their farm estates, from which the rich drive away the free citizens whom they would have to pay for work."

Lucius said "Tiberius I see you are passionate about helping the middle-class people of Rome, that is honorable, but be careful not to make policies that could threaten the rich's prosperity too much too quickly."

Aelianus passed his finger through the flame of their table's candle "Tiberius you have truly noble intentions, you may gather with your supporters at my tavern whenever you desire."

Often they returned and prepared speeches for Rome's public to inform Romans that he intended to work for them while enjoying Aelianus' fine wine and delicious foods, Tiberius' popularity soared with the common plebs and veterans of Rome, and as more and more senators dined at Aelianus' establishment, the fame of his tavern and inn increased as well.

Chapter XIX Aelianus

133 BC

The world of Rome was changing internally, though most did not realize it. My master had become connected with Tiberius Gracchus, a most ambitious member of the Roman Senate. Tiberius was working on land reform that would adjust Rome to help the poor and homeless of Rome, this would bring powerful enemies to Tiberius and Aelianus. Tiberius and Rufus worked tirelessly reaching out to colleagues in the Senate to try to come to a proposal that would be able to find compromise but still achieve the core of their goals. Rufus would listen to the veterans he met on the streets and relay ideas with Tiberius, Lucius, Aelianus and Linus crafted many proposals.

While Tiberius worked on his writings for the new law for the senate's vote, Linus occasionally met with Rufus at Aelianus' inn for wine and a chance to relax. Following these meetings Rufus occasionally stayed at Aelianus' very late. On nights when they did not meet, Aelianus would train Pris in various sword fighting techniques as it helped him to consider what was going on while he taught her.

One day Aelianus, Pris and her children went to the fish & farmer's market in the Roman Forum to buy food supplies for Aelianus' inn. Near the entrance of the forum speaking before a crowd at the Rostra, listening to Tiberius who told the crowd, "...Wild beasts that roam over Italy have their dens, each has a place of repose and refuge. But the men who have fought and been injured or killed for Rome and Italy enjoy nothing but the air and light; without a house or a home they wander about with their wives and children homeless and those without families form into violent gangs. It is up to us; it is our duty to do something to help them get back on their feet. I pledge that I will legislate on the matter of the homeless legionaries. I have written a proposal for a law called Lex Sempronia Agraria..."

The crowd of Roman citizens roared its approval. As they passed through the crowd, Sarth looked at Pris "Mother, what is going on?"

Pris looked down, "Rome is going through a great transition it seems."

Sarth asked "Will that impact us?"

Pris looked at Tiberius in the distance "I hope not."

Aelianus looked back at them, when they got beyond the crowd and into the market, he stopped to say "This could have a big impact on Rome, and thus on all of you. Tiberius Gracchus will soon Speak before the Senate. Tiberius sees his opportunity to improve the lot of the poor...."

Pris half-smiled "That's nice master, but how does that impact us?"

Aelianus tried to explain, "The law would reorganize control of the public land that had been conquered in previous wars that have been controlled by the state, it will impose rights for poor Romans and veterans to possess more than 500 jugera of the public land. For the rich, any land that they owned above this limit would be confiscated by the state."

Pris gave a mystified look, "How does that impact us?"

Aelianus cleared his throat, "It means that we will need fewer slaves for farmhands, meaning a decrease in slavery, that is how it will impact your kind."

Aelianus reflected for a moment as Pris stayed silent, then he said. "Slavery is an awful institution, but it will take a long time before we can eliminate it completely."

Pris wondered "Is it possible that Rome can do without slaves, I wish it but I have a hard time believing it possible."

Aelianus shrugged, "Probably not for a long time, Romans love the power it gives them over other living beings. Still Tiberius' efforts are a step in the right direction."

They purchased the supplies they needed and returned from the market. Later that evening, Senators Tiberius, his brother Gaius, Rufus, Crassus Maximus, Publius Mucius, Lucius Mummius, Linus Scippio and Appius Claudius came to Aelianus' inn. While enjoying the wine and food. Pris listened to them formulate the proposed law which would forfeit illegal possessions to the public land, for which the Senate would be compensated.

At Rufus's invitation Aelianus attended the Senate gathering as his aide. As predicted, many of the senatorial elites opposed the law. After speaking with the senate for the law, there was great opposition from those whose families had gained vast estates over the last 50 to 100 years. They claimed that Tiberius was seeking a redistribution of wealth, upend slavery, and rob them of their hard-earned work. One claimed that this law would thereby shake the foundations of the Republic and incite social revolution. Tiberius Gracchus argued that redistribution of re-confiscated public land to the poor and homeless in Rome would be a very fair action and save it from revolution, rebellion or dictatorship. Tiberius argued to give the poor at least plots of 30 jugera upon which to support themselves and their families, that redistribution would create more wealth and would make those populations eligible for taxation and military service. Thus, Tiberius' law sought to solve the twin problems of increasing the number of men eligible for military service (thereby boosting Rome's available military strength) while also providing farm land for homeless war veterans.

During a midday break, Linus Scipio took Rufus and Aelianus aside, "I have learned that a former centurion named Vicidius Marcellus Paullus has been encouraging Senators to vote certain ways. He works for Tiberius' cousin-law, Senator Publius Cornelius Scipio Nasica."

Aelianus felt a wave of shock as Linus continued "Publius is a relative of mine and Tiberius by marriage, Vicidius is connected through his family to many rich Senators who had known his father and a few his grandfather."

Aelianus looked around concerned Vicidius was there and might see him, but Vicidius was not to be found. Linus continued "Vicidius has made a good impression on the

Roman praetor of Greece as an efficient tax collector. That praetor introduced Vicidius to Nasica.

Senator Vicidius Marcellus Paullus

Additionally, Vicidius inherited his family's large estate of land and fortune. Nasica approved a license for Vicidius and his cousin Tiberius to be co-owners of a brothel, the Shady Star."

Aelianus nodded, "I heard somewhere that Shady got new ownership a year or so ago." Aelianus looked around again

"Vicidius is ambitious, he is clever; he and Titus spared no time inviting Senators to have free service with their best whores, making sure to have those Senators sign their names and family seals to the proposals Nasica is in favor of. Tiberius joined them.

Rufus asked "How did Vicidius get connected to Nasica?"

Aelianus reported "Nasica's father is an old friend and if my spy's right, an old lover of his mother. Through that connection Vicidius was given an assistant position. I understand that Vicidius intimidates rival supporters."

Rufus nodded, "I've seen him make speeches in favor or against specific Senators. Vicidius is clever, he knows that politics is his road to real power."

Aelianus acknowledged "I suspect that he has the ambition to do dirty work to gain personal power by knocking off rivals, though I don't have more than rumors and a personal experience of him."

Rufus said "So it's possible Vicidius may have moved to trap those who have families to blackmail them into voting for or against specific proposals. Clever Nascia, We must be careful."

Aelianus' eyes opened a little wider, "Vicidius…. I had a bad relationship with him. He recklessly led our manipular into a death trap, during the battle, it was the end of my brother." Rufus' face flashed concern.

Tiberius acknowledged with a pause and nod, "My sources tell me that Vicidius has convinced a number of other wealthy senators to be staunchly against these land reforms I am pushing for."

Rufus agreed "I concur from my sources too. The Senate has many conservative elements who are strongly against these agrarian reforms."

Aelianus spoke up "Vicidius can be very persuasive and intimidating. Such a man might be used to try to intimidate you Tiberius, and your supporters."

Over the next few weeks, Vicidius watched where Tiberius met with his friends for their gatherings, he followed Rufus or Tiberius to Aelianus' tavern. The tavern had six separate rooms in the inn's first floor against the wall with small tables for guests to meet privately, and 8 tables in the open room.

On the particular night that Vicidius came to the establishment, that was when he saw Aelianus, first time since their fallout in Greece, busy helping Pris and his other servants serve food and drinks. Aelianus did not notice Vicidius who had been greeted by Pris on entering. Pris saw Vicidius and could sense there was something sinister and intimidating about him.

Vicidius felt delighted on finding Aelianus' inn, it was too much to bear. He waited for Tiberius, Rufus and other Senators to leave. An hour later Vicidius finished enjoying his drink then he decided it was time to menace Aelianus. The inn was still crowded and busy, Vicidius had planned to wait until most of the customers had left, however the bar had only steadily become more crowded full of happy customers who were laughing and having loud conversations. Helga and Pris were serving tables food and wine, a lively game of dice was being played out at a corner table with a small crowd of patrons cheering the game on.

Aelianus did not notice Vicidius as he was explaining the wine and night's food dishes to a newly arrived couple. The temptation was too great.

Vicidius walked up to him. "Ae-li-anus... you are a friend of Tiberius you gay coward". Aelianus quickly turned to look at Vicidius, his hands closed into fists and his kind appearance switched to be on guard. The tavern quieted down as many people were watching the two men talk. One group of men were all veterans who had been coming to Aelianus' tavern for months as his business grew for construction jobs as well as to dine. Two of their friends were guards at the tavern ready to deal with drunks, they approached from behind Vicidius.

Aelianus paused a second, grinning "Are you still having trouble with the ladies Vicidius? Your face looks even less attractive than a leper".

Vicidius' face reddened, "I am enjoying multiple women, but that is not why I am here talking to you. You are an associate of Tiberius Gracchus; the Senate won't approve his reforms and I bet Hades' gold you nor he will be around much longer."

Aelianus shrugged "All men die, some never truly live. I live for Rome and to make Rome a better place."

Vicidius scoffed "There is no place in Rome for a coward."

Aelianus looked Vicidius square in the eyes and yelled "Do you want a piece of me Vicidius Marcellus Paullus? Do you want to be embarrassed by me again?"

Vicidius hesitated. Aelianus waved his hands out "If I win you will show all Rome that you are a pathetic fighter and lower than a snake's belly. I have tens of witnesses here. Are you ready to be humiliated? Go ahead, I have faced death a hundred times and I, Vicidius, am still here. I piss down Hades' throat and ignore his gold, just know that if you pull your gladius I will clean the floor of you, you have never bested me once."

Vicidius smirked, "Your days are numbered, and I know where to find you". Vicidius walked out backwards to the door watching Aelianus constantly pointing at him, "This is not done".

Aelianus walked after Vicidius yelling "And close the door on your way out, we don't want your odor in here!"

Aelianus walked after Vicidius, his shoulders swaying, hands moving as he walked, head held high, he went to the door that Vicidius had left open and closed it. Aelianus turned to everyone smiling "I guess he was raised in a barn! A round of a goblet of wine for all." The customers all cheered.

Aelianus immediately went to his blank scrolls. There he grabbed his feather and ink, and penned a warning: *Tiberius, I have received information that the Senate may not approve your reforms, your life is potentially in danger. I have learned that against the advice Rufus and I gave you that you have chosen to sidestep the Senate altogether by approaching the Plebeian Assembly which supported your measures. I must warn again that this action may insult the Senate and alienate many Senators who might otherwise show support. Know that by skirting the law against powerful opponents, your life could be in jeopardy.* Aelianus had his veteran bodyguard Marcus hand deliver the message to Rufus.

Rufus explained to Tiberius that Aelianus was right. "It will take longer, but going through the Senate would be a safer path forward."

Tiberius shook his head "I want to pass this legislation without any more delays from the Senate, those corrupt crony crows are happy to argue the laws to death, meanwhile every day is a struggle for Rome's homeless veterans."

Rufus, scoffed, "True but rushing in gives a threatening image, one that those who oppose this law will spin to make the ignorant violent and hostile. You must listen!"

Tiberius put his hands on Rufus' shoulders "Do not worry. This must happen. Give me your support. We will not fail; our veterans will protect me, depend on it."

Rufus shook his head "It is not good to risk your life. We must negotiate a way forward."

Tiberius countered, "This was a challenging situation, with half the Senate in the rich's gold purse, any tribune could veto a proposal, preventing it from Senatorial approval and being laid before the Assembly. I must bypass them."

Rufus cautioned Tiberius, "To do so would make them claim you are grabbing ultimate power like a dictator!"

TIberius said "These proposals are by now well known by the opposition and should not be a shock, they will listen to what's best for Rome."

Rufus said "My spies tell me that Senator Nascia has had Vicidius speak privately with his allied members in the Senate. It is rumored that Vicidius has persuaded Tribune Marcus Octavius, to use his veto against you."

Tiberius looked at him, "I will counter him."

At the Senate that day, when the charges of usurping power were placed by Octavius, Tiberius raised his hands at the assembly, "It is to our brave veterans and legionnaires that I must risk everything. They gave everything to Rome, so Rome must support them, yet Tribune Octavius is obstructing, acting contrary to the wishes of his constituents. Octavius has violated a basic tenet of a tribune, which was to ensure the total protection of the people from any political or economic oppression by the Senate!"

Octavius shook his head and remained resolute in his opposition to Tiberius' law. Octavius said: "Tiberius is overstepping his power as a Tribute; our veterans are serving Rome for the glory of growing our republic."

Tiberius waved his hand at Octavius, "See without any validation or deep concern, Octavius makes broad accusations to snuff out this proposal before the Senate can even vote. I motion that we vote to unseat Octavius and hold an election for his replacement."

The people began to vote as to whether or not to depose Octavius, but he vetoed the vote, as was his legal right as tribune.

Rufus spoke up "Let us negotiate further so we may...."

Tiberius pulled at his hair, "No, there is no other way, remove Octavius from the Senate as he is obstructing legitimate legislation."

Several members of the Senate grabbed Octavius and escorted him from the Senate floor, as this was happening, half the Senate went into uproar at the forcible removal of their man from the Assembly's meeting floor as Tiberius proceeded with the vote to unseat Octavius.

Chapter XIX Aelianus & Rufus

133 BC

The Senate had over time become unwilling to compromise due to the many wealthy uncompromising senators who stood to lose with Tiberius' legislation. The seeds for violence and the end of the Republic had been planted. During this time, my master came to fully trust my mother, and for a time it seemed that life would be normal. Rome's Republic had slipped into oligarchy and leaders resorted to violence and scandals to silence opposition.

Rufus came over that night exhausted by all the riotous behavior at the Senate. Aelianus was puzzled, "Why cannot Tiberius simply make the proposal for his law?"

Rufus explained "The forcible removal of a tribune violated Octavius' right of sacrosanctity. A tribune cannot by law ever be physically touched by an opponent, yet that is what happened."

Aelianus hit the table, "Damn...."

Rufus smirked, "Yes, these actions have Tiberius' supporters worried, if anything happens that could be even spun as remotely illegal, it means anyone who assisted Tiberius would stand to be in jeopardy.

Aelianus ran his hand through his hair "That does not seem good for us."

Rufus agreed, "It gets worse, Tiberius has further used his veto on daily ceremonial rites that tribunes conduct, such as the opening of key public buildings, markets and temples instead of moving to dispose of Octavius."

Aelianus squinted his eyes, "Why, what is he doing that for?"

Rufus shut his eyes, then leaned back against his chair looking at the ceiling, "By law, Rome's buildings required both tribunes to agree to open public facilities, now through these actions Tiberius has effectively shut down the entire city of Rome's commerce."

Aelianus raised his eyebrows, "This impacts all businesses, trade and production. I can understand trying to shut down and boycott to a point, but now it is also impacting common businesses, not just the rich. This was playing with fire, even my tavern is officially closed."

Rufus' eyes widened as he nodded, "Yes and it looks like Tiberius will continue to do this until both the Senate and the Assembly pass his laws. The Assembly, fearing for Tiberius's safety, has decided to have a group of veterans guard him, can you hand pick several men to do this?"

Aelianus smiled, "I know the right group of veterans who can protect Tiberius and escort him. Just make sure he doesn't move until we can get to him."

Rufus said, "That's good because Tiberius Gracchus' overruling of Octavius's veto was not proper, afterwards his supporters took Octavius outside and beat him, that was illegal. My source tells me that his opponents are determined to prosecute Tiberius at the end of his one-year term which could have severe consequences. This is because he violated the constitution when he ordered his men to use force against Tribune Octavius."

Aelianus poured more wine. "Is there more news?"

Rufus nodded "After the exit of Octavius, Tiberius was next confronted by Titus Annius in a stand-off, Annius is a renowned orator and has many supporters in the Senate."

Aelianus acknowledged "I have heard Annius' speeches at the market, he is quite a speaker."

Rufus continued "Well Annius argued that Tiberius is grabbing for absolute power as Tiberius physically removed Octavius."

Aelianus shook his head as Rufus continued "Tiberius told me later as I was leaving that he realized you Aelianus had warned him of this at this very tavern, that his actions against Octavius could and has caused him ill repute among the Senate and even among some of the common people."

Aelianus spoke directly "Among common people of Rome, the law still is the law. Tiberius must listen, it was all assumptions before, but the death of Sagonius, Tiberius' man should be warning enough. My sources told me that Sagonius was poisoned." Rufus frowned as he nodded.

The Senate made a decree that all businesses would be reopened. A few days later Vicidius came by Aelianus inn again laughing about how Aelianus' friends were dying all over. Aelianus' guards began to move towards him, but he smiled and walked away. Tiberius felt the time to seize his opportunity was in hand. Showing strength for the people of Rome could gain sympathy with the people, against Rufus and Aelianus' concerns, Tiberius dressed in mourning clothes and paraded his children in front of the Assembly, pleading for the protection of himself and his family. Tiberius sought to repair the perception of his error against Octavius by arguing that the office of the tribune, which was held as a sacrosanct position, could be challenged if the holder violated his oath. To support this, he reminded all that other sacrosanct office holders were seized when they violated their duties, such as Vestal Virgins or the Roman kings, by doing so the state benefited from their removal.

Rufus told Aelianus "Tiberius is truly ambitious, he has pledged to protect himself further by gaining veteran and military supporters, that for re-election to the tribunate positions in 132 BC, that the term of military service would shorten, he proposes to abolish the exclusive right of senators to act as court jurors and will propose to include other social classes to be jurors. Further Tiberius proposes to admit allies to Roman citizenship, all of these moves are popular with the people's Assembly, but many in the Senate will ardently oppose."

Aelianus said "Seems like that could be popular."

Rufus shrugged "We shall see. After the drama at the Senate, Tiberius went outside to the market where he continued to promote his proposals to the people of Rome, including that he had fears for his safety and that of his family. At the end of which he rallied a large group of homeless veteran supporters who are now camped outside his house to ensure his protection."

Aelianus nodded, "I walked by Tiberius' home earlier and saw one veteran I remember from the legions, named Septimus who plays a harp to keep the men entertained. I have offered to give them all my inn's leftover food and wine each night."

Rufus smiled, "You are generous my man, but we must be careful. This movement is good, but it has the potential to explode and it's anyone's guess who will end up on top."

Chapter XX Aelianus & Pris

133 BC

While events in Rome had become ever more intense, Aelianus wanted more companionship when Rufus was busy. As he fully trusted Pris, understanding her sharp intellect and kindness. Aelianus spoke with Pris about business, politics, relationships and other matters. In order to get a break from the volatile situation, my master started to take us fishing about once a month. The first trip would be unforgettable.

Fish

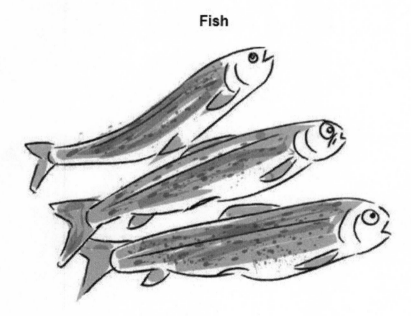

One day, Aelianus said that he wanted to go fishing, that it had been ages since his last time. Luciana and I were excited to get out of the house and my master seemed to really need a moment to have some peace and reflect on ongoing issues.

Aelianus had Pris prepare a meal for everyone, then told Pris to come along to write down his dictations and to take care of us kids when he wanted to focus on fishing. When we arrived Pris said "Wow, such a beautiful place, all the trees make me almost feel back at home."

Aelianus said "I love coming here, it is peaceful and I can relax here."

Aelianus had brought his bow, he tied an end of the line to one end, next he baited his hook on the other. To keep the fish as fresh as possible, he had brought a bucket, filling it with water that the caught fish would be held in. Many times, the fish bit off the hook, but sometimes not.

Master fished for a few hours speaking with my mother about tavern supply, wine and the politics of Tiberius. They sat there for a long while, Luciana and Sarth played along the river, suddenly Luciana noticed a green frog off to the right upstream on the river bank. While Sarth was stacking rocks on the river side, she started tip-toeing over to try to catch it, it turned and leaped into some bushes.

Pris called "Luciana, don't go too far" An excited voice called back "Yes mother!"

Aelianus chuckled, "Ah to be young. Watching you and your children is heartwarming for me, I never knew my mother…"

As Pris and Aelianus talked about his childhood, Sarth started to follow Luciana, but she turned and glared at him, so Sarth returned to Aelianus to listen to his master's childhood story and await an invitation to make a few fishing attempts.

Aelianus saw Sarth waiting nearby and smiling, handing over the line "The fish do not like me today, maybe you might have some luck."

Sarth smiled ear to ear taking the line, they sat there for a few minutes, suddenly the fishing line jerked violently, "I got one!" Sarth shouted.

"WOW, this is a big one" Aelianus exclaimed as he pulled in a big Salmerino del Trentino fish, it was about the length of the master's forearm, purple in color with white dots along its body.

Sarth placed the fish into their bucket, "We are eating well tonight" Aelianus shouted joyfully.

Suddenly we heard a splash of water and Luciana's scream. Aelianus and Pris started running in the direction of the scream thinking Luciana may have fallen into the river. A few rough looking men appeared out of the bushes, the smallest one in back was holding a wet Luciana, they all had their gladius swords brandished, turning a happy day ugly.

Their leader was a tall man covered with tattoos, pointing his sword at Aelianus he barked "Look what we dragged from the river! If you want her alive, you will give us your money, your stuff and your woman and don't think about trying for your gladius over there or this kid's dead."

Aelianus signaled Pris to stay back looking at the bandits, "Well stranger, let's talk".

Aelianus brushed off the dirt from his toga while walking slowly towards the bandit holding his hands up at his shoulder height, his shoulders broad and swaying a little with each step, his head high. Aelianus smiled "You see I did not grab for my gladius; I am unarmed. Now why don't you all let the girl go, I can pay you, and then go away before someone gets hurt?"

The bandit leader was shocked, never had his victims threatened him, was the girl not important to him? Aelianus kept slowly approaching and stopped just within sword reach. The bandit leader yelled "Fool, do you want to die?"

Aelianus just smiled.

The leader frowned and his sword arm went back across his body, coiled back to strike in a head level swing, "Very well die y…"

The bandit's blade swung out in one continuous fluid motion, Aelianus sidestepped left towards his attacker's sword arm while strike blocking the attacker's sword arm with his right arm at the wrist, swinging the blade arm downward in a circular motion with his right arm Aelianus next reached his left fist above his head then struck down on the attacker's sword arm as it swung down near his legs.

245

Aelianus continued the swing off his left side with his left arm, as this was happening his right fist shot up smashing the attacker's jaw which emitted a loud crushing sound and a couple teeth with blood flying out. Aelianus' left hand next came up around the attacker's sword arm, wrapping the arm inward towards Aelianus' chest while the sword was sticking out over Aelianus' left elbow, Aelianus stepped back hooking his right hand down on the attacker's sword arm wrist dislocating the attacker's grip while pulling the sword away from the attacker, disarming him.

The attacker yelled in pain grabbing his now broken jaw, Aelianus kicked him in the stomach with his right foot, the attacker fell to his knees as Aelianus swung the attacker's sword in the air catching it into his own hand.

The second attacker yelled as he rushed up "You cannot kill my broth…"

Aelianus in a flash deflected the 2nd attacker's sword's stab with a downward arching block which had an ear-splitting clash, then after he parried the attacker's blade in a single movement that almost looked like a fast dance Aelianus reversed arched his blade slashing across the man's throat sending a spew of blood in the air.

The man fell dropping his blade grabbing his throat choking on his own blood as life left him, Aelianus spun and seeing the leader on the ground pulling a dagger from his belt, nimbly shifted his stance squatted on his left knee with his right leg stretched out, in a single movement Aelianus stabbed his gladius into the leader's heart, whose body immediately began to jerk as he howled in brief pain as Aelianus pulled the blood red blade out of his dead attacker's body.

Aelianus grabbed the 2nd bandit's gladius which had been dropped. Now holding two gladius swords Aelianus stood up, the last bandit was a younger man who began trembling. Aelianus paused, pointing his left sword at the man he yelled "Give me the girl unharmed and I will let you live or would you want to meet Hades painfully as well?"

The man stood there a moment, released Luciana and ran off.

Aelianus kneeled down, "Come to me child, it is alright". Luciana ran over to him as he gave her a big hug, she began to shake and began crying.

Pris had rushed over and hugged Luciana and laid a hand on her shoulder, "Thank you Aelianus."

Aelianus looked up, "You must never hesitate in such moments. Well, it has been a busy day, let us return home".

On the way Aelianus talked about how dangerous the world was. Turning to Sarth Aelianus smiled "How old are you now Sarth?"

Sarth had his arm around his sister Luciana, they were startled "We are 9 years old master."

Aelianus looked at Pris "I am sorry they were in such a situation and had to see all the blood, and death. One doesn't normally experience such things at such a young age.

Pris bowed her head "You didn't plan on those bandits and you saved them from death. That is what matters".

Pris began to hum "We are one with nature, we leave to feed our families taking only what we need, oh nature please give us the prize and a safe trip home."

Aelianus looked at her listening to her sing in Cimbri, touching her behind her shoulder he remarked "I like how you sang that song, what does it mean?" Pris explained it to him.

Along the way home Pris saw some purple and red mushrooms growing alongside the dirt path before they got to the main road. She stopped the party and began picking them.

Aelianus looked over "What are you picking those for?"

Pris looked up, smiled and said to all of them, my grandma Fiona taught me, these purple ones can be brewed into tea, great for fevers, pains and headaches. Those red ones over there are poisonous, we can mix them up with cheese and sprinkle them to kill the rats."

Sarth chimed in "Purple good, red bad"

Pris nodded. Aelianus' eye lit up, "Wow, good to know."

Pris was about to stand up when she noticed the flowers around that area, as she picked a handful, she said "These are Arnica flowers, they have great medicinal value for aches and pains.... and they smell wonderful."

Aelianus smiled "Tell me children, do you like dogs?"

The kids cheered, Aelianus continued "Great because we are getting a new one when we get home."

Chapter XXI Pris & Quintus Gaius Traianus

133 BC

Aelianus was a great socializer, he became good friends with several Senators and his quick wit caused all to want to invite him to their social gatherings.

The following evening Sabina had gone out and Rufus sent word that Tiberius was hosting a party at his home villa. Many Senators would be there, Rufus wanted to have Aelianus join him. Aelianus had Pris join him to be his assistant if needed. Aelianus had once bought an attractive red toga dress for Sabina which Sabina had hated and had not even tried on. Rather than throw out a perfectly good dress, Aelianus had given it to Pris, who looked stunning in it.

Pris at Tiberius' Party

Pris wore that dress to the party. Tiberius, Tiberius' wife, and Tiberius' younger brother Gaius, greeted the guests as they arrived. Aelianus noticed many people looking at Pris smiling. Aelianus smiled saying to Pris "You are stunning my dear."

Tiberius saw Pris and gave her a big smile "You are the loveliest servant in all of Rome, you always know which wines I love best, welcome to my home."

Pris smiled back thanking him and tried to be unobtrusive in the back of the gathering as the various Senators all talked politics with Tiberius and Gaius. Gaius voiced his opinions strongly as Aelianus and Rufus listened about the options of how the Roman republic could best proceed in these times. Senator Linus Cornelius Scipio arrived, greeted Tiberius and began speaking with Aelianus and Rufus as well about the proposed changes. The wives of the Senators were all talking laying on couches as their collection of children had gone into a backroom to play. Pris was standing within hearing range of Aelianus, though she was not paying much attention to their conversation, bored of the political discussion that was ongoing. A knock at the door, and another two Senators entered giving their greetings to Tiberius' wife as they came in.

Pris was listening to the music from the harp that an older daughter of one of the Senators played, she smiled, it was truly lovely. *At least I can listen to that for a while,* Pris thought. Suddenly she had a tap on her shoulder, Pris turned and saw the man who had paid to sleep with her years ago.

The man smiled "I thought it might be you…. how are you?"

Pris was stunned, she thought she would never see this man again. Instantly Pris felt a mixture of bittersweet feelings. For some reason his friendly smile and handsome appearance started to rub away the pain and sadness that she felt. Pris immediately thought *Quintus! Oh, keep it together*, "I am alive thank you."

Quintus nodded, "You look to be in good health. We didn't really get to know each other before. I am Quintus Gaius Traianus, I am the Senator of the 8th district. I must say…. I have not forgotten about you, it was special…. You are Pris right?" Pris nodded.

Quintus smiled "Are you still working in that tavern & inn?"

Pris gave a half smile, "Yes, my current master is Aelianus Treneca, Cyprian's son." Pris considered *Should I tell him about our two children whom he had fathered with me?* Suddenly from behind Quintus, a woman's voice interrupted them, "Dear, who are you speaking with?"

Quintus turned around, "This is Aelianus' slave dear; her name is Pris. She is very knowledgeable of Aelianus' wines, she served me wine once at her inn. I was asking about those."

Quintus' wife hardly noticed Pris as she waved her hand, "That's nice." Turning to Pris she said "Slave, I would like some wine."

Pris bowed her head and went for the wine.

Quintus said that he would join the political conversation and his wife sat with the other wives. Pris brought her wine to which she hardly noticed. Pris turned to QUintus' direction and looked at him for an instant before walking to the back of the room. *Has he not forgotten about me? He is married? Oh my, how to feel about this?* Pris could not lie to herself, part of her did find Quintus attractive, he is a Senator, she could easily love him. But she thought *I am a slave, it's impossible, and I don't want to be his mistress.* That would be too dangerous. Pris felt something and looked over to see Quintus looking at her a couple times during the party, but she tried to be as inconspicuous as possible.

A few hours went by, Aelianus, Rufus and Pris returned home. Aelianus mentioned how he had a slight headache, so Pris made tea with the purple mushrooms for him. Aelianus was really impressed and requested she make some for his predicted hangover.

That night while cleaning the kitchen, Ingrid the old slave woman sat down feeling winded. Pris and Helga let her rest and gave her some water. A few moments later Ingrid fell over dead. Pris and Helga cried loudly causing Aelianus to come to the kitchen to see what was amiss.

Helga closed Ingrid's eyes "Now you are free."

Aelianus arrived and cried as well. Pris looked at Aelianus, *he is the only Roman I respect*. Teana the 70-year-old Carthaginian woman came in and wept too, she spoke to

Pris and Helga "Ingrid had been his wet nurse, no wonder he grieves."

Rome

3

That night Pris dreamed that Quintus was trying to run away with her from some unknown assailant, they got lost and separated in a gray stonewalled maze. Pris could hear him calling out, his voice echoing. Next she heard the voices of her children with Aelianus calling for her to go in a different direction, after searching through the maze she found a staircase that took her up above the maze, in the distance she saw prince Volker of the Saxons beaconing her from a grassy hill to come to him, but she felt a

---

[3] Image of Ancient Rome, Copyright Free:
https://www.flickr.com/photos/psulibscollections/5832221541

dangerous presence somewhere in the maze with the knowledge that she had to go through it again.

Pris hurried down the stairs she heard her mother's voice saying "Pris run!" Pris ran across a hallway of fur trees that suddenly became Roman columns, she heard her children's voices calling "Mommy don't leave us!" Pris looked back to see images of her children with the bandits at the river standing a ways back. Pris turned around and rushed towards them only for them to disappear. Pris shouted "Sarth! Luciana!"

Pris woke up in a cold sweat. She immediately went to her sleeping children to kiss their heads.

Chapter XXII Power Plays

133 BC

When the day for the vote of Lex Sempronia Agraria arrived, many of his supporters assembled at the Capitol. Tiberius set out, not heeding many ominous omens. As the tribunes were being assembled, a skirmish broke out on the outskirts of the crowd as Tiberius' supporters were attempting to block Vicidius and a group of Tiberius' opponents.

Fulvius Flaccus a sympathetic senator and friend of Rufus, was able to make his way to Tiberius to warn him that the Senate was seated and plotting to kill him, having armed slaves and their men since they could not convince the consul, who was a friend of Tiberius, to do the deed. Tiberius' men then armed themselves with clubs and staves, prepared to meet any violence. There was a great amount of noise and shouting from the clashing groups and a brawl ensued.

Soon Tiberius tried to shout above the din, gestured to his head to signal his life was in danger. Vicidius saw this and knew it could be implied to be a sign requesting for a King's crown and ran back to the Senate to report his idea of the signal. At this moment, Rufus exited the Senate's building and saw Aelianus as he was entering the Roman Forum. Rufus yelled "Aelianus, go and get more security, I will return to the Senate to get more help!" Rufus and Aelianus rushed off to their tasks.

When the Senate heard Vicidius explain how Tiberius was signaling himself to be a king, the opposition became outraged by Publius Cornelius Scipio Nasica, Tiberius' cousin by marriage. Nasica was the newly elected Pontifex Maximus, he did not want to be associated with a would-be king or dictator. Nasica exclaimed "These actions by Tiberius showed that he desires to make himself king!" Nasica went to the consul "You must take action!" The consul refused, "Tiberius is not a traitor, we must negotiate." Nasica girded his toga over his head, shouting "No! The consul has betrayed the state!" He turned to Vicidius, "Let every man who wishes to uphold the laws and loves Rome follow me!" Nasica led a group of senators including Vicidius towards Tiberius and his supporters.

In the resulting confrontation, Nasica, Vicidius, Praetor Popilius Laena along with some Senators and hundreds of their other slave guards attacked Tiberius and his supporters. The Roman Forum became a mess of hundreds of people brawling. In the fray Tiberius was beaten to death by Vicidius and others with clubs and staves and many of Tiberius' supporters were similarly hurt or killed. More than 300 supporters of Tiberius were slain that day by bats, stones and staves, but none by sword. Once Tiberius's group were defeated, the dead were collected and their bodies were thrown into the Tiber River. Vicidius did this intentionally knowing that such an act would deny them a proper funeral.

Aelianus had returned to the site with 20 armed men, but it was too late, he saw Tiberius' body being thrown over a bridge from a distance and decided it best to stay alive.

Aelianus and his men returned to their inn, sorrowful and angry.

Following the massacre, Praetor Popilius Laena with Vicidius' help tried many of Tiberius' surviving supporters. These people were often executed or sent into exile without a trial. A few who tried to fight were arrested, executed or assassinated. Vicidius enjoyed catching these followers, his favorite thing to do was have a captive sewn up in a bag with poisonous vipers and thrown in the river.

Chapter XXIII

133 BC

Once Tiberius was dead, we were all in jeopardy, my master was playing a dangerous game. However, Aelianus still felt he had protection through his connections.

Senator Rufus was protected by several powerful Senators and Rufus protected Aelianus stating that though they had talked to Tiberius to propose a more moderate bill, one that would not threaten the rich, they were not hardcore supporters. Aelianus was unhappy to be untruthful, however with all the murders and summary executions going on, Aelianus was grateful just to get through this alive.

Vicidius tried to paint Aelianus in a bad light before the Senate, he claimed that Aelianus was an ardent supporter of Tiberius, however he had no proof and Aelianus simply countered that he is a tavern owner and could not control who came into his establishment for good wine and food. Indeed, Rufus and many others of the Senate had also enjoyed meals there, the overall consensus agreed that Aelianus was a veteran and patriot from his time in the legions, that he was a friendly soul who welcomed all Romans to his establishment. Unless they had more proof, they would not kill an innocent man. Aelianus wanted to speak with Rufus, but it was risky for him to be on the street, not knowing if some Roman would recognize him as a friend of Tiberius or not, so he came to Pris.

Aelianus said to Pris "There is a need for me to communicate with Rufus and others who were supporters of Tiberius, however if I am seen by the wrong person on the streets, it is possible that I could be killed. I don't think anyone would recognize you or your son Sarth. Could you deliver this scroll to Rufus next time you and Helga buy food for our tavern?" Pris looked at Aelianus and agreed.

During the months that followed, whenever there was an urgent need Pris would take Sarth to the market for shopping and put any scrolls from Aelianus into the mail drop at Rufus' door.

During this time, there was an uproar and backlash among the people and among the homeless veterans as more of them identified themselves as Tiberius supporters their anger continued for many weeks.

Eventually at Vicidius' suggestion the Senate attempted to mollify the people by allowing a modified version of the agrarian law Tiberius had championed to go into effect. The Senate cast a vote to replace Tiberius's position on the commission; the job fell to Publius Crassus, father-in-law of Tiberius' cousin Titus. Listening to Crassus and Rufus, the Senate threatened Nasica with impeachment and consequently reassigned him to Asia to remove him from Rome. The veterans and most people made no attempt to conceal their hatred of Nasica, accosting him publicly, cursing him and calling him a tyrant. Nasica was despised and outcast for turning his back on the veterans and people of Rome, he died a few years later near the city of Pergamon (modern Turkey).

Chapter XIV Duty calls

132 BC

A few months after Tiberius's death, Aelianus was visited by Senator Mummius in his tavern.

Aelianus received him warmly, "Good to see you, Senator!"

Mummius wore an unhappy face, "Aelianus" he said as he reached into his robe and pulled a scroll. "It pains me to tell you this being that you have already done your duty for Rome in war. There is a revolt going on in Sicilia, it started small, a year or so ago. If reports are true, a Syrian slave named Eunus who has been claiming to be a prophet, captured the city of Enna in the middle of the island with 400 fellow slaves."

Aelianus looked at him in mild shock, "Back to the legions?"

Mummius nodded his head, "We need as many experienced veterans as possible, and this will show all of Rome that you are still fully loyal to Rome."

Aelianus nodded, as he asked. "Have the reports we've read not been true that the local governor stamped them out?"

Mummius shook his head, a local army of town watches were dispatched, but they were smashed. Soon after that disaster, another leader named Cleon, stormed the city of Agrigentum on the southern coast, his horde slaughtered the population, our spies report that he then joined Eunus' army and became his military commander. Eunus has even proclaimed himself king, under the name of Antiochus."

Stallion and several other cohort units are going to be resurrected, but that will take some time. If this revolt is not crushed quickly it could spread across Italy and beyond. We need experienced veterans to go down and train the town watches to be ready for battle."

Aelianus acknowledged, "How soon?"

Mummius shrugged, "Once they have gathered enough veterans, a few weeks at most."

Rufus came to Aelianus that night, they drank into the night "Aelianus, why are you so quiet tonight?"

Aelianus gave a half grin "I've been recalled to the legion, Slave and gladiator revolts in Sicily have erupted, Mummius called it the first Servile war."

Rufus said "You've already served nearly 20 years active and reservist in the legions in the Princep heavy infantry, you don't need to go. I can pull a favor or two in the Senate."

Aelianus shook his head, "No, I have experience, not many do. I must go.

Rufus gave him a look so he explained, "The danger of being associated with Tiberius probably has not ended with his death. I suspect that the people who had orchestrated his death also want me silenced. You are protected by your position, but I am not. I know Vicidius, be very careful of him."

Rufus stayed quiet for a moment, then said "Is there anything I can do while you are away to help with your tavern or winery?"

Aelianus looked at him, "Sabina has no interest in running the tavern or winery, I will have Pris manage them, she is very clever. If you could just check on her daily to be sure all is well, that would be helpful."

Rufus nodded, "I will give you a couple more guards while you are away, they will be told to protect all in this house."

Aelianus smiled "Thank you."

Rufus moved to him "Now be careful and return to me."

Chapter XXIV Vicidius & Sabina

133 BC

Aelianus left Rome with a hastily assembled legion made up of veterans and many green recruits. Aelianus didn't talk much about personal feelings except what was needed as a typical centurion; his feelings were still torn by all that had happened around Tiberius and the future of Rome. Aelianus' manipular they marched South from Rome. They were involved in a major defeat, which Aelianus survived, after fighting in another couple battles, his legion was one of many that partook in crushing the slave revolts led by Eunus. Though Aelianus did not enjoy killing, he was good at it.

A few days after Aelianus had departed, Sabina was at a market shopping. It was there in the Roman Forum that Vicidius approached her. They spoke at length and when Vicidius invited her to speak with him at his home, Sabina quickly accepted. Vicidius' home was a large villa that was located at the top of one of Rome's seven hills. There was a balcony from his dining room that overlooked much of the city. They had some wine.

Vicidius looked at Sabina who smiled after a mouthful of wine. He said "Sabina like Aelianus, I served in the legion and now that I have been elected as a Senator I feel strongly about preserving the power of Rome for those who are guiding it towards its great future." Vicidius handed Sabina a small bowl of nuts and said "Aelianus was an indirect supporter of Tiberius Gracchus, he is a threat to what Rome is."

Sabina shrugged, "Aelianus is serving Rome now in Sicily to put down the revolts, but he doesn't care about me. He is as good as dead for all I care."

Vicidius grinned a little, "Sabina you plainly care nothing of Aelianus nor the danger your husband is in or of the events which had befallen Tiberius."

Sabina thought for a moment, then she touched Vicidius' facial scar, Vicidius moved back surprised. Sabina said "You are so distinguished." Vicidius stood wide eyed. Sabina said "Tell me about that…"

Vicidius said "A mark of battle, I killed a king getting that….

Sabina smiled, "You are a perfect match for me, I need a powerful man."

Vicidius lost his calm face a moment then shielded his surprise. Vicidius said "Now is the greatest time for Rome, I will do so many things for its greater glory…."

Sabina listened further as Vicidius told her about his plans to make Rome the greatest power in the world, how only he had the ambition to do what fools like Tiberius, Rufus and Aelianus could not in order to keep Rome strong and that it was their duty to eliminate any threats to Rome's power external or internal.

They were drinking wine and enjoying the view of Rome from his balcony. Vicidius could not wait any longer and made a pass at her. Sabina received him for what would become several sexual marathons over the day and throughout the night.

Months went by and Aelianus returned from his duty in Sicily. Aelianus returned to Rome, a veteran of two wars, his shield and armor showed the signs of battle. Aelianus was happy to be home and away from the legions. Aelianus saw Pris first, "Where is Sabina?"

Pris responded "I believe she is shopping."

Aelianus set his things down and sat, "I served honorably, my unit had been transitioned to protect Rome. A week ago I retired from the legion"

Pris clapped "Good, now you can take care of your home" Aelianus smiled.

Aelianus said "Pris, you are now a 25-year-old woman and your children Sarth & Luciana are what 7 years old?" Pris nodded. Aelianus smiled watching her, "Thank you for taking care of things while I was away."

Aelianus looked at her and her twin children. Luciana was playing a harp, Sarth brought him some wine. "Your children, their eyes were of different colors, the right blue and left brown. Remarkable!" Pris smiled.

Aelianus recalled his promise to his grandfather and attempted to reconnect with Sabina, however no matter what he did, there was always some reason that she would find to decline and or yell at him about. Aelianus occasionally came to the kitchen late at night, sweat covering his body.

On one such night Pris was using the bathroom and exiting the toilet saw him awake in the dining room. Aelianus poured a goblet of wine refilling it as footsteps approached from behind, looking behind him he smiled "Ah Pris, what are you doing up?"

Pris smiled, "That is a question I have for you master."

Aelianus motioned to an empty chair, "A nightmare, so I woke up."

Pris looked at him concerned "Are you awake because of Sabina? If so...." Pris smiled, "I have a mixture that you can add to your wine, it might make you both feel excited to embrace each other."

Aelianus looked at her, "Hmmm, perhaps I'll have to try that, go ahead and put some in this."

Pris smiled, "You will be very excited master." She went away and returned with a leather pouch.

Aelianus raised an eyebrow, "Perhaps if she will receive me.... If it will help, it is what must be done." He looked at the powder, "No, I am awake due to nightmares, of battle, of killing, of my brother being killed..."

Pris nodded as she opened her pouch she carried and poured white powder into his goblet. Aelianus rolled it around, Pris put her hand on his forearm thinking *If I can get them to become loving, it would be a miracle for me and my children.*

At that moment Sabina entered the room. Sabina eyed them sitting together, her voice came out icy "What are you two doing together here?"

Aelianus stood up "Wife, I had a nightmare, and I thought to sample this delicious wine, would you like to try some?" Sabina gave an annoyed look so he continued.

"Pris had just listened to me recount my nightmare of battle. Care to join me and try this fine wine?"

Sabina pointed her finger at Pris "Why did you summon her to listen to you? You are sleeping with her aren't you Aelianus!"

Aelianus shook his head as he walked over offering the wine goblet, "No that's silly dear, I...." Sabina slapped away the goblet, wine flew through the air and landed all over the floor as the goblet clanked against a wall. Aelianus was stunned and she slapped him next.

Aelianus grabbed Sabina on her arms, "Dear you are mistaken, I...."

Sabina slapped him again "I don't want to hear your lies and you should not be wasting our wine on your sorrows!"

Aelianus frowned "We own a winery; do you have any clue how much wine we have? If you want to be tight, you should be asking for my permission before you go on your expensive shopping sprees!"

Sabina looked at Pris "Slave, clean up that mess and then get out!"

Then she turned back to Aelianus, "I am so sick of you whining about your duty, you cannot even be a man and satisfy me, yet you are all too happy to talk to that slave! And the minute you return to Rome you leave your junk all over making my house filthy."

Aelianus yelled back "Woman you have no idea what conditions I lived in while I served in the Legion or how many times I faced death? Yet where have you been since I came home? Why could you not say one kind thing to me now that I'm here?"

The argument between them lasted a long time, eventually Sabina stormed out of the room shouting vile profanities she returned to their room and slammed the door.

Aelianus was enraged, he called on Pris to come in to refill his wine goblet. As he was waiting for it to be filled, Aelianus looked at a bowl of olives, he put an olive in his mouth and, not thinking about it while he swallowed, deep in thought. Next Aelianus tossed an olive in the air, caught it in his mouth, but began choking on it.

Pris, remembering when she was young how Rúna her mother had once saved Krull her father from choking on food, she immediately rushed over and from behind reached her hands around Aelianus hugging him from

269

behind and making a fist with her hands began pumping his chest in and upward, after the third pump the olive flew from Aelianus' blued face saving his life.

Once Aelianus could breathe and speak again, he thanked her for saving his life, and said "You are the best slave a man could have."

Pris looked unhappy and said "Slave, is that all I am to you?"

Aelianus shook his head, he said "If you agree to continue to work for me. I will free you and your children and make you all my paid servants."

Pris gave a sideways grin, "And Helga." Aelianus said "Fine."

Pris then agreed.

Aelianus said, "Great I will pay you, and Helga, the same that I would have to pay a normal servant."

Pris looked at him, Aelianus shrugged, "Plus 25% each month to cover back pay."

Pris smiled, "Deal."

Chapter XXV Sarth and Luciana Complications

129 BC

My master came to fully trust my mother, and for a time it seemed that life would be normal.

Four years passed, Aelianus kept sleeping with Rufus, meanwhile his wife Sabina clandestinely continued to sleep with Vicidius. Sabina had many admirers in the Senate and became an extra set of eyes and ears for Vicidius at Senatorial parties she attended. Aelianus learned of some of these activities through Rufus and other Senators who dined at his tavern.

For a man who was not receiving any respect or love from his wife due to his gay nature, he instead received advice and support from Pris. Pris believed that friendship with Aelianus meant security for her and her children. Aelianus fully trusted Pris and appreciated her sharp intellect. Aelianus listened to Pris now about her viewpoints on business commerce, philosophy, politics, and other matters.

Aelianus brought Pris and Helga to his office one morning. "Pris I want to apologize to you that Cyprian had made you sleep with Senator Quintus when I was gone."

Helga smiled, "Thank you master."

Pris shook her head, "You had no control over the matter, that was when Cyprian had been master, besides I have two beautiful children who are all mine. You have been like a father to them. Furthermore, I am more grateful to you since you saved me and my children from certain death when we went fishing together."

Pris and Helga walked out, Helga asked "What do you think about that?"

Pris said "Aelianus is a kind master; yet I feel conflicted, Germania will always be home."

Helga nodded "I hope he frees us, we could travel home together."

Pris nodded, "I think he might, if I continue to help him. Rome will always be strange, dangerous, we will always be barbarians to Romans." Helga nodded as they set up the breakfast table.

Sarth and Luciana had overheard them talking, Sarth asked "Mom Rome is where we were born, can you not love it? It is a beautiful and impressive city."

Pris shrugged, "Rome has impressive aqueducts, marble buildings, but it will never be my home, not in my heart." Sarth made a face, Pris continued "But Rome did give me two gifts, you two my beautiful children!"

Helga smiled as she reentered the room, "That's true Pris totally loves you children Sarth and Luciana!"

Luciana smiled as she folded the napkins "Mother is how all good mothers should be of their children."

Pris smiled and returned to the kitchen, Helga came in "Are you alright?"

Pris shrugged, "I miss my father and sister, I was robbed of them, of life at home...."

Helga put her hand on Pris' shoulder "Stop sister, we must stay patient. One day, but not yet." Pris nodded.

Pris said "Aelianus asked her if there was anything he could do for her, I told him that I hoped to get her freedom, to become a freedwoman, to leave Rome eventually."

Helga asked "What did he say?"

Pris responded "Aelianus told me that he needed me for his business but would allow me to gain nominal freedom under him as his servant, not slave."

Aelianus' voice filled the next room, "Good morning young children!" Pris and Helga entered the room with bowls of porridge, cooked eggs and toast.

Aelianus asked "Where is Sabina?" Helga said "She has a hangover, I think she might be sleeping in this morning." Aelianus shrugged, and began eating food.

Pris asked "Master, you told me before that I could be freed, was that something you are serious about?"

Aelianus smiled, "Oh, I forgot to tell you about that, I have all the paperwork done to free you and your children and Helga on the condition that you will promise to stay as my servants. I will pay you going forward and you can live in his residence until you both have enough money to move into her own place."

Helga smiled broadly, "Master, I have nowhere to go back to, I accept your offer."

Pris nodded, Sarth and Luciana cheered, then Aelianus said "Why don't you feed your kids Pris, they look hungry."

At that moment Helga heard Sabina's summing bell and went to assist her.

Pris brought her children to the kitchen. They asked her "Well Mommy, does this mean we stay in Rome?" Pris nodded "For the meantime, until you both are a little older. Then we will return to Jutland."

Luciana said "Mommy, I'm not sure I want to go, neither does Sarth. Aelianus has done so much for us. I love the dolls Aelianus got me. I love how he taught me about flowers, he taught me how to plant tomatoes, carrots, grape vines, how to harvest the grapes, how to smash them for making them into wine, it was so much fun!"

Pris nodded "Aelianus said you are a smart girl and that he might see if you want to become a winemaker."

Luciana's eyes opened wide "That would be so much fun! I love squashing those grapes!"

Pris had a hard time falling asleep in bed that night, she looked at her sleeping children and sleeping Helga.

Chapter XXVI Pris

129 BC

By this time Aelianus would send Pris to the market to purchase supplies weekly, occasionally with Helga or with one of his guards. Pris' Latin had become fluent, she still had a slight accent, but Aelianus had helped her to learn how to read and write as it helped him with business matters.

Aelianus was a decent business owner, and he came to realize that Pris was really clever. Pris had become proficient at her Latin, philosophy, mathematics, along with her charming sense of humor. Pris suggested certain types of wine to go with certain types of food in a set menu, Pris had suggested small improvements for his inn and tavern in an organized way to be sure that the old food was always served first, that the meats had been salted. At her idea, small bells on each table for customers to summon their waiter, she was good at keeping an inventory of all the wine and other stored food ingredients like salt or flour. Pris was organized and watched over tavern details whenever Aelianus could not. Aelianus was good at keeping the customers entertained, Aelianus was very charming to all, welcoming them to his restaurant.

Often Aelianus had to travel to and from the tavern inn from his vineyard, on such occasions he typically left his guards to protect his house, however since Tiberius was murdered, he knew that anyone who had supported Tiberius was in danger of assassination. One night walking home with Pris in the darkened streets of Rome, Aelianus felt that someone was following him.

Aelianus looked at Pris, "I am so lucky to have you with me."

Pris looked at him "Why master?"

Aelianus smiled, "You are my secret weapon; you are great in recording wine inventory counts and shelf-life information. I have also been surprised to see how fast you've learned swordplay."

Pris smiled "Really?"

Aelianus smiled "Yes an assassin would never suspect you as my secret bodyguard." She felt the handle of her gladius that was underneath her cloak.

Aelianus kept looking into the shadows as they walked and continued talking "At first you were unable to defend against my strikes, but not anymore. I am proud of you."

Pris smiled "True it seemed like no matter what attack or defense I did you could deflect or block and perform a counter and soon be holding your wooden blade at my throat. No matter what I did it seemed like your wooden blade would end up inches from my throat or heart."

Aelianus smiled "You are now nearly my equal in swordplay. And I've seen Sarth improve greatly as well."

They walked in silence for a while, they stopped at an intersection as a line of legionnaires marched by.

Aelianus smiled, "You've begun to hold your own against my attacks. I've been noticing that strategies and simpler attacks that once had worked against you are now being blocked more often than not."

Pris pointed to him "Yesterday I was able to keep you at bay for a long time…. 10 minutes before we finished."

Aelianus smiled "I, I had to be really tricky with you, you are really catching on with the sword".

Pris smiled back "I almost had you."

He gave a laugh, "Almost? Almost is not the same thing as did. My my… we are getting ambitious."

Pris asked Aelianus about his time in the legion, about how they fought. About Sicily… Aelianus spoke of the manipulars, how they marched, the equipment, what harm was there in telling her his old soldier stories?

After returning home, Aelianus called for Sarth to come over just before their practice session. Aelianus paused, "Sarth my boy, you've become so good with your sword, I want to give you this wooden sword to always have."

Sarth's eyes lit up "Really master?"

Aelianus laughed "Yes, dear boy, you are a natural. Keep it with pride, you have earned it."

Sarth looked at it for a long time, "May I keep it in the armory? I don't have a place for it in my room." Aelianus nodded.

That night after Sarth and then Pris had practiced swordplay with Aelianus. Pris watched Sarth go upstairs for bed then turned to Aelianus.

Pris said "Master, my children at 12 now. When they are 16 I will take them from Rome and travel home."

Aelianus was torn inside, he stuttered his response "V..very…. well." He nodded eyes closed, "Thank you for letting me know and for giving me a little longer. Do you know if life will be better for you all in Germanica? There is danger there too."

Pris nodded "Life is dangerous anywhere master. But I will never be anything but a barbarian among Romans."

Aelianus nodded and gave Pris a short hug. Aelianus asked "Shall we practice some more?"

Pris grinned "I may get you this time."

Sabina had been quietly watching them from the time they started practicing swordplay from above on the 2nd floor through the atrium. Their swordplay had become almost like a dance with Aelianus naming certain moves.

Sabina heard him yell "Ah so you are trying to use the Spartan attack, well I shall use my block and Achilles counter strike" Aelianus said while Pris laughed.

For a long time, neither was able to best the other with counters and recounters. Aelianus smiled at Pris across their swords as they blocked and dodged each other's strikes.

Sabina stared at their laughter and dance-like movements and lover-like holds. Her hand started to shake, spinning some wine. Swallowing a large mouthful of wine that partly rolled around her mouth and onto her dress, Sabina stormed off in a rage to bed alone. A twisted vile sense of jealousy captured her, almost blind with fury. Inside her room Sabina moaned "Why should he be happy, while I have to sneak around with my lover and that fool listens to that slave more than he does to me?"

Helga quietly left Sabina's room.

Another who watched Aelianus and Pris practice was Traaz from the stables. Traaz was thoroughly impressed, "Aelianus is too good with a sword...." he said to a horse, "There is no way I could beat him 1-1. What must be done?"

Chapter XXVII Pris & Traaz

129 BC

My master's mistakes were closing in. Perhaps if he had sold Traaz and/or divorced Sabina, events might have gone differently.

The next evening in bed Vicidius asked Sabina "Why have you not divorced him?"

Sabina said "I never loved Aelianus, but until I met you, I had found the situation convenient. I will not divorce him to be an ashamed divorcee."

Vicidius asked "Because a gay husband was unwilling to take care of you?"

Sabina exclaimed "Yes! A woman needs a man to be manly. I deserve better than this!" Sabina looked at their hands intertwined, "Aelianus is a useful tool, he never touched me, he never even argues, it is almost like we are not married, but siblings."

The next day Sabina, on her way to go shopping at the market saw Vicidius yelling and beating a man who owed him money. It was obvious to her that Vicidius was cruel to anyone who crossed his path the wrong way, yet he had always been charming to her.

Sabina was attracted towards those who are powerful and made friends with those in power. One such friend and neighbor was the wife of a senator, who introduced her to Vicidius, not knowing they already knew each other. Sabina wanted to be more than his mistress. *Vicidius is now a Senator, tomorrow a Consul perhaps? Vicidius is a man of action, so what if he had to murder a few people to get to where he is. That's the way of things. But I cannot have him as my own unless I am single, that is why since Aelianus won't divorce me, he must die, that is the only way.*

Arriving home Sabina heard the servants talking about an incident that had happened to Pris while she was meeting with Vicidius. Apparently Pris had gone to fetch a bucket that was in the stables. Traaz had trapped Pris inside the stables and tried to force himself on her, but Pris had somehow gotten away. Curious as to what happened, Sabina asked Pris what had happened.

Pris, surprised by Sabina's sudden look of concern, told her that Traaz had grabbed Pris by her throat in one hand and her left wrist forcing her hand down on his privates. Traaz had said "You're gonna feel me inside" with a smirk.

Pris said "I felt disgusted, but I smiled and nodded so that he would loosen his grip a little, I felt his tool through his clothing and he released her hand wanting me to continue, then I made fists with my hands and they shot up striking either side of his arm of the hand on her throat just above his elbow."

Sabina was shocked "Wow that must have hurt him!"

Pris nodded "Yes, I saw a flash go across his face. His arm went limp as he released my throat and then I immediately kicked him in his privates as hard as she could. Traaz fell to the floor curled over, his pain must have been immense"

281

Pris angled her head "I soon had a knife at his throat. I told him "Touch me again and I will nail your tool to the wall'."

Sabina asked "Then what happened?"

Pris shrugged "Traaz was curled on the floor whimpering in pain, so I left him alone in the stables."

Sabina smirked thinking how Traaz had let Pris get the best of him thinking *Well, she might have got a lucky shot, but if Vicidius ever goes on a trip…. he still is great for sex.*

Arriving going into her bedroom Sabina came out where she overheard Aelianus yelling at Traaz. "Traaz, you have been a servant of my family for many years, and by Mars we pretty much grew up together." Aelianus had Traaz tied up to a post, he was holding a whip and he was wearing his sword. Traaz had several lashes that were bloody on his back. Traaz moaned in pain from each lash.

Aelianus positioned his face inches from Traaz's. "If you touch Pris, Helga or any other of my servants again you will be gone. If I find another weapon in your room, you will be sold to the gladiator ring, if any harm befalls any of the women of this house, you will be crucified. Do you understand?"

Traaz nodded, saying nothing. Sabina assumed that Traaz had often tried to get Pris to fool around whenever Sabina was not an option; she did not care if Pris was raped by him. Traaz and Pris were both slaves in Sabina's mind, slaves have no value. Better to be dead than a slave Sabina thought.

Aelianus pointed to Pris "Apologize!" Traaz looked at her and smiled. Seeing this Aelianus whipped him for a long time until finally Traaz yelled "I am sorry, please... stop!"

Aelianus stopped and he walked to Traaz, "Fine, but know this Traaz, one more incident and I will have you as a gladiator, really enrage me and you will be crucified."

Aelianus looked to his guards "Take him to his room, give him some medicine and wrappings to heal his back."

Traaz was unchained by the guards and led back to his room, Traaz looked scornfully at Aelianus as he was walking off. *This is not over Aelianus, I shall have revenge on you and the world for subjecting me to this life of slavery.*

Sabina followed Aelianus upstairs to the dining room. Aelianus turned to her, "I used to overlook it when he killed a rabbit or mice. But I learned that Traaz sexually assaulted Pris, and then after she fought him off he killed Goro...."

Sabina shrugged thinking, so he killed a dog, it was old.

Aelianus shook his head in shock, "I should sell him to the gladiator ring."

Sabina only laughed looking at Aelianus, "Traaz is a slave, he is in chains, he knows what will happen to him if he becomes violent to us and Goro was old, he was no longer useful."

Aelianus objected "There was something odd about Traaz, before the assaults I thought I could overlook his faults, however after these incidents, I am doubtful that Traaz can be trusted. We should get rid of him."

Sabina shrugged saying "We have nothing to fear so long as Traaz sleeps in a locked room at night. Traaz is very strong, we need him to work on our horses."

Aelianus argued "Don't you see? Traaz has attempted to rape our slaves. You could be next. We should sell him before something happens."

Sabina raised an eyebrow, "And how will we get the horses taken care of?"

Aelianus motioned outside "We could hire a homeless veteran to do his work"

Sabina looked at him "No I do not agree, those veterans cost too much money."

Aelianus argued with Sabina further, but she would not agree with him to sell Traaz. They argued for hours about it.

Aelianus became angry about it, Sabina slapped him "You will do what I say in matters of this house!"

Aelianus knew he could divorce her, but he had promised his grandfather Justus, he had given his word to try to carry on the family name.

Sabina looked at him in disdain, threw her glass of wine at him and stormed out of the room, he sat there a long time then went to bed.

Sabina had gone to bed in a guest room, but she could not sleep. I must do something to get me tired, that idiot won't help me... Sabina started drinking wine, then on a thought, she went to Traaz's room drinking wine.

Sabina said in an annoyed voice "Guards outside, stay close in case I call." Sabina looked at Traaz and laughed, "Oh chained up are you? You are pathetic, oh I wonder if you realize you'll never be free."

All at once she took off his lower clothing, rubbing him. Sabina got him aroused, and laid onto his bed. Traaz, seeing her invite him, eagerly went to work inserting his male part into her female part. It wasn't long before he became a little too rough strangling Sabina's neck as he pounded his tool into her, Sabina moaned and laughed in ecstasy, but Traaz began squeezing her neck violently, she quickly pulled a small knife she had hidden in her toga and put the blade to his throat. Traaz froze completely and released her throat; Sabina snickered "Oops! This knife scratches and slices so easily." Sabina playfully scratched his throat with the blade. "If you do not please me I will scream rape, and you will be crucified."

Traaz backed down and pulled out and stood up.

Sabina practically yelled "What are you doing? I did not say stop. I am not done yet. You had better not finish before me or I'll slice you!"

Sabina walked to the door and told a guard to bring her a whip. Traaz stood next to his bed and whipped him hard a few times.

Traaz, shaking with rage, "That hurt! Alright, alright... I will do whatever you want!"

Smiling, Sabina still holding the knife in one hand and the whip in the other, commanded "Traaz lay on your back. You are a strong and handsome slave, but must be taught who's boss!" Sabina whipped him again a couple more times.

Traaz yelled "Ow! You are the boss!"

Sabina licked the whip marks on his chest, then wrapped the whip around his throat, choking him as she hopped on top of him and getting him hard again, then rode him and was scraping the blade on his leg. Sabina smiled and then yelped in ecstasy when she soon experienced her own explosion that sent waves of freakish pleasure that she savored. Sabina took the whip away from Traaz's throat.

Hopping off, Sabina chirped "You made me happy, so you will live slave". She left, leaving Traaz on his bed. Sabina smiled at Traaz as she closed his door, smirking as he looked confused and angry.

Sabina locked the door.

Sabina thought in bed as she was falling asleep, *Aelianus is holding me back and Pris also has to go. It does not matter that Aelianus' relationship with Pris is nonsexual.*

Aelianus will not divorce me, so he must be killed, I need Vicidius to marry me…. If I get him to fall in love with me, then get me pregnant, that could seal the deal, then my future will be set; easy…..

Chapter XXVIII A trip to the Market

129 BC

The next day my master needed to go to the winery. He sent my mother and all of us to the market, it would include a fateful meeting.

Aelianus came to Sabina "Dear we need more food supplies, can…."

Sabina laughed, "No, I will go to the temple to pray all day long, Helga will buy some accessories for me after she has finished cleaning my room."

Aelianus pulled at his hair "Sabina, that isn't fair, you've gone to the temple everyday for the last two weeks!"

Sabina stuck her hand in his face and walked towards the front door.

Aelianus simply rolled his eyes, "Shall you return before dusk?" Sabina walked out without answering his question and slammed the door to the street. Aelianus took out a coin and flipped it, sex it said…. he laughed to himself.

Aelianus lightly brought his fist down onto the table nearest him. He whispered to no one in particular "She would find excuses not to do anything… too busy or too tired or it was too hot, too rainy, etc."

Pris set down a plate on the table, "Master Aelianus do you need me to go?"

Aelianus looked at Pris and nodded "You I trust. As you know, a key of this tavern is that the food is always fresh. If it is not eaten within a few days, we give it away to homeless veterans. We need fresh food ingredients to be bought and delivered back to the tavern early enough that our cooks will be able to have food ready for the next days' meals."

Pris nodded "Understood, yes my inventory list will ge useful."

Aelianus grinned, "Damn you're good. Yes go to the Juno market at Palatine Hill, buy everything on this list at the market and return, there are several items we need in bulk, those are to be delivered, payment on delivery of the remaining items. I would ask Septimus, but he is cooking today's meal for us now." Aelianus handed her a scroll, she nodded.

Pris asked "May I bring my children? They would like to go too." Aelianus nodded.

Aelianus said "Thank you Pris. I think Sabina uses religion as an excuse not to perform needed tasks. I would ask Helga, but Sabina has her cleaning Sabina's room, that could take all day."

After Pris thanked him, gathered her kids and left in their wagon.

Sabina felt even more annoyed; *Why should I be stuck with this gay useless husband? There will be no children, no future with him. Yet, it is impossible for me to divorce him.*

No matter how angrily I yell at him, Aelianus never becomes violent. Without some physical evidence a divorce would be impossible, actually even then it was unlikely in Roman law, the husband is dominant. No, there is only one way, I will meet Vicidius and it will be settled; Aelianus, Pris and her children must all die. But I do not want to get my hands dirty with blood or watch them die of poison, watching them squirm and twitch in some unsightly gruesome way. Sabina made her decision with a smile on her face, *I will ask Vicidius to do it with Traaz. I have a spare key, Traaz has a reason to do it... and then I could be free!*

Sabina had walked to the end of the block and turned the corner to go South. Aelianus watched her as she turned, he waved and she ignored him. Septimus asked "Boss, is everything alright?"

Aelianus responded "I don't know, something's off. Bring me Traaz." Aelianus went to Traaz "Traaz, if you follow Sabina, tell me who she meets, where she goes, what she does and if she eats or drinks, then report all back to me, you will be back in my good graces."

Traaz nodded and followed after her.

A few blocks away, Sabina walked towards Palatine Hill, she stopped not far from the market that Pris and her children would be shopping at. At a corner near a small temple of Hades, she prayed to the God of the underworld for his services. She finished her prayer then pulled out a scroll that she had written last night.

Turning around suddenly she spotted Traaz lurking in an alleyway and walked right over to him. Sabina shouted "Traaz.... come out."

Traaz came out in the open. Squeezing the handle of her knife in her toga, Sabina said "Slave, I want you to go to Vicidius' residence. When he returns home, you are to follow his instructions."

Traaz stood there and said, "Aelianus sent me to watch you."

Sabina laughed, "Do you really care what that fag wants?"

Traaz shook his head, Sabina smiled "Good, soon he will be gone and if you help me, I will give you your freedom."

Traaz bowed his head. Sabina gave Traaz a scrolled letter, "This is for Vicidius if you open it you will die, if you give it to anyone but Vicidius I will see you crucified."

Traaz took the scroll and bowed saying "By your command."

Chapter XXIX Unforgettable Encounters

129 BC

The day we went to the market to buy supplies was an unforgettable day indeed.

Pris, Sarth and Luciana arrived at the market early one sunny day in their horse-pulled cart. There were always many families and children at the market, there were hundreds of tents under which all manner of goods were being sold. The market was located in a huge open plaza of grassy grounds surrounded by a 6-foot brick wall which had the shape of an octagon the length of a large building.

The Romans had built one entrance at every other section to control who could come in or out to reduce the chance of a thief escaping. The octagon had fountains at a few corners to give the people inside somewhere to sit or cool themselves from the heat. In one section everything was some type of food, animal species or ingredients. In another section homemade craftsmanship of soaps, wood carvings, artwork and an array of colorful clothing was for sale. The tents had owners who, some were from Rome or Italy and others were merchants from as far as Iberia, Syria, Greece, Egypt, Pontus and Aksum.

Pris invited her children Sarth and Luciana to come with her. The children had just turned 9 years old and could help in carrying smaller items home. It was a very hot and crowded day at the market.

Luciana spotted and gleefully said "Sarth looks at the cute Rottweiler puppy!"

Sarth smiled at the puppy, but then saw an alluring young lady who was walking the dog ahead of two guards.

Pris was negotiating the price of salt as her kids went to greet the puppy and the girl for a moment.

Luciana reached out her hand and started giggling when the puppy began licking it. Luciana petted the dog behind the ears saying "hello" to the young lady who was about their age.

Sarth smiled as he paid his attention to the girl, "That's a cute puppy you have, what's your name?"

The girl smiled, "I am Atia…"

Sarth and Luciana meet Atia

293

Atia's bodyguards who had been looking for adult threats moved to separate the children, but Atia shook her head waving them away.

Sarth had seen them and asked, "Should we not talk?"

Atia smiled, touching Sarth's hand, "No we are not supposed to, but I want friends, what's your names?" Sarth and Luciana told her.

Atia looked at Sarth and Luciana's eyes, "Your eyes are amazing, I think they are different colors, brown and blue?

Sarth nodded "We come here every day to buy supplies for our master's tavern, how about you?"

Atia grinned looking him in the eyes "I don't get out much, I...."

Atia's mother Claudia who had been at another tent telling her slaves the types of fresh produce that she wanted and the amount of money she was willing to spend on fresh eggs. She had turned to see her daughter talking to Sarth and Luciana.

Atia continued "...... I live in a big house on Capitoline Hill" Sarth's eyes went wide, "That's where we live too".

Claudia knew immediately that her daughter was speaking to children who were obviously slaves as they did not look ethnically Italian, and they wore simple clothing of a lower class. It was plain as day with Atia's daughter wearing the latest toga fashion, a golden ornamental hairpin, and a jeweled collar brooch.

Claudia quickly moved to separate them, Claudia yelled at her guards "Evander, Felix, you fools, I do not want Atia to mix with barbarians, they might be pickpockets!" Evander separated the children as she moved to grab Atia's hand to lead her daughter towards the tent she had been at.

During this commotion, the big Rottweiler puppy got excited and started jumping lovingly trying to lick Claudia's face. Claudia started swatting at the dog, "Down! Bad dog!"

As this was happening, the dog accidentally bumped into Atia and she fell over into the grassy ground. Unknown to her, her golden ornamental hairpin fell out of her hair.

Sarth and Luciana moved to help Atia stand up, but Claudia yelled at them "Stay in your place, we do not need you".

Pulling Atia off the ground, Claudia catapulted Atia to her feet and then yelled at her guards "keep my daughter away from those filthy children!"

The guards became a physical barrier and Claudia led her daughter followed by a servant. Atia looked back sadly as she was being led away. Sarth and Luciana, oblivious to Claudia's discrimination waved goodbye as Atia returned a goodbye wave to them.

Sarth heard Claudia saying beyond the crowd "Do not ever let barbarians like them bother my daughter again!" After

they had disappeared into the crowd Sarth looked down
and saw the golden ornamental hairpin right next to his foot
that had eight dark little sapphires across the ridge.

Sarth grabbed the hairpin as another child walked up about
to grab it. Sarth pushed the boy down, and without asking
permission ran off after Atia yelling "I'll be right back
Luciana" not listening to his sister yelling after him not to
go.

Atia's Hairpin

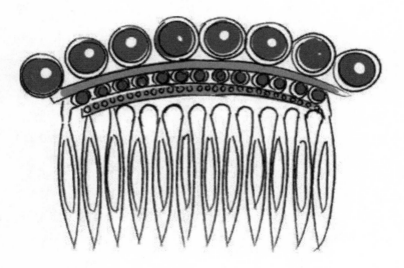

He went in a straight line thinking they would have just
gone in the same direction, but he just saw more and more
crowds. Sarth ran through the crowd of people trying to
catch up, he ran by a bald tattooed man who wore brown
leather armor, black boots, clothing, a black cape nearly
bumping into him before disappearing in the crowd. The

two warriors wore medallions around their necks indicating they were friends of Rome.

A Roman Legatus Commander dressed in impressive armor approached the tent with six guards and three slaves, "Hello friends, where are you from and what is your price for your high-quality salt?"

The ugly seller nodded his head, his voice raspy "Yes sir, we come a long way from Noricum, King Zoran of the Tauriscion sent us on this trade mission to sell salt to you Romans. 10 talons per pound of salt."

The Legatus agreed, "Done. I will buy 25 pounds plus an extra 50 talons on delivery if your men could deliver it to my garrison's storehouse."

The ugly seller smiled, "That can be done, what address and name?"

The Legatus said "I am Carbo, this is the address."

The ugly seller smiled "I am Wador, these are my men Raez and Ubel, they will deliver this shipment."

Carbo looked at the salt, "Is there anything else you sell?"

Wador smiled wider, "Slaves, salt and weapons."

Carbo smiled "Ah, well Rome has needs for all those." I am a Legatus Legionis, the overall Legionary commander of Rome's garrison, we must have a reliable source of salt. We already have multiple suppliers, but we need more. If your quality is good, we will pay well for it"

Wador smiled, rubbing his hands, "We are men of business and we aim to please."

Carbo signed a receipt for the salt with his ring as a stamp. He looked at Ubel. *That bald tattooed man is quite fierce looking, was it my grandfather's brother...…? Yes, it was, who fell to one of those stinking fur covered Gauls, these Celts look almost the same.* Carbo said "Very well on delivery I shall have payment ready." Then he and his guards walked off.

Ubel needed to use the bathroom so he started walking, excited to try using a Roman toilet.

Pris and Luciana ran into Helga at the market in their search for Sarth. "Helga, what are you doing here?"

Helga looked bored, "Oh Pris! Sabina is running low on a few of her hair brushes that broke, so I've come to buy some new ones. What's wrong?"

Pris exclaimed "Sarth is missing, he went to return a girl's hairpin, but has not come back."

Helga's eyes went wide as she glanced around, "Ok, I will go look for him. Maybe you and Luciana should stay here in case he returns?" Pris agreed.

Sarth arrived at a fountain; it was elevated on a higher platform that was surrounded by steps. There were columns all around it, and there was the brick octagon border wall behind that, the wall was about 7 feet high. The fountain's columns had vines growing all over them which gave a little bit of seclusion from the bustle of the market. There were a few legionaries splashing water onto themselves due to the heat, Sarth jumped onto the edge of the fountain to get up to see, a legionnaire yelled at him asking where he was going, Sarth ignored him and ran up to a cart of goods climbing on top.

From there after looking for a moment he saw Claudia scolding Atia in the distance, her slaves standing in company watching. The legionnaire had run up saying "Stop kid!"

Sarth leapt over the other side of the cart and ran through the crowd leaving the legionnaire behind. By the time Sarth reached them, a man dressed in expensive toga had joined Claudia, and she was explaining to him what was happening as he listened with a focused expression. "..... I led her away from some ragga muffins and it was only after we got here Atia that realized her hairpin was missing."

The man looked surprised as she continued

"The golden ornamental hairpin your grandmother gave her." Claudia had a scowl on her face, "This is what befalls when you insist on wearing fancy accessories to the market and then mix with lower classes, they rob...."

At that moment Sarth walked up. "Atia! I was searching all over for you," They all turned, "....you dropped your hairpin."

Claudia was about to say something when the man motioned to her to be silent,

Atia was beaming the man spoke first his voice was very gruff "Thank you young man, as my wife was voicing her deep concern over this item's loss, it has been in my family for a long time. I am Senator Linus Cornelius Scipio, do you know my name?"

Sarth shook his head, giving him the hairpin.

Linus smiled and receiving it continued "The Scipio's are quite well known, my uncle defeated Hannibal and the Carthaginians, have you heard of Hannibal?"

Sarth's mouth fell open and eyes wide "Hannibal? Hannibal is at the gates, that Hannibal?"

Linus chuckled deeply, "Yes, my boy, the very one." Another chuckle "So you've heard the mother's tale. Yes, my grand uncle crushed Hannibal and his Carthaginian army at Zama. This hairpin is from Carthage, it was what their princess had worn, a gift from him to my grandmother, his sister, and from her to my daughter."

Linus had his hand on Atia's shoulder lovingly, "And what is your name my little man?"

Sarth swallowed, "Sarth sir, Sarth de Treneca".

Tapping Linus' shoulder Claudia hissed "See! Sarth of house Treneca? He is absolutely a slave."

Linus raised his hand without looking at Claudia directly, "Well my fine fellow" Linus handed Claudia the hairpin, looking at Sarth then at Atia then back to Sarth, "You are our little hero today, a Scipio never forgets their friends, should you ever be in need, come find us".

Sarth smiled a little, "Where can I find you?"

Linus grinned broadly "A good question, you can find us at the large villa #15 on 5th and Romulus on Capitoline Hill."

Sarth's face beamed "I live at the Happy Moon on Capitoline Hill and know that villa, we walk by it on the way to this market."

Linus' eyes widened as he gently nodded, "The Happy Moon, well that IS a great tavern and inn, I have been there a few times with my colleagues from the Senate. So, your master must be Aelianus, is that right?"

Sarth acknowledged. "Well, boy that man is a patriot with more lives than a cat. Go home and tell your master to deliver one of his finest barrels of wine to my home to be paid on arrival. I will give you my address written on this scroll so you will have my villa's address. I will need the scroll back; can I trust you for this delivery?"

Sarth nodded, receiving it smiling.

Linus continued "Good. You shall make a fine Roman. Now say goodbye to my daughter, your mother must be in sheer panic with you missing".

Linus motioned Sarth to Atia who had been looking from Sarth to her dad and occasionally to her mom.

Sarth smiled, "I am happy to have been able to help you, Atia " he said, feeling a little nervous having her parents there listening.

Atia smiled "As am I Sarth, thank you for delivering my hairpin, you are my hero".

He smiled again, then said goodbye waving again to her and receiving one in return.

Sarth then hurried back in the direction of where his mother and sister had been.

Linus smiled, turning to Claudia "A fine lad, doesn't hurt to be nice".

Claudia responded "I'm not blind. That boy may be nice, but he is not in our class, he is of barbarian blood, not our equal." Linus looked at Claudia about to say something but suddenly turned to sneeze.

Claudia, not missing a beat, turned to Atia "If we see him again you must treat him like a servant, he is not and cannot ever be your friend, is that clear?"

Atia looked at her mother then back toward where Sarth had disappeared into the crowd feeling heartbroken "Yes mama."

Ubel was returning from the bathroom, delighted about his experience. Marvelous invention, I will talk King Zoran into hiring Romans to make bathrooms in Noricum. As he walked, he noticed a young woman looking across the crowd seeking someone. *She is wearing simple Roman clothes, her blonde hair, perfect curves, height and the shape of her nose, all perfect. Oh, how I miss sleeping with such women. She is so much like the women of my homeland, the Cimbrians.* Ubel thought moving closer.

Ubel walked up and a few steps away recognized Pris. His sonorous voice sounded like a little earthquake "Ah young one, so I have found you."

A feeling of dread swept through Pris as she turned her head. "Ubel…."

He smiled in a way that was unsettling, "Yes it is I, my you have grown. The last time I saw you was at the feast after our hunt. I had heard about what happened to your parents, pity."

Pris instantly thought *Father too?* Anger swept through her "You…. traitor, you helped the Swabians raid our caravan. I saw you."

Ubel shook his head, "You must have seen someone else, young one, I was in the village when that occurred. Why would they receive me? The Swabians do not like our kind."

Pris shook her head, "No it was you, your tattoos and bald head are unmistakable you filth."

Ubel shook his head, his hand on the hilt of his sword, "My my, such a tough woman you've become, but we are in Rome not in your daddy's village. I could kill you and your girl here now and Krull wouldn't know a thing about it. Romans don't value slaves"

Pris shook her head, "I am property, damage or kill me and it's akin to doing likewise to my master, you would not escape. I can speak Latin, can you? There are legionnaires all over this place, you would never escape alive."

Ubel started to speak as Pris smiled "They nail criminals like you on trees. You would make a fine tree ordainment"

Ubel looked around; he had seen the crucified prior to entering into Rome. Ubel had seen many legionaries in pairs of four patrolling throughout the market; he even now saw a double column of legionaries marching nearby. Ubel breathed deeply as he fought the urge, of wanting to slice her in half. He was able to control himself and smirked, "You are a slave, living is worse than death for you. I will let you stay a slave."

Ubel backed up and left, he smirked, "I will not be crucified for an annoying girl you are not worth it. One day soon Pris, you shall be mine."

Luciana cringed, "Mommy, he scares me."

Pris realized that Luciana was shaking, so she gave her a hug. Pris watched the crowd long after he had disappeared. Pris had been clutching her knife in her robes, so tempted to stab him, revenge was within a few feet, but he never came close enough. Ubel had a sword and failure would have jeopardized her children.

The market was packed full of people, Sarth made it back to where his mother and sister had been, but they were not there now. Panic struck him, he had told them he would be right back, what could have happened? Sarth returned to the fountain, the legionaries were no longer there, instead he arrived to see a richly dressed man heavily kissing and groping a woman in the corner, where vines were completely blocking the view from those in the market. Sarth decided to give the lovers their space, stood to the market side of the vines hoping to catch a glimpse of his mother and sister waiting as this was a place they had agreed to go to if they ever got separated.

From inside the fountain area, he could hear the sounds of the lovers groping and sounds of pleasurable moaning becoming more intimate, similar to what Sarth had heard once before late at night when he had awoken to use the bathroom, he had walked by a guest room door and heard similar moaning by guests at Aelianus' inn. Giggling Sarth couldn't help but try to catch a peek. What was the man doing to her to make her moan like that? This could be educational... Sarth thought.

The pair had turned and now the man's face was towards him, both of them were kissing with their eyes closed. The man had a scar that went from his eyebrow to the bottom of his cheek, the woman pushed him downward and began talking as the man went below and she opened her toga.

Between moans, Sarth overheard Sabina's familiar voice say "Tell me Vicidius, I am so tired of waiting to marry you, how and when will you kill Aelianus?"

At that moment, an elderly man approached Sarth from behind and hit him with a walking stick and yelled at him "What are you doing shame on you for watching the lovers young fool!"

Sarth got hit a couple times with the staff before he started to run away. By this point Vicidius had come out of the fountain area and saw Sarth running away into the crowd, Vicidius ran after, but there were too many people in the crowded market.

Sarth was running through the crowds towards another fountain corner thinking perhaps he had mixed up the meeting place, and suddenly his mother grabbed him. Pris hugged him tightly "Where have you been Sarth, I was going frantic!"

Pris held Sarth not letting go "I love you Sarth!"

Luciana hugged Sarth from behind as Pris said "Ich liebe dich Sarth" over and over in Cimbri.

Vicidius dashed in pursuit for a few paces, but it was no use, the boy whoever he was gone. *Was it that fag's servant boy? Vicidius had seen Sarth once when he went to the inn to spy on Tiberius and his group.*

Sabina approached him "What is it?" Vicidius shook his head, "All I know for certain is that I spotted a boy who looks like he could be one of your slaves."

Sabina shrugged, "They came here today to buy food for our market, just like we came for our snack…"

Vicidius said "We shouldn't have come here, too risky. If he was Aelianus' boy he may have overheard your request.

Sabina scoffed, "Next to a crowded market, even if it was him, do you think he could have heard me whispering?"

Vicidius said "The boy could have been the same kid I saw in the Happy moon, he was about the same height, hair color and age."

Sabina said "Even so, there is no way that the boy could prove anything, even if he was the same and heard everything, there was no proof a slave could put forward, except alert his master…. And who cares if Aelianus cannot sleep?" She said giggling.

Vicidius gave her a hug, "We must move quickly, Aelianus has friends in the Senate." Sabina rubbed his tool, he smiled and nodded, taking her hand they returned to their horses near the fountain.

Helga had found Pris and Luciana together in the market as they were departing. When she saw that Sarth was safe with his mother, Helga laughed and ran her hand through his hair "You gave us such a shock."

The Sun started to give pink rays as sunset began. Sarth apologized to her for searching for him and again to his mom, giving them both hugs. Luciana came over and they held hands walking back to the wagon. Helga showed them the hair accessories she had bought for Sabina then they all hopped into the wagon. Riding in their cart on the way home, Pris and Helga listened to Sarth tell them about what had happened to him. Sarth said "Mom I can remember every detail of her face, her smile, the little dimple she had on her cheek when she smiled."

Luciana agreed, "Atia is so nice Mommy, the clothing she wore was so pretty…."

Sarth thought about his encounters. The thought of Claudia, the encounter at the fountain, he now was concerned if he had heard what he thought he had heard. It had been a little noisy from the market, but to tell him that his wife wanted him dead and intended to marry someone else…. They listened to Luciana talk at length about her new friend.

Pris had bittersweet thoughts listening to her daughter's excited voice. She looked at her children, *They do not yet quite realize they are slaves, she thought sadly. There is no chance my boy could ever be in love with that girl, or my daughter be a friend of her. Her family would never allow it. Aelianus has been such a benevolent master to them, they have been sheltered. What to do about Ubel? He is alive… Was he truthful about father? I must be sure he doesn't know where to find me.* Pris turned right at an intersection where they normally would go straight.

Helga saw that Pris and Sarth were not being as talkative as normal, "Anything wrong, are we taking a different way home?"

Pris shrugged, "I want to take a slightly different way home."

Luciana said "Mommy talked to a scary man at the market."

Helga said "Oh, is everything ok?"

Pris nodded and looked at her son "Sarth love, what's wrong?"

Sarth looked at his mom, "After I returned the hairpin, I was searching for you two but there were so many people that I couldn't see very far, so I went to a fountain to stand on the steps to see above the crowd."

Pris kept looking at him, Sarth continued "I suddenly overheard a couple's heavy kissing and I turned around and saw it was our mistress, Sabina with another man. Worse, she said that she wants to marry the other man and wants to know when the other man will kill our master."

Pris put her arm around Sarth in a half hug, they hurried back towards their tavern with their cartload of purchases. The Sun had gone down over the horizon and light was quickly fading to the darkness of night.

Chapter XXX Attack at the Tavern

129 BC

An encounter with old enemies....

Turning a corner, their tavern was in sight, suddenly from the shadows Ubel stepped out, his outline appearing lit by the moon and a few burning torches that were posted in the walls of buildings. Ubel shouted out, "Time to die " his sword already pulled out.

Another man Pris immediately saw was Raez, the man who had transported her years ago. Raez attempted to grab the horse's reins, but Pris cracked the reins and the horses took off. Ubel grabbed the back of the wagon and Raez was knocked back. Pris heard Wador's voice from the darkness yell out "Don't let those whores escape!"

Helga saw a whip lash out towards Pris, but with the wagon moving it missed her and lashed Ubel's arm who screamed, the whip inadvertently pulled Ubel off the wagon.

Pris and Helga started screaming for help as they arrived at Aelianus' tavern. Helga heard Ubel yell "Idiot!" as she grabbed the children and rushed them inside the tavern.

Helga screamed on entering the door and Aelianus emerged from the building with his two guards, they were all armed with gladiuses. Pris grabbed a gladius that they carried in the wagon and hopped off, seeing her help she yelled "Aelianus, those men are trying to murder us!"

Ubel was already charging at them from across the street; Raez had also run to within a few yards and fat Wador approached from behind all of them. Wador yelled in his raspy accented Latin "Give us the two women or we kill you Romans!"

Aelianus raised his sword, "Come take them!"

Raez pulled his own whip out and tried to whip Aelianus by the neck, something he loved doing to adversaries, Aelianus saw it coming and slashed his gladius through the air and sliced the whip in half. Aelianus then charged at Raez, the closest opponent. As Aelianus charged, Raez dropped his whip cursing, pulled out his sword and the two began fighting fiercely.

The guards attacked Ubel and Wador and instantly the street was full of combat. Ubel became locked with his opponent.

Wador waited for his guard to attack him and threw dirt in the guard's face, blinded, the guard stepped back but Wador saw an opening and laughed as he stabbed his sword into the man's chest, Pris had run at Wador, the memories of him whipping her still in her mind. As soon as she saw him throw the dirt, she screamed, but the guard did not have enough time to react.

As the dying guard was falling over, Pris attacked Wador. Wador tried to pull the sword out of the guards' chest, but his victim in his dying moments had clung onto the sword's handle. Wador struggled to pull the man off and Pris was on him right in front of her, she slashed high and his head went flying. Pris next ran over to Aelianus to help teamed up on Raez.

Aelianus yelled "Not this time girl, stay back". Raez had been struggling already against Aelianus.

Aelianus' sword thrusts were so precise that every time Raez tried to slash it was parried. Aelianus blocked above and below, he appeared to be toying with Raez. Aelianus started laughing, calling Raez pathetic.

Raez tried to strike towards Aelianus' chest, he blocked the thrust and then kicked Raez in the stomach and then slashed down to knock the sword out of Raaz's hand then held the blade to Raaz's throat.

Aelianus looked over as did Pris from Wador's body at Ubel.

Aelianus was surprised that Ubel had just killed his other guard.

Pris screamed "No!" and prepared to charge at Ubel.

Aelianus yelled "NO!!"

Raez looked, realizing that Aelianus was distracted, he lunged for his sword. Aelianus frowned at Raez, "You fool!"

Raez picked up his sword, saw Aelianus motion to him beckoning Raez with a welcoming nod holding his sword at ready, Raez panicked and ran away. Aelianus smirked and cocked his head "Coward!" saw Raez run into the darkness of an alley.

Aelianus smiled seeing a column of Roman legionaries that had appeared from around the corner about a block away, Aelianus waved and yelled at them,"Help friends!!" Seeing the column of 30 legionnaires switch to double march approaching their position, Aelianus turned his attention to Ubel next, he hurried over towards Pris who screamed "traitor!" now attacking Ubel, their swords clashed with each parry the other.

Septimus came out of the tavern with a gladius in his hand and also charged towards Ubel.

Aelianus' voice boomed "If I get over there, you're dead."

Ubel looked over, seeing that the fight was lost, he defended against a sword thrust of Pris' then kicked her stomach sending her backwards. Seeing Aelianus was closing in and legionnaires not far behind, Ubel ran off down the street to where they had first attacked the wagon. Ubel could hear the legionnaires following behind. Ubel rendezvoused with Raez where they had left three horses, he jumped onto his horse and then they rode off into the night.

Back at the tavern, Aelianus looked to Pris, "Are you alright?"

Pris, still feeling dizzy nodded, "I'll live. Those were the slavers who had sold me into slavery. That bald tattooed man who ran off orchestrated an attack on my parents which killed many including my mother and maybe father."

Aelianus looked back to where Ubel had gone, then to Pris, "So a little revenge tonight dear girl. We shall toast some wine to celebrate being alive." Aelianus saw that Pris was starting to shake a little. He said, "The shakes, the first time one kills that happens. He put his hands on her shoulder, "You did great." Aelianus looked up to see a Centurion was approaching and said to her, "Pris go inside, I will handle this."

Aelianus walked to the Centurion, "Friend of Rome, thank the Gods you arrived. My slave was returning from the Market when our wagon came under attack by those bandits."

The centurion looked at Aelianus, writing down this summary, then asked Aelianus his name. As Aelianus told him the Centurion's mouth opened and eyes went wide…. "I knew I knew you from somewhere! Aelianus! It is I, Marius Caesar. I was a new recruit in Stallion legion with you, you were my centurion!"

Aelianus took a hard look, finally remembering one face out of 660 he had commanded. "Yes, indeed! You have risen in the ranks old comrade!"

Marius looked around, "It appears your swordplay skills have not waned at all Aelianus!"

Aelianus laughed, "It is like dancing, once we get good at it, it becomes like breathing."

Marius nodded, "And this is your tavern?"

314

Aelianus waved his hand, "Indeed, the Happy Moon, please come by anytime." They saluted each other and Marius ordered his men to send an alert to the wall guards about the remaining two bandits.

Aelianus went to his two dead guards, he had servants take the goods off the wagon and then had their bodies put on the wagon. Aelianus returned inside. Pris came over and hugged him, then told Aelianus about the threat that someone was with a woman who sounded like his wife and that she had asked when a man named Aelianus would be killed.

Aelianus was silent for a long time, finally he said "Good to know. Thank you, I will need to hire new guards, we will get a new dog tomorrow, we have my own sword, the locks on the door and our secret weapon pointing to Pris."

Pris said "But why not go to the authorities?"

Aelianus gave a bittersweet smile "What proof do we have? The name Aelianus is not an uncommon name, your boy did not get a great look at their faces, even if one of them had a scar, that is not unusual for any veteran of the legions, and your boy told you that there was a lot of noise from the market. Even if he was totally sure, we have only the word of a 9-year-old servant boy, it will not hold in court against a Roman citizen. All we can do is be sure our guard is up."

At that moment David arrived with a delivery of wine from Aelianus' vineyard and Sarth remembered to give the scroll of Linus to Aelianus to purchase one barrel of wine.

Aelianus took the order, thanked Sarth, and gave the order to his deliveryman to prepare and send a barrel of wine to Linus Scipio. Aelianus turned to Septimus, "Thank you for protecting my tavern, Helga and the children like I ordered. Where is our dog Max?" Septimus took a big breath, "The children were frightened, so we kept the dog with them. If I had sent the dog out or joined sooner, maybe…"

Aelianus shook his head, "If you had, we might also have a dead dog. I love those children, you did what I ordered." He then turned to David, "I need to start making arrangements for the funerals of his two guards. Talk to me later. Helga, see to David, he's probably hungry."

Helga came over, "David, do you want the usual?"

David smiled, "If you're bringing it I'll take anything."

Helga smiled then went to Pris "I took Luciana to her bedroom, Zoe is with her, but she seemed scared, you might want to let her know you are ok."

Pris nodded, took Sarth by the hand and then went into the building to Luciana's bedroom.

Helga turned to Aelianus, pulling out a scroll from her purse. "Master I nearly forgot, on the way to the market I ran into your friend, Senator Rufus, he gave me these scrolls for you to read."

Aelianus took the scrolls and as he read them his face went white.

Helga touched his upper arm, "Are you alright?"

Aelianus looked at her, "Rufus says he has uncovered a plot by several senators listed in a conspiracy that links them as being behind a planned murder of Tiberius and his supporters. This, if true, would prove that Tiberius was not killed by an out-of-control mob that the Senate investigation claimed. Rufus asks me to hold onto this information until he has a chance to speak with me. We should alert Tiberius' younger brother Gaius of this. Thank you dear, you have done well. Please take these scrolls up to my office, place them in my lock box. Afterwards, you can eat with David if you're hungry."

Helga bowed her head and taking the scrolls, went upstairs.

Chapter XXXI Aziri, Daminian & Tykie
129 BC

The African merchant and his sailors....

Aziri, Daminian| & Tykie

The next day, a trio of men arrived at the tavern that Pris had never seen. Their leader was a black man, tall and muscular, his skin darker than any Pris had ever seen, like a night sky color Pris thought. The two Mediterranean men looked a little different from each other. The man on the black man's right side who wore a black toga looked like he could almost be Roman or Greek, in his facial appearance.

The man to the black man's left was wearing a white toga and wore a beard, he had a more Middle eastern complexion. Their clothing was functional, that of sailors. Pris led them to a table near the back as they had requested, while welcoming them to the tavern. The black man was wearing clothing that looked well worn, not Roman, pants with a large shirt that was worn over the top of his pants. The shirt had splendid star like emblems on either side of fine embroidery that surrounded the neck and went down the front of the shirt, of such fine make that Pris had never before seen and he wore several necklaces and rings.

After gazing in amazement at his shirt, Pris said "I like your shirt!" She produced a rolled paper for them "Here is a menu"

The black man spread it out, looking at Pris and giving a smile, "I would like to eat a bowl of soup with bread and wine. These two will have the same" he said with a thick rolling accent that she could not quite place.

Pris called the order to Helga who saw the party and acknowledged, then went into the kitchen. Septimus was playing music in the corner, the tavern was full. Pris went to the wine storage and returned with three goblets and a large jug of wine.

"Ah, those bottles look great, thank you dear." The black man said. Pris poured their wine, the black man said "Please call your master, tell him Daminian Tesfaye is here".

Pris nodded her head and called for Aelianus. Pris went away and came back with wet hand towels. Daminian asked "What are these for dear?"

Pris answered "To have clean hands sir for eating."

The three men shrugged and Pris began handing them out, at that moment Aelianus arrived at their table "Daminian! Greetings, it has been a long time".

Daminian stood and they gave each other a friendly embrace before they all sat at their table. "Too long my friend, please join us for a meal. I am now captain of a larger trireme called the Seawitch."

Aelianus smiled "You came at the perfect time, after lunch and before dinner. I happily accept. Pris, I will have whatever they're having."

Pris relayed the order, then returned to assist another table, but stayed in the room. Pris watched their group while working, she noticed the other two were also dressed differently than Daminian.

The man in the white toga had straight short black hair and tan skin, he had a youthful look unmistakably of Mediterranean ethnicity, his toga clothing was white, he had tattoos on his arms, one earring in each of his ears, his eyes were mischievous, he had a magnetic smile, he appeared at ease as he casually saw all.

The other man in a black toga was dressed in a Spartan style, his muscular body was solid, his jaw was chiseled, he held a masterful pose, his hair cut short and he had a very focused look.

Daminian was saying "These are two of my men Aelianus, you know Aziri, my 1st mate?" he said motioning to the man in the white toga.

Aelianus laughed, nodding, "How could I forget? So, you have a former gladiator and Carthaginian as a sail hand? Impressive."

Daminian laughed "Yes, the very same former gladiator that you threw at me in Sicily."

Aelianus looked at Aziri, "And what is your last name?"

Aziri grinned, "Aziri Hiero." Both felt nostalgic surprise and respect from seeing someone at a pivotal moment of one's life.

Aelianus smiled nodding. Daminian next pointed to his other man "and this is our very handsome Tykie Nabis of Sparta, my 2nd mate." he motioned to the man in the black toga. Aelianus looked from Tykie to Aziri.

Daminian turned to his men, "Men this is my friend Aelianus. Many years ago, I was sailing from Carthage to Taranto, my ship had hit a storm and we lost a few hands due to the rough seas, though we did not sink. A couple days later, we came upon Aelianus and around 15 other Romans floating in the ocean, his ship had not been as lucky in the storm."

Tykie's head shook, "Poseidon strikes any who dares into his realm."

Daminian nodded "Yes, so we saved Aelianus, his brother, another few Romans and their commander, a man named Vicidius."

Aelianus smiled "Yes, we had been floating for two days with sharks, had you not come along I would not be here".

Daminian looked around "Is your brother living in Rome?"

Aelianus shook his head, his pain plainly on his face, "Decimus was… killed in action at the battle of Corinth in Greece".

Daminian shook his head and touched his heart saying "May he rest in peace".

Tykie said "I am sorry to learn of this, many were killed in that siege, my father and two uncles fought in those battles allied to the Romans. Your brother has seen the end of war". Aelianus smiled bitterly and nodded. They raised their goblets and saluted each other.

Aelianus took a long sip of the wine, putting it down he smiled saying "So a trireme? Those are large ships, which must be perfect for your merchant business".

Daminian nodded, "Yes, I have upgraded. My earlier ship was only half the size, but I was able to purchase this former Cornithian war vessel from a Spartan ship owner and convert it to a speedy trade ship, it frightens away most pirates."

Aelianus was surprised "A Cornithian ship, and Spartan owner, how did that come about? Weren't all of Corinth's ships destroyed or captured by Roman forces during the Achaean War?"

Daminian shook his head, "The captain of this ship had been attacking Roman war vessels in the Ionian Sea when Cornith came under siege. When they returned to Corinth for resupply, they saw the city under siege and decided to conduct a diplomatic mission to Sparta to try to urge the Spartans to switch sides to support the Achaean League against Rome and save Corinth."

Tykie chimed in "My father is the King's advisor, we knew that the Romans had beaten Carthage, beaten Epris, beaten Macedon. Our king believed the Romans would beat the Achaean League, he knew the Romans were too powerful and had no love for Corinth, Athens or the Achaean League, so my King decided to capture and claim the ship in port."

Daminian smiled and continued "Yes, so it had been used as a merchant ship by the Spartan King for the past 13 years. We bought it from the King. The most amazing thing about the ship is it has a secret advantage!"

The two crewmen looked at each other as they drank another mouthful of wine looking at the tavern's other patrons casually. Aelianus' raised his eyebrow, "What might that be?"

Daminian's smile beamed as he lowered his voice to a whisper, "We have the speed of the Gods."

Aelianus raised an eyebrow, "Well, so it is a fast ship? Good, I have a large amount of my great red wine at my vineyard looking for a home."

Daminian smiled "Good"

Aelianus continued "I also have a few friends in high places who might be interested in purchasing some of your ivory as well, one is a senator named Rufus. Rufus is in the middle of trying to make laws by the late Tiberius Gracchus for land redistribution for Roman veterans. A cache of ivory would give someone like him leverage with his opponents, to ease the chariot wheels."

Tykie made a face "I don't believe that is a Greek saying."

Aelianus smiled, "No I just made it up".

Daminian turned to Tykie, "Make a note to have Hector take some samples to Senator Rufus tomorrow."

Aelianus spoke up "Rufus often comes to this bar, if you want, I could present the samples to him?"

Daminian pulled a sack out from under the table "That sounds good, please let him look at the contents of this sack".

Aelianus took the sack, opened it and saw several pieces of ivory inside, closed the bag and handed it to Pris, "Please put this on my office table and then return here".

After Pris walked off, Aelianus asked "How urgently do you hope to sell the ivory?" Daminan said "Any paying customer".

Daminian asked "Aelianus, we are seeking a certain man who might be a buyer. His name is Titus Paullus, we understand he owns a brothel."

Aelianus was taken aback, "Titus Paullus?" Aelianus paused, "There are many reputable buyers who I believe would pay; although I believe Titus Paullus would buy as he has a blacksmith who specializes in making ivory sword handles. I must caution you that he is a cousin of my old manipular's centurion Vicidius Paullus, now Senator Paullus. Titus is protected by Vicidius, they are dangerous men."

Daminian smiled, "Interesting, we have business with Titus, don't we Aziri."

Aelianus' looked at each of them, "They are some of the most dangerous men in Rome. Titus was a centurion in a different cohort in our legion than mine. As you said, Titus now runs a brothel in the South of the city on Aventine Hill. I know that he bought large amounts of ivory then sold it all in the form of sword handles a year or so ago."

Aziri asked "How do you know this?"

Aelianus answered "I know many Senators, through my friend Rufus and his colleagues. I saw the swords at a dinner party hosted by Senators. It's funny how word travels among senators. Once they enjoy my wine, I learn all kinds of things."

Aelianus cleared his throat, "Give me a few days and I am sure many will want to buy your ivory; they always look at such transactions as appropriations of someone else's money. I will set up a meeting for you. How long do you plan to be in Rome?"

Daminian responded, "The plan is five days."

Aziri's face grew determined "Aelianus, I must meet with Titus, it is important." He opened a scroll and allowed Aelianus to read it.

Aelianus acknowledged "Ah I see, there is Titus' name as the buyer. Ok Aziri, and all of you. But you must go to the meeting armed, they may try to rob and kill you as they may actually pay. About other buyers, I will speak with Rufus when I meet with him later today."

Daminian smiled, "Perfect, thank you old friend."

Chapter XXXII

129 BC

My master's war in Sicily was pivotal in creating the trio of Sailors. They would become a loyal team on an amazing ship.

Pris returned with Helga bringing their food and wine. The food was placed on the table. Tykie said "Wow, it looks and smells far better than what we have on our ship!" Aziri rubbed his hands eagerly.

Helga smiled, "Our specialty." Another couple customers came in and sat at another table, Helga went to serve them. Pris was about to go over there as well but Aelianus motioned to her to stay.

Daminian smelled the food "Ah, I love it!"

Aelianus motioned to Pris to come to him, as he looked at his guests he spoke into her ear, "Let's see this ship of theirs." Pris nodded.

Daminian said "Lets eat!" They tried the food, then quickly devoured it each of them moaning and slurping as the food was consumed.

Daminian shouted, "That is the best meal I've had in years, not since Sparta have I eaten so well!"

Aziri smiled "Our compliments to the chef!" Helga came out from the kitchen and gave a bow.

Aelianus said "Daminian, I would love to see this ship of yours, may we see it?"

Daminian smiled "Absolutely." He set a bag of coins on the table, Pris took it, looked in the bag and smiled. Then tossed it to Helga. They all walked out of the tavern together and turned towards the Tiber River.

Looking at Aziri, Aelianus said "The Gods have a sense of humor, and so we meet again". Aelianus looked ahead, then to Aziri then ahead as they walked while waving his hand at Aziri "It took a moment to recognize you Aziri as you've cut your hair and have a beard" Aelianus motioned to his own shoulders "Last time I recall your hair came down to here."

Aziri ``Yes, we continue to breathe. Even surviving that revolt, it is hard to believe my eyes".

Aelianus agreed, "yes, Mars has a funny way of throwing men at each other. I am so pleased that we did not kill each other".

Daminian raised an eyebrow and motioned with his ring filled hands back and forth towards them "Wait what? Tell me how did you two first meet? My memory was you brought Aziri to me at night on my ship and told me to keep him hidden until after I shoved off, that's all I know".

Aelianus nodded. "So, I was recalled to active duty after the rebellion started in Sicily."

Aziri said, "It began in Agrigentum in the south. Many Roman town watch troops were killed, and our masters."

Aelianus nodded, "Yes, but then Tauromenium revolted as did many other cities and towns, many civilians were killed but there was no legion in Sicily. So I and many other veterans were quickly formed into a manipular in Southern Italy and then quickly sent to Sicily to help pacify the revolt. We were the first battle hardened unit to arrive, though some had been out of service for years. The other manipulars had been reserved units which had not yet seen action."

Aziri smiled occasionally, nodding his head. "It's true the Romans we first killed could hardly march together and were not clever."

Aelianus was silent a moment thinking about rebellion. "Shortly after our manipular's arrival in Sicily, our Legatus Legionis, the overall commander got violently sick and had to stay under medical care." They stopped at a corner as a line of Roman legionnaires marched by.

When they passed, Aelianus continued, "The Legatus' next in command had been a political appointee, Senator Domonic Leana, a man who's still in power today."

Leana didn't know what he was doing, So the Mayor suggested he order to cover the most area, he ordered us to split up into subgroups. Of the 660 men of my manipular who arrived, 44 were assigned to each of the 15 towns to train and rebuild more effective town watch units. Our main goal was to provide security to Syracuse and other towns

329

still under Roman control until more experienced Maniple units arrive from Italy and Greece."

Aziri snickered, "That strategy didn't work out so well."

Aelianus looked at him and nodded "There weren't enough of us, the slave revolt spread and had crushed Catana's town watch garrison, they killed the governor of the island who had gone there to inspect their readiness."

Pris asked "What of the governor's family?"

Aelianus just shook his head. Then continued "Catana is just a day's ride north of Syracuse. The mayor declared he would not allow another city to fall. I think he wanted to receive some military glory for himself."

Aziri nodded "That fool of Syracuse thought it was his chance to grab glory, we had a spy who passed us information about it."

Aelianus listened, "I later suspected as much. I had warned him that pushing our men out too quickly was dangerous, as the town watch were not front-line troops and had no battle experience. We had 10 units of town watch. Sadly, he did not listen to me, he ordered Domonic Leana to lead five of our units to Catana. With our own Legatus deathly ill, Domonic Leana became our de facto Legatus."

Daminian asked "He was that bad?"

Aelianus scoffed, "He didn't even know how to order us to turn left or right."

They turned a corner going across an intersection leaving Capitoline Hill the ground gently sloping downward towards the river. From here they traveled near central Rome where the tall pillared buildings stood in the distance.

Pris asked "What's a Legatus?"

Aelianus was in deep thought and did not answer.

Tykie smiled and said to her "A Legatus is what the Romans call a general."

Aelianus realized they had stopped walking and talking, he became himself and continued "Apologies, I was just recalling events. We were marching along and Leana, our new Legatus, saw gladiators on horseback. He had us charge after them."

Tykie said "One infantry unit Going after mounted men, that doesn't sound good."

Aelianus said "I know right? They led us to an enemy formation on the top of a sparsely tree covered hill. Where we stopped. I had hoped he wouldn't do anything foolish."

Aziri laughed, "Nope."

Aelianus sighed, "The enemy all turned and showed their bare asses at us calling us cowards."

Daminian laughed. "Too much pride."

Aelianus nodded, "So brilliant Domonic Leana had us attack up that rocky hill, with the gladiator slave army in a defensive hilltop position."

Aziri nodded and spoke up "Many of those gladiators had been experienced soldiers and warriors from conquered enemies in earlier wars, we were eager and ready for the tin cans, ahem, Romans."

Aelianus acknowledged, "Truly, they knew how to fight in battles and how to fight as coordinated units. As arrows began to fly, I formed us into testudo as we closed in as the other units did."

Pris asked "What's testudo?"

Aziri chirped up testudo makes them look like a Tortus, they hide behind their shields from all angles."

Aelianus nodded then continued "The enemy fired arrows, slung rocks and threw larger stones as we got close. Then when we were near the cusp of the incline and the ground began to flatten, the gladiators charged down the hill, we were nearly exhausted just marching up in our armor.

Aziri nodded, "Yes, we knew it."

Aelianus grimaced, "When they were on us,they were slammed into our formation, we had not carried pilum javelins as our Legatus had not supplied them to a town watch unit. We clashed and were at a disadvantage, their skill plus my men were all tired, I kept my unit's organization intact as best I could."

Aziri nodded, "Yes you did hold and fought for a long while, perhaps an hour we killed your men one by one"

Aelianus shrugged, "The enemy were experienced warriors on higher ground, men being killed in front of someone who has never seen battle and never killed, and weariness causes panic. Once in the fray, panic can overpower any soldier if the odds are too challenging."

Aelianus looked at Aziri, "Your side had the advantage, when men were killed those behind could not hold their shields in place. They panicked and ignored legate Leana's orders to stay in place. Too many fell under the enemy's blades, one by one those in the back of the formations all turned and fled. Then Leana our Legate also fled, it was a disgraceful display."

Decimus asked "Then what happened?"

Aelianus waved his hands, "The reinforcements of the gladiator army came crashing down, and the units that had been engaged with our other Roman units which were smashed quicker turned to attack my last remaining group. They killed the wounded and dying Romans that littered the ground as they came."

Pris asked "How did you survive?"

Aelianus said "Seeing that all was lost, by this point, I was also fighting, a few veterans and I were still up. I yelled for a fighting withdrawal of our men as it would not be able to hold off the entire enemy army. We began to quickly withdraw, however with so many other Romans fleeing away at both sides, the enemy attacking us as we withdrew, the last of my men fled. I killed two more who attacked me then ran down the hill zig zagging. I dropped my shield when I started running, I went so quickly that my helmet fell off too."

Aziri said "I knew those two men, Aelianus, they had been revengeful, wanting to kill every last Roman they could."

Aelianus shrugged, "War is hell. So I ran downhill with some arrows landing around where I ran, I spotted a large boulder with a few trees around it. I could hear men running after me."

Aelianus motioned to the ground, "There was a dead roman soldier who had been hit by an arrow in the neck during our attack. I grabbed his gladius sword and turned to the shouts and sound of footsteps beating down behind me."

Aziri grinned, "You were a fast runner."

Aelianus continued "I turned to fight off the three gladiator enemies who had chased after me. Three spearmen rapidly approached trying to catch up to me. Wielding two swords I stood my ground in a defensive position as the first two men lunged at me in an aggressive manner."

Aziri said "You were quite formidable."

Aelianus said "I parried with my swords knocking their spears away as I closed into them, suddenly I spun and slashed with my left-handed gladius, catching one of them between his breast plate and his belt."

Aziri nodded "I can see it like yesterday. A fountain of blood spewed as he screamed and fell"

Aelianus said "With my right sword, which had parried his spear away, I sliced his spear in half then kicked him over. Then I threw my right-handed gladius at the third attacker, it landed in his throat. I had disarmed the second man; his helmet had fallen off when I kicked him over."

Aziri interrupted "At that moment he could have killed me"

Daminian asked "Why didn't you?"

Aelianus said "I saw that he was just a kid, not much different than a friend I knew in Rome. This young boy sat frozen, I held my blade pointing it at him and nodded."

Aziri commented "I sat there expecting death, but he didn't finish me." He motioned to Aelianus continuing "To save a life when in defeat is the mark of a truly honorable man."

They had walked to an intersection, Aelianus pointed to the right "This way to the Tiber's port."

Daminian said "Yes, Seawitch is that way."

Aelianus scratched his head "Now where was I.... Right, I had Aziri on the ground, I saw more of his comrades coming from a distance, having caught my breath, I decided to spare his life and ran downhill again. I ran and ran, I kept running."

Aziri motioned hands together "Thank you for not killing me."

Aelianus grinned. "I did not stop running until it grew dark and I could hide behind a tree far down the road from where the hill's fighting had happened. I caught my breath and continued onto Catana with a few other Romans who had survived.

My luck must have been good because there was no sign of any cavalry. If they had, I would have never left that place."

Aziri said "Our men who had horses had gone off to get reinforcements. We had thought there were more of you."

Aelianus sneezed, "Ah, war. Well the Gods remind me of my mortality". The men chuckled. Aelianus looked at Aziri again "So, we still live, friend. We have had some interesting encounters with you and I."

Aziri agreed, "You have my continued thanks for not killing me on that battlefield."

Aelianus shrugged, "At the moment I felt exhausted, you looked young and I've never enjoyed killing simply for the sake of killing".

Aziri marveled for an instant thinking that moment.

Aelianus raised an eyebrow as they shared a mutual respect for each other. "Then a few days later reinforcement legions arrived from Italy and Greece, finding no opposition, the other legions went onto the next city to seek out the enemy while one came to Catana where I and the remnants of the town watch were. We had thought the town safe, but the first evening as our column marched through the town as a building had caught fire, we arrived thinking to put out a fire, but your men suddenly appeared from all directions in a trap."

Daminian and Tykie were surprised, Tykie spoke first "you two fought each other twice?" Aziri and Aelianus both nodded. We had just been reinforced and formed together, new recruits and the survivors of the earlier disaster.

"There were hundreds of them, I was leading the manipular, the men were not ready, most were novices, only one other veteran legionary, a man named Marius Caesar who I knew was a dependable soldier was the only other man I was confident about. We were marching through an intersection from the town square towards the walls, when suddenly rebel gladiators came at us from 4 directions.

Our men engaged and for a moment we thought we would mop them up, but then arrows started impacting us after our unit had spread to engage the attackers on the ground. I had already become engaged fighting against three attackers, blocking and counter attacking. I rapidly killed two, then this third one...."

Aelianus pointed at Aziri "He and I began fighting and parrying with each other. Many more of his comrades went to his left, while our swords clashed, parrying and blocking.

Aziri is great with a sword, but so am I. I saw him motion some of his comrades away, I knew it was him and I."

Aziri nodded, "We had a long fight, neither of us got an upper hand."

Aelianus continued, "A long fight ensued, but being attacked on four sides, we suffered many losses, the men of my manipular, Marius Caesar ordered those still alive to fight in circle formation, that means shoulder to shoulder facing outward."

Aziri nodded, "We had killed about half of their men by that point."

Aelianus nodded, "Our men began to waver. Suddenly we got lucky, their leader was killed by Marius. The attackers started to flee on all sides. I commanded Marius Caesar to keep fighting retreat, but due to being cut off by Aziri, a few other gladiators attacked me."

Aziri agreed, "They wanted to take care of you so that I could help them."

Aelianus said "I kept spinning and fighting like a mad man. Finally, this one ....", Aelianus pointed to Aziri, "Got lucky and hit my helmet's crest, which made it fly off, then he yelled, wait I want to talk and backed up."

Aziri nodded "I pulled off my helmet and said 'You spared my life the other day, so I now spare yours."

Aelianus shrugged, "War. They had let me go. I walked back to my men thinking I would be killed, but no one tried to cut me down. Luckily for us, two legions had arrived in Catana; another cohort came around a corner a few blocks away, so Aziri and his remaining comrades fled. Then we reasserted control on the city. A week later, the two legions with us in reserve went out where there was a huge battle at a river."

Aziri nodded "This time we had not been ready, they attacked our camp at first light; it was a massacre."

Aelianus said "The Legatos, was again Leana, he spared none to repair his pride. We killed most of them and those who surrendered were crucified."

Aelianus stopped as Daminian and Tykie looked at both of them. "A week later I was back in Syracuse, in charge of another reconfigured manipular. We were patrolling, the city as it was and is the main Roman controlled port city of the island. A boy ran up telling us that an assassin had snuck into his house and was about to hurt or kill his parents." We hurried over to his large home and went into the house. I sent my men rushing through the open gate door, they were under orders to take the criminal alive if possible."

Pris asked "What happened?"

Aelianus said "As they rushed inside, I remained outside but soon noticed a person jumping over the wall from inside, trying to escape. I ran over and followed him around a corner, and he tried to jump me, but he had no sword. I saw that he was wearing a Roman uniform, and so I demanded an explanation. And it was him again…." Aelianus pointed to Aziri.

Aziri shook his head, "I was in shock as well."

Aelianus said "I could hardly believe it. Aziri told me that he and his sister had been slaves at this house and that he needed to save her. About this time, my men caught up to us and I told them that I would take him in for questioning. Instead, I walked him to your boat Daminian. I figured I owed him a life."

Pris nodded following along. "You are honorable Aelianus."

Aelianus smiled "On the way Aziri told me more about the master, why don't you share Aziri?"

Aziri agreed. There was a column of Roman soldiers marching by on the street. Aelianus looked at them with a smile, "It's ok Aziri, they will not hear unless we grab their attention, they're too busy listening to their centurion's cadence."

Aziri looked at Aelianus and nodded looking forward up the street ahead of them. "The master's name was Domitius Atilius, he was the centurion who during the 3rd Punic war, led an attack on my family farm outside Carthage. This happened while I was still a young boy, our father had been defending the city. Atilius beat my mother after they had killed my grandfather for attempting to defend us, they pillaged our home for valuables. Atilius then killed my grandmother for complaining. Then when he found our aunt

340

who was prettier than my mother, pleaded for them to stop he took her inside and raped her. Domitius, I never forgot his face. He brought us to his farm in Sicily as war trophies, my older sister, mother, aunt, and I were pressed into slavery. I was soon sold to a gladiator owner."

The others stayed silent listening to Aziri "After my fellows and I escaped and rebelled anything seemed possible for a while. Then when we were beaten, I and many ran into the forest beyond the river. I went to Syracuse, the city at night where my first master's home was. At night, I climbed the city wall and killed a Roman guard on top of the wall while entering the city. I took his uniform and then returned to my old master's home's wine cellar. I came upon his family while they were at dinner though their boy had not been at the table. Domitius looked to be in shock when he saw me."

Tykie asked "Wow, what did you do?"

Aziri's face became bitter, "I demanded to have my mother, aunt and sister. Domitius laughed and said that my mother and aunt had both died from his fun…. Knowing that he meant his sexual and physical abuses, and seeing his smug look and all those years he treated us like property, I demanded to know where they were." Domitius yelled, "Your mother and aunt are dead." I yelled again "And my sister!" I swung my blade stopping inches from his wife's neck, Domitius still did not talk. His wife screamed "Domitius sold her, we have the bill of sale in that drawer." Aziri said "I had to get information out of him, so I stabbed him in his leg above the knee and yelled "Who to?"

Domitius whimpered in pain crying "A man named Titus, Titus Paullus, a Roman from Rome."

Aziri Said "I told his wife to bring me the bill of sale, it showed that the sale had happened some years earlier."

Aelianus asked "Many slaves are sold like that."

Aziri said "I asked him why he had sold her, he yelled that he was tired of fucking a dog. His wife pleaded for mercy, I turned my attention to her for a half second and Domitius suddenly tried to grab a knife that sat on the table, so I reflexively killed him. I thought for a moment about killing his wife too, she had never helped us or treated us like anything but slaves. My rage was so intense, yet I couldn't in the end, I am not an animal like them. Then I heard Romans banging on the door below so I fled.... I dropped my sword, it landed in the garden below as I landed on the balcony, and didn't couldn't go back for it"

Azizri looked at Aelianus, "I must find my sister Zaina Aelianus, I have done hurtful things, but she is innocent."

Aelianus nodded, "The things we do for love."

Aelianus looked from Aziri to the others, "I would have let Aziri go at that moment, I owed him my life, but with the city full of newly arrived reinforcements, the city was swarming with Romans. The only good way for him to escape was via your ship, so I delivered Aziri to you."

342

Daminian nodded, "Yeah, you showed up with this young man. He was a great find; he is a great fighter and a true Carthaginian pirate."

Aziri smiled nodding at Tykie, Tykie rolled his head then mock coughing and said "hooey!"

Aziri looked at Aelianus solemnly "Can you help me?"

Aelianus scratched his chin, "Titus Paullus…. The expectation of all in the legion is to follow orders, to be merciless, we killed on order, period. Titus was different, he enjoyed it, loved to hurt his victims, to draw it out. He would toy with them until he got bored and would finish them."

Aziri nodded "Yes, that seems about right for most Romans."

Aelianus said "Vicidius and Titus took pleasure in crucifying captives." As Vicidius is a Senator now, that makes Titus almost untouchable in Rome."

Daminian asked "How do we find Titus?"

Aelianus said "Finding Titus isn't hard, he manages the Shady Star which his cousin Vicidius Marcellus Paullus owns. If Titus bought your sister, she must be working there at his brothel. When you Titus, he is average height, strong, full head of hair. He has two lightning bolt tattoos on his forearms that strike through the letters SPQR.

Aziri looked grim; "Can you introduce us?"

Aelianus nodded, "I cannot get near them, I do and they will know you are a friend of mine and they will not want to do anything with you except maybe kill all of us; but Pris can guide you all to their brothel."

Daminian said "Pris will do fine. We really appreciate your help Aelianus."

Aelianus nodded, "I do want to be clear though, as these are powerful men you will be meeting, if your meeting goes bad, they will not be merciful. If you are caught alive, they will likely torture you and then crucify you all on crosses. Are you all ready to make such a risk?"

They saw a passing slave cart go by, Aelianus motioned with his heads towards it, "That is the least of the consequences that could happen."

Daminian nodded, as did Aziri and Tykie.

Chapter XXXII Loyalty as a matter of honor.

129 BC

The call of blood....

They came to a street that had construction going on, and so had to go around it via different streets. Making the first turn Tykie looked at Aelianus, "You say Titus enjoyed inflicting pain, how so?"

Aelianus looked at him "Our legions were to put down the slave revolts, after we defeated the slaves under Eunus, Titus convinced our Legatus to have all the male slaves who were captured at Enna to fight each other to the death, a last gladiatorial game. Those who refused were crucified. While that was going on, the Legatus also ordered the men to rape all the female slaves they captured before they were sent back in chains."

Aziri's hands turned into fists not saying anything.

Aelianus continued, "I became disgusted by it all, I could not find pride in wearing the legion's uniform anymore."

Aziri nodded "I saw such things from Romans in Carthage, impossible to forget. After we were captured and transported to Sicily and forced into slavery; our master Domitius did not wait long before he raped our mother. I threatened him the next day with a knife, I was 10 years old. He sold me to a gladiator slave owner the next day."

Pris looked grim, "That is horrifying."

Aelianus paused, "I have no doubt that your sister has experienced all kinds of physical and sexual abuse, if she is still alive, she will need you to support her, please prepare yourself friend."

Aziri nodded, "Understood"

Daminian smiled, "We can handle them. Thank you for your help, I am in your debt."

Aelianus turned to Daminian, "There is a risk of death, and I won't be there to help. Why are you doing this?"

Daminian said "For my part, I owe Aziri a life debt, and there may be some coin to be acquired."

Chapter XXXIII Seawitch

129 BC

They journeyed across Rome to see Seawitch and then for the meeting with Titus.

It was a hot day, they walked the remaining blocks of the bustling city, past columns of Roman soldiers marching, of merchants selling various wears, of citizens in togas walking here and there going about their business, men, women and children of all ages. They turned back onto the main street and continued downhill and it opened at the Tiber River where there was an expansive port with a few trireme ships moored to the South of the bridged Tiberina Island. There were a few smaller merchant ships and fishing boats moored there as well.

Daminian pointed to his ship with pride "I present you to the Seawitch, the large trireme at the end of the dock with the folded black sails." As they were squinting from this distance Daminian continued "It is the one which has the delivery cart that is receiving boxes now."

They walked down the dock, from a distance Seawitch looked like any other Trireme. Up close Seawitch looked more or less like a normal trireme, though this one was longer. Daminian said "My ship is bigger than most Triremes."

Pris asked "How big?"

Daminian yelled "Tykie!"

Seawitch

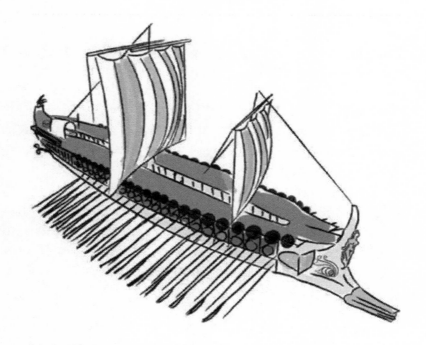

Tykie answered "The typical length is about 37 meters; her length is closer to 45 meters. Her beam is approximately 5.5 to 6.5 meters, the weight of most triremes is around 45 tons, this one is around 50 tons."

Pris smiled "Oh my....."

Tykie smiled "She has a massive mainsail mast in the middle and a slightly smaller mast forward of that. The front of the ship has a metal ram at the ship's nose and a wooden female figurehead."

Aelianus noted "All triremes typically have three lines of oars along the side of the ship and these ships could carry around 200 persons if I recall right."

Daminian nodded "Impressive friend."

Aelianus smiled, "I've seen some very fast Greek sail ships, what makes her special?"

Daminian smiled nodding, "True in normal cases, but not against her, my ship is easily the fastest ship in the Mediterranean. Even the Romans and Greek vessels cannot out sail her."

After looking over the ship Aelianus noticed many slight differences. Aelianus squinted and pointed to the figurehead, "Easily the fastest? Well I see there are some differences to this ship. Is there a pipe poking out of the figurehead's mouth?".

Daminian smiled, "Yes my friend, this ship is one of a kind."

Aelianus scratched his head, "How ever did you get this ship in this port without it being impounded by the authorities?"

Daminian smiled, "I saved a Senator from a pirate attack off Southern Italy a couple of years ago. I told him that I would be happy to deliver his ivory shipments at a discount so long as he provided me with safe passage in and out of Rome. It is good to have friends in high places." Aelianus nodded as he and Pris stood before the Seawitch.

While Aelianus and Daminian were talking Pris smiled and whispered "Such a beautiful vessel, a way to a different place and freedom."

Tykie asked Pris "What did you say?"

Pris said "Nothing"

Aelianus asked "A question, this ship has only two oar lines instead of three, and they did not go back quite as far as she had seen in other similar ships. There were wooden covered windows near the back. Why is that?"

Daminian smiled and motioned them to board. They arrived on the main deck of the ship. Daminian spoke with the watchman as they came on board, meanwhile the group briefly looked over the whole ship. A line of black shields lined each side of the ship along the deck. Up forward the ship looked basically the same, it was a little longer and a little wider, an extra mast which was not too uncommon.

Tykie asked "Have you been on a ship before Pris?"

Pris shook her head "This was the first time for me on any ship, such an exciting adventure."

On the large wooden ship with two great central sail masts, neatly coiled rope rigging laying at certain places on deck, there was a stairway at the fore and aft of the ship, just before the captain's helm. A crew of roughly 180 men were all busy stowing provisions that he had purchased earlier in the day and some other crewmen were bringing boxes out of the hold down to the dock for the delivery carts. Many smiled at Pris, one sailor whistled at her. Pris smiled, then she pointed to the line of crewmen with the boxes. She asked Aziri "What are they unloading?"

Aziri shrugged "An Ivory delivery for Captain's Senator friend; he paid for his share when we arrived earlier today."

Daminian came over to them, then as the group went aft.

Aelianus spotted more differences, he asked "What are the round small shield size pipes emitting from the hole that goes into the lower deck and the other odd pipe that goes out the back of the ship for?"

Aelianus saw a strange tube that was going through the deck behind the captain's helm, "What's this?" Aelianus asked.

Daminian said "For shouting below when I am on top deck"

Daminian laughed, then Aelianus pointed to a small raised square box surface raised about 3 feet level with the exterior railings, from another ship this pipe would be barely visible, from the dock it was out of view. The back pipe was covered with black ash. Aelianus looked inquisitively at that wondering what it could be for.

Daminian patted him on his shoulder "You are perceptive" Smiling,"Those are the mouth and ass of our lovely beast. Follow me"

Daminian waved them all to follow him to the lower deck. Daminian continued with his speech pointing out how the captain's cabin had been reduced in size to that of a normal crewman's space, the rudder's helm control wheel moved to the front of the aft space ahead of the opening. "After Tykie joined my ship as its engineer, he made some very special improvements to our lady. That is why I said we have the speed of the Gods earlier…"

Daminian pointed at Tykie "His uncle was an autistic engineering genius. The man is super quiet, he flaps his hands and sometimes repeats what he says, sometimes it seems like he is speaking to himself….. he can give the impression that he is slightly touched by the Gods."

Tykie nodded saying "Perseus is, he created a prototype steam propulsion system that is unlike anything in this world."

Aelianus "A prototype steam propulsion system engine… What is that?" He asked, intrigued about the engine, he sensed that he was about to see something significant.

Daminian held up his hands "Before I answer, when Tykie joined my crew, he explained it over a few hours cause I didn't believe it was possible."

Tykie said, "Once Seawitch was Daminian's, we put her on drydock for six months while my uncle told us where and how to make improvements to the original ship. We also added metal framing like a skeletal basket on the bottom of the ship to give the ship more power and strength."

Daminian said "Tykie's uncle made this our prototype engine, we retrofit it into the back of our ship, it works…..

Amazing." He kissed his fingers towards it. "I even have more space for provisions, need less oarsmen for only when I don't use this engine and my engine makes us about twice as fast as any other ship out there."

Aelianus looked on in awe "This ship really works, powered off of steam?"

Tykie smiled nodding as Daminian said "We did our first major test run from Sparta to Alexandria in Egypt, then came directly here from Egypt with a supply of goods from Aksum via Egypt."

Aelianus "So this engine makes this ship fast, and you can still carry as much Ivory and gold?"

Daminian nodded, smiling, "Yes friend we have a bounty of ivory, we wish to sell our ivory and purchase Roman wine that we can sell elsewhere."

Aelianus rubbed his hands "I can supply you with that!"

The party passed the 2nd deck where there were lines of oar seats and weapon storage rooms. They continued below to the lowest third deck, and Daminian explained this was their crew's quarters, cargo, and food storage and a small galley. They walked forward to aft, Aelianus saw Daminian's Captain's cabin was up front, which was unusual and there were two unusual metal rods that went from aft along the ceiling all the way forward to the front. Daminian pointed out "Those tubes go to the wooden lady at the Stern."

Aelianus saw that in the aft, where there normally was the very spacious Captain's room, this had been divided into two rooms, the first contained a large supply of wood and a smaller supply of black stones. The 2nd room at the very back contained a large brick box sitting on marble.

Seawitch's Steam Engine

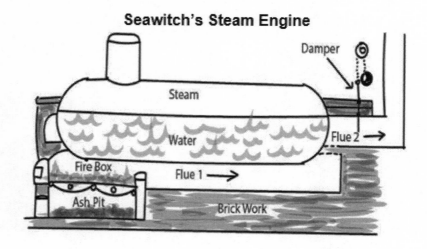

Tykie pulled off a cloak cover from the engine, "Connected to a metal shaft that is turned by the steam that pushes the pistons, the main shaft goes through the back of our trireme, her engine has metal rods that send steam forward and a main exhaust above." Aelianus was fully in awe and curious "The steam engine? Metal shafts, metal forward rods, pistons? What are those things?"

Daminian laughed, "If you like, I will take you out to the ocean to show it all to you one day my friend. I like your inquisitive mind. Now, while I am happy to show you our ship, and the engine, its design stays behind closed doors, and I will sell the plans to the Roman government after I have retired."

Aelianus remarked "A ship that is powered by oars or a steam engine?" Aelianus was amazed and curious about the machine in front of him. It basically looked like a huge cylinder box, there was one large tube that went into the ceiling, and a square chimney that went up from the brick box below the cylinder. There were two metal cans the size of drums on either side of the main cylinder, these drums had metal rods that stuck out of them and went aft where they connected to wheels that had interconnecting teeth. These wheels connected to a main huge shaft that had teeth groves around the connecting part of the crankshaft much like a wedding band on a finger leaves a mark. The main crankshaft went straight out exiting the ship through a water tight metal surface.

Daminian smiled, raising his eyebrows "Impressive, isn't it?"

Aelianus said to Daminian "I am impressed. You are right, this is radically different, potentially it could greatly benefit business."

Daminian said "Exactly, whenever they see my ship in daylight, they must think she is a normal trireme powered by oars, when we use our steam engine…" He laughed "perhaps they think we are on fire or a scary sea monster." At night, they will never know how we outpaced them."

Pris asked, "Where does this pipe go?"

Daminian motioned with his hand, "Into the water my dear, that is our spinning oar or as Tykie likes to call… a propeller, because it propels us forward".

Pris nodded in understanding. There was a chain hanging down from the chimney and the large tube that went forward. The machine was truly unlike anything either of them had ever seen before and they stood there in awe for a minute. Below the large metal cylinder. There was a small metal door opening into a brick furnace that was below the cylinder sitting on top of a ceramic block. Aelianus pointed, "Is that where the fire happens to heat the water and make steam?"

Tykie nodded, "Yes, this engine can burn wood or coal as fuel and then the mechanism transfers the heat produced into circulating boiler water."

Aelianus looked at a stack of boxes of black stones sitting picking up a stone, "Coal, what is coal?" he asked inquisitively.

Daminian laughed, "You can think of it as black magic. There are tribes that live on a large island that has beautiful white cliffs and lots of rain. Rome has not got to the far North yet, but I have. They traded these black stones they called coal, which produce immense heat, much hotter than wood. It normally takes time for it to heat up, once it is hot, it is surely impressive. And I can pour oils on it to make it become hot faster."

Aelianus picked up a piece as Daminian continued "During very critical moments I use this-our best stuff. The people of those islands were happy to trade a great deal of that black magic for the Greek wine and Egyptian beer which we introduced to them."

Tykie interrupted, "So, this system heats the water into steam sufficiently then the steam pushes the inner mechanisms to spin the metal rod that is our rear spinning oar, that propels the ship."

Aelianus squinted his eyes trying to imagine it all in action.

Tykie said proudly "We still have oars and sails as we may not have enough coal for long distance voyages given, we carry wine or other cargo and we need to do more sea tests but first results show that, it approximately doubles maybe even triples our speed beyond what we normally get from oar & sail speed, and we can sail for days on a full furnace of coal."

Daminian waved his hand like a fan, "Ready to see the ivory?"

Aelianus nodded looking at Daminian straight in the eyes with a smile, "Absolutely partner."

Chapter XXXIV Sabina's departure

129 BC

Fateful events for good and bad.

Sabina returned home shortly after Aelianus and Pris had left with the sailors. She walked to the tavern's kitchen and spoke with Septimus and Helga. "Septimus, Helga, I will be traveling to our beach villa today, Helga, you are coming with me. Septimus, you will stay here with Octavian and Morbius and the dog. Take care of customers, Aelianus will be back later. Helga, we will need food and wine at the villa."

Helga raised an eyebrow, Master Aelianus said specifically that all the wine at the tavern is for the tavern, but we could go to the winery and get more there."

Sabina said "Ok, we could use David too, he will help manage you slaves while we are at the villa." An hour later, Sabina got into a wagon and departed.

Sabina thought on the way to the winery, *The tricky issue of the actual murders, multiple murders in this case. I have not experienced this, but when Mom and Dad died in a fire I was old enough that I knew I must create my own destiny. Uncle was an elderly fool, we argued about everything and it was his idea I was married off to Aelianus over some old family war debt. I must control my feelings, Aelianus' life will be ended just as if Traaz were heading off to kill a stray dog infected with rabies.*

Sabina thought *If Traaz succeeds I am free. If he does not, we can assume he was just a murderous slave. If Traaz tries to double-cross me, Vicidius will kill him. I am just speeding up departure dates so that I can remarry a man who will give me children and act like a man. I married Aelianus expecting him to fulfill my needs and he clearly has no intention of doing his required job. I want to be married to a powerful man and Aelianus has merely been a stepping stone for me on my way to power and the luxury that wealth affords.*

Helga saw that Sabina was smiling in the wagon on her way out of the city.

Chapter XXXV How is it possible?

129 BC

On Seawitch, plans for a new future.

On the Seawitch, the party had walked from the engine room to the cargo hold. The very handsome Tykie gave an overall summary for their guests, "My uncle Perseus is a man who is very aloof…"

Pris asked "How so?"

Tykie smiled "We would often see him talking to himself about the designs of the universe, physics, engineering or advanced math, he would excitedly talk about such things delightfully, then he would stop realize people were watching him and say hello before returning to his in-depth conversations, his stuttering speech impediment, his hands shaking each other and head occasionally shaking all by himself.

Pris looked at him, "We had such a man in my village, he seemed to be possessed by the spirits."

Tykie nodded "Some people would look at Perseus and think he is mad, but he is touched by the Gods, he is a genius. Since he was young, he had often invented strange gizmos that made sounds or blew water in the air for the delight of local children."

Pris smiled, "He sounds wonderful."

Tykie nodded, "He was, long before the Greek-Roman war, Perseus said he believed Epris showed that even under a gifted general, the existing Greek army style was obsolete compared to Roman armies. Greece was weak with Alexander's spin-off Hellenic kingdoms still fighting each other and he wanted to protect Greece from Roman conquest, which he suspected given they had already conquered Greek kingdoms in Southern Italy and Sicily. Perseus created the design for this machine on scrolls in his home in Sparta."

Aziri interrupted, "But the Spartans are traditionalists, aren't they?"

Tykie nodded "Yes, that is true, our King just looked mystified when Perseus brought the designs and the idea to him."

They arrived at the cargo hold, showed Aelianus and Pris the large amount of ivory they had brought, minus what they had sold to Tribune Publius Crassus.

Aelianus smiled "Very nice. Ok, I will trade you 60 barrels of wine for half of this ivory"

Daminian shook his hand, "Done, when can I have it here?"

Aelianus looked at Pris and back to Daminian "I can have the barrels here at your dock by…. Sunset tonight."

Daminian smiled broadly "Then I shall have the amount of ivory you want, delivered to your inn?"

Aelianus shook his head "No to our vineyard and winery, there is more storage space there".

They shook hands both smiling "Done and done" they each said together.

Pris made sure to walk close to Tykie while this conversation happened, "Then what occurred with Perseus?"

Tykie looked at Aelianus and Daminian, Daminian looked to Aelianus who nodded, so he continued "The Achaean League had sent word to our King that they wanted Sparta to join them in a war against Rome. Our King sent my father and uncle Perseus to Corinth to negotiate a peace mission, to achieve victory through peace. Our King agreed that anything was worth a try, and my uncle thought the Corinthian King and his advisors there might be interested buyers for his steam engine to give them technology that could improve their ability for fast trade, thus improving their commerce standing without any war with Rome."

Pris asked "What happened"

Tykie shrugged, "Their King and everyone in Corinth's court King thought Perseus was mad, they said they did not trust a Spartan nutcase and claimed that if it was so good why wasn't his own King utilizing it. Perseus' anger at the King's rejection, he called them "obsolete dinosaurs" destroyed any chance to invest their funds into creating something new that might fail."

Aelianus spoke up "I suppose they thought they just needed as many hoplites as possible…"

Tykie nodded "The fools had no idea what they were walking away from."

Daminian spoke up waving his hands, "It is all about the sale, in how one presents a product. He should have shown why they needed his product to the right people. To do that one must have the right connections".

Tykie shrugged "No matter. My father felt they might become captives, and so when they left the palace and agreed to return for dinner, they instead immediately left the city. Not long after they left Corinth, they watched the League's armies march South, following carefully they watched in horror as the Corinth army lay siege on Sparta. We think the probable Corinthian King had hoped to intimidate Sparta into joining them, thus gathering enough hoplite men to fight as his hoplites in phalanx formations in their foolish war against Rome."

Aziri spoke up "That was his strategy? Hilarious, Spartans don't fear anything."

Tykie nodded saying "They laid siege for a few weeks, tried to assault Sparta once, but were repulsed. They then lifted the siege to march North once the Roman troops had arrived."

Pris wanted to clarify "So, Greek armies were fighting other Greek armies?"

Tykie nodded as Aziri cut in "Did Sparta win?"

Tykie ignored him, "Greece was never under the control of one kingdom, the closest was under Philip & Alexander's Macedonian era, but even then..." He looked at Aziri "Sparta had remained independent. So, when my father and uncle returned to Sparta, they were briefly received by our King as he was leading his forces out to fight against Corinth. My father and uncle Perseus returned home to my family."

Aelianus asked "You say your family is related to the King?"

Tykie waving his hands in the air said "Well, our King is a distant cousin of my father's, he wanted to know what was going on, but also if his cousins were mistreated. Spartans are even more traditionalists than other Greeks, but our family was of course interested, so Perseus described his machine to all of us at dinner one night. I was so captured by his descriptions that he showed me a design copy of his prototype engine."

Tykie stared straight ahead at no one in particular while pointing his index finger in the air "Never discourage anyone... who continually makes progress, no matter how slow. -Pluto".

Aziri rolled his eyes, Tykie raised his eyebrow and went on, leading the group back upstairs "A few days later my uncle thinking no one wanted his blueprint, starting to plan to travel to Alexandria to deposit his invention's plans in the library there, but the night before he was to sail, we all had a goodbye dinner for him. At that dinner our King arrived with his new friend Daminian, the friendly merchant who had spoken his way into the King's good nature."

Daminian smiled "I merely sold him some Iberian weapons that were made of the finest metal, he was very happy with them and invited me to join the dinner".

Aelianus chuckled "You do have a way with people "

Daminian nodded, smiling "Absolutely."

Tykie continued "Daminian and I spoke at that dinner during which he offered to have me join his crew. I am the 2nd son of my family, so my father accepted. As my first act as a crew member, I told Daminian about the engine after he had hired me. Daminian was interested and so Perseus and I spent the next 7 or 8 months retrofitting the ship he had purchased from our King.

We did our first trial run going first to Alexandria Egypt where Perseus bid us farewell, he decided to share his ideas with the scholars there. We next met with my cousin who had come from Aksum, we collected our ivory from him and received it in exchange for the Greek and Roman wine we had.

Leaving Alexandria, we went first to Carthage, then after we traded in Iberia, we journeyed to trade in Britannia."

Pris turned to Aziri "You've been back to Carthage?"

Aziri nodded, "It still bears the scars of war and genocide, when Rome sacked it, they truly devastated the city, there is only rubble there now. All the original Carthaginians were either killed in battle, slaughtered in their homes or hauled off to slavery, the Romans spared no one."

Pris asked "Did they truly do such things?"

Aziri nodded his head "13 years ago, the Romans stormed my city of Carthage, and sacked it, they raped, murdered, pillaged, everyone I knew as a child, every single person suffered that fate. Of the soldiers who surrendered, the Romans kept their captured defenders in groups and then they slaughtered all of them plus many of our civilians... anyone who resisted. It was only when the Romans had tired of killing, they decided to enslave those of us who were remaining. Now all of the old Carthaginian territories have been taken over as Roman provinces in Northern Africa."

Pris looked on at him in silence, having been a slave.

Aziri said "When we went there, I was hoping somehow that the rumors about the city may have been untrue, that the city may have started to revive, but now there are only burnt-out ruins."

Aziri stopped talking, lost in thought. Aelianus, having listened in, looked to Aziri, "I am sorry for what happened to you, your family and your people friend."

Aziri nodded "It was not you, and I killed many Romans in Sicily to even the score. My father and uncles killed Romans in the last war for Carthage."

Pris listened, thinking about how Aziri had gone through so much suffering whereas Tykie's life had been relatively calm, and about her own experiences, the thoughts of *How can I ever accept or be accepted by Rome? Do I even want to be? Kept going through her mind.*

Daminian decided to change the subject, "So what do you think of this ship?"

Pris thought about it, looking at the ship "She is beautiful" she said.

Aelianus rocked from one side of his foot to the other while rubbing his chin. This was more impressive than the aqueducts he thought "This ship is amazing, I have seen many, especially how your engine is unlike anything I have ever seen before. Daminian, I imagine this would beat any pirate ship in a race."

Daminian laughed "Most assuredly"

Aelianus smiled "Your ship will work great for my imports and exports. I would love to take a ride on your ship once with this engine running".

Daminian smiled, "Next time we go out, if you like you may come too, a night ride to the coast perhaps?"

Rubbing his hands, Aelianus' excitement bubbled inside as though he were a young boy. "I would love that."

They walked topside and overlooked Rome from the ship. Aelianus said "As you are a friend Daminian, please be very careful with Titus and his men, they are handpicked veterans who have always been thugs as his brothel's security. They are all good fighters, merciless to those with whom they pull their blades. I know of a man who tried to buy the freedom of a whore he fell in love with only to have them kill him as he didn't have enough money. Then Vicidius legitimized the murder by putting the dead man on a cross."

Daminian rubbed his head, "This man who hates you, he is powerful but has not killed you?"

Aelianus nodded "My contact told me that after the war, Vicidius and Titus bought a whorehouse and inn, a source of income for them. Later his mother used her network to connect him to work for a corrupt and powerful senator she knew in the Senate. He started out as a military advisor, or really if my sources are right as their political hitman. From there, he helped kill several Senators a few years ago in a coup d'etat. Then in the very next election he filled the seat of one of those who had been slain. Since then he has blackmailed many in the Senate to vote for his proposals while he rounded up many who were involved with the coup, yet I am allied with a Senator who also has very powerful friends. That and I believe he is afraid to fight me one on one."

Chapter XXXVI Plan of attack
129 BC

A dangerous path…

Daminian nodded "Our first objective is to find out if Aziri's sister is there."

Aziri said eagerly "And if she is to save her."

Pris asked "What's her name?"

Aziri looked at Pris "Zaina."

Pris acknowledged as Aelianus motioned down below "Ivory is really valuable here, Vicidius would benefit from a large supply. Titus should be eager to purchase a great amount." If they do own Aziri's sister, he might offer to exchange her to you for the ivory. If there are too many guards."

Aziri tapped his sword handle, "If he has my sister…. I won't be peaceful around them boss."

Daminian nodded, "I understand. You will be fine."

Aelianus looked at Aziri "I would not trust that guy more than a snake, he is not the only person who wants ivory."

Aziri shrugged, "But he probably is the one who has Zaina."

Aelianus cautioned "Give me a couple days, I will ask around, perhaps there are other buyers. If all goes well."

Daminian raised his hand, "In a few days if you may have more buyers that I can sell to, if all goes well, yes that would be great."

Aelianus nodded, "Very well, be careful."

Daminian smiled, "Yes good times are here now thanks to your help. Here is a signed purchase order, payment of ivory on the receipt of 30 barrels of wine."

Aelianus said "May I have a scroll, writing utensils?"

Daminian snapped his fingers as he responded "How soon can you deliver the wine?"

Tykie left them for a moment.

Aelianus smiled "My men should be able to make the delivery this afternoon. I had 30 barrels already staged at the dock warehouse right there" Aelianus pointed to a large building next to the river.

Tykie returned with the materials, Aelianus wrote on the scrolls for a moment then using the ink on his ring, pressed it to the scroll. "Now, this scroll will grant you permission to take possession of the wine, please have the ivory delivered to the same warehouse. The wine is ready for export. You can have 30 barrels of that shipment."

Daminian shook Aelianus' hand "Perfect, it will be done today then".

Aelianus pulled out a scroll from his Toga. "Here is a basic map of Rome, my inn is located here on Capitoline Hill, over here is Titus' location, the Shady Star tavern & brothel, it is located over here on Aventine Hill. If Vicidius is there, he will probably help defend the brothel, but killing him would bring all of Rome's security on you if you're identified and he gets away."

Daminian nodded "Thanks for the warning. Helping this really helps us out."

I will stop by your inn again in three days for a meal, then it will be three to six months before I am in Rome again."

Aziri said "Truly Aelianus, thank you."

Aelianus happily said "I owe my life to Daminian for saving me from the sea, and to you Aziri for sparing his life in battle, it is a matter of honor. It will be good to see you in 3 to 6 months, that will be either picking season, or we can drink together either way. In the pricking season we can head out to my vineyard and crush grapes together."

Daminian and Aelianus shook hands. Then they walked down the gangplank and up the dock from the ship, Pris remarked how lovely the city looked from the river, the birds flying through the cool air as dark clouds approached from the distance.

Turning to Pris, Aelianus instructed her to guide them to the Shady Star, and then to wait near that location to guide them back to their ship. Aelianus gave Pris a scroll that said that she was conducting an errand for him and he gave her a dagger in case anyone tried to stop her.

Aelianus rubbed his hands, as he thought walking towards home, *If this steam engine works as well as Daminian claims there could be great profits with less risk for me to be had. I could bring products to market faster than my competition, if it truly can outrun pirates and hostile navies, there could be astronomical profits to be had.* Aelianus thought.... *Tonight, I will have to speak with Rufus about this.* Aelianus thought breathlessly as he turned a corner. *With mountains of treasure ahead even Sabina should decide to be kind again...* Aelianus thought, *this will be the start of a great future for me and for our Roman Republic! Now to get home and prepare for Rufus' arrival....*

Chapter XXXVII Vicidius & Livia

129 BC

No other choice....

Vicidius was in a hurry, he had to get home, change into his armor, grab his sword, his horse and then travel across town to his rival's home. He did not know if Traaz would succeed, Aelianus was a great swordsman, admittedly one of the best Vicidius had ever seen. If Traaz messed up, and somehow alerted Aelianus, it was sure that Traaz would lose in a fair swordfight. As they had planned, he must strike at Aelianus while he slept, and only after Traaz had killed the guards. He had also made sure to tell Traaz to kill Rufus if he was there. They had planned that after all was done, they would meet at the Circus Maximus in 5 days. Vicidius had arranged a safe house for Traaz to stay just down the street. Rufus was the unknown, if he was not there, Vicidius would have to go to Rufus' villa afterwards and murder him. Rufus was getting too close and knew too many powerful senators.

As Vicidius grabbed his gladius off his wall he heard his mother's elderly voice, she was all dirty wearing her gardening clothing "What are you doing?"

Startled, Vicidius held his gladius a moment before turning to the voice. Seeing the old woman who was once pretty, "Mother I am dealing with a problem, one that threatens my goals" Vicidius said.

Livia scoffed "Dealing with problems by use of a gladius…
to grab power? Great power requires great responsibility"
she urged.

Vicidius snorted "No, Great power requires great ambition,
control and ruthlessness. It is a dog-eat-dog world, and
Aelianus stands in my way."

Livia grabbed him by the shoulder, "Why do you go after
this man?"

Vicidius looked at her "He is working towards goals that
would support the Gracchus policies, policies that would
strip us of our land and holdings. Aelianus was one of
Tiberius Gracchus' main supporters."

Livia shook her head "I warn you son, it is not always wise
to strike for a quick and easy target, even if you succeed,
violence often returns to be the wielders undoing".

Vicidius waved his hand up "I am defending our family,
trying to grow our power mother, easy for you to lecture!"

Livia slapped him "Don't you think for a moment you could
be where you are without what I did for you."

Livia put her hand on a chair's back, "Your grandfather
Lucius Aemilius Paullus was a Consul of Rome twice, in
219 and 216 BC. He gained glory and power when he
defeated King Demetrius of Pharos, in the Second Illyrian
War. On his arrival back to Rome, he was awarded a
triumph."

Vicidius interrupted her "See, he grabbed power and it brought him glory!"

Livia rolled her eyes "Wait, oh how quickly power got to his head, I remember my grandmother pleading with him when I was a child. She urged him not to do anything beyond the law, yet oh power and opportunity can be fleeting as the changing weather. His so-called friends were quick to abandon him when he was subsequently charged, along with his subordinates, for unfairly dividing the war spoils. Yet they all did it."

Vicidius looked his mother in the eye, "We have benefitted from those spoils, and thanks to his connections in the Senate he was acquitted. Then those same idiots came begging him to fight Hannibal once their replacement generals were all annihilated!"

Livia snorted "He was a fool to attack Hannibal, that man was a master on the battlefield. He should have let that Carthaginian brute starve stuck inside Italy and then have Hannibal come at him in desperation."

Vicidius ignored this "I don't have time for a military lecture!"

Livia shook her head "You think that acquittal saved him for the moment, either from dishonor or perhaps death, but it also encouraged him to try to regain glory and he became more aggressive in his risk taking when he led Roman forces against Hannibal at Cannae only to get slaughtered."

Vicidius said "Death is better than dishonor."

Livia paused, picking up a golden Illyrian artifact that was centered on their table she continued "Do I need to remind you how our family honor was shattered by his defeat?"

Vicidius shook his head but she stopped him from talking, "That defeat caused your father to become a drunk, which did not raise our family status."

Vicidius was about to say something and Livia put her hand over his mouth, "We are where we are now because I slept with the right people while your father was wallowing away as a drunk, and I killed a few people who threatened us." The old woman paused, watching Vicidius' reaction she continued "One doesn't always need a sword to kill."

Vicidius scoffed, "Is there a point to this history lesson, I will be late!"

Livis said "There is only one thing worse in Roman culture than to get caught for being greedy, that is to suffer defeat on the battlefield. Your father carried the shame his whole life and tried to escape his responsibilities by being a drunk."

Vicidius interrupted "That was not his fau…"

Livia slapped him "Do you understand that I sacrificed and risked my whole life so that you could return our family to glory and NOW what do you do? You murder Tiberius Gracchus, perhaps the most famous Senator of our day because his land reforms threaten to take away a little land from newly conquered lands that elite families who don't need them and then you've gone around murdering his supporters?"

Vicidius was stunned "…Now you intend to murder one of the most well connected, beloved and famous Roman patriot war veteran who half the city loves his tavern and whose lover is an influential Senator simply because he may have been connected to Tiberius and what… insulted your fragile ego long ago? Or is it because you are fucking his wife?"

Vicidius said "That's not…"

Livia interrupted him, "Such a confused face, I know about your men's attempted attack on him when he was fishing. Sloppy."

Vicidius looked at her, "How do you know all this? You knew about the men I sent to kill Aelianus at the river?"

Livia looked at him and then shook her head, sighing, "You really need to hire better mercenaries, Vicidius, those men were outmatched."

Vicidius stood wide eyed, "The one who ran off, was he yours?"

Livia thinly smiled "He ran away, and then he came to me, because I paid him."

Vicidius put his hands on the table, not sure if he was furious that his activities had been discovered or if he was relieved that it was his mom that had discovered him and she was not disowning him. A wave of seething anger overcame him not knowing how to react, but he would not let himself lash out at his mother, she was the one person who had protected him through everything. Raising his head she looked into his eyes again, as he said "There is one more murder beyond his that must be done, Aelianus probably does not know it, but his lover Rufus has information that could destroy us. Rufus has learned my identity as one of the hitmen who killed Tiberius and many of his supporters, that it was not just Publius Nasica Serapio."

Livia interrupted, "Why did you help kill Tiberius? That was too risky!"

Vicidius looked at her like she was stupid "I had to, my contacts are all elite Senators who own huge land estates, while we will be impacted, some of their estates were liable to lose 50% or more of their land under Tiberius' proposed law, they knew that I was ambitious and had military skills. Serapio was the pontifex maximus, he was a firm conservative, like his father and his cousin Scipio Aemilianus."

Livia shook her head "Lucius Scipio publicly supported Tiberius, doesn't that mean…"

Vicidius finished her thought "Yes that famed family is split between supporters and opponents of Tiberius. And his name saved him from the purge."

Livia said "My sources informed me that Serapio and his cousin Aemilianus disagreed with Lucius about how to deal with Tiberius, Lucius wanted to negotiate, but Tiberius was not going to slow down."

Vicidius shrugged "Tiberius pushed powerful men too far and too fast, so they turned to Serapio to stop him, but he did not have the skills to do it all alone so he tasked me to do most of the dirty work. We then led the opposition to the tribune of the plebs Tiberius Gracchus."

Livia asked "So why are we in danger if you and he did what the Senate wanted?"

Vicidius stammered, "Not all of the Senate wanted that done, just about half. Then when things got out of control, I made sure that Serapio took the fall as the one who finally murdered Tiberius. I planted the staff I used for killing Tiberius in Serapio's home."

Livia was calculating all this information against what she already knew "Why did Serapio not attempt to betray you?"

Vicidius said "I have had Serapio blackmailed for years, he has been a frequent customer at my brothel and owed me a large gambling debt. Also his mistress is an employee of mine, to expose him would mean a humiliating divorce and shame on his family and his descendants. Serapio agreed to stay silent about the half of the Senate who had supported him and also about my involvement on the condition he be exiled to Pergamum near Asia to avoid his prosecution by Gracchus' supporters in the Senate."

Livia looked at Vicidius, "Did you have anything to do with his death? He died soon after arriving in Pergamum or so I read."

Vicidius was wide eyed again then slowly nodded, "Wow... You are well informed. I made a trip over there for a visit, I couldn't take any chances of him changing his mind. I met with him at his villa, we drank wine until he got drunk, then I gave him a drink of water that would be his last, then placed his body in his bed to make it look like he had died in his sleep"

Vicidius rubbed his hands in the air as though cleaning them.

Livia nodded, understanding.

Vicidius continued, "I have had well established spies, Rufus told a servant of his who is one of my spies, that he will meet with other Senators with proof soon. Some of these Senators are on my payroll. Rufus has offered them a huge amount of Ivory as payment for their agreement to pursue this information."

Livia said "Be careful, these men could set you into a trap."

Vicidius said "Those twits may betray me once they have their hands on the ivory. But I cannot kill half the Senate, yet to allow Rufus to keep talking to Senators with proof or no proof, can kill me or my career just as easily,

Livia nodded "A lie if repeated enough to the right people can be deadly. Those Senators have too much power."

Vicidius said "Even though I am a Senator now, if they feel I am a liability, they will eliminate me too. I have to stave off this information in order to keep my hands clean and protect us from the others."

Livia nodded, "Our family must not be jeopardized. What about the law?"

Vicidius cut her off "The law is what powerful men make it. I could be crucified."

Livia nodded understanding, she touched Vicidius tenderly on his face tracing the scar that went down his right cheek "Then make sure there are no mistakes and you gain the power you need to keep us safe. Blackmail or kill Rufus into being quiet and silence Aelianus, but be careful, he is dangerous with a sword as your bungled fishing trip attack showed us."

Vicidius nodded, grabbing his sheathed gladius, "I have already put the plan into motion, it will happen tonight."

Livia responded regretfully, "If it must be done it must be done, but we are dealing with great risk, if they come for you, I will not be able to protect you"

Vicidius nodded, "I shall not fail mother." Vicidius gave her a kiss on her cheek and left.

Chapter XXXVIII Personal history

129 BC

Introductions....

Pris led Daminian, Aziri, Tykie, and three of his men who were of Daminian's guards and two sailors who were carrying a trunk of ivory to the Shady Star where they would meet with Titus Paullus. They waved to Aelianus who headed back towards his tavern in the opposite direction.

As soon as they were out of sight Daminian asked "Pris tell us about herself."

Pris told them her background story, about being abducted and made a slave. "Rome will probably always feel alien to me, Aelianus has been a kind master, he has been kind to my children, he has taught us how to speak Latin, read, write and do math and other subjects while allowing me to speak with my children in my native tongue of Cimbri."

Pris ran her hand through her hair, "At first I felt violated by Cyprian, Aelianus' father by being forced to have sex with a Roman senator, but I got two beautiful children, by him, and I love them." Pris directed them to stay off the main avenues and onto back roads, "Although I have a pass, I am not sure if such a large group of non-Romans would not cause attention."

Daminian nodded agreement. "It must have been terrible; to be a slave. Yet yes, children are life's best treasure."

Pris turned the conversation to Daminian, "I must say that I am astounded by you, I have never seen a man with such amazingly dark skin, you are handsome!"

Daminian smiled, "Thank you young one."

Pris giggled and continued "I am so happy to know you, and you have such an incredible ship. Please tell me about yourself."

Daminian told her about himself. "I am a seafaring trading merchant from the Kingdom of Aksum."

Pris looked away from the road and focused on him "Aksum, where is that".

Daminian smiled "Do you know how Egypt borders the Red Sea?"

Pris nodded "I have never been there, but Aelianus has told me stories about the Egyptians, their pyramids and the Red Sea."

Daminian smiled "Yes well, the kingdom I was born in is called Aksum, it is South of Egypt and it controls the area of the Southern half of the Red Sea. That location has made Aksum a very influential Kingdom in that part of the world, much like Rome. It holds sway over the Southern half of the Red Sea, into the Indian ocean and its trade goods can be found even beyond that.

Tykie spoke up "It is a trading juggernaut whose gold and ivory make it a vital link between Egypt and the Far East."

Daminian continued "The kingdom is similar to Egypt, it has developed special buildings of massive stone obelisks, which are temples. Some of them are huge, roughly the height of 20 men....

Pris asked "Are you from a noble family of Aksum?"

Daminian smiled, "No, my father was born a fisherman, my parents married young and I was the last of eight children."

Pris smiled, "Your parents were a healthy match."

Daminian smiled bitterly. "True they made many children, but we did not always have enough to eat. So, one year when my father and his two brothers had a great catch. They saved all the extra fish they could by smoking and salting the meat, then they worked tirelessly to sell their products in the market. They did not make huge profits after feeding all of us, but our lives slowly began to improve."

Pris pointed out the way to Palatine hill.

Daminian continued "So, my uncle and father used the extra profits to start a trading business. My uncle's friend was involved in hunting animals such as elephants, rhinos and others, he proposed we sell some of those catches to the Egyptians. They began selling to a merchant in Egypt whom they met at our city's market. Things began to improve for our family finally, still not much because we were a large family. My older brothers and sisters all grew up and got married. A few brothers went off to do their own businesses, a farmer, a hunter, a couple became soldiers, my three sisters all started having children of their own, two other brothers became fishermen, then it was my turn."

Tykie motioned to Daminian, "This is interesting, a rags to riches story!"

Daminian acknowledged and continued "My mother died due to a fever about this time, and my father remarried; they soon had a new child. By this time, I was married, but fate soon took her ...." Daminian paused.

Pris asked "What happened?"

Daminian looked at her as he wiped a tear away, "She and the baby died in childbirth."

Pris said "I'm sorry..."

Daminian nodded "I mourned for a long time, months went by and finally when my father was away on a trade mission with one of my brothers. It was then that my father's wife came to me. We started drinking and talking, she made a pass, but I denied her. When father returned she told him lies. I tried to argue, but he did not believe me."

Tykie said "Wow captain, sad story..."

Daminian said "My father said that I must join the next merchant ship to go to Greece via Egypt to sell our goods with my uncle as captain. Our products were ivory, incense, iron and gold. We stopped first in Egypt, we sold our many goods in their market in Alexandria, and we purchased Egyptian perfumes and fabrics. We were enroute to Greece from Egypt when a storm hit us. My uncle was on topside trying to tie down the mainsail that had come loose in the howling wind. The ship rocked from a sudden large wave that hit us. We took on a large amount of water and I was helping to bail water out. It was only after an hour of fighting the storm that we all realized that my uncle had been blown overboard. We looked for days circling in the same water's area however we never found him".

Tykie whistled "Damn, sometimes Poseidon takes us without warning".

Daminian nodded his lips, cringed for a moment, "He was a good man." Then he continued, "The sales in Greece were a success, the Hellenistic kingdom of Athens was hungry for new and interesting items, we made a big profit."

"After Athens, we returned to Egypt and sent word about my uncle's death. The Sea is your favorite lover, and she can be the merciless monster; like any woman." Daminian laughed with bittersweet sarcasm.

Pris touched his arm "My family, in Germania many are fishermen too, sometimes they don't return."

Daminian smiled, "Life sometimes pushes us into roles we did not see coming or even want. In a way it propelled me to become Captain. My father was hurt by the loss of his brother. They used to argue so passionately when they were together, but my uncle's death was very challenging for him. By this time, his new younger wife had given my father two new children. I did not feel comfortable staying, so I began conducting trade missions. A few years went by;

I was trading between Sicily, Greece, Iberia and even to Britannia. It was on a return trip to Greece from Iberia when I first met Aelianus."

Pris pointed to the very handsome Tykie, "Is that when you two met as well?"

Tykie nodded and Pris blushed a little, she then said:" We are now halfway there" Daminian acknowledged, rolling his eyes while smiling.

Tykie said, "Well, Pris, I am Tykie Nabis, the Spartan and Daminian's 2nd mate. My mother is of royal Macedonian blood, a distant descendant of Alexander's family the King of Macedon. She was married to my father in a political alliance, as he is a younger cousin of the King of Sparta. They had quite an age gap, at their wedding my father was over 35 when my mother was 17, but they were in great health and had five children including me."

They all stopped a moment at a crossroads as a chariot sped past and Pris looked at Tykie ``Macedon, I have heard of that country ...." Tykie smiled "The Macedonians are from Northern Greece. Under Philip the 2nd they conquered most of Greece, except Sparta, around 200 years ago. Then under Alexander the Macedonians conquered the whole Egyptian and Persian empires all the way to India which is at the far end of the Hellenistic world. They may well have come back for Rome had Alexander not died of a fever shortly after conquering all that. Without an heir his empire fragmented into Civil wars."

Pris asked "So your father is a cousin to the King of Sparta?"

Tykie nodded, "Yes, and as cousins they grew up together. My father was one of the men who urged our King not to join the Achaean League, the alliance of Greek countries that fought and lost to Rome,"

Aziri poked "I thought you said that Spartans were always war hungry and are great fighters?"

Tykie picked up a tiny pebble saying "Take this Carthaginian!" and threw it at Aziri which he deflected off his shield laughing.

Pris giggled "I have read many of Aelianus' scrolls, one which talked about a great Spartan King who fought off the Persian empire."

Tykie nodded "Yes that was King Leonidas who led a Greek coalition of 6 to 7,000 Greeks including 300 Spartans vs perhaps 100,000 to 200,000 Persians, that was roughly 350 years ago, when Sparta was at her heyday."

Aziri smirked "Yes, but the Spartans have never changed their style of warfare and about 250 years ago the Spartans were soundly defeated by the Thebans at the battle of Leuctra!"

Tykie showed him a fist "True, Sparta has not been a major military power for some time though we still have had our military traditions even when the Romans showed up. The

Achaean League tried to push us into war to fight Rome, because Sparta is awesome. Yet our current King is wise, knowing Rome's reputation of having beaten Epirus, Macedon, Seleucids and Carthage, he listened to my father who urged our King to not fight against Rome. After the Romans soundly defeated the Achaean League, Rome recognizing that Sparta had selected peace made Sparta a free city again."

Aziri broke in "Tykie's viewpoint of Roman power is that it has some benefits, and he doesn't care too much either way. Tykie just wants to travel and get rich. He is very philosophical, he drives us nuts with his quotes of Socrates, Aristotle and Plato among others, he OFTEN quotes some Greek philosophical crackpot."

Tykie laughed, looking at Aziri "If they were crackpots, why do so many non-Greeks quote them?"

Tykie then looked at Pris, he grinned. "A few years after the war, Daminian arrived offering trade for his goods, my father advised our King to open trade with him and so Daminian and I met at his welcome feast. We spoke at length and being that I have siblings and am not an only child, my parents agreed to let me seek my own fortunes. Unlike some Spartans, I always loved the ocean, so it was a great opportunity for me."

Aziri laughed, "Tykie is only half a member, half the time he is quoting someone."

Tykie pointed at him "That's cause the engine is running right most of the time; and the only true wisdom is in knowing, Aziri, that YOU know nothing."

Aziri pointed at Tykie making a fist while Tykie turned red in the face with laughter."

Daminian's other men all broke out laughing as he said "Ah gods, what would I do without this entertainer? Well played."

Pris clapped, "Hysterical"

Tykie spoke loudly, barely able to control a straight face. "That was Socrates who knew...."

Aziri pointed at Tykie saying "Courage is knowing what not to fear. That's Plato."

Tykie clapped; my cultural lessons have finally stuck in that thick Carthaginian head of yours."

Daminian, laughing at these two, raised his hands, "Enough bickering you two. Pris you already know Aziri's story, these three in the back are Felix, Jason and Taron, Felix was muscular with red hair a man from Iberia, Taron, is from Egypt and Jason the one in the back of our group with the long brown hair is our Seleucid madman, he loves to talk aloud while he fights. All great fighters, who have survived many adventures with me".

Pris nodded, turning a corner Pris pointed ahead. "We are getting close to the Shady Star, it is the fourth building at the far end of that square ahead."

Daminian nodded, "In that case, from here, walk a little behind us, Pris stay near that fountain that is outside the building, keep a lookout on how things are going, we might exit in a hurry otherwise we should be out within an hour."

Pris nodded. Pris let the group walk ahead and then followed at a distance to a fountain where she started speaking to an elderly homeless woman who was sitting there. Pris kept an eye on the group as they got closer to the Shady inn.

The Sun had nearly descended from the sky as they walked past the fountain and towards the building with its large pillars holding the front roof of Doric Roman architectural style at the front of the building that surrounded the front and side. It was a tan four story building that had a simple tavern on the ground floor and three stories above. The side facing the street were all rooms and the back side had no visible windows. The sounds coming from the floors above communicated that it was a very busy brothel on the upper floors. Behind the entry building, there was a connecting building going up four stories, each level had balconies and rooms inside. They noticed a large cart which had double horses attached. There were men loading barrels of something from a side door of the building. Daminian, Aziri, Tykie and the others walked towards the front entrance of the building.

Chapter XXXIX The Brothel

129 BC

No turning back…. Be careful of what you wish for.

As they arrived within a short distance from the building a few men approached them. One of the men, dressed in a brown toga whose hair was cut in a military style, squinted his eyes as he tilted his head asking "Ello, are you all here for our ladies?"

Daminian grinned "We desire an audience with Titus Paullus, we are interested in selling our bounty of ivory."

The thug leader nodded, "Titus will probably be pleased."

Daminian continued "Afterward we will want to celebrate for one lady for each of us."

The thug smirked "Very well, any special requests?"

Daminian nodded "Yes, I was informed that your brothel has a Carthaginian whore, I want her, I have yet to enjoy one of their kind. The others will take any female so long as they are young and healthy"

The thug nodded, "Very good." One of their men turned and went inside the building. They waited outside the entrance as Titus' two men eyed them for a long time, the sun went down and finally the man who ran into the building came back and motioned to them all to follow him inside.

Daminian and his group followed the man inside while the other two guards stayed at the entrance. They entered the building into a large hall that had stairs at the far end going up towards the brothel above. There were a few women, each talking with different male customers each sitting on long sofa chairs. There were two guards standing outside the room at the entrance.

Their guide led them past these people into a large dining room to the right where two men sat at a table. One man was in his 40s, he was dressed in a white toga with a black band, he was muscular and had a sharp look about him. There was a bald man sitting next to him in a brown toga, the bald man looked to be about 10 years older. There were four more guards in the room, two on the left and two on the right. In a far corner, there was a bar where a woman was wiping washed glasses with a rag. Daminian and his men walked up to the occupied table, their footsteps causing the floorboards to squeak.

The man with the white toga spoke as they entered "Greetings, I am Titus Flavious Paullus. I understand you have ivory to sell?"

Daminian nodded, "Yes that is true, I was informed that you are a buyer".

Titus smiled, "Correct, you have any samples?"

Daminian opened his bag and pulled out ivory samples, placing them on the table in front of them, "Here they are."

Titus told the man with the bald shaved head "Ori, pass me that big one." As the other man did so he passed the piece of ivory with his right hand, and doing so Titus' forearm showing his tattoo of lightning with SPQR on it became visible to Daminian and Aziri.

As Ori passed the piece of ivory to Titus.

Daminian said "Also as I told your man outside, my men and I have traveled a long way, we would like some female companionship. I have a special taste for Carthaginian women."

Titus smiled "We can help with that; I have one Carthaginian lady perfect for you and many more for your group" he snapped his fingers and one of the guards left the room.

Daminian smiled "Good, meantime I have a ship full of ivory, how much will you purchase?"

Titus said "We have 100,000 denarius aureus here for a down payment now. I can have another 100,000 by tomorrow. Remaining payment on delivery." Titus snapped his fingers and guards brought over a large box, opening it.

Daminian looked at Tykie "Check it."

Tykie walked over to the box, Titus nodded so the guard opened the box, gold light reflected out of the full box. Tykie whistled "It appears to be all there."

Daminian looked delighted saying "That will be enough."

A woman came into the room with a tray of glasses and a pitcher of wine. Setting it down on the table, Titus told her to bring in their available ladies. A moment later a line of ladies entered the room, each was scantily clad in light togas which deeply revealed their chests and other body parts. Although all of them wore smiles, there was a fear that could be sensed of their not wanting to be there. Titus had stood up to point the ladies out. The last one to arrive of the group was skinny, average height, tan skin, she had long black hair, she had whip scars all over her body's tan skin and looked to be in some dazed state of shock, Aziri saw her and immediately knew it was his younger sister Zaina.

Daminian looked at Aziri, Aziri nodded drawing his sword. The six of them pulled their swords as they were attacked by Titus, Ori and the brothel's guards. The women screamed and rushed for the door; a couple of ladies jumped behind the bar; Zaina still stood there not comprehending what was going on.

Aziri had been the first to engage and his strikes were parried blow for blow against Ori.

Titus had pulled his gladius sword and was in the midst of swordplay parrying back and forth with Daminian.

Tykie had engaged with one of the brothel guards with his xiphos sword, they parried each other back and forth. Tykie dodged left, grabbed his opponent's sword as it shot past hit in a missed stab, wrapping his arm around his opponent's sword arm while pushing forward he dislodged the sword from his opponent's hand. The man reached for his dagger, but Tykie having grabbed his opponent's dropped sword, pivoted back and double stabbed the guard who screamed in agony as he fell from the double sword thrust.

The guard fighting against Taron was an experienced veteran, he stepped back as Taron attacked him dodging Taron's slash; he then stepped in and fatally stabbed Taron, the guard's blade going deep into Taron's heart.

Jason deflected the attacks of the guard who attacked him first, then kicked the guard who had just stabbed Taron. That guard was knocked down for a moment, Jason pulled a knife and while his first opponent locked swords with him, he stabbed him in the stomach. Turning, he then threw his knife into Taron's killer's chest.

Felix engaged with two guards near the door, but these two were strong opponents and they were battling to a draw.

Aziri and Ori had battled each other into the main room, there were women and some other Roman customers running for the door. The two guards from outside came in to see what was going on. Aziri dodged a slash that hit a pillar, he and Ori's sword dueling went back and forth almost as if in a dance. It ranged all around the room, the two guards joined in, but Aziri was too good, they could not land a blow on him, he spun and laughed, elbowing, kicking and hitting them as he fought them all almost dancing around objects. In the process of this dance of death he spun slashing the throat of one attacker and stabbed through the belly of another. Then he started focusing solely on Ori. Ori went upstairs and Aziri followed him where they again engaged in battle.

Meanwhile, Daminian had continued fighting with Titus, in the process a torch lamp was knocked over and landed on top of a table, which caught fire.

Tykie, during this time, was fighting against his attacker who knocked one of his swords away, but while their swords were locked, Tykie grabbed a large glass off the top of a table with his free hand and smashed it on top of his opponent's head, dazing him. Tykie kicked his opponent, grabbing his xiphos sword off the floor and killed him.

Felix was fighting two opponents, one of them turned and engaged against Jason, Felix was defending against his opponent, but then another guard came in from the main room and stabbed Felix from behind through the liver.

Tykie had seen the 3rd opponent rushing up behind Felix and had yelled "Felix watch out...." But it was too late. Tykie let out a yell "Noooooo!!!" He grabbed another sword and again holding two blades attacked all three men yelling "You cannot do that to my friend!!"

Fighting with trance like fury of a possessed Spartan warrior, Tykie yelled in Spartan Greek "*Molon Labe*" quoting King Leonidas meaning "Come and get them" he engaged all three deflecting the closest guard's sword with his right blade, and stabbing him with his left, then pivoting to block the 2nd man's blade during which he pulled out his left blade and it came down in an arche landing deeply into the guard's helmet, the guard twitched and fell, all was done so quickly the guards had no time to react. Tykie was now able to engage the one who had backstabbed his friend Felix, the guard lunged his blade at Tykie, who hit the sword from underneath the hilt sending it flying with the guard losing a finger. Tykie then took both of his swords and stabbed them deeply into the guard's chest. The man stood there dying, but he did not fall quickly so Tykie pulled out one sword and sliced his head off.

Titus had dodged one of Daminian's sword thrusts and kicked him in the stomach and hit him on the back of the head with his hilt. Daminian fell, unconscious.

Titus turned and saw that Jason was just finishing his attacker, and that Tykie was going berserk on three guards dispatching them one by one. Titus pulled a dagger and threw it.

Jason had just turned from his kill and tried to dodge the knife, but it still hit him in his left shoulder.

Titus turned back to finish off Daminian but he was suddenly struck by a stone to his head. Titus fell over and did not move. At the doorway stood Pris with a slingshot in hand.

Tykie and Jason saw her and offered their thanks. Tykie went to Daminian, seeing him out cold, Tykie grabbed a pitcher of water from the bar and threw it on Daminian, waking him up. "I always wanted to do that" he said with a laugh.

Daminian woke up, as he was getting up Pris went to Jason to remove the knife and make a makeshift bandage. During the battle Zaina had shrunk into a ball, shaking in fear. There were many whip markings all over her back and a branding slave mark on her back as well. Daminian told Pris and Jason to help Zaina to the cart as he took out some rope and tied Titus up then carried him out.

Tykie went over to his friend Felix, who was bleeding out. Tykie held Felix's hand, it was cold, he was delirious "Father, I…. come to the-e" he whispered as blood poured out of his mouth and the opening in his back. Tykie shouted, "Felix, HANG ON, WE CAN SAVE YOU…." But in that moment Felix's eyes shut and his spirit passed. Tykie shouted "NOOOOOOO!"

Pris came up and touched Tykie's shoulder, "I'm sorry for your friend, but we have to get out of here".

Daminian told Jason to see if the wagon was still outside the building. He and Tykie carried Felix and Taron's bodies and put them in the cart.

Chapter XXXX Wins and loses….

129 BC

They came quickly back, Daminian led a bound Titus out the door. Above Aziri and Ori's swords clashed back and forth, Aziri's laughter could be heard as he kicked Ori in the stomach then spun around to kill a guard who had burst into the room and then Aziri spun around again to defend Ori's next attack at him, seemingly in one movement.

Daminian and Tykie ran back into the building, ran across the hallway back into the room. A few moments later they appeared hauling the chest that contained the gold. Daminian yelled "Aziri, stop playing with that creep we need to get out of here!"

Aziri glanced down from where he was fighting on the second floor, he saw them carrying the chest across the floor via the atrium. Suddenly two more guards entered the room to join Ori. Ori's breath came in quick heaves, but he kept a determined face. Aziri was a little surprised that Ori was still alive and fighting vigorously, though neither he nor Aziri was able to beat the other. Aziri yelled: "Daminian! Can we stay and finish these clowns?"

Daminian and Tykie were nearing the doorway to go out, he shook his head yelling, "We have lost two already, and Jason is badly wounded. We have your sister; we leave now!" Aziri smirked about how Ori had battled him for a good 10 minutes without either of them having an advantage until he had got a lucky slash on Ori's leg just before the last two guards had come from above.

Daminian commanded again "Come now, your revenge has to wait!" as he and Tykie went out the door.

Aziri growled, "Another time then Roman filth!"

Aziri kicked a chair that flew hitting Ori, he then ran jumping onto the railing of the Atrium, and kicked off it. Flying through the air he caught a large round iron chandelier that held for a moment before the chain broke by his weight. Aziri fell down with the chandelier landing on top of a sofa with the chandelier crashing on top of a marble table that had a priceless flower vase. The table and vase were destroyed with a metallic echoing boom that saw Aziri bounce off the sofa in a ricochet, his body flew crashing against a wall. Laughing "Wow, that was great!" Aziri yelled. Quickly Aziri started running for the door as he heard guards approaching from the upstairs stairway.

Aziri ran out after his group who were all outside, he noticed that night had come. He hopped into the back of their commandeered two-horse wagon. Jason was at the helm with Pris. Titus, Daminian and Zaina were in the middle with their dead comrades, Tykie and Aziri were at the back of the wagon with a few empty wooden wine barrels. Aziri yelled "I'm in!"

Pris set them off, the wagon quickly picking up speed. They got about a block down the street when they saw a chariot rapidly approaching from behind. Pointing at it, Daminian shouted "Time to lighten our load".

Tykie and Aziri knocked over one of the empty wine barrels pushing it off the edge of the cart. The barrel landed and exploded. The next one he pushed bounced and the chariot had to swerve in order not to run into the barrel, but it was not stopped. The driver and his companion were able to get going again as the cart turned a corner now heading rapidly after them in the direction of the river. The chariot started to catch up again and so they dropped the last barrel, this time the chariot had nowhere to swerve and the barrel hit the right wheel exploding and the wheel shot off hitting a building. The chariot skidded along on one wheel, the driver and passenger jumping out as the chariot rolled out of control and then slammed into a building. Pris led their wagon through a couple more backstreets with turns before finally slowing down to stop behind another wagon full of hay.

They could hear Roman soldiers marching at double pace going towards the direction of the Shady Star, they pulled a tarp over the back of the wagon as a group of legionnaires marched right past them. It was important not to draw attention after the Romans had passed by, Pris said to the others "I'm happy we got out of there alive. Your ship and the port are straight ahead, but I will get out here and return to Aelianus' tavern; good luck to you!"

Daminian said "Pris you saved my life, I am in your debt. After the events of today, my ship will be leaving tomorrow at first light. This creep Titus we have has powerful friends. If all went as planned, Aelianus' wine should have all been onboarded by this evening. You may come with us if you wish." Pris smiled, "I am tempted, but my children are here as is Aelianus."

Daminian nodded "Let Aelianus know that I am leaving no later than dawn tomorrow, I will return in six months. You have until dawn my dear to make your final decision. Any longer and I would be jeopardizing my ship."

Pris nodded and turned to Zaina gently touching her shoulder "You will be alright now" Zaina smiled a little and then suddenly gave Pris a hug "Thank you."

Aziri hugged them both, then Pris climbed off the wagon "Good luck my friends."

The group all waved to Pris as Tykie urged the horses to start walking again towards the river and their ship was now in view.

Pris hurried back to Aelianus' tavern and thought of home remembering her father's voice and his prayer: *"We are one with nature, we leave to feed our families taking only what we need, oh nature please give us the prize and a safe trip home."*

Pris got about halfway to the tavern when she started shaking. It was the first time that she had seen so much death in many years. Flashbacks of the battle of her childhood leapt into her mind, her mother's death, her kidnapping, all of the years of slavery, the fishing trip, all these things came to her mind. Even now, walking through Rome wearing Roman clothing, and speaking fluent Latin, she still stuck out like a sore thumb. Everyone here was Italian, tan skin, brown or black hair.

As she turned a corner, at a crossing a bored centurion stood with his legionnaires, they held torches and were questioning everyone who passed. The centurion asked her for her walking pass. His six men all looked like they had nothing better to do. She produced the scroll Aelianus had given her for free passage. The legionnaires were all wearing the standard Lorica Hamata chainmail vests, they all wore red capes, the centurion wore ocreae protective leggings worn on his shins, his men had plain metal helmets, this centurion's helmet had a red transverse crest that went from ear to ear. They were all armed with spears, gladius swords and daggers. "Hello pretty slave, where are you going?"

Pris smiled "Returning to my master from the market". The centurion raised an eyebrow circling Pris ``You have no products, did not buy anything?"

Pris replied "My master ordered me to buy fresh eggs, but the market was sold out".

The centurion grabbed her, rubbing her down all over her breasts, side of her body, all the way between her legs "You do not have any weapons, do you?" He touched her excessively, "We had reports of a disturbance across the city."

Pris controlled herself to not become angry, feeling violated from this rub down, responding, "I could not create such a disturbance."

The centurion smirked, too busy enjoying the grope to pay attention to what the woman said "Ah, what have we here, a sling and a dagger?" The Centurion pulled out her weapons.

Pris responded "Those are standard lengths, law says that we may have them with our master's approval, you can see my master's waxed imprint on the scroll."

The centurion dropped the dagger and sling to reread the scroll "True, I see that. Well, there are your little picker and squirrel stone chucker, pick them up and be on your way."

As Pris bent over to pick her items off the ground he slapped her ass. "Have a nice day now."

The centurion said turning not looking at her or seeing her face flush red as he walked back to his men who roared in laughter giving their centurion high fives.

Chapter XXXXI Subhuman

129 BC

The last night of servitude....

Pris walked on, feeling violated, the centurion had touched her everywhere. How dare he disrespect me so, I am not even human to that animal, Pris thought. Pris had to step into a side alley to regain her composure.... "That perverted twit! Revenge with a whip would be delicious...."

Pris returned to Aelianus' tavern, it was closed as Aelianus was expecting Rufus to arrive this evening.

Septimus was just exiting the tavern, *"What's wrong deir, ya all right?"*

Pris looked at him and sighed, "Maybe you'll understand. A centurion felt me all over at a check point on the way home. It is so hard to not shout at men like him... I cannot mouth off or even report such violations."

Septimus put his hand on her shoulder, "True deary, in the minds of most Romans, aside from myself, Aelianus and Rufus, you are still a slave and of inferior ethnicity."

Pris said "I know right? I can do everything right for the rest of my life here in Rome, but I have no real security here. If I am raped by a centurion or even a normal Roman citizen on the street, I have no legal rights or power to redress any grievances, except to say thank you. If a Roman kills me, my children would not have any justice. If a Roman centurion killed my children over some crime, there would be no power for me to help them."

Septimus shrugged, "It isn't much better for us poor folk either love."

Pris nodded, "I've seen. Also Roman women will never accept me as one of their own. As long as I live in Rome I will be an outsider, and it took the events of today for me to finally decide that I cannot tolerate this situation any more."

Septimus looked at her sideways, "What will you do?"

Pris shrugged, "Aelianus told me before that I could have my freedom. I think I will take his offer and take my kids back to Germania."

Septimus said "Hmmm, well love, I will be going to a certain tavern tonight that is close by. He pointed down the street to another establishment. "I have always wanted to visit my old legionnaire friend, he lives in Mediolanum up North so if Aelianus agrees I can escort you at least that far. I will drop by here tomorrow morning just in case."

Pris smiled "Thank you Septimus. Enjoy your night tonight."

Septimus gave her a hug and walked off towards a lively tavern a few buildings down the street.

Pris entered into the Happy Moon, she saw that most of the slaves had gone with Sabina. Pris had expected that Sabina would be surrounded by her servants waiting on her hand and foot having Helga help her try on various gowns and jewelry. As Pris went through the tavern and into the home section, she said hello to the two guards who were posted at the entryway Octavian and Morbius, Roman legionnaire veterans whom Aelianus had hired to be his personal guards. Pris asked "Octavian and Morbius, do you know where Sabina, Helga and the other servants are?"

Octavian said "Sabina and most of the servants left for the beach villa hours ago. Septimus stayed to cover until Aelianus returned, then Aelianus sent him home for the evening. Aelianus is inside his office."

Aelianus looked alarmed, "Thank you for telling me. Tell the guards to be extra careful tonight, Vicidius might think I was behind the attack." Pris nodded "Very well master, I shall let them know".

Pris nodded, then greeted their Rottweiler dog, Maximinian.

Pris went to Aelianus, told him about what had happened at the Shady Star, about Titus, of Daminian's decision to leave at dawn, and confirmed that they were expecting Senator Rufus this evening and that he wanted to be served dinner.

Pris saw that Sarth and Luciana were in the garden playing. When Pris entered the kitchen, she looked through Helga's backup cooking scrolls. Pris read through a few recipes before finding the one Aelianus had requested based on what they had available. Pris saw her own cook scrolls that she had copied, one for Aelianus and another for herself. Pris started grabbing ingredients for the meal, she was slicing some vegetables when she saw that Helga had left a note for her that read:

Pris,

Sabina arrived home while you and our master were out. She has summoned us to go to the beach with her.

This is all very sudden, I've no idea when we will be home. It is strange because she has not informed our master.

Be well.

-Helga.

Pris read it, strange that Sabina had left suddenly, she usually liked to have her servants pack days' worth of clothing at least a day or two beforehand, but that was not the case last night.

After a few minutes Pris fed the dog, then went into the kitchen to make dinner. hey came to the kitchen after smelling the sweet aroma of Pris' cooking tomato sauces and spices which would come together to make a tomato-based sausage bean noodle soup, with a chopped cranberry vinaigrette arugula salad and toasted garlic sourdough bread that Pris had made a couple days earlier.

Rufus loved Aelianus she knew, they both loved Pris' cooking. Ingrid and Helga had taught Pris many types of Greek, Germanic and Celtic ethnic foods, Pris had picked those up over time and learned a number of Roman-Greek and some Germanic dishes similar to what she remembered her mother making. Pris said "Luciana dear, we will have company for dinner tonight, please get your harp ready in the dining room and do a little practicing before our guest arrives."

Luciana smiled, "Yes mamma."

The soup was beginning to bubble and bread was in the oven when Pris opened a blank scroll in which she penned a goodbye letter to Aelianus.

Sarth came into the kitchen "What are you writing mom?"

Pris took a deep breath, "I'm writing a goodbye letter."

Sarth sensed the seriousness of her response "To who?"

Pris' mouth contorted, "It is truly hard to write as he had been such a benevolent master." Pris started to tear up…

Sarth asked "Why must we say goodbye? He saved us twice…"

Pris said "Aelianus is the only Roman I trust, but we will never be accepted as Romans. It is time to take you and Luciana North, we will live with my father among the Cimbri in Germania."

Sarth asked "Do you think Aelianus will let us leave?"

Sarth nodded "I believe so. If Aelianus gives us a pass, we could travel without harassment."

Sarth asked "If Aelianus refuses?"

Pris said "I have another way for us. Those sailors who came to the tavern today."

Sarth asked "What sailors?"

Pris shook her head "Don't worry about it. Why don't you go prepare your stuff?"

Pris then went into the library carrying the scrolled message in hand and gave the message to Aelianus.

Handing the scroll to Aelianus was very hard. How would he react?

Aelianus read the scroll and a very sad look came over his face, he grimaced, but nodding, he said "This is something I have hoped to put off for another few years, but I understand… Rome is dangerous even for me. We cannot control fate, just try to swim with the current. I will write a pass for you and your children to use to get through Roman lands; but first…" Aelianus surprised her, he gave her a big hug. "So, my dear, tonight we will be celebrating your goodbye feast for you all as you leave for a new life." Aelianus stopped, his voice became halting, his speech strained. "You are the woman… I have loved…. as much as a sister. As much as…. I loved my late grandmother. Farewell then dear Pris, tonight will be our final hurray."

Pris nodded, also feeling bittersweet tears of joy and sadness "Thank you Aelianus, you are a fine man, I hope you will continue to have a great life".

Aelianus nodded and they hugged again. Holding his tears back, Aelianus smiled "Now then, let us celebrate tonight. My only request is that you leave copies of those wonderful cooking scrolls of yours."

Pris nodded, "I made copies of them for you weeks ago, they're in the kitchen."

Aelianus nodded, "Excellent, there is a cart of hay beneath the balcony to feed the horses that you can take, there are three to pick from, you may have two."

Pris took a deep breath, "I ran into Septimus when I came in, he has offered to escort us up to Mediolanum tomorrow morning if it is alright with you."

Aelianus nodded, "That will be fine. I will have Septimus take you to Mediolanum and from there he can arrange for a guide to take you Northward. Mediolanum is the most Northern Roman city in Italy, next to the Alps, so it will be on your way home."

Pris nodded, smiling "Thank you."

Aelianus smiled, wiping a tear away "Alright then, well before dinner, I need to finish up a few things before Rufus arrives, Gods know I get little done while he is around. I want a large bottle of my best wine with a couple goblets in my study." Pris went downstairs, brought back the wine to

Aelianus and then she returned to the kitchen to attend the soup.

Rufus arrived and after greeting the guards, the children in the garden and the dog, came over to greet Pris to smell the soup. "My word Pris, you make masterpieces every time you cook. Marvelous, you are without a doubt the best cook in Rome."

Rufus gave Pris a smile then asked where Aelianus was, pointing to the library Rufus then called through the Atrium "Aelianus!" From across the villa Aelianus yelled excitedly from his office "Rufus, come here! I want to share something extraordinary, opportunities await us!" Rufus went up the stairs and into the study where Aelianus waited.

After Rufus arrived, Aelianus told him about the ship and then next told Rufus that he had freed Pris and given her passage to return to Germania with her children.

Rufus frowned, "I shall miss her cooking. Be sure to get her to give you copies of your favorite recipes!"

Aelianus nodded "Done." They enjoyed the wine and soon Rufus' toga was thrown on a chair as they began their love making in the study.

Pris meantime had packed her own and the children's bags.

Chapter XXXXII Aelianus and Rufus

129 BC

A pleasant evening....

When finished, Aelianus and Rufus came out to the dining room hungry for food. Pris giggled noting, Rufus had arrived tonight wearing his purple toga to Aelianus' study, but that they had stayed there quite a while as their sounds of love making had ensued, when they came out he was not wearing his purple robe. Clearly they came out holding hands as happy lovers; enjoying each other's company completely.

Pris brought their food to the dining room and was delighted to find a bag of gold coins with a sealed official pass for their travel through Roman lands and a thank you note from Aelianus. Pris prayed to the Gods that Aelianus would be alright and that she and her children would travel safely.

Pris served Aelianus and his guest Senator Rufus dinner. Aelianus asked "Pris, first I would like your children to also eat. Then if Luciana would play her cithara that would be wonderful."

Pris clapped, the children came out of the kitchen, Aelianus asked "Have you both eaten?"

Luciana smiled as the children both said "Yes Aelianus."

Pris asked "Would you play for them?"

Luciana played the cithara masterfully for them as Sarth stood by ready to refill their wine.

Aelianus clapped his hands after tasting the soup and food "Absolutely perfect!"

Rufus said "This was the best meal I have ever eaten."

Pris was very pleased.

As they all listened to Luciana play the cithara; Rufus told Pris "You and your children are wonderful people and that our Roman Republic would be lucky to have her continued friendship in the future."

Chapter XXXXIII Traaz strikes

129 BC

The snake strikes....

The clouds parted that evening and a full moon shone on Rome. Two men met outside a large home on the West side of Rome near the Tiber River. Traaz was standing on the ground and had been juggling his knives in the air when Vicidius rode up, his hands and chest were covered in blood, there were signs of lots of blood on his clothes as well. Traaz wore a hooded cloak, leather armor and everything he wore was either a dark brown or black color.

Vicidius looked at him, "All good with Rufus?"

Traaz laughed, "Rufus was not there, but I took care of his staff, they will never be a concern again."

Vicidius nodded, *all for the greater good, Traaz did what had to be done.* Vicidius gave Traaz a scroll "This will protect you if I am away and you get caught."

Vicidius was eager to have the operation start, sitting on his war horse wearing Roman armor and weapons, finally revenge would be his. Vicidius said "I noticed there are wine barrels next to the stable entrance. You should block the back stable door with one so they cannot escape that way."

Traaz nodded "Yup, no prob."

Vicidius motioned towards the tavern, "Well, now that you are warmed up, go do it."

Nodding, the assassin sheathed his knives and walked across the street, pulling out keys that opened the front gated door. Vicidius sat on his horse, a minute later a column of legionnaires passed him, not stopping. He looked at the tavern and house intently. Slipping inside the assassin closed the door but did not shut it completely. In the tavern, the assassin pulled a rag out of his pocket and poured clear liquid on it. The house dog came over wagging its tail, the assassin walked over to it calmly, knowing the dog, "Here Maximus, good boy…" he placed the rag on its mouth violently and held it there as the dog struggled desperately for a moment then fell over limp.

As it died Traaz giggled gleefully, "No more picking up your dog shit! Filthy animal!" He waited to be sure it was dead by holding the rag to the dog's mouth for a long time after it had gone limp. He then went towards the taverns and villa's connecting door.

Meanwhile Aelianus and Rufus happily enjoyed their best wine in his Lycurgus wine goblets as the melodies of Luciana's cithara harp poured out. Aelianus was in an exceptionally good mood. Sarth had stood by the back wall ready with the wine and water. After Luciana's skillful playing, Aelianus and Rufus applauded loudly at the table.

Aelianus said loudly "Marvelous dear!"

Traaz, the assassin, used the cover of the music to hide his steps. He entered the entryway for the house and pulled

417

his two daggers. Jumping through the connecting entryway, Traaz stabbed both the guards Octavian and Morbius at the same time in their necks. Both were choking on their own blood unable to scream, only gargling hissing sounds came out of them as their bodies twisted in agony and then fell dead to the floor. Traaz immediately grabbed them, one in each hand, catching the bodies as they fell to lighten any noise. Traaz rubbed his hands, giggling, then looking around hid the bodies next to rose bushes out of view from the second floor. Traaz hurried to the stables to spend a little time with the horses. "Beautiful beasts" He hissed.

After playing for a while Luciana missed a cord, Aelianus saw Luciana yawn before she started playing again. Aelianus walked over clapping as he said with a happy drunk voice, "Ah my young treasure, you are simply magnificent" he gave her a kiss on her head and then turning to Pris who had just returned from the kitchen with a dessert cake, "My dear, your children seem tired, they will need energy for their travels tomorrow. Send them to bed for the night".

Pris smiled and nodded, Motioning to her children "Time for bed children."

Sarth and Luciana both hugged Aelianus. Then Pris led them to their room.

Luciana said "Momma, I will miss Aelianus."

Sarth agreed, "Yeah, Aelianus is such a good man."

Pris thought for a moment "I know, we were lucky to have him. You have to trust me that we will be happier and safer where we are going."

Sarth asked "Will we ever return?"

Pris said "Rome is powerful, I will tell our people about Rome. Perhaps the Cimbri can be allies with Rome, perhaps trade with Rome via my friend Daminian's ship? We must return home."

Pris did not blame the Romans for her captivity, but she knew that if she stayed, she would never truly be Roman or at ease here. It was the looks she got at the market and wherever she went from other Roman ladies, the treatment by the Roman legionnaires, like the centurion in the street, they just would never see her as an equal human being. Pris' unquenched anger was focused at the ones who had captured her, it was that traitor Ubel, his Swabian friends, and Raez the Taurisci who had whipped her. They were the ones who had originally kidnapped her and murdered her mother all those years ago.

Pris recalled her killing Wador, he had been such an evil merciless man. May Hades burn his soul for eternity. Pris thought. Pris' mind went back to Krull and Tuli. Did father survive his wounds? Is he and Tuli still alive? Pris had not forgotten what he looked like. She hoped for the best and smiled as she thought hopefully in a few more weeks we might all be reunited again!

Pris led her children down the hall looking out into the atrium over the garden thinking of what needed to be packed for their journey and decided she would be extra fast cleaning in the kitchen tonight before she went to bed. Pris was too excited to sleep and knew that her children would only be able to sleep a few hours before they all would get up early, finish packing and then leave by wagon with Septimus, exciting as the journey with Daminian's ship would be traveling with Septimus seemed safer than traveling by sea.

Pris made her children use the bathroom and then put them to bed. She thought again about how different and advanced Roman life was in comparison to the village life she had grown up in, how she would miss Roman bathrooms, and baths. Pris planned to ask Tykie if she ever met him if he knew how to make a Roman style toilet, wishing she had asked him before.

After her children were in bed, Pris returned to the dining room where Aelianus and his guest sat talking about business and political developments while still enjoying more wine. Pris put some dirty plates on a cart, it had been a long day. She glanced down and noticed that their dog Maximus was missing, and the dog had not come begging for food during dinner, strange as that was, she assumed Maximus must be asleep in the tavern or maybe the guards had fed him? Pris just wanted to get the dishes washed before so she could start preparing for her journey.

Aelianus came over to the kitchen, there he gave her a last hug. Aelianus' face was quite red from the wine and he was wobbling in his walk "My dear…. Thank you for everything. How soon will you leave?"

Pris tried to smile, "As soon as you can prepare the wagon and have Septimus ready."

Aelianus nodded, "Understood, Septimus will come in after his breakfast. I will have the wagon ready by then."

Pris nodded "That will be fine. Oh I want to remind you that Daminian is leaving tomorrow at dawn, but he said he will return in about six months."

Aelianus nodded. "Understood. You know, letting you go is one of the hardest things I have ever done. You will always have a friend in me no matter where you go or how long we are separated." Aelianus sighed, he gave her a kiss on her cheek, then he gave a wine impacted smile "Now Rufus and I are off to bed".

Pris watched Aelianus and Rufus walk to the master bedroom holding hands. Pris then went to the table to collect dirty plates. From the shadows of the stable the assassin Traaz hissed "About fucking time, this place stinks." He then realized that he had stepped in horse shit.

Pris carried the collected plates to the kitchen and began to wash them.

In the children's bedroom Sarth woke up. "Oh no!" Sarth whispered, "my practice sword, the one Aelianus gave me... I cannot let that get left behind!" Sarth got up, seeing Luciana was asleep he walked out of his room determined to get his practice blade. Sarth went downstairs to the armory which had a bathroom next to it.

From Aelianus' bedroom Pris soon heard the sounds of love making from inside. *My myyy, so much energy tonight she thought.* She continued scrubbing the plates, bowls, goblets and silverware in a cleaning bowl thinking about her life that she had somewhat enjoyed while living under Aelianus' care.

Suddenly she heard a shrill piercing yell from Aelianus' bedroom followed almost immediately by Rufus' screaming "No!" followed by another scream.

Unlike the sounds of love making, these were the same type of screams that she had heard at the Shady Star, of the fishing trip, and of the battle she had experienced long ago. Horror gripped her for an instant, then her protective instincts as a mother and Aelianus' lessons about taking control of a situation kicked in, she grabbed a sharp cooking knife.

Outside, Vicidius thought he heard screams coming from the back of the house. He thought *"Is that Traaz who has succeeded or did Aelianus kill Traaz?"* He paced his horse irritably back and forth, then galloped over towards the back of the house wanting to recheck if the stable exit had been blocked by Traaz as he had requested, it hadn't.

Cursing Traaz, Vicidius dismounted and moved a large wine barrel to sit in front of the stable's door; it was very heavy. Vicidius had been fighting the urge to urinate, but couldn't wait longer, so too some time to do this.

Finishing, Vicidius thought "Perhaps I should go in himself, he had his sword out and gently felt the barn door, but remembered his plan. No, if Traaz succeeded, all is well. If he failed, Aelianus is likely awake with a sword in his hand, I might not win against him. Besides, if I don't go in, Aelianus would likely think Traaz had independently tried to kill him.

Chapter XXXXIV Time to escape the Assassin...

129 BC

Time to escape the Assassin....

Fearing something awful, Pris left the kitchen with a large knife in hand, she could not go directly to her kids room as it was blocked by a large stack of wine barrels. She ran across the hallway floor of the atrium past the dining room and looked into Aelianus bedroom from the opened door. With shock she saw Aelianus' twitching body on the bed, his back was oozing blood from the fatal stab wound and Senator Rufus who had been receiving Aelianus during their love making had lost his head.

The cloaked assassin stood there breathing heavily, his gladius' blade shinny with blood as the two victims' blood was still gushing all over the bed, the assassin seemed to be enjoying all the blood as he stood there laughing with his hands spread out. Blood was everywhere, and a little had sprayed over Aelianus' own gladius that hung from the wall above the bed.

Pris ran towards her children's room. In a panic, she wondered why the dog had not barked any alarm about the assassin. Pris ran as fast as she could, suddenly she heard a high-pitched nasally voice yell out "Hey!!" Then she heard the sounds of a man starting to chase her from a distance behind. "You're dead!!" The assassin yelled after her.

As she rounded the corner, she saw ahead a very sleepy-eyed Luciana come out of her room, she asked "Mommy what's going on?"

Pris screamed to Luciana in Cimbrian language "Where is Sarth?!" she swept Luciana up and glanced into her kids' room as she passed it.

Luciana cried "He is not here!"

Behind them the assassin had just turned the corner and was catching up, "Come here!" he yelled.

Pris saw that Aelianus' office door was open and she ran in carrying Luciana immediately she slammed the door closed and swung the large wooden lock in place to bolted it. She led Luciana to the balcony, hearing the assassin ramming himself against the door cursing loudly.

Luciana gasped "That bad man is Traaz!"

Pris nodded, "His high-pitched voice was unmistakable. Ok, there were only two ways out of here, we either go back through the door where the assassin is or over the balcony."

Luciana said "What about Sarth?"

Pris shook her head, "I will have to go back for him." She grabbed the purple toga that Rufus had left on Aelianus' chair, Luciana watched as she tied it to a small pillar holding the balcony's concrete hand rest. There was a cart full of hay below that Aelianus had purchased for the horses. Suddenly there was a ringing sound, it was the servant summoning bell which was in Aelianus' room. Pris told her daughter "Hang onto me!" Once Luciana grabbed onto her shoulders she went over the side and scaled down the wall for a few feet, then dropped into the cart full of hay. Pris could still hear the ringing from inside where she and Luciana had landed in the hay filled cart below. For a moment, Pris briefly thought Aelianus might be ringing it, but then decided that was impossible. *With that wound, and that much blood, my dear master is surely dead.* The clucking sound of a horse's approaching trot came to Pris. *We do not have much time*, she immediately got herself then Luciana out of the cart. Pris quickly smoothed the hay to look like it had not been smashed, then they ran across the street to hide between a neighbor's house and some bushes.

From their hiding place behind an alleyway's entrance Pris saw a Roman officer appear around the corner a few moments later on horseback, he rode over and waited across from Aelianus' tavern's main entrance. Pris thought *"That Legionnaire is not a night watch patrol, he is waiting for something, he must be in on the attack!"* The officer held an unlit torch, seeing a posted lit torch on the wall, he lit it which illuminated his face, she could just make out that he had a scar that went from his eyebrow to the bottom of his cheek, gasping she recalled that Vicidius' face was identically scarred from when she saw him at Aelianus' tavern.

Vicidius' attention was on Aelianus' home not the street, though he quickly noticed the hanging toga flapping in the wind; he started looking around the building that was Aelianus' home. When Vicidius rode around the far corner, she thought He must be checking the back entrance. Pris waited a few more moments, every ounce of her screamed to go back to save Sarth, but she had no sword and no idea if Sarth was alive, if the assassin would catch and kill her and then what would happen to her children?

Pris struggled to hold herself, her hands shook.

Luciana asked "Momma, should we go back for Sarth?"

Pris yearned "If I go back and I am killed you would be in trouble. We can only hope Sarth is hiding inside, we need to get help."

Luciana nodded "Sarth is great at hide and go seek, he might be ok!"

Pris hoped, "He is also clever, I think he just rang the summoning bell to save us. It is only 15 minutes to the river if we take the alleyways, Aelianus' friends are there. We must get help. Let's go now."

They hurried over into the alley when Vicidius rode back around the other side of the house. He circled back stopping in the main street, where he looked around for a moment, then he returned to stay across from the main entrance, he kept looking around, but mainly watching the home.

Pris didn't risk any more time, Pris nudged Luciana to start hurrying towards the river. After they had gotten well into the alley and the shadows, Luciana asked as a whisper, "Why didn't we ask the legions to help us?"

Pris shook her head, "We are not Romans, and one of the killers is Roman or at least he was wearing an officer's uniform. We will go seek help from Daminian and his men, then return back here for Sarth."

Pris thought I will go back for him with or without their help, but first I must save Luciana. Pris knew this alley well she had taken many times, it was too narrow for a horse, and it would take them straight towards the river, they stayed in the shadows hurrying briskly towards the Tiber River. Pris wanted to hurry, so she carried Luciana on her back as she ran towards the Tiber seeking Daminian's ship.

Back at the house, two men in dark clothing rapidly approached Vicidius and called him out; both were out of breath. "Vicidius, …. we've been looking all over for you…. The brothel was attacked, your cousin…. Titus was taken captive, our gold was stolen, dozens of our men are dead. Aside from those killed, several of our whores have also fled."

Vicidius looked at him in brief shock, "What? Who did this? Do we know where the attackers went? Ori, tell me how?" Ori tried to catch his breath, "...It happened when they had a meeting with a gang posing to be ivory sellers. That gang had an African leader."

Vicidius nodded, "Ok, do we know where they went?"

Ori nodded "After their attack a pair of our men chased after the commandeered wagon in a chariot, one survived a crash, he was unconscious, but he woke up an hour ago, he said they seemed to be heading towards the river. Our men found our wagon down by the docks and saw the same African on top of the trireme logged in as the Seawitch."

Vicidius nodded, "Ok, good work Ori."

There was a sudden high pitched nasally scream from inside the building. Pointing to it Vicidius said "Ori and Magnus go inside and check on our man, and the targets Aelianus and his lover Rufus. Confirm if Traaz is alive or dead, and if both targets are not already dead. If Traaz our assassin is alive, bring him to our safe house, if not, leave him. Then report your findings to me at the dock."

Vicidius started to gallop off, turning right at the corner to head towards the river.

Chapter XXXXV Pris & Luciana
129 BC

Time to escape Rome....

At the end of the alley, they came to a wide street. A group of 12 Roman soldiers were marching by the side street. They waited until the patrol had marched past; as soon as the legionnaires were a safe distance down the street, they crossed the street and hurried down the alley until it opened to another street. This time they could see the port in front of them and down the dock they could see Seawitch still moored in between a few other merchant ships.

Luciana asked "Mommy, will Sarth be joining us?"

Pris said "Yes, we won't leave without him."

Looking both ways, it looked clear, so they exited the alley and ran to the entrance of the dock. Suddenly from behind them Luciana said "Mommy do you hear that?" A man galloping on a horse approaching from far behind them still on the street.

Pris nodded "Yes, let's go!" they could hear the clap-pity-clap of a horse's hooves at full gallop. They started to run down the dock. They heard the man who began to yell at them in Latin to stop. Pris picked Luciana up and continued running down the dock. Daminian's watch saw the activity and called for Daminian.

Daminian hurried over to the watch to see Pris running towards them on the dock clinging to her child, and a Roman on horseback was galloping in pursuit after them as he came through the entrance to the port.

Pris and Luciana arrived at the ship, shouting urgently "May we come aboard for sanctuary?"

Daminian came to the top of the ship's boarding ramp and said, "Yes, come aboard! What is going on and where is your son?"

Pris pushed Luciana onboard as she shook her head, tears flooding out, "They murdered Aelianus, I need to go back for my son!"

As Pris pleaded, the galloping sounds from the Vicidius' horse could be heard.

Aziri yelled "Roman horseman racing from the gate towards the dock and rapidly approaching!"

From the horse Vicidius stopped once inside the port and his horse reared on its hind legs as he waved his sword in the air and yelled at a group of Roman infantry who were marching on the street, "Men of Rome, follow me!"

Daminian looked in that direction, he saw the legionnaire charge again onto the dock, then he saw the column of Roman infantry following him through the port's entrance. The horseman yelled again as his horse put its first steps onto the start of the dock. "Halt! Do not attempt to leave!"

Daminian yelled "Damn! We cannot stay, come aboard Pris!" He grabbed her wrist as she began to argue. Daminian judged, *Aside from Pris and Aelianus, Titus is below decks in chains….*

Turning to Aziri, Daminian yelled "Use your bow and kill that horseman!"

Pris said "Wait!"

Daminian said "No we go now!" He faced his crew, "Attention Crew, immediate departure, shove off!!" Then he turned back to Pris "No time to save your son, we depart!"

Pris shook her head "Nooooooo!!!!"

Daminian motioned to Tykie "Take her and her daughter below, bring them to Zaina."

Tykie grabbed her as Pris resisted, Luciana began to cry.

Daminian urged "You have your daughter, if we stay, we are all dead."

Aziri had already grabbed his bow and arrows and was getting into position to fire along with three crewmen who were doing likewise. Aziri smiled as he pulled back his arrow, aiming he then shouted "Time to kill the little Roman!"

Daminian turned to them and yelled "Loose!"

Four arrows shot out, one missed, Aziri's arrow struck Vicidius in his breast plate's upper left corner near the left shoulder, the two other arrows shot by the sailors hit the horse which screamed and fell over catapulting Vicidius through the air. He crashed landed into a cart full of fish, which had been unloaded from the neighboring ship.

Aziri swore "Don't shoot a horse you morons!" He turned his eyes sadly from the dying animal.

Nodding his approval and turning, Daminian put his hands to his mouth and shouted, **"ALL HANDS MAN YOUR STATIONS, EMERGENCY DEPARTURE!! TOP CREW UNTIE THE DOCK LINES. OARSMEN PUSH OFF STARBOARD SIDE, ONCE WE ARE OFF, AHEAD FULL OAR POWER!!"** Daminian next turned his position to yell down the shout tube "Tykie, **ASSUME YOUR POSITION IN THE ENGINE ROOM AND FIRE UP THE STEAM ENGINE WITH BLACK MAGIC AT ONCE.**" Daminian turned slightly and yelled **"Aziri at the helm, steer us out per my command, Seawitch goes to sea now!!"**

The crew untied the dock lines, brought up the ramp and pushed their ship away from the dock, the main red sail was untied and opened fully into the gentle wind. "Engine with coal loaded, fire set!" Tykie reported from below.

The ship started making headway under the power of the oarsmen.

On the dock, dozens of Roman infantry ran to the fallen horseman. They reached Vicidius and slapped him awake. Vicidius was stunned, then he yelled, "What is that pain?" He realized he had an arrow sticking into his breastplate.

A legionnaire said "Centurion, are you alright?"

Vicidius said "It must not have gone through the armor, but I feel a terrible stabbing pain. There is a small pin prick." Vicidius yelled furiously "Aaarrrrrrrgggggghhhhhhhh!!" He pulled out the arrow, the legionnaire said "Wow, lucky, it barely got its tip through."

Vicidius saw a parked chariot near the gate of the pier and yelled "Make way!" He then ran for it.

Pris joined Luciana and Zaina in the captain's cabin.

Luciana teared up "Mommy!"

Pris held her as she started shaking herself. Pris shook and tears flooded her vision, holding Luciana Zaina tried to say something, but Pris could not understand her. Zaina then gave both of them a big hug.

The sounds of crew members running around above as they reacted to Daminian's commands were met by sounds of the beating drum of the drummer setting the pace. Seawitch was making fast progress towards the city's wall gate that protected the city from the outside. The steam engine's heat pressure quickly increased as the water inside the tank came to an intense boil. "Engine ready" Tykie called from below, "activating our steam engine!" he reported.

Daminian rang a bell and commanded "Blow the forward horn and switch to the forward exhaust.'"

From the front of the Seawitch exhaust smoke suddenly poured out of the Seawitch's figurehead's mouth and two gusts of white steam screamed out of her nose like a mad dragon loud enough to wake the dead "Hhhhhhhhhrrrrrrrrrrnnnnnnnnnnnk!!" the entire city of Rome within hearing range shuddered inside their homes afraid some monstrous Titan of the Gods was attacking their city.

Daminian yelled "Oarsmen pull in oars!" The rear engine began to quickly spin the main shaft the ship quickly picked up speed pushing away water with the ship quickly gaining speed. He yelled again "Bowmen on the main deck." The oarsmen brought their oars in and grabbed bows, they came to the top deck taking positions along the sides ready to shoot their arrows.

Up ahead at the edge of the city, the walls lined the perimeter and archers whose wall battlements guarded an exterior threat, but there was no defensive surface for a threat coming from within, their walkway was open and they stood looking warily at the approaching demonic looking ship that was blowing a black smoke screen from the figure mount's mouth and the shrill loud bursts of white steam from its eyes as they prepared trembling arrows into their bows.

One legionnaire started shaking and yelled "Perhaps the Gods turned that ship into a Titan or some sea monster?"

Another yelled "We have not seen or heard anything like this ship!"

The horn blew again "Arrrrgh, what is that demonic blowing sound and smoke… Can you see it?"

Another legionnaire yelled "The smoke is screening the demon ship!"

By this time Vicidius had ridden his chariot to the city side of the wall, he climbed the stairs and ran past some archers to where the river gate guard was posted, the man was standing there holding the gate lever, his face looked pale. Arriving, Vicidius saw a dozen legionnaire archers shaking, he barked commands "What are you all doing? Start shooting at the ship!" He turned to the river gate guard, "Close the gate!"

The river gate guard said "Centurion, the river gate was made to keep enemy ships from entering the city, it had never been tested by a ship ramming it from within and that is a demon ship!" He yelled his pointed hand shaking.

Vicidius yelled "We need fire arrows. Where's the oil and fire?"

A legionnaire said "We were not expecting the need for oil provisions!"

Covered by the smoke screen, Daminian ordered "Archers shoot at targets on the wall, loose!" Hundreds of arrows shot out, several Roman archers on the wall were hit at their elevated wall positions, many died. Vicidius jumped to the floor of the wall's walkway, a few arrows landed around him. A few arrows were fired at the ship though none hit any sailors as the smoke was thick.

Daminian ordered "Engine room, blow the horn again!" He grinned at the visibly frightened Romans on the wall "Brace for impact!"

At that moment Seawitch rammed through the gate, a loud explosive noise blasted and rocked throughout the city and valley beyond.

Vicidius cursed "Damn ship!!" He ran across the river on top of the wall then down the wall's steps then he jumped onto another legionnaire's horse and charged towards the ocean.

Daminian yelled down the hole "Tykie, switch to rear exhaust".

Down below Tykie pulled a chain and suddenly the smoke switched to billow from behind the ship.

Daminian saw Vicidius galloping ahead along the road.

After smashing through the gate, Zaina looked at Luciana "She has fallen asleep." They lifted up Luciana and laid her on Daminian's bed. She said "I will stay here with her if you want to see what's happening." Pris said "I am concerned about what was going on." Pris touched Zaina's shoulder and said "Thank you." She gave Luciana a kiss then went topside.

Pris went to Daminian, he was watching Vicidius galloping ahead Pris asked "Can we shoot him with an arrow?" Daminian shook his head, "The road is just out of range."

Pris asked "How long before we reach the ocean?"

Daminian turned to her "30 minutes."

Pris asked, "Can that horse beat us there?"

Daminian nodded, "Beat us, yes, horses can gallop about 4 times faster than we sail. Catching us is another matter."

Pris sat down at the stern and as the rest of the crew maintained their stations. Daminian came over and put his hand on her shoulder, "Be strong."

Pris talked without looking at him, "I cannot stop thinking of Sarth, of Aelianus, Rufus, the guards and our dog. This was not supposed to happen." Tears began to roll down her face.

Daminian nodded and said to her, "Your son may yet live. Are you sure about Aelianus? Do you know if…." The way Pris' eyes flooded with tears as she shook her head told him the answer before she said anything, more tears ran down as she said "He was murdered."

Daminian cursed loudly "Damn it... He was my friend…. Do you know who did it?"

Pris nodded her head, he had been wearing a cloak, and was in the dark when I had a good look at him, but he had a very high-pitched voice, it was unmistakable, it was Traaz, one of the slaves Aelianus owned. But there was another man, a legionnaire waited outside the house. Legionnaires do not sit in front of a house for no reason

438

when patrolling. I noticed while serving dinner that he had been outside our home for at least a half hour before Aelianus' murder.

Daminian crouched down feeling shared sorrow with Pris who was kneeling with her arms wrapped around her knees sobbing, putting his arm around her back after a moment.

Daminian gently said "I have other friends in Rome, a senator who might help. I will send word. Perhaps the killers will be caught."

Pris looked at him "One man is Traaz, Aelianus' former slave. The other I am not sure, though I know a man named Vicidius hated him."

Daminian nodded, "That could make sense given our brothel action earlier." He looked back into the darkness hiding where Vicidius was riding, though they could faintly still hear the hovels clapping along the road. Daminian said "Meantime, my dear, it is not totally safe here, there is not much for you to do now, please go below and protect your daughter." Daminian watched her go below, then returned to the Captain's wheel.

Pris went below, and saw Luciana was still asleep.

Zaina smiled, "I will let you two be alone."

Pris laid next to Luciana whispering "I love you Sarth!" First in Latin, then she switched to Cimbrian *"Ich liebe dich Sarth!"* Pris said over and over in Cimbri.

Chapter XXXXVI Daminian, Tykie & Aziri

129 BC

From the Tiber to the Mediterranean Sea....

The Seawitch was running at full speed as it neared the mouth of the Tiber where it flows into the Mediterranean Sea. Seeing two Roman triremes closing in ahead, Daminian yelled down the tube, "Tykie, all ahead full, adjust to forward exhaust!"

Throwing in a fresh batch of coal and pulling on the screaming horn, Tykie pulled a chain and suddenly the mouth on the figurehead of the Seawitch began blowing plumes of smoke and Tykie blew the horn sending out white steam from the figurehead's eyes as Seawitch quickly picked up a high speed which was unlike anything an oar powered ship was capable of.

Vicidius had gotten to the beach 20 minutes before, and boarded a Trireme and had gotten out to sea in record time. The two Roman triremes were both approaching from the South of the bay in their attempt to block the Seawitch. Vicidius was on the first ship and was closest towards achieving a blocking position, however Seawitch was now going full blast, and blowing smoke out and screaming on the steam horn again, it was simply too fast for the triremes. Sailing along, powered by steam, Seawitch moved at more than twice the speed of the Roman vessels.

The Roman sailors and marines on the two triremes were terrified wondering where in the seven hells had this fire breathing sea monster come from. Seawitch quickly sailed past the Roman triremes just out of archer range. One of the crew on Seawitch showed his moon at the Romans. Vicidius furious at being outplayed screamed angrily at his captain to do something. He yelled "**I WANT THAT SHIP!**"

On Seawitch Daminian yelled down the yell hole, "Switch to rear exhaust!!" In the dark of night their cloud of smoke quickly made the air a hazy black. Quickly the Seawitch disappeared. Occasionally the Romans could hear Seawitch blowing her horn in defiant liberty of her foes until it was far out of range.

When they were sure they were safely out of range, Daminian gave control of the ship to Aziri and went below.

He found Pris laying with and sleeping Luciana. Daminian kindly beckoned Pris, she followed him from the room to where Zaina was sitting at a small table where he always ate meals.

Daminian said "My ladies, we are safe, we have outrun the Romans. Being that this ship is full of men, I want to offer my cabin for you all to stay in for the duration of this voyage. If you need to come to the top deck, it is fine for short periods. While I trust my crew, it will make me feel better if you all stay there in my room."

The ladies nodded.

Daminian asked "Pris, you said before you are from Germania, do you wish to return there?"

Pris nodded. Daminian smiled, "Very good, well I can drop you off in Southern Gaul at Massilia, it is a Greek controlled port city, the best place to take you."

Pris asked "Do we need to be concerned about landing at Massilia?"

Daminian smiled "It will take many days for word to arrive from Rome, it will be impossible for them to know where we went, and besides, Massilia is a Greek-Gallic city, not Roman. I supply them with trade goods, so their king has always been very easy going about my presence."

Pris nodded "Massilia then, and thank you."

Daminian "Very good. We will arrive in a few days."

On the first day of their voyage, they buried their dead friends Taron and Felix at sea. During the voyage, Zaina gave support to Pris about the loss of her son and Pris gave Zaina her support for surviving rape and torture.

Down below in the storage deck, Titus received repeated beatings from Aziri. Seawitch sailed past five small and one huge island.

Daminian brought the ladies top side, the steam engine was off and the ship was being powered by oar and sail. Pointing to port Daminian said "That is Corsica, once a Carthaginian colony, now an island nominally controlled by Rome. We have found an old abandoned Carthaginian fort on the far North side of that island and converted it to be our little hideout."

They stopped at their hideout to pick up food supplies and a day later returned to the sea.

Sailing away from Corsica, the ship made great time, gently rocking in the calm sea. The sea was a clear blue, and the sky meeting the seas in the distance were so clear that Pris was almost able to forget about all her worries, the gentle rocking of the ship was a little hard to get used to at first, but after a day it felt like being drunk without the nasty feeling of too much alcohol in one's system.

The next morning after leaving Corsica, Aziri was shocked at the cage in the rear of the ship; he found that Titus had picked the lock of his cage and strangled his guard. Aziri immediately sounded the alarm. The crew searched everywhere, they realized that Titus must have jumped overboard during the night, he was not on the ship. It could take hours or days to circle back and no telling if they would find him.

Pris found some happiness watching Luciana watch dolphins swimming and jumping alongside the ship. Daminian walked over and grinned watching Luciana as well.

Pris said "Thank you Daminian for saving us."

Daminian bowed and said "Of course, I owe you a life debt from the brothel, and Aelianus had been a friend of mine."

Pris asked him "Do you know anyone in Massilia?"

Daminian said "I do know some people there who will be able to connect you to a guide into Germania." Pris smiled as they continued on to Massilia.

Daminian asked again about Aelianus death, Pris gave a full accounting of the night when Aelianus had been murdered, that she suspected that her son had somehow saved them through distracting the assassin with Aelianus' room bell and that they were separated in their escape.

Daminian comforted her saying that "Your son Sarth might live, it sounds like he is resourceful, he might yet survive. I may not return to Rome for a long time, but I will send word from Massilia to ask my contacts and friends in Rome if they can find out any information. If I can find out anything I will return there to get a hold of him, if I get a hold of him, I will bring him to Massilia and send word to you."

Chapter XXXXVII On the Sea

129 BC

Aziri, Tykie, Jason, Zaina, Pris and Luciana were eating breakfast the morning before they arrived in Massilia. Pris said "Good news Luciana, we arrive today!"

Luciana smiled, "Why is Massilia safe, aren't there Romans there?"

Pris shook her head, as Tykie explained "The city was founded by the Greeks around 570 odd years ago in 600 BC. It is a bustling port city with some marble Greek style buildings, and a marketplace."

Jason nodded "Massilia sided with the Romans against the Carthaginians during the 2nd Punic war, and so the Romans have allowed it to stay independent. There are no Romans in the city."

Luciana asked "Have any of you been there before?"

Jason nodded, "We have ported there before child. It is safe."

Daminian came below to grab some food. Aziri came forward, "Daminian, my sister needs a stable life, I am the only family she has and she has been continually sea sick. We will also be getting off at Massilia."

Daminian nodded, "Understood my 1st mate, you have been a great sailor and friend. I will let you collect your things and give you payment. If you ever want to rejoin the crew you are always welcome."

The Seawitch pulled into port, the ladies came to the top deck. They saw a long wooden dock that led straight to a street that went along the port area. From the center street, which had marble buildings leading up the street to an open square. On a hill behind the open space a Greek style marble building could be seen at the top, along the way an amphitheater, a temple and a stone wall with towers went around the city.

As their seamen tied down the lines of Seawitch to the dock, Tykie pointed to the bustling commerce in the city for Pris and Luciana to see, he beamed "You see, we Greeks have come very far."

Aziri yawned "True but Greek influence is being eclipsed now by...."

Tykie shook his head "It will never be eclipsed!"

Aziri laughed, "We shall see Spartan."

When all was ready Daminian, Aziri, Tykie, Jason and Zaina escorted Pris and Luciana ashore they walking to a large building that had a warehouse facing the port, they walked to the street side of the building which looked like the front. Entering inside they met an older gentleman. Daminian smiled "Syrus! Great to see you partner!"

Syrus smiled and they shook hands. "Daminian! To what do I owe the pleasure?"

Daminian smiled "I would like to introduce you to some precious people of mine. First, Aziri and his sister Zaina, they are leaving my ship, Aziri is a great swordsman and friend. Next I have two passengers, Pris and her daughter Luciana. They are traveling to their homeland in Germania."

Syrus acknowledged, a tall fat man of around 50 years with a large blackish graying beard "Aziri, Pris, this is Syrus, my friend and trade partner of many years. Syrus is of Greek descent."

Tykie greeted Syrus in Greek and Syrus' eyes went wide, "You must be Spartan."

Tykie nodded. Syrus turned to Daminian, "I have not heard his accent for a long time, wow."

Daminian motioned to Pris "Syrus, this is a dear friend of mine, she and her daughter are traveling to the far reaches of Germania. As a man of honor, do you have a reliable guide who can take them to Germania?"

Syrus nodded "Yes, I have such a man, however while he can take them to the Southern edge of Germania, I don't think he would be willing to go through it. Germania is extremely dangerous to outsiders."

Daminian turned to Pris "I wish I could tell you that I would travel up past Britannia next week, but I do not have plans to go even that far for another several months earliest. You and your daughter can stay with us on Seawitch in the Mediterranean, or you both can stay at our port on Corsica

Island. Life on a ship is not exactly a safe place for children, and the island is so small you will be tired of it in less than a few weeks."

Pris smiled and kissed Daminian's cheek, "Thank you for the offer my friend, Germania is home for me and will be for Luciana. There I have a better chance of survival than anywhere else."

Daminian smiled, "Well in that case here are a couple bags of gold coins. They might come in handy."

Syrus cleared his throat and yelled "Navar come here!"

From a backroom they heard a deep voice say "Alright" heavy footsteps caused the floorboards to creak, a door opened from behind a screen. A truly large man who had long black hair that fell past his shoulders appeared he was wearing rough dark leather clothing, leather armor and a dark green cloak. Daminian noted that Navar's forearms were about the size of his own thighs.

Syrus pointed to the small giant, "This is Navar, my swordsman and guide. He is part Greek and part Gaul, and a very trustworthy man. Navar has been to the edge of Germania before."

Syrus said "Navar, you are needed to transport this lady and her daughter to her home village in Jutland, the far Northern side of Germania."

Navar paused for a moment, "That's far up North, rugged country; should not be a problem."

Syrus smiled "Navar is skillful, resourceful and loyal. He will do his best to return Pris and her daughter home."

Syrus told Pris "I owe Daminian a big debt, he helped me start this business. Navar is yours to help you for this trip, he is ready." Navar nodded.

Pris was overwhelmed with mixed emotion, Sarth was still back in Rome, possibly dead like Aelianus. Yet she had Luciana, and Daminian had been a perfect gentleman, and his crew had risked death to bring her and Luciana to freedom. "Thank you..." Pris said, "I do not know what else to say".

Daminian said "At times like these, thank you is more than enough. May you have a safe journey home. We travel the Mediterranean, and we are based in Corsica. I come here to trade at least once or twice a year, also for supplies and news, perhaps we will meet again."

Pris nodded "I would like that. For saving us, I wish to give you this medallion. It is a symbol of my people, if you have this my people would think of you as a friend."

Daminian touched his heart "Thank you."

Jason said "Pris here is some food for your trip. It is called beef jerky, it will last a long time."

Pris responded "Thank you Jason."

Tykie next handed her a xiphos, his Greek sword. Pris looked at them "I cannot...."

Tykie said "Yes you must, I have another and you may be in need of a good weapon…."

Aziri interrupted "This one's better, this is a Carthaginian style bow and a quiver of arrows. This bow is smaller than most, it is easy to use on horseback. It is a good ranged weapon; I've used this bow to hunt many times".

Tykie finished "As I was saying, a great sword is at times necessary." he gave Aziri an annoyed look, who shrugged smiling.

Pris grinned "Thank you all."

Daminian told Syrus "As I mentioned earlier Syrus, Aziri and his sister Zaina have decided to disembark from my ship as well. If you need a great fighter, Aziri is one of the best swordsmen I've known. Please also give aid to his sister Zaina as they will need a place to stay as they settle in this city."

Syrus agreed, "I have just the lady to introduce to Zaina, she owns a restaurant and could use a good waitress. Aziri and Zaina can stay in my guest room until they find a place to live. Aziri, I could use your services while Navar is guiding Pris up to Germania." Aziri nodded, "Very good, we shall collect our things from the ship and return here later." Daminian nodded, "Well I shall be back within a few months to check on things." Syrus smiled, "Good, perhaps I will win that ship of yours." Daminian shook his head smiling "Never".

Stepping outside Daminian, Aziri, Tykie, Jason and Zaina gave Pris and Luciana parting hugs and they returned to their ship. Pris saw Daminian and Tykie speaking with and then shaking hands with Aziri before Daminian's group headed back to the ship. Pris, Luciana Aziri and Zaina waved to them and then returned inside Syrus' shop.

Chapter XXXXVIII Navar

129 BC

Within an hour everything was ready. Pris had bought some food supplies, blankets and a canteen from Syrus, and a bag to carry it in. Syrus led them back behind his shop, there were three horses and his guide Navar. Aziri and Zaina gave Pris and Luciana final hugs and then they set off North.

They traveled through farms and then forested lands. Eventually they arrived at the Alps, the mountains were almost impassable, so they traveled towards the center of the Alps gaining much elevation.

At first, they traveled during night, with the road going North from Massilia going from stone to a dirt road and eventually ending in a broad meadow where a farmer's land ended. Pris noticed from a distance that the people now lived in very basic farm homes, the men worked their fields some without wearing any shirts, their hair was long.

Navar grinned, "Those are Celts Mam."

Where the road ended they faced the untamed woods of the North. They had ridden mostly in silence since their initial greeting. The closer they came to this area the more at home Pris felt, Pris felt a joy she hadn't in years, "Oh this is so lovely!"

Navar of Massilia

Luciana looked at everything "Mommy, this land is kind of scary."

Pris rode next to Luciana, she started talking about the beauty of the landscape, pointing out the lovely mountains approaching in the distance, the rivers they passed and the gentle hills as the road became dirt and eventually the path became overgrown with tall grass. They had arrived at the base of the Alps where they found a tall waterfall leading into a river that cut between the forested hilly land. It was starting to get dark. Navar looked at her with a nervous glance, "The terrain ahead becomes dangerous, it would be best for us to camp for the night."

Luciana had been practically falling asleep in the saddle, Pris agreed. "Yes, let's do that."

Navar pulled the saddles off their horses that they could use as pillows, the under blanket they would sleep on top of, and he pulled blankets out of a sack that he had brought along. Navar made a campfire from some twigs and his flint.

Pris had been waiting and waiting for Navar to say something for hours but he had been very quiet. She finally asked him "I am not a talkative type, but you are truly a quiet man. Is everything alright?"

Navar nodded, "Apologies miss, I normally travel alone. Is there anything you want to know?"

Pris shrugged, "Sure, how does the terrain go from here?"

Navar said "The road continues to go high up and we will be able to look over deep ravines."

Pris said "I am just happy that we are passing through during Summer."

Navar nodded, "Impossible in Winter. Though we will still need to be cautious."

That night the howling of wolves woke them up. The horses began to panic as they too knew danger was approaching.

Navar drew his sword and put a torch in the dying fire, as the torch flared to life, they could see the eyes and outline of a pack of wolves approaching.

Pris drew her bow and shot the most visible wolf in the front of the pack. The other wolves stopped.

There was a sound of the wolves fighting and then soon it was quiet. At first, they all stayed awake, but after the horses calmed down, they figured it was alright to relax.

Navar told Pris to get some sleep and he would switch watches with her in a few hours.

Pris took the watch at Sunrise, allowing Navar to sleep for an hour as she watched the rising Sun turn the sky from dark to purple to pink to blue.

The radiance of the view was spellbinding, from here at this elevation, there were not so many trees and she could see several mountains nearby and in between the mountains she could see a large beautiful lake over a ridge they had passed by to her left far below them.

When Navar woke, Pris pointed to the lake saying "That is truly beautiful."

Navar looked and nodded, "Indeed it is, but there is a tribe that hunts and fishes in those grounds. They are nominally allied with Rome, but I did not want to take any chances, the fewer people we meet on this journey the better."

Navar broke out some deer jerky, dried pear slices and bread from his bag. Pris did the same from her supplies. Luciana awoke with a startle, Pris comforted and fed her.

Navar gave them some deer jerky, he was happy to see their faces turn happy as they bit into the food, Navar smiled hearing the mother and child making happy "Mmmmm" sounds. He said "I base it in a sugar and wine sauce before I smoke it." Navar smiled at them as he watched, Pris looked at him questioningly.

Navar said "Apologies, I see great love you have for her, but I also see great pain, what happened to you?"

Pris spent the next 20 minutes explaining their story, omitting many details like the steam engine which she didn't think he would understand or even believe. Navar listened at length; Pris had finished at the part when they met Navar.

He nodded saying "The Gods give and take from mortals. It is only what we do with the time that we have to make the most of our lives."

Luciana woke up started, Pris gave her a hug, "It's ok dear, it's ok…"

Navar grimaced as he put more wood on the fire.

Luciana said "Mommy, growing up, I was often happy, I enjoyed people. Now in the dream, I kept seeing flashes of my life go by, Master Aelianus gone, and Sarth too? Why did those people attack us?"

Pris shrugged, "We may never know. Sarth did a very heroic thing, he made the bad man leave us so we could escape."

Luciana nodded, hugging her mom, then slipped back into sleep.

Navar didn't say anything, but Pris spoke anyway "She is still trying to come to grips with the fact that her former master, who had been more of a father figure to her is dead, that her twin brother Sarth whom she loved beyond anything may also possibly be dead." Pris had to stop for a moment.

Navar said "You don't know his fate, so you can only hope for the best."

Pris nodded, "Even if he is not dead, we may never see each other again."

Navar said "Perhaps, but stranger things have happened, don't give up hope."

Pris nodded and smiled "Do you have a wife or family?"

Navar shook his head "Not anymore, my wife passed away five years ago in childbirth and the baby was stillborn."

Navar ran his hand through his hair and rubbed his face as he said to Pris, "Last night we were lucky by your good shot, you probably killed the Alpha male of the wolves ... but they might come back."

Pris asked "Will they return?"

Navar nodded "Wolves are like people, they generally hunt within a range of their dens and hunt every day for their food. We must keep going, we can try to stay high to avoid the humans, but there might be more danger from the mountain, or we can risk going down to the valleys, but there could be danger there too."

Pris nodded "Let's stay high for now until we find no other path forward, then turn downward."

Navar nodded "Very well."

Luciana said "Mommy the sunrise is so beautiful here!"

Pris nodded, "Yes, and we can see so far across the valleys between the mountains. Come child, time to get on our horses, we've a long way to go."

Chapter XXXXIX Pris, Luciana & Navar

129 BC

Up and down mountains they traveled. They proceeded along the side of the mountain for a few hours over rough terrain but came to a place where the horses could not go up or continue forward. As the way down was not really steep, they walked the horses downward to where the land flattened enough to mount the horses again.

Pris Haas

This was where the trees greeted them in a huge forest, in the distance the land gave way dropping far below, there was beauty as far as the eye could see.

They proceeded North and Northeast as their path took them. There was a steep rocky hill that had the width of about two horses standing nose to butt that had a very subtle decline as they continued down this mountain. Navar said that the path would level out at the bottom and they could choose to either go around the next mountain or there was another higher path. Making their way down the mountain Pris was teaching Luciana about their tribe as she remembered it. Luciana asked "May I ride closer to the side, I want a view of the mountains."

Pris looked at Navar who shrugged, and so Pris responded "Alright, you may, but not too close to the edge of the road."

Luciana said "Yes Mommy."

Luciana watched the view, she was silent as Pris spoke with Navar. Luciana reflected on all that had happened, back in Rome.

Tears rolled down her face again as Luciana began to weep.

Pris rode over, "Are you ok?"

Luciana didn't respond, then said "Mommy I know you have always wanted to return to the Cimbri, but I fear going there; Rome is all I know."

Navar looked at her sympathetically.

Pris rubbed her back "I promise you will love Germania Luciana, it will become a new home for you. It will be safe and you will find happiness there."

Luciana looked up through her tears, "Do you really know that Mommy, will everything be ok?"

Pris looked at her hard, "Yes, you will adapt to Germania, it might be hard at first, it is not Rome, but it will be more liberating, and someday you may become a bridge between our cultures or at least a content woman."

Luciana glanced at the horizon, then back to her mom, her eyes blurred by her tears. Pris gave her a cloth to wipe her eyes. Luciana said "I hope so, I will try."

The trees with the sun rise coming through them shining a brilliant light, "I pray we will see Sarth again."

Pris nodded, biting her lip as she looked far ahead, "Sarth is a survivor, if anyone would have a chance, it would be him. We have to keep hope no matter what".

Chapter L (50) Luciana

129 BC

Danger on the trail…..

For a long while she held Pris' hand, both feeling solace through their shared grief and love as they overlooked the forest covered canyon which had a river far below. Navar farted loudly, Pris looked at him with a little annoyance and he tried to pretend that it had been the horse.

Suddenly Luciana's horse bucked screaming, a snake had struck out at its foot from behind a small boulder. The snake had bit at the horse's foot, but the horse had seen the snake's head snapping out just in time to buck its forelegs. Luciana's horse killed the snake in its trampling, but as it reared, Luciana was thrown from her saddle as she had not been holding her reins tightly while looking off at the horizon. Luciana flew through the air behind them and over the side of the road dropping below the road.

Pris' scream echoed across the distance
"NOOOOOOOO!!!"

Luciana's horse took off like a shot down the road as Pris and Navar circled back rushing to the edge. They looked down and saw that Luciana had landed on the side of the cliff on a flat boulder that edged out from the face of the cliff about 20 feet below them. She was lying on her stomach, her head resting on her left arm, she was not moving nor crying.

Navar pulled a long-coiled rope out of his saddle bag. Giving the reins of both horses to Pris he yelled "Hold the horses, I will climb down for her."

Pris nodded "Please save her!"

Holding the middle of the rope, Navar put the rope through two rings on the saddles of the two horses, then he threw the rope uncoiling it, then tied the middle of it to the saddle horn, then with two lines of rope he wrapped them between two rocks that poked out from the edge of the road and the cliff before he stepped in the middle then wrapped the ropes around his waist, then stepping over the lines he put the lines in between his butt and through his legs, he slipped off his boots going barefoot, then he pulled the two lines up in his right hand to give himself a seat holding him as he rappelled down the face of the cliff. Navar yelled "Hang on kid, don't move, I'm coming!" He rappelled slowly downward. Every step seemed to send small rocks downward.

Wind strongly hit them as Navar closed in and got closer to Luciana.

Navar breathed "Merciful Gods please let this child be alive" He turned Luciana over to check her and she suddenly screamed out in pain. Navar yelled "She's alive! Her left shoulder is dislocated, she had bruises all over her face, her hands and perhaps elsewhere." Navar looked at her some more, "It seems Luciana's left arm must have cushioned her head at impact.

Luciana began crying.

Navar asked her "You did great girl. You're a survivor! Can you move your toes?"

Luciana did this while crying.

Navar smiled "This is good, you will be fine! Not many could do that after such a drop girl, you are a strong one."

Luciana smiled through her tears. Navar gave her a piece of jerky, "It is not safe here. Bite down on this, I must carry you, but it will be painful."

Luciana nodded, biting down on the jerky.

Navar picked Luciana up and hugged her to his body and tied a rope around her to him, it held her head on his shoulder and he called up, "Pris, now slowly have the horses move away from the road to pull us up." The rocks at the edge held the rope while the horses pulled the rope up.

Pris breathed her father's prayer "We are one with nature, we leave to feed our families taking only what we need, oh nature please give us the prize and a safe trip home."

Navar carried Luciana up the cliff, his adrenaline allowing him to ignore the pain from sharp rocks cutting his feet. They made it up the side of the cliff, Navar held Luciana who was whimpering from the pain in her arms and shoulder.

Navar shouted "She has a dislocated left shoulder, grab my saddle blanket" Pris jumped off her horse, pulled out the blanket they had slept on and ran over to them.

Navar set Luciana down on the blanket.

Pris hugged Luciana, who was still crying, her shoulder visibly popped out of place.

Navar went back to his horse. Cutting a small length of rope, he grabbed another smaller bag. Returning to Luciana and Pris, he pulled out some paper and put the herbs on the paper, rolling it and licking the paper.

Next, he grabbed some dry nearly dead weeds that were also in his bag, he next pulled out his pipe, put some of the weeds into it then pull out his flint and sparking it on the weeds they caught fire, he took a puff, then smoke escaping from his mouth he told the whimpering Luciana to puff the pipe as he had saying that it would dull her pain.

Luciana took a puff of the pipe and she suddenly stopped crying the smoke coming out of her mouth as her mouth slowly changed from a painful grimace to a relaxed smile.

Navar smiled and his voice sounded different as he said "There ya go."

Pris looked at Navar thankful he had taken her pain away wondering what the dried herbs were.

Navar next looked at Pris "We must reset her arm; this will be painful for her. You must hold her as I pull it back into place."

Pris nodded, holding Luciana, Navar grabbed her arm and in a sudden jerk pulled it out causing an audible snap. Luciana shouted out briefly at the sharp pain, but then she felt better taking another puff from the roll.

Navar reached into his bag and pulled out some rolled up bandages which he used to wrap up his slashed feet. Next he pulled a large cloth from his bag tying it around Luciana's neck and her left arm saying "This should hold your arm in place allowing your shoulder to rest."

Pris hugged Luciana, kissed the side of her head, she looked up to whisper a thank you to him to which he smiled. A wave of relief sweeping over them all. For the rest of the day they sat together on Pris' horse, Pris holding Luciana who sat in front.

After a half hour they came upon Luciana's horse that had bucked her off. Although none of them blamed the horse, Luciana did not want to ride him again, so they transferred all of their gear to that horse to carry while the group of three rode on the other two horses.

Chapter LI Survivors

129 BC

The group continued on; Pris and Navar were speaking about whether it would make sense to stop early and hunt for some fresh food or to keep going and survive off jerky. Luciana spoke up "Mommy, my shoulder hurts, can we stop?"

Pris nodded, the road had opened up into a small meadow.

Navar said "This is a good spot, we can stop for the night."

Navar looked at the saddle that Luciana's original horse had carried, he said "Bad news, some of the food is missing, some of the food must have fallen out when this horse bolted. Perhaps I should go hunt?"

Pris agreed, "Yes, I'll make a fire, see if you can find a rabbit, squirrel or bird that we can eat for dinner."

Navar said "No problem" he pulled out his bow and quiver of arrows. Getting onto his horse, he tossed his bag of herbs to Pris, "For her pain, put it in the pipe like we did before. Smoke in small amounts because there isn't more than what's in the bag. So smoke some now, then stop and only smoke it when the pain is intense." Navar smiled then rode off on his horse.

Pris prepared the pipe for Luciana and after she had smoked and her pain subsided, During this time Pris positioned her sword, bow and arrows to be readily accessible. That done, Pris collected some wood and built their campfire and using the flint, started it, then she sat next to Luciana. Pris spoke with Luciana in Cimbri, "How do you feel?"

Luciana responded "I feel better now. Mommy, tell me about Grandpa, what is he like?"

Pris smiled "Your grandpa was loving, brave, the tribe's chief and a great hunter. He took me hunting and taught me how to sword fight. But what I remember best was how loving he was to me, to my mother and my sister."

Luciana asked "Was aunt Tuli like you?"

Pris smiled "Tuli loved to follow me around, she was very kind and she loved to sing."

Pris then spoke about her village, "People in my village were all like a big family. Almost everyone knows each other at least a little bit. It is not like Rome where most people don't know each other." Pris stopped speaking for a while.

Luciana asked "Are you alright Mom?"

Pris said "Sorry darling, I was just thinking about my mother. I have never fully got over her loss. Let me tell you more about our music and food...." Pris spoke at length about her tribe's culture, music and foods of her tribe.

They were holding each other exhausted and fell asleep as it started to become late in the day as the Sun was beginning to set. Pris woke up, she saw Luciana was fitful in her sleep, so Pris hugged her daughter again, petting her hair and hummed softly. Luciana's sleep calmed down and she slept peacefully again.

Pris put a log on their campfire and after looking around to see that the rocky meadow was empty she soon fell asleep too. Pris saw Aelianus in a dream, he was smiling at her "You can make it Pris" his apparition said in Latin. Pris started to respond, to thank him, but Aelianus' appearance turned concerned, urging her "Pris wake up!"

Pris awoke to the sounds of horses approaching. The Sun had nearly set, light was dim but still enough to see across the meadow. Pris turned over and opening her eyes saw five bandits on horseback approaching their campfire. They were wearing ragged pastel browns, green and blue clothing and mismatched armor. Each of these men had beards and long hair. They started spreading out as they approached her at a slow trot. One of them said something familiar, then Pris remembered a word in Celtic she learned from Helga it meant "women" and the others started laughing, one was carrying a spear, another was armed with a sword, the other two had arrows in their bows as the closest one started making kissing sounds, and another was humping his saddle while saying something while another made the sound of "Uuum Humm".

Pris drew her arrow in her bow, immediately the two with bows also drew their arrows into firing position. The one carrying a sword drew it as he hopped off his horse and waved his free hand around, motioning to his friends as he said something to Pris in a threatening tone.

One of his men aiming a bow at Pris was laughing and making kissing sounds. An arrow suddenly stuck through the bowman's neck and the kissing sounds and laughter turned into a gargled scream. An arrowhead appeared on the other side as he fell off his horse.

The other bandit on a horse with a bow in hand turned to shoot at the attacker, but before he could pull his arrow back, a second arrow flew through his chest and stuck out his backside, he also fell off his horse.

The third and fourth bandits turned their horses to attack the approaching combatant, as the man with the sword started to run towards Pris.

Pris judged instantly on who to shoot at and fired her arrow hitting the third bandit carrying a spear in his side under his right arm just as a second arrow struck him in his chest. He fell off his saddle, but his foot got caught in a stirrup and he was dragged along the ground by his horse.

The fourth bandit also holding a spear charged towards Navar as Navar was charging at him. Pris fired her second arrow at the bandit but hit his horse and he was thrown through the air landing hard onto a small bush.

The bandit who had dismounted carrying his sword was just a few paces away, he charged at Pris, she dropped her bow and pulled her own sword out as the swordsman's blade swung and clashed against her own blade's block.

Across the meadow, the bandit had landed on his butt onto a bush. He groaned as he rolled off and got up. The bandit's spear had flown through the air and was sticking blade down in the ground several paces away from him. Still on his horse, Navar charged up to him as he pulled his sword.

Navar swung his sword at the bandit and the two swords made a loud clash as they struck at each other. Navar passed him after their swords clashed, he jumped off his horse and charged at the man, they engaged in an aggressive parry for parry battle.

Similarly Pris was parrying her attackers' swings as though in a trance, Aelianus' lessons were like a natural rhythm; she could hear his voice as she parried the bandit's sword with her own. After a few clashes, she blocked her attacker's sword and with whip-like reflex she sliced off his extended sword hand and then immediately stabbed him in his chest with her blade, he screamed and fell over dead.

Pris saw that Luciana had awakened and had a horrified look as she picked up her bow and tried to get a shot at their last attacker, however Navar's large body was blocking the shot.

Their last attacker had not been able to land a strike without it being parried. The attacker was no small man, but he was quite as strong as Navar. Navar was pushing down hard on the swords and the attacker's sword arm was tiring, so his left hand shot to his dagger and he tried to stab Navar in the stomach with it.

Navar saw this and dodged to his left away from the dagger which still stabbed into his clothing on his right side. He kicked the attacker in the stomach sending him backwards, then swung his sword hitting the attacker's unsteadied sword sending the sword off left. Navar instantly curled his wrist around not waiting for the blade to return and swung his blade in reverse, connected the blade perfectly between the attacker's helmet and his chain mailed shoulders, the last attacker's head went flying with pieces of neck for several feet as blood burst from his body like a fountain, his body fell over to the ground.

With the last attacker killed, Navar whistled for his horse which came over to him in a brisk trott. He went over to the bandit's horse which had been shot by an arrow, it was dying, but in pain, so he finished it off. Navar looked around to see if any more attackers would be coming out of the tree line, after a moment he rode over to Pris and Luciana to see if they were ok. Seeing they were alright he smiled, "Glad you both are alright and that I had not tried to get another animal."

Luciana asked "Why did you have to kill the horse?"

Navar smiled sadly, "It was in pain, it was dying, I didn't want it to suffer."

Luciana nodded.

He tried to get Luciana's mind off the killing as she looked visibly shaken. "Guess what's for dinner?" Navar showed them the rabbit he had shot as he pulled out his knife.

Luciana looked at him until he started to prepare their meal. She turned to her mother and asked "Do many Northern warriors have long hair?"

Pris smiled, but before she could respond Navar winked at her saying in his thick accented voice "Only the best ones."

Pris smiled as she walked over to the dead to retrieve arrows, adding the bandit's arrows to their own.

Luciana looked at the attackers then at their horses, pointing she said "What will we do with the other four horses?"

Navar smiled, they can now carry our gear."

They ate their food, then went to sleep and slept there overnight without further incident.

Chapter LII Sanctuary

129 BC

The town in the mountains......

The next morning, they got up with the dawn and within an hour had traveled to the bottom of the mountain. It was a little foggy, but they saw a small bridge that crossed a calm part of the river. The expanse around the town had been turned into wheat farms, using all the available flat land in the valley's short distance to where the next mountain shot up steeply seemingly to the clouds.

Pris asked "Is this town alright? I am concerned about what could happen."

Navar raised his hands to assuage her concern "It should be fine, I have come here before to trade goods."

Pris and Luciana followed Navar's look as he pointed at the town. Across the stone bridge past the rocky connecting ground, they saw the town's main iron door with a timber Gatehouse above the iron door. There was a tall wooden wall made of logs surrounding the town. As they got closer, more and more of the town beyond the wall became visible. This town looked like it probably had around a thousand people.

Navar said calmly, "I have been here before to trade furs, this is the main home of the Tigurini clan, a part of the Helvetii tribe. We should be safe with them."

Pris nodded "Can you confirm if it is safe?"

Navar nodded, he urged his horse forward to cross the bridge while Pris and Luciana stayed behind in a tree covered area.

Navar appeared on the bridge, some girls who had been down by the river saw him approach and they ran into the town's entrance which had two large doors standing open as archers were patrolling along the top of the walls. To the left the path continued into the fields, leading to the mountain in the far distance. To the right, just a short distance from the bridge the town's wall came up to the edge of the river where the bank went down and became a short gravel beach front. The beach cut inwards into the town area in a tiny bay where there were several canoes, with some larger boats.

By the time Navar was across the bridge five men came out of the village on horseback. Pris saw Navar wave and then spoke with them at length. After a moment the men escorted Navar to their position. Navar motioned to the leader saying "Pris, this is King Tor, leader of Sion which is this town. He is king of the Seduni Celtic tribe."

Tor smiled broadly and said something while motioning a welcome. Tor was a bearded old bald man who had a patch over his left eye. He wore polished chainmail armor, a red cape and blue shirt and trousers. Tor looked like he must have been a strong man long ago, but now was pretty fat.

Tor gave a close look at Pris and Luciana. Meanwhile Navar continued "The Seduni are trade partners with the Romans, but are not controlled by them, at least not yet."

Tor said something, Navar waited, then translated "Tor welcomes us as guests to his village. His granddaughters alerted him of my approach as he and his men were about to leave for a hunt."

Tor saw Luciana and became concerned, saying something in Celtic to Navar while pointing to her.

Navar said "I told Tor of your daughter's condition at the bridge and he says now that he has an able cleric who can look at her shoulder and give you medicine for her pain".

Pris smiled, raising her hands together and bowing her head "Thank you generous king."

Tor laughed, saying something at length in Celtic as his face turned a little pink,

Navar cleared his throat saying "Well, Tor says anything for someone so lovely as you. He says they will have a feast tonight to welcome us as his guests."

Tor spoke in Celtic and one of his men rode back to the village, Navar translated, raising his eyebrows "His warrior has gone back to wake up their old cleric, apparently the man might have a hangover."

Pris thanked him again as they all rode across the bridge to the town.

When they approached the Gatehouse King Tor yelled something Navar whispered "He is telling the town that we are his guests and to be courteous to us while we stay in their town."

Tor yelled again and suddenly a man with five hounds appeared with another twenty men on horses who had been in a stable area. Tor then turned to them all and smiling said in very poor Latin "See you night."

Pris nodded happily and said: "Thank you."

Tor smiled, not waiting for the translation rode off with his twenty-four men, followed by the hounds.

The group of horsemen were all holding bows and spears.

Chapter LIII King Tor of the Seduni Celtic tribe
129 BC

A safe place in the mountains.......

As they watched Tor and his hunting party leave, a warrior on horseback approached from the center of town and waved them to follow him. He led them through the hillside town where people wore clothing not too unlike what Pris remembered of her own village long ago. Unlike in Rome or Roman lands, the warriors here did not march in lines and were all unique in their clothing and weapons. The streets were on a steady hillside that sloped upwards; eventually leading to the mountain beyond them.

There were many women walking with their children, some commerce of trade going on in one area that had many tents, people buying various goods and must be a market. Finally, they arrived at a large building where their guide dismounted and brought them inside.

There was a large entry hall that had four doors, two on either side of the main room and one near the backside. There was a large table, four fireplaces two at each side wall. At the far end of the room was a small throne.

Navar said "King Tor has welcomed us into his own house, this is a great honor." The warrior led them to the door of a side room, opening the door they saw a double bunk bed.

The warrior said something to Navar who translated smiling "This man asks if you and I want separate rooms or to sleep in the same room." Navar said something in Celtic and motioned to the neighboring room.

Pris motioned to herself and Luciana "We will be sleeping in the same room."

Navar was surprised as the warrior waved them all into the same room and left Pris said looking at Navar in his eyes, "This doesn't mean we are sleeping together, right?"

Navar shrugged, Pris said, "Anything unwelcomed and my knife might hit something of yours that is important."

Navar laughed, "No problem, I'll sleep on the floor."

They were unpacking their things when the old cleric knocked on their door.

The old man waved at them, he had brought a case. The old man motioned to himself saying something. Navar said "He says his name is Cillian, he is their cleric. A medicine man." The old man walked over to Luciana, he examined Luciana, through Navar asked her "Hello girl, I need you to slowly and gently move your arm until you feel any pain." He moved his own arm in a slow circle.

Luciana moved her arm a little but winced in pain.

Cillian hummed a "Umhum" touching and looking at her shoulder and other scrapped up body parts. He smiled, said something in a kind manner, then spoke in a concise manner to Navar who nodded.

Navar translated "Cillian says it was definitely dislocated." He gently felt her shoulder nodding. "He says she was lucky, no broken bones." Cillian smiled at Luciana, he then gave Pris an ointment. Then through Navar he said "Rub this on her wounds" and then he yelled in Celtic towards the door. An older female servant came to the room with a small pot of some hot water.

Navar said "Cillian told her to bring this for the tea."

Cillian showed Pris how much to use to prepare it and not long after drinking it, Luciana fell into a peaceful sleep. The old cleric smiled, examined her shoulder again and said something which Navar translated "He says the best thing for her is to get plenty of rest, to drink this tea when the pain is too strong. Use the ointment on her wounds, it will make them heal faster. That she needs to eat food." Keep it in a sling for 3 to 4 weeks, try to keep the movement as little as possible at first. Let her move more after that time. It might take 6 months for it to fully heal."

Pris thanked him and gave Cillian a hug before he left. Cillian's face blushed a little with a big grin.

Navar put his things down. "None for me?"

Pris laughed. Navar said "Well I'm going to head to the market, do you want to come?"

Pris said "No thanks

That afternoon King Tor's hunting party returned with two dead boars they had killed. The boars were cooked over the chamber's two large fireplaces. When ready the boars were then cut up and slices were brought to each guest by young women. On the plates the meat was served with beer, boiled potato and greens. The large table had several impressive warriors of varying ages.

Luciana had awakened and so she came out with Pris and Navar at the table. Tor was seated next to his wife Amilia who was an old woman who smiled a lot, but didn't say much. Tor motioned to a young man and woman who were seated to his left. Navar translated "This is their son Prince Thoran and his wife Lori."

Pris smiled and toasted Thoran and Lori. Thoran was a young man of average height, thick arms, he had a clean-shaven face and long brown hair as did many of the warriors in the Hall.

Thoran smiled at Pris who smiled back.

Tor asked Navar to share their story, so Pris told Navar to tell their story, he nodded and then spoke at length to Tor and Amilia as well as members of the royal family. During Navar's long relay of events, Tor and Amilia's faces went from concerned to surprised to sympathetic as it all was described. Amilia put her hand on Pris' without thinking a couple times.

When finished Tor said through Navar's translation "This land has seen many wars, now we are at peace. We trade with the Chatti Germanic tribe, the Chatti have traded out goods as far as the Saxons. We also trade with nearby

Celtic towns as well as the Mediolanum, a Roman city to the South."

Pris' excitement was raised when she heard the name "Saxons", remembering they were the tribe that her father's mission was to all those years ago. "How do you get to the Saxon tribe from here?"

Tor continued through Navar's translations "They are across mountains, then across the Black Forest and follow a large river North beyond that. We don't know their exact location, somewhere close to a large river. These mountains…" Tor said, pointing his finger around, "…they keep us isolated but safe."

Navar cautioned "The Saxons are a collection of hundreds of tribes unified only by the same language, sometimes they war against each other."

Pris said "My father took me and others to a Saxon tribe for a trade mission long ago."

Navar grimaced, "Unless you know for sure which Saxon tribe it was, we may or may not be walking into a trap."

Pris nodded, "Such is our life, but I am a Germanic woman, they are more likely to let us pass if I do the talking, we….".

Navar overtalked her "Should be fine? We should be careful Pris, you were kidnapped by a Germanic tribe, the Swabians, right? The Celts or Romans did not capture you."

Pris nodded, "True" Tor asked Navar a question, he responded, then Tor said through Navar "King Tor says that he will have an escort guide us to Chatti lands in the Black Forest. From there we will need to try to get further North."

Tor announced something to all those present, the warriors at the table all began speaking with each other. One of them said something to the King, Tor responded and then waved them all back to their food and the meal continued.

Pris asked Navar "What was said?"

Navar shrugged, "They asked how far North the escort will go and what they should do if attacked by one of the tribes."

Pris asked "What did he say?"

Navar scoffed, "Fight like Hell."

Navar was listening to the King speak for a while then Pris asked "What did Tor say?"

Navar replied "King Tor announced that the escort will be a voluntary force and that they should not attack unless absolutely necessary."

Ameilia privately asked Tor a question to which he whispered a response. Navar heard and his eyebrow raised, but he did not say anything as he drank some beer.

Tor said something to Navar who turned to Pris "The journey is very far, we must travel passed many mountains, valleys and lakes before we will reach Germania, that will take at least a week. The escort will guide us there."

Pris raised her glass "To King Tor the wise, thanks for your generosity."

Tor smiled nodding. Pris leaned over, "What did the Queen say to the King earlier?"

Navar glanced at Tor who smiled, he said something to Navar.

Navar nodded to Tor and said "Sometimes a mouse can save a fox from a trap and sometimes a fox can save a mouse."

Pris nodded and toasted the King.

At that moment Tor's granddaughters came to Pris asking something, Navar said they wanted to show Luciana their new puppies, Luciana got excited and gave Pris a pleading look. Pris nodded so Luciana went off with them.

Pris was conscious that many of the warriors eating in the hall were looking at her longingly.

Amelia noticed these looks too and said something happily to Tor who then smiled and relayed it to Navar. Gently shaking his goblet of beer Navar waved an open hand at Pris, "King Tor and Queen Amelia say that the men all see such beauty in you."

Pris smiled, "They are too kind."

Pris turned to Navar, "Kind as they are, I can only think about returning home. It is a reunion with my family that I have thought about more than 10,000 times. I think about what could have happened to my dad and my sister. Tuli could be married and a mother by now."

Navar nodded "I can understand, and you have come so far towards getting there. Those answers will come, but not yet. For now, tonight we are here, we don't know what may or may not happen tomorrow, just enjoy this moment."

Pris smiled in between bites of her meal of boar meat and enjoyed her beer.

Chapter LIV A festive evening

129 BC

A delicious feast led to enchantment.......

As dinner came to a close, King Tor clapped his hands and loudly said something to which the crowd cheered. Servants came in and began pulling apart the large table into quarter pieces and then placing the pieces gently on their sides at the four sides of the room, next the chairs were moved to be placed along the length of the rooms and a group of men left the room then reentered in a few moments with musical instruments. They began playing a lively happy melody of stringed instruments with a couple men using flutes and another man on drums. Several of the men started dancing in large circles with the ladies in the middle of the circles spinning as others cheered and clapped. The dancers moved their bodies in unison to the fast-paced rhythm as the men danced in larger circles around them.

Suddenly the dance circles split into pairs and for a while the dancers of men and women circled each other closely before they all reformed into large circles again.

Pris said "Wow Navar, I have never seen this exact dance though I remember my parents dancing together." Pris hid her feeling of sadness by drinking a big gulp of beer, then gave a smile.

Navar leaned over and squeezed her hand, "You must not blame yourself. We cannot change the past, your mother would want you to be happy."

Pris looked at him and smiled as a tear fell from her face. She quickly wiped her face and then they watched the group of dancers as they danced. "Yes she probably would."

Now Luciana returned with Tor's granddaughters who looked concerned. Luciana said "Mommy, my shoulder is painful again."

Navar signaled Cillian, the old cleric who had been drinking ale. They took Luciana to bed. After Luciana had drank some tea and fallen asleep, Cillian said "It might help a little to gently massage her shoulder when it is not too tender. She should be fine for tonight."

Cillian showed her by giving Pris a quick gentle shoulder massage to show her how and where. Pris smiled "Thank you both again Cillian and Navar. I think I will go to bed as well."

Navar nodded "I will return to the hall, the dance was intriguing."

Pris whispered "Good night" as she closed the door.

After Navar returned, he was soon dancing with a local lady. He was the biggest man on the floor, and yet she enjoyed his agile dancing.

King Tor and the Queen clapped watching them. Suddenly the song turned slow, King Tor and his wife joined, the other dancers gave them the center of the stage. Navar started to back away only for the lady to grab him and they continued dancing in a side area sharing smiles as they danced.

Pris lay next to Luciana thinking again about what would be awaiting them in their journey ahead. Pris quickly fell asleep next to Luciana from the mixture of beer and exhaustion.

Chapter LV An early start

129 BC

A refreshed start for their journey......

Navar did not return to their bedroom that evening. The next morning he arrived early knocking his hand gently on their door asking permission to enter. Hearing his solid tapping and deep voice, Pris came to the door still a little sleepy from the beers, "What happened to you last night Navar?"

With a sheepish grin Navar said "An angel found me in the dance, we danced and danced, then afterwards she brought me to her room."

Pris smiled giggling "Oh, happy times for you then! Well Luciana and I will be ready to leave soon."

Navar nodded, "I will be ready as well. The King has left instructions that we are to eat before we leave. I advise we do so as it will be back to jerky and rabbit meat soon enough."

They came to the hall, where a table was prepared for them. Navar asked a servant in Celtic, who said that "King Tor and the Queen were still in bed."

Indeed a faint snoring echoed from their closed door. 20 men to Chatti lands. Pris, Luciana and Navar ate some eggs.

As they ate, an attractive brunette woman came over to Navar and while holding his hand said something, he responded in Celtic gently to her and she gave him a note and then pushed his head back before she kissed his mouth.

Pris waited until they had finished their kiss, then Pris asked Navar to ask her if she could give them a metal bowl.

Navar asked the lady and she went away.

Pris asked "What is her name?"

Navar had closed his eyes as she walked away still savoring the kiss and said half in a dream "Eileen."

Luciana and Pris smiled, Pris then said happily, "You have a reason to return here."

Navar nodded, "Yes I do."

Cillian the old cleric came by and examined Luciana again, he said something which Navar translated to "Luciana should be fine to travel, he requests that she keep her arm in a sling, and her hurt arm to a minimum." Pris nodded.

Cillian had brought a sheet of brown colored fabric, Navar translated "This is clean, it has been colored by roots. Tie it around your girl's arm."

Chapter LVI Into the mountains and beyond.
129 BC

Their journey restarted into the mountains....

Prince Thoran sat on his horse wearing an impressive set of armor, sword and provisions with the party of 19 similarly prepared warriors. The party exited the great hall, Navar asked Thoran a question, Thoran responded which Navar translated "He says that he has decided to join us on our journey." Pris gave a short bow of her head, "Thank you prince!"

They departed from Sion while the Sun was still low in the sky. Tor's granddaughters waved to them as they left the town, Luciana said "They are kind people."

Pris agreed, "I will always be thankful to those people."

They traveled around mountains that Navar was less familiar with as he had only come this far North a couple times. The party rode around tall mountains and across small valleys for a few more days. The mountains were simply colossal, their shadows stretched over whole valleys, they rode past large lakes and small villages most of which were full of farmers and some fisherman. The views of the landscape were breathtaking throughout their journey, though they found very little flat land. Almost every inch was a gentle slope that led to an immense mountain nearby. There was still plenty of snow on the mountain tops even in the middle of Summer. Snow melted water dropped thousands of feet making stunningly beautiful waterfalls that led into the rivers and lakes of this land. They rode past a few large lakes heading North, after that they found a large town next to one very large lake that three rivers fed into. Prince Thoran said through Navar "That town's name was Zurih, it is a part of our Seduni Celtic tribe."

Pris thought the area was breathtaking, but they were in a hurry to get to Germania. Further along the way they saw some deer in the distance, but the deer quickly ran away from the party.

After two weeks of steady progress the party arrived at a river, the edge of Germania. The mountains of the Alps had begun to decrease into steep forest covered hills and rivers at their Northern side.

Pris asked to stop before going further. Navar asked "Is there anything wrong?"

Pris looked at the Northern horizon then looked at him, "My tribe is at the ocean; past all the tribes of Germania, it would be dangerous for you, Prince Thoran and the escort to travel all the way to my village."

Navar shook his head "We will be fine."

Pris shook her head, "No hear me out. After Luciana and I arrive, it will be perhaps more dangerous for you all to travel back without me. Navar, you've been an amazing guide, you saved Luciana from the cliff and again from bandits. I cannot thank you enough, but from here the way to...."

Navar shook his head "No Pris I am loyal to my word..."

Pris held up her hand, "It's ok, I can hold my own in a fight, and the way home is that way."

Navar asked "How do you know? What if you get lost?"

Pris pulled out her metal bowl from a saddle bag. She dismounted at the river and scooped it full of water. Then pulling out a needle from her knitting kit, she began to sharpen it with her knife at one end. Next, motioning to a wild rhododendron bush nearby, she handed Luciana her knife "Please go cut off a stem of leaves from the bush."

Luciana returned with a leafy stem. Pris pulled off a big leaf and placed it on the water then placed the metal needle she had been scraping onto the leaf, which turned and then stopped. Pris said "North is that way, home that way."

Navar had dismounted and came over to her "You are correct, your father taught you well. But can you both get there safely without an escort? Other than Germanic tribes, as well as bears and wolves are in those woods."

Pris nodded, "We should be fine, but traveling with a group of non-Germanic warriors might be more dangerous."

Navar wanted to disagree, but Pris held up her hand; he could tell that her mind was made up, with a struggle he took a deep breath and then said "As you wish".

Pris smiled, "Hold on" she went to her saddlebag and gave him a bag of gold that Daminian had given her. "You were truly awesome, thank you friend." Pris gave him a hug.

Prince Thoran had listened to the whole conversation in broken Latin he said "You strong woman. Be careful!"

Reluctantly Navar nodded and accepted the bag then remounted his horse, he thought a moment then motioned to one of the pack horses that was carrying food rations. "This one carries enough food for the two of you to get home if you ration and eat small meals. There is small tent gear and here is a short sword on the horse for Luciana in case it's needed. That should be all you'll need. I hope to see you again Pris."

Navar looked at the girl "Luciana you take care of your mother! I pray for you both to have a safe journey. Good luck!"

Then he and the escort rode back in the direction of Sion.

Chapter LVII Germania and new dangers

129 BC

Finally Pris and Luciana arrive in Germania.....

Pris and Luciana watched them leave. Pris looked again at the needle and thinking about the hundreds of Saxons tribes ahead, Luciana saw her and asked "Mommy, is everything alright?"

Pris nodded "I was just thinking about how the Saxon language was similar to my native language, it will be interesting to speak and hear it again."

Luciana nodded as they mounted their horses.

Pris thought *"It has been years since I spoke or heard full conversations in Cimbri, much less Saxon languages."*

Luciana asked "Are we sure this is the way to go?"

Pris nodded "Although I am not really familiar with this exact place, grandpa's hunting survival lessons point the way home. I'm confident we will be fine and are headed in the right direction. There are no Romans ahead anyway."

Luciana didn't say anything.

The rising sun was adding beautiful rays of light through the forest and on many forested hills ahead of them. Luciana said "It's truly beautiful", she said looking across the natural beauty across the stretched horizon.

Pris nodded "This is just the beginning, the forests are full of beauty and wonder, we are more than halfway home."

They descended down the side of the mountain in a gradual way, they had taken note of where a river cut through from the mountain down into the land below. They stayed near the river as much as possible with their horses, but in some areas, they needed to backtrack to other paths. They made their way slowly around the mountain, so it was never truly steep, however it was slow going.

Luciana asked "Mommy, tell me more about home? What kind of food do they eat? What kind of music do they enjoy?"

Pris smiled as she told more about her home. They neared the lower part of the mountain, here the area was full of trees as far as the eye could see and the forest was dark... Pris had tried to avoid the forests as one cannot see very far ahead, but there was no other option.

Entering into the forest, the sounds of forest animals were constant, Luciana kept looking around in the direction of birds, owls and other chirping sounds. Her face showed her excitement. The floor of the forest was a maze of brush, downed logs and small trees... The light was hardly visible even during the day due to the constant tree cover overhead. They continued forward traveling through the forest as the trees became so condensed that they could not see anything but trees and brush covered ground. The sound of water rushing between rocks became audible to them.

Pris motioned in that direction, "Let's head that way, I can make another direction reading."

Luciana nodded "Yes mama. Can you tell me mama, how were you kidnapped?"

Pris told her the story in a little more detail. "So, you were captured by Swabian warriors?"

Pris nodded her head, "Yes, they were merciless, they murdered my mother and many others in the caravan, they...." Pris looked ahead, the trees were beginning to clear, beyond it there was a river.

They came to the last line of trees and looked out over the river. It was a bright day and it was as though humans had never stepped in these lands.

Pris looked at Luciana "Stay here in the tree line where it's safe."

Luciana shook her head "It's so dark and scary in these woods, can I please come with you?"

Pris put her hand on Luciana's shoulder, "You have to stay here for a little while, I will go down to the river, if it's safe I will let you come out."

Luciana looked disappointed and worried, "Alright." She got off her horse and led it into a grassy area behind the trees.

Pris got off her horse and from behind the trees looked around along the river, it was a wide river full of rocks that the water endlessly flowed over and between, the river's water was rapid giving a loud refreshing sound of water rushing over and around the moss-covered rocks. On the far side of the river another view of endless silver fir, pine and beech trees continued in a broad expanse.

Pris grabbed some leaves off of a bush, then she came out from the tree line and looked around. It was wonderful to feel the sunshine and absorb the expanse of natural beauty ahead of her. All appeared safe, then she saw a bridge made of wood far downstream. Pris turned and whistled for Luciana who came out from her hiding place.

Luciana joined her as Pris took her metal bowl out and soon had an understanding of where North was. After she was putting the bowl away, Luciana grabbed Pris' arm pointing up the river "Mama, look"

Pris turned to look up stream and saw three men approaching them from a distance on horses, they were armed with bows, arrows and swords. Worse, these men were wearing all black, like those who had killed her mother and the others so long ago, their braided hair and shaved heads were unmistakable, Pris said "Swabians!"

Just before Pris turned her attention to Luciana she saw one of them pulling out some rope from his saddle. As this was happening, she heard one of them yell the same thing she remembered from long ago, "Fang sei ein!" Pris turned her horse yelling to Luciana in Latin "Flee! They mean to capture us!"

Pris and Luciana started to gallop down the river, as they did Pris saw another one of them coming at them from the tree line to her right. Pris did not like these odds, she knew that they would only be able to flee on this clay-muddy terrain for so long before these men caught them, even now the warrior who approached her from the tree line was closing in on Luciana who had been closer to him. When he was just within ear shot, Pris heard him yell "herkommen!"

Pris hoped he had his focus on Luciana and maintaining control over his horse and on the terrain. Pris heard Aelianus' words *"we must never hesitate at such moments."* Pris yelled "Flee Luciana!"

As she waited another second until their pursuer was nearly on them, she drew her Xiphos sword from its scabbard on her left side turning her horse pivoting and nearly colliding with her pursuer just as his horse caught up to them. She turned so quickly and her sword came out without warning that he had no time to see it or even pull out his own sword, his left hand had been outstretched to grab Luciana, his right was controlling his horse. There was coiled rope and a sword near his torso. Pris' blade sliced under his outstretched left arm and ran through his chest out through the other side; the momentum of the horses at full gallop made the blade cut through his leather armor, flesh, bone and body as if it were made of butter.

The warrior screamed as blood sprayed from the huge slice in his chest and back, blood poured out of his mouth, his dead body fell off his horse.

Pris galloped uphill sensing that Luciana had continued galloping downstream, now on higher ground from their other pursuers and still seated on her horse, she sheathed her sword in its scabbard, then drew her bow and fired three arrows at the other pursuers as they all charged toward her; those men fell off their horses, killing two and perhaps the third. The fourth man had been behind the other two and was too close for her to pull an arrow, so Pris threw her bow down and redrew her sword.

Their swords clashed and then were locked, but the attacker was a little stronger than Pris, holding her blade against his, he kicked at Pris from his saddle, connecting to her stomach, she fell off her horse.

Pris' horse trotted away as the last Swabian jumped off his horse. Pris was already up, her blade in hand, blocking her attackers' overhead slash. Using the blade's momentum she deflected the blade to the side, then using a singular movement Aelianus had taught her, she twisted and slashed her own blade back towards her attacker. It was such a perfectly timed movement, like dancing that it went past her attacker's guard and slashed across his throat. Blood sprayed over Pris as her attacker dropped his sword, clung to his throat a moment, then fell.

Pris swung her blade all the way around again this time she slashed through her attacker's neck sending his head flying with his fingers, more of his blood landed on Pris.

Pris, now the last one standing, she wiped her bloody blade on the dead attacked. She looked up to see that one of the

Swabians who she had shot with an arrow was still alive, he screamed in agony.

Memories of her last encounter with the Swabians flooded her mind, of how they had killed her mother and others of her tribe, of the ground that had turned red from so many who had been like family to her. Pris thought about finishing the screaming man, she started walking towards him, her blade red.

She heard a horse approaching, looking over to see Luciana approaching holding Pris' horse reins.

Luciana spoke "Mother don't, we don't need to slaughter them and be as merciless as they are."

Pris remembered when her father told her "*When we cannot trust men or women or beasts, this we can trust*" Pris looked at Luciana, then nodded.

They rode away from that place following the river, arriving eventually near a large lake where they made camp. The next day they traveled around the lake enjoying the view, then they followed a river from the lake to a waterfall that was about the height of five adults standing on each other's shoulders.

From the cusp of the cliff behind some bushes and trees next to the bank at the top of the Falls, they looked down and could see a village below. There was at least a thousand people in the village, it was a scene, not unlike the memories of her own village, people were working in their little yards attending to their plants, others were riding here or there on horseback, children were playing games, women washing laundry, warriors here and there at defensive positions talking to each other or looking bored.

Luciana looked at Pris "Mama, can we go to that village?"

Pris shook her head, "The clothing they are wearing, their braided long hair and shaved heads, it is the same as those men I killed yesterday, they look like Swabians."

Pris motioned to Luciana, "Let's wait until nightfall and then go around, it is too dangerous."

They waited an hour, but then while listening to the sound of water go over the falls, Luciana who had been looking at the horizon and surrounding scenery noticed several Swabians warriors walking up the far side of the waterfall on the opposite bank.

Luciana whispered loudly "Mama, look! Aren't they Swabians?"

Pris looked in that direction "Yes, it looks like they have fishing gear in their hands, but they are approaching this direction." At that moment shouting was heard down below, Pris and Luciana saw all the Swabian warriors turn their attention back to the village so they did too. Below two riders had approached their town's fortified gate and were yelling to the tower. Pris saw that one of the men had an arrow through his shoulder, instantly she recognized that he was one of the men who had attacked them before at the river.

Pris turned to Luciana "We need to move now!" Pris and Luciana crawled back from the cusp of the cliff and then hurried back to their horses. They got on their horses and then headed East along the river and away from the Swabians.

They traveled through thick forest that slanted slightly downhill, eventually they came to a path that was wide enough for two horses and had stones laid in certain places. The path leveled off where it came to a fork.

Luciana looked at Pris "Mama, which way should we go?" Pris was about to answer when a pair of young women, a few older women and several children, who by the look of their loaded baskets, had been berry picking, a look of fright appeared on their faces seeing Pris' sword and blood-stained clothing.

The women carried staves but no weapons. Pris knew immediately that these women were Swabians, for a moment all froze, sounds of the forest animals chirping broke the moment, Pris pointed to the other way down the fork, Luciana kicked her horse hard and galloped that way with Pris following close behind.

Chapter LVIII A good life

129 BC

Three men sat at a river holding spears watching women and children from the village as they pulled and collected a woven basket net trap that had sunk into the river due to rocks inside. Gisbert looked at Volker, "What is it brother, you've been so quiet today?"

Volker grinned "I have been in deep thought brother, life has been fairly good."

Volker Ragnarr

Konrad laughed "I would say so, a life of hunting, fishing and farming vegetables needed for our village."

Gisbert nodded "Yeah, and thanks to you Volker, no wars in how many years?"

Volker grinned "Father set things up well with our neighbors, we have been lucky. But with so many mouths to feed, I wonder how long it will last."

Konrad laughed, "The Cherusi fight among themselves, the Chatti worry about the Celts more than us, we are allied with the Anglos, the Swabians have enemies all around them..."

Volker nodded, "All the same, I want every man to hunt and practice with their swords or axes each day."

Gisbert laughed, "Sure brother, we can suggest it, most people will practice, but I think it will come after harvesting food for many."

Konrad asked "Is that all that has you quiet, isn't there more to the story?"

Volker shrugged as he picked up a rock, "I saw her again; last night in my dreams."

Gisbert put his hand on Volker's shoulder "I remember her too, brother, the young Pris."

Volker nodded, "I should be over her, now with all that's happened, but it has been impossible to truly forget her."

Konrad nodded, "A first kiss can do that, and she was a truly pretty one."

Gisbert said "That may be so, but you've a great life now brother. Time to let her go."

Volker nodded, "I don't dwell on her night and day, I'm fine." He threw his rock in the river. Volker thought *"Whatever happened to her? Is she still alive?"*

Konrad picked up a rock and threw it across the river, "I remember Volk when your dad, our King, told you days after Pris was kidnapped about how her group had been attacked and that Pris was taken. She is probably dead friend. The Swabians are not kind to their prisoners."

Volker nodded, "Those damn Swabians…. If they hadn't attacked that caravan, Urix, the leader of the Cimbrans wouldn't have gone to war against them, we wouldn't have gone to war against them and maybe Cerdic, might still be alive."

Gisbert said "We cannot change the past, Cedric died in battle against the Swabians, he had a good death."

Volker nodded "True."

Konrad said "He would have been king, but with his death, the responsibility went to you old friend when your dad passed….. The last thing he did was have me married to firm up alliance with the Chatti and assume leadership of their tribe."

Gisbert said "Well Volker, you have been a great king, I have no desire for it, and LInza is a great wife for you."

Volker smiled, "Lucky you are brother."

Gisbert smiled saying "You're our leader, I'm just a fighter."

Volker sighed "It is a heavy responsibility, in a few more moons there will be a regional collective tribe meeting in which the leaders of each tribe will meet to discuss ongoing events, negotiate trade."

Gisbert said "and sometimes declare wars."

Volker nodded, "Hopefully not."

Konrad threw his rock in the river, "Still for the time being, we are a strong tribe, our people are happy, our beautiful queen Linza is pregnant with your child. Times are good, oh leader." Vollker laughed. They examined the net, seeing they had caught 30 fish.

Volker's house was a large, long wooden building, on a small hill inside his village, which contained forest trees here and there. The house was over one hundred years old. The house was just a little larger than the rest of the houses in the village. Volker's house had a large hall on the main floor for receiving important visitors or when the tribe decided to gather for meetings, but there was a fence surrounding the building. Volker said "Tomorrow we will go on a hunt, make sure to spread the word around the village to remind our hunting party."

Volker had awakened just before dawn, he kissed Linza, his sleeping wife on her head before he went downstairs.

He was greeted by their servant Alice; she was a happy old woman.

Alice said "Good morning King Volker."

Volker nodded to her "Morning, is breakfast ready?"

Alice smiled, "I have eggs ready for you, my king."

Volker sat down at the table. Soon she came over, poured a glass of water and placed a plate of eggs, carrots and sweet bread before him.

After his meal, Volker exited from his large house. It was a foggy morning and still pretty dark outside.

The smell of the forest with the mist was strong, and the forest echoed with the sounds of various birds and animals waking up. There was a large group of friends and warriors who had gathered this morning as he had requested.

Volker nodded to his friends Konrad, Klaas, Oliver, Mattias and Hans who were in front of the crowd. Volker's brother-in-law Rax had joined them. "Good morning, all, good morning Rax, I trust you slept well?"
Rax nodded, he motioned towards Volker's horse while making a slight bow. A mighty muscular warrior, his bald head shaved.

Chapter LIX The hunt

129 BC

The hunt....

The whole group consisted of 10 friends and another 50 warrior guards who had brought 30 dogs waiting for Volker on their horses outside his house. They were all dressed in warm fur clothing wearing leather armor and capes. The group had been talking quietly with their warriors similarly ready. Each warrior had packed a couple days provisions, they had tents and pack horses for extra gear and a few to carry back the animals they intended to catch.

Volker mounted his horse then spoke to the group saying "Friends, thanks for coming out early as I requested three days back. Today we hunt for our village's festival. We need fresh meat, deer, boar, bear, turkey or whatever large animal you come across. We need at least three or four large kills to provide enough food for our people. The hunt will be to the South in the mountain's meadows near a river."

Rex asked "Is it far from here?"

Volker shook his head "Not far, it is a wide place where a fire happened long ago, animals are often found there."

Konrad joked "It's easy to hunt, should be no problem for you Rax."

Rax looked at Konrad unamused.

Volker looked at them, "It is the festive moon in three nights, so we will split into three groups to hunt across different sections of that meadow. We will meet back here within three days with whatever you can get. The group that catches the biggest animal will win first beers at the festival. The group cheered.

They rode past several houses that made up their village, and departed through a main gate. From there, they rode through the forest, in which he had lived all his life. They all knew every tree, the moss-covered jagged rocks in the rivers and the large waterfall not far from their homes.

The sound of the water falling over the falls was always something they enjoyed, Volker thought this would be a relatively ordinary hunt. Would they find deer or a bear or a boar? Whatever the case, he had a feeling they might find something special. They rode for an hour and arrived at a large meadow where a forest fire had burned down many trees' years earlier.

The trees in this area were not able to grow tall because the deer would eat the saplings. They stopped, dismounted from their horses, the fog was beginning to dissipate as they waited for an animal to appear from the mist as they usually did, they began rechecking their bows, making sure their arrows were in perfect condition with the thoughts of returning home with some beast for a feast.

Chapter LX The balance of life.

129 BC

Pris and Luciana had ridden a whole day from the fork on the path, no sign of the Swabians following them. From there, they slowed their pace a little, not wanting to gallop near another hostile village.

Arriving at a large lake, Pris made another compass check and from there slightly redirected themselves. They went through an endless forest, the sounds of animals, birds and an occasional rabbit or squirrel sighting to add a little joy. Eventually they came to a river where Pris made a new compass reading and they continued on their course. Each day had the same pattern, in the morning Pris would prepare a meal from the food rations they had brought. Pris would then pull out her metal bowl, rinse her face and Luciana's. After which she would pull out the stem and remove a leaf, sharpen her needle and place the needle on the leaf. The needle would point in the direction they were traveling. Whenever possible they traveled along rivers. Finally, as it became dark, they would camp near the river to supply themselves with fresh water.

After two more days' travel they came upon a large meadow as the sun was setting.

Luciana stopped her horse, "Mommy, can we camp here tonight?"

Pris looked at her, "It is safer near a river darling."

Luciana persisted, pleading "Well, it would be so nice to be able to see some stars without any trees blocking our view."

Pris looked at her in the eyes "Is the forest scaring you?"

Luciana nodded, "Please."

Pris smiled "Very well, we will camp here tonight."

They set camp, made a small campfire and enjoyed a meal. They watched the stars, Luciana fell asleep while Pris stayed awake a little longer, her face showing her in deep thought.

They woke up the next morning and it was very foggy.

Pris could hear the sounds of dogs approaching. Immediately she woke up Luciana, "The Swabians, they may be coming!"

Not desiring to be caught by hostile warriors. They hopped on Pris' horse as Luciana's horse had gotten loose in the night and was in the meadow a good distance off.

They did not have time to spare for cleaning up their tents and started to ride. They rode off on their mare, the sounds of hounds and horses in their wake with rays of the sun just starting to rise over the tops of the Alps behind them in the distance.

Chapter LXI The hunt begins

129 BC

Volker's party arrived at the meadow after an hour's ride, the Sun was now fully up above the Alps to shine through the sky; black crows were flying ahead of them cawing ahead of them. As the group entered the meadow Volker, divided his group into thirds, 15 men went South, 15 North. Volker and his party of 30 would hunt the central meadow. The groups headed into the meadow, as they got towards the center of the meadow, Volker's dogs started barking and were released.

The dogs started running off in a direction towards the opposite side of the meadow. Volker and his men followed, expecting an animal ahead. They went over the ridge of a slight hill where instead of a deer or a slumbering bear, he could barely make out two figures through the remaining mist. There was an adult woman and a girl who had just hopped onto one of their two horses and started galloping away towards the meadows far side. Volker and his guards charged after the two women.

One of Volker's men started to aim his bow, Volker yelled "No! Don't shoot, I want them alive!"

Volker's horse quickly ran ahead of his guards as his stallion was the fastest horse of his group. He started going full gallop, leaving his guards following behind even at this distance he knew he was catching up to the pair of ladies.

Just as the ladies entered into the forest's path, Volker got into calling range "Halt, who are you? Why are you in our lands?"

Pris ignored the yelling at first, but as Volker's powerful stallion continued to close the distance to her mare, she felt down to her sword hilt.

Volker called again "Stop ladies, I will not harm you!"

Pris turned her head a little as she called to her daughter in Latin "Luciana he doesn't seem threatening. Go just beyond the river, I will deal with him there!"

Volker called again "Hey you stop, let's talk!"

Pris thought, *"We must get to a place where I can defend myself, if necessary, just have to make it to that river before his stallion catches us…. His voice sounds familiar, older, but familiar; could it be?"*

Luciana and Pris reached a shallow river and crossed immediately. Pris turned around on the far side as Volker's horse arrived at the other side. Pris had slid Luciana off her horse and pulled out her bow and arrow in a single movement, a move Aelianus had once taught her.

Luciana hopped off and drew the sword Navar had given her, she hurried over to and waited behind a nearby tree shaking. Volker then caught up and stopped his horse at his side of the river, finding Pris across the small slow rocky river waiting on her horse, her arrow locked and aiming straight at his chest. Volker slowly raised his hands to the air grinning, "Wait friend, we mean no harm."

It was at the word friend that Pris relaxed her arrow a little. Saxon was close but not exactly the same language as Cimbrian, it had been 17 years since Pris had heard Saxon, the accents and some words were different in this German dialect. The word "Friend" was the same and that was a start.

Pris looked at him now with both eyes, "Have we met before?" Pris could not remember his face. Volker the boy had short blond hair, this man had short brownish blond hair up top, the sides of his head were shaved, he wore a full short cut beard and had a solid muscular body, Pris saw that he had tattooed arms and hands that looked magical. He wore a wolf belt over his shoulder and a necklace of wolf teeth, a fur over his right shoulder, his leather clothing, cape and chain armor bulging from his muscular body. The sword he wore at his belt looked large and powerful; he wore a ram's horn across his body.

Pris took a chance, speaking in Cimbri, she yelled "I am Pris Haas of the Cimbri, I am looking for Volker Ragnarr of the Saxons."

Volker sat there a moment and he laughed, responding in rough Cimbri, "Well you found me!"

Pris could hardly believe it, taking her arrow's aim off his heart and seeing him as a person, she asked their first question "You enjoy horses?"

Volker nodded "I love them".

Volker and Pris both started laughing as Pris put her bow and arrow away. She looked at him continuing in Cimbri "Is it truly you under that beard?" Volker rode his horse across the river "Yes, it is me, I am older now. Your accent has become even stranger than before." He got to the point that they were right next to each other, their horses heads were near the other horses' butts.

Pris looked at him, his face had grown handsome, but she sensed a seriousness that was not there before. Volker looked at Pris, stunned by how the cute girl he remembered had turned into such a shockingly beautiful woman. Volker felt a yearning that eclipsed anything he had felt for her during their childhood, or for any woman he had known since.

Volker froze looking at her for a moment, then swallowed hard and asked "I... We thought you were dead. Where have you been and what brings you here?"

Pris kept looking into his eyes, she moved her hand through her hair without realizing it. Such a long time since she heard his voice, it was husky now, his German Saxon accent's sound mesmerizing her "It's a long story."

Volker felt a warmth inside him, he had not felt this giddy in ages, meeting her again made him so happy his smile beamed, his face not far from hers "Well then, let's go back to the meadow and talk about it."

At this moment the other members of Volker's party rode up. Rax was the first to arrive, seeing Volker and Pris in an almost romantic like state, immediately eyed them questioningly. Within seconds his other friends arrived one by one, Konrad, Klaas, Oliver, Mattias and Hans they smiled.

Volker turned his horse to the group, signaling them to halt "This is lady Pris of the Cimbri, our allies. I have not seen her in many years, she is our friend. We will escort her and her daughter back to the meadow."

Pris understood all of the words except "Allies" was a word in Saxons she had not learned. Knowing that they were safe, Pris whistled and Luciana came out from her hiding place.

The group returned to the meadow, they passed where Pris and Luciana had slept earlier, they went to Volker's campsite across the Meadow, not far from a thick forest. One of Volker's warriors had fetched Luciana's stray horse and others had collected Pris and Luciana's stuff bringing it all to where Volker's group had camped the night before.

Others of their group had laid out a tent cover to sit on. Once that was done, Volker told his 15 warriors to go hunting; they took their six dogs with them. That done, Volker turned his attention back to Pris, motioning them all to sit, his 10 close friends sat in two semi circles to the sides between Volker and Pris. Volker said "We are all very interested to hear your story."

Pris relayed her life story starting with the diplomatic trade trip when she was a girl, how she joined her sister without her parents knowing when they first met the Saxons. Pris continued with the Swabian battle afterwards, her kidnapping, the frightening trip in a caged wagon to Celtic lands of being whipped, of Helga who had saved her, and then onto Rome.

Pris told them about her life as a slave under Cyprian, about how she had been raped and had her twin kids. Pris told them how Aelianus, her second master, had been kind, more like a father who taught her some swordplay. Pris talked about the brothel raid, the last dinner with Aelanus, how Sarth who had always been somewhat independent was missing when the assassination happened, how she suspected that he saved them by ringing Aelianus' bed bell and that she didn't know his fate.

Pris said "He was such a brave good boy, there was no one else alive in the house, the bell ringing could only have been him…." She had to stop, she felt tears coming.

Volker touched her shoulder "You did well. You protected your daughter, your son protected you both. That was a very brave and honorable choice for him."

Pris wiped away some tears before telling them about how they fled to Daminian to get help, but that they had to escape Rome on his ship. Pris spoke of Navar, King Tor, Prince Thoran and the journey North.

When she was done, Volker sat a short while then leaning forward and holding her shoulder he said "Life may throw unimaginable challenges at us. It is not that we encounter such challenges but how we rise and the path we choose to travel that defines us."

Pris nodded, smiling "Aelianus sometimes would say we have to fall down so we can stand up."

Volker nodded, "Yes, I agree. Well, Pris, I have to tell you about myself, I have had a much more ordinary life. After your caravan was raided, your King Urix and your father joined forces with my father and we warred with the Swabians. It was vicious, my brother Cedric was killed. Yet we won, because Cedric was killed, I was tapped to be heir. I was pushed into an arranged marriage with the Chatti clan's Princess Linza. She has been my wife and our Queen for about two years; and she is now pregnant."

Pris smiled, feeling a little sad "Congratulations! She is a lucky woman."

Volker nodded, "I was not planning on getting married, but I was duty bound. I had already fallen in love once and lost out, the idea of falling in love again seemed somehow wrong. Yet I had a duty. Linza is my wife, I owe her my loyalty and my love."

Pris nodded "I understand, life has continued on. Well, she is a very lucky woman."

Volker smiled and motioned to his group members who had just returned with a deer they had killed, he looked back at Pris "You and your daughter must stay with us at least long enough to celebrate at our festival and your return to

Germania. After the festival my men will escort you to Jutland and your Cimbrian people."

Pris grabbed him happily on his forearms "Thank you!"

Volker smiled, "It's the least we can do." He turned his head looking across the meadow "And it looks like one of my hunting parties has caught us some dinner."

Pris followed his gaze to where about 100 yards away she saw hunting party of 15 men were returning with a dead boar being hauled on a pack horse.

Chapter LXII Uninvited company

129 BC

Time for a reckoning..........

At that moment, out of the woods 20 Swabian warriors emerged. Volker and his group of 12 all mounted their horses and turned to face this large ominous group of black armored Swabian warriors that now approached them.

When they got about ten horse lengths apart, two of the Swabians continued to ride a little further ahead approaching them. The larger one had a bear skull as his helmet, his shoulders had skulls on them, his black armor had a black cape attached that blew in the wind. The man who rode with him had a shoulder that was bandaged, but otherwise wore similar armor and color as the other. The rest of their group approached on their horses close behind the first two.

The larger one bellowed out in a language Pris could barely understand, she did understand "I am Günther, a few days ago, at a river....," He said a few words she didn't understand, then pointed to Pris "...she killed three of our men, another wounded...."

It suddenly hit Pris though, Günther had the same skull cap as one of the men who had attacked her parents convoy all those years ago, his armor was the same.

Volker listened and then said something in his language and his group began to laugh. In a calm voice Volker said out loud in Cimbrian "He says you killed three of his men

521

recently, that he wants to burn you at the stake. I will not let them." Volker next yelled to the two, "If you want her, you must fight through us!"

Günther put his fingers to his lips and blew a whistle. Another 20 warriors emerged from behind Volker's group at the other side of the meadow and began approaching them. Their leader barked orders to Volker pointing at Pris though she didn't really understand.

Volker laughed, shook his head and drew his sword.

Günther yelled and he and his men started to charge.

The Swabian Leader, Gunther the Champion

Volker yelled and his group pulled their bows and arrows firing a volley into the charging warriors, several of them fell off their horses. Volker then put his hunting ram horn to his lips and sounded it out three times loudly, he yelled "Charge!!" He galloped at their leader.

Konrad, Oliver, Mattias and three of their guards close behind Volker immediately engaging the Swabian leader and his warriors. Rax, Pris, Klaas and Hans and their three other guards turned their bows towards the 20 Swabians who were attacking from across the meadow, in an instant arrows shot out causing three Swabian warriors to fall. Volker's party let another volley of arrows loose, five more of the attackers fell, they drew their swords as the Swabian reinforcements hit them from the side. Volker had charged at Günther, but two of his bodyguards rushed up and he battled with them with his shield and sword.

Volker was a champion with different forms of swordplay, on a horse, or off a horse, with a shield, or without. He aggressively attacked the guards, quickly killing them. Meanwhile Klaas and Hans of his party were killed. Konrad and Oliver were each fighting enemies, eventually the entire party was fighting, Oliver used his dagger and killed an enemy while they were locked with their swords, then threw his dagger killing another. A third Swabian warrior rode up as this happened and attacked Konrad who parried a few strikes and slashes, but then the warrior deflected his blade and Konrad's arm and blade vibrated from the strike, he took his attention off his enemy just to steady his hand, but in that moment the Swabian warrior did a second slash and sent Konrad's head flying. Volker saw this, "Noooooo!" he yelled as he attacked Konrad's killer.

The two charged each other and fought, parrying each other's blows and Volker grabbed his opponent causing both men to fall to the ground. Volker jumped up a little faster than the enemy warrior and had an advantage of slightly higher ground. The two of them continued parrying each other's blade thrusts and slashes. Volker moved his sword around in a crazy eight pattern, beckoning this warrior to engage. They clashed again, their swords ringing off each other with each parried blow.

Günther began swinging a chain that had a loud whistle on the end, it emitted a loud piercing sound. At the noise, another 30 Swabians charged out of the woods, seeing this, Volker kicked his opponent down and then yelled to his men, "Everyone battle our way out of this meadow, let's get to the trees away from them" Volker yelled pointing to the closest tree line that was away from the approaching Swabian reinforcements "We must use the trees!"

Their group fought their way through in the direction Volker had pointed, where the Swabians were not present. As Pris and the others pulled back to their new defensive area that was thick with trees, Volker, Oliver and Rax fought off Günther and his warriors. Volker pulled out his ram horn again, as he did this the warrior who had been kicked down caught up to Volker, they restarted their battle as Volker retreated backwards. Pris arrived at the tree line, seeing that Luciana was safe in the tree cover, she pulled out her bow and began firing arrows at the Swabian attackers killing many.

At that moment Navar appeared on his horse at full gallop with Thoran and 19 Seduni warriors all on horseback following him as they charged towards the Swabians who were now in the middle. Navar pulled out his bow at full gallop and began shooting arrows killing Swabians from behind.

Volker was still battling his opponent at the tree line, his opponent seemed tired and a slash was done somewhat sloppily, Volker grabbed the enemy's sword arm at the wrist and then plunged his own blade through his opponent's heart.

Volker blew his horn again, suddenly six dogs jumped out of the forest followed by 15 of Volker's warriors who had gone hunting charged their horses from across the meadow heading towards the battle raged, the group leader blew his horn in answer, giving Volker and his men additional confidence that help was coming. As Volker's last opponent fell, another Swabian warrior attacked him, but Volker was able to dodge and the blade hit a tree. Volker counter slashed his blade across the side of that enemy's stomach, mortally wounding the Swabian. He backed away as blood sprayed, his face in shock, dropping his blade he fell over.

Pris had just killed another opponent with her bow. As she did this, Günther, the bear-skulled leader charged at her.

Pris heard her mother's voice, Rúna say "That one" as she saw Rúna 's ghost pointing at Gunther. Pris shot at him with another arrow, but his horse had run over some ground that was slightly lower and the arrow bounced off Gunther's armored shoulder pad. Throwing her bow down as he jumped off his horse, Pris avoided his initial attack dodging right of his overhead slash and engaged him in battle. Pris, knowing Günther had attacked her people, and was responsible for her mother's death, felt an uncontrollable sense of vengeance erupt in her. Pris parried Günther's attacks again and again.

Navar, Thoran and the Seduni warriors had by this point had caught up to the back of the Swabians. They attacked the Swabians, some who had turned around. The 30 Swabian reinforcements had arrived and split, some attacking Volker and Pris' group, others attacking Navar and Thoran's group. Navar jumped off his horse, engaging the Swabians in battle Thoran was knocked off his horse, then similarly was fighting.

At this point the six dogs attacked the Swabians and several more Swabians were hit by arrows from the hunting party before they plowed into the fighting on their horses. Günther on the other side of the fighting attacked Pris ruthlessly. Pris countered his slashes with moves she had learned from Krull and perfected with Aelianus. After he had blocked her low, she pulled back her blade looking to swing high, Günther raised his sword to block there, but as Pris swung, she adjusted her swing's angle midway sharply downward, her blade cut into Günther's chainmail covered breast, he cursed as the mail broke in places and his side soon had a slash that was bleeding badly.

Pris tried to stab for the kill but Günther blocked her strike and their swords interlocked. "Why did you attack my parents?"

Pris shouted in Cimbrian, Günther looked puzzled, Pris hit him in his wounded side, he yelped in pain as she moved her blade pointing towards his neck, Günther clutched his wound while defensively parrying her attacks. Their swords clashed then locked. Pris yelled "Why did you attack our convoy outside the Saxon town near a river all those years ago?"

Günther's eyes lit up as he replied in Cimbrian "You? You are Cimbrian? You were there?"

Pris knocked his sword away then pushed her blade close to his neck, "Why??"

Günther replied "A man named Ubel had a blood pact over our late king. Ubel requested we attack a Cimbrian convoy, he promised us riches in payment for his blood debt."

Pris was stunned, a Swabian warrior rushed in and attacked Pris with his ax, as her attention went to the attacker Günther, seeing an opportunity, ran back to his sword, then seeing Pris was busy fighting his warrior, he mounted his horse and galloped to find protection with his men.

Pris parried her new attacker's blows, then finding an opening she deflected his ax and slashed across his shoulder, jaw bone and cheek. Blood erupted; the attacker broke off.

During this time, the fighting between the Swabians and the Seduni group had become totally intermixed. Thoran was fighting against one Swabian and another Swabian went to attack him from behind. Navar saved Thoran by slicing the Swabian in half, but while that happened, the Swabian who was clashing swords with Thoran got a lucky strike on Thoran's shield, he kicked Thoran in the stomach, knocking him down. The Swabian was about to finish him when Navar threw his sword into the attacker's chest, then picked up an axe and defended Thoran from other attackers until Thoran could get on his feet again.

Volker now had a clear path and rejoined Pris in fighting off attacking Swabian warriors.

Günther, behind his men and bleeding badly, looked to where Navar, Thoran and the Seduni warriors were off to the right flank still killing many Swabians. Gunther saw how the Saxon hunting party had hit their left flank and that his warriors were now bottle necked between three groups. Looking at his own wounds, and seeing they had lost dozens of men and had many more injured. Gunther yelled "Swabians retreat!"

The other remaining Swabians pulled off their attack and ran for their horses and retreated. The Saxons and Seduni groups killed a few more Swabians as they tried to run off.

Volker turned to Pris "You injured their leader and that turned the tide, and now they have retreated. Good job!"

Pris grinned with agreement, wiping her bloody blade on the cape of a dead Swabian. "We all did well... and look, my friend Navar and the Seduni showed up!"

Volker saw them and grinned broadly saying "Navar is a fierce looking warrior, they all are."

Pris agreed, "I learned a little more about them from their leader. Do you think he will die?"

Volker looked back "Hard to say, perhaps."

Pris looked in that direction too, "He was one of the leaders who attacked my parents all those years ago."

Volker smiled, "Well you gave him an injury he will never forget."

Navar and Thoran came over, Pris looked at them thankfully. "What, what are you doing here?"

Navar smiled, "I was returning with Thoran and the Seduni escort to Sion. We camped that first night and I heard a deer being attacked by wolves. A fawn was calling for help,

I found the mother deer dead and the wolves were circling around the fawn that stood on top of a large rock. As I watched pulling out my bow, a large stag with huge antlers suddenly jumped through the trees and killed many wolves causing them to flee. I took that as a sign that you might be in trouble, that you would need help. Thoran wanted some adventure, so we returned to where we parted in the mountains and then I tracked you here."

Pris smiled, patting his shoulder, "Wow, thank you both. This is King Volker and his Saxon men. King Volker, this is Navar, Thoran and their Seduni escort."

Navar smiled "May I continue to escort you home?"

Pris nodded, Volker said "I will have my men escort you all to Pris' village. After that they will escort you, Navar, Thoran and your men back to the Alps." Navar and Thoran thanked Volker then they all went to mount their horses.

Chapter LXIII A feast to celebrate

129 BC

They traveled to Volker's town and celebrated that night with several hundred people. Volker ordered sixty of his men to escort Pris, Navar and Luciana to the Cimbrian lands. Volker asked his friends to lead the party. The two other hunting groups that had gone out had also returned, one with a dead wild boar and the other with another deer.

Volker's wife welcomed their guests into their home. They enjoyed the town over the next couple days. Volker had his cleric look at Luciana's shoulder.

On the eve of the festival, hundreds of townspeople gathered among musicians playing, the food being cooked, they feasted on the meats that were provided with fresh beer. Luciana felt a little odd in this world that her mother seemed so at home in. Pris saw that Luciana was looking nervous, so put her arm around Luciana and together they enjoyed the music and dancing. A few girls about Luciana's age came over to her wanting to show her how to dance to their music, soon even Luciana was laughing and dancing among them.

Volker's sister Christina, having heard of the battle, arrived during the celebration to check on Volker. She and Gisbert saw Volker looking at Pris, "Sweet brother." Christina said, "Good to see you and your old friend again."

Volker watched Pris throughout the celebration, he kept seeing her and feeling anguish inside. Navar, Thoran and the Seduni enjoyed the food and drink. They stayed close to Pris, though they did not talk to her much.

That night Volker had a hard time sleeping even though he had only drunk one beer at the feast, normally he would drink three or more at a feast like that.

"What is wrong with me?" Volker thought again, I have not seen Pris in 20 some years. I am married to Linza, my wife, and she is pregnant. *"Why do I still think about Pris?"* Downstairs, Pris was asleep when she awoke to Luciana crying and shaking.

Pris shook Luciana awake, "What's wrong dear?"

Luciana started crying, "Sarth! I cannot forget about him"

Luciana continued. "He survived somehow, but then he was scared and suddenly there were dark figures all around him and around us. Then I woke up."

Pris held Luciana for a long embrace, "I promise you Luciana, somehow I will reunite you and Sarth, if he is alive, you will see him again."

The next morning Volker woke up early, put on his brown pants and green shirt with a cape that was the current style and exited his house. Oliver, Navar as well as four of Volker's best warriors were there waiting as two more were approaching from the road. Oliver waved "Morning Volker, you are up early."

Volker nodded "I did not sleep well"

Oliver nodded understanding; he had been a close friend of Volker's since childhood. "Don't worry, we will get her home safe."

Volker nodded "The ladies are about to eat breakfast, have you all eaten already?"

The men all nodded "Alright then, they will eat and then will be coming out. It may be a while."

Volker returned back inside, he knocked on Pris' door, "your escort is here Pris, are you and your daughter awake?"

Pris came to the door, "We are awake and ready for breakfast."

Volker motioned towards the kitchen "Alice will see to your needs over there".

After Pris and Luciana had eaten they thanked Alice and were greeted by Linza the queen who had just awakened. Linza came down her belly the size of a large ball. Alice went to her as she said that she would like to eat some eggs. Alice went to work and Linza looked at Pris and spoke in Saxons "So you are the girl my husband met all those years ago?"

Pris smiled "Much time had passed since then and you have now started a wonderful family. I'm happy for you."

Linza smiled, Volker came in, kissed Linza's cheek and greeted Pris; "Are you ready to go?"

Pris nodded her head, Volker smiled "Very well your escort is outside".

Volker walked them out, he greeted Novar and Thoran.

Volker then smiled at Pris and Luciana, "I hope to see you both again before long. You will always have a friend in me Pris."

Pris smiled back "Dear King, you are and always will be my treasured friend."

They rode off into the forest heading North escorted by Volker's men, Navar, Thoran and the remaining 12 Seduni warriors. Volker watched them leave; he and Pris shared a final wave to each other. Pris thought she saw him sucking in his bottom lip. He waited until the trees made them disappear from sight then he went back inside his home.

They traveled with their escort of 60 Saxon warriors North for another week, they traveled through the Saxon and Angle lands back to the Cimbri in the Jutland region.

Chapter LXIV Almost home

129 BC

They traveled to Northern Germania.

The Summer weather was temperate and Pris and Luciana who had been used to Rome's hot and humid weather throughout the year felt cold. Pris remembered the weather from when she was a child, but the wind greeting them coming from the ocean was a welcome reminder of where she had come from. The sights and sounds were still the same.

They came out of the trees seeing the rocky ocean shoreline that was instantly familiar, Pris got off her horse and ran to the edge of the familiar cliff that overlooked the ocean. The wind was gently hitting the group and the sound of waves crashing against the rocks along the shoreline, gulls flew above them calling to each other. In a million ways the scene was the beautiful familiar place that Pris remembered. Pris looked to the west to where her fortified home was at the edge of the last hills that dropped steeply to a peninsula that had a bay sheltered from the ocean.

Pris could see from this distance that her town had grown to perhaps a thousand people, but was largely as she remembered it. There were people who were working in the fields to the South where she had once been attacked by the bear, behind the village to the East opposite the ocean there appeared to be wheat fields, along the bay there were men busy on fishing boats.

The group rode down the well-traveled path at a semi-gallop, Pris wanted to return as fast as she could, Luciana did too. Oliver smiled; he could see they were at the right place. The path led into a short stretch of woods, then when they arrived near the farmland that went to the town Oliver said "Party stop. It is time."

Thoran nodded, "She can get home safely from here."

Navar smiled at Pris, "I am glad I can know that you are both safe. Now I can return to Sion, and then maybe to Massalia. I will let Daminian know you got home safe should I see him again."

Pris thanked Navar and gave him a kiss on the cheek.

Pris thanked Oliver, Thoran and the Saxon-Seduni escort. Navar gave a last wave then he galloped his horse following after Oliver, Thoran and the Saxon-Seduni escort back South from where they had come.

Pris and Luciana rode along the road towards the gates of her town.

Pris mentioned the spot where her friend had enraged a bear long ago; they rode into the open fields that were full of rows of crops. An old farmer was directing his field hands in the harvest, He waved to Pris thinking how familiar she looked.

At the closed gates the guards on the wall loudly called for the gates to be opened. Warriors in the towers to either side of the walls and on the walls looked, shouts were heard from inside and the doors opened. Several warriors approached Pris and Luciana. Pris called out in Cimbrian "I Pris, daughter of Krull Haas, am home, let me and my daughter into this town."

One fierce looking warrior who had a muscular body, long red beard and long red hair removed his helmet, Pris recognized him, "Karl is that you? You survived the bear!"

They both laughed as Karl said "Oh my! Pris, is it really you?"

Pris laughed as they gave each other a friendly hug "So good to see you old friend!"

Karl shouted, "You are alive Pris! Oh my, we need to get you inside, who is this lovely girl?" Pris motioned to her daughter "This is Luciana."

Karl grinned broadly "Excellent. Well, Lena will be thrilled to see you again. She is now my wife!"

Pris smiled, "That's wonderful."

Karl turned to the other warriors who were younger than he and didn't recognize her, "This is Pris you fool, Krull's eldest daughter!"

The warriors cheered, "Welcome!" A large crowd of people came out to see with the older ones recognizing Pris shouted for joy and soon the crowd began to cheer as they walked into the front gate amongst jubilation.

Chapter LXV Krull

129 BC

After so many years my mother and grandfather would find happiness.

Krull Haas

The old man was working in his home, his once bright red hair had begun to fade to gray at the sides of his head. Krull Haas ran his hand through his hair, then petted his loyal dog Spike. Krull was still very fit and active, now just past his 64th year. His town of Husum had grown substantially during his life, Krull had been a proactive leader, attending to the needs of his village, and the population had flourished under his leadership.

A knock came to his door, Krull had been working inside his own house rebuilding a wooden chair. Krull answered the door, he saw his old friend and commerce advisor Sveinn, Bryn and Rob were standing outside with a jug "We've come by to see how you are old friend, what are you doing inside?"

Krull smiled, waving them inside, "I have been working with my hands, fixing this old rocking chair." Krull loved to see a project start and then to feel the joy of accomplishment when it was done correctly.

Sveinn smiled "Perhaps you could share it with a woman?"

Krull smiled a moment. "You know old friend; I have not gone after a woman in ages."

Sveinn shrugged, "You are not dead yet?"

Rob said "Much the shame, let's drink!"

Krull enjoyed the distraction, the thought of using a new chair led him to feel tears as the old chair that this one was replacing had been built by himself with his daughter Pris shortly before she was taken, his wife killed and his world turned upside down. The old chair had been repaired so many times, but it had finally been crushed under him when Krull was in a drunken stupor a few weeks ago. Having thought again about Rúna and Pris. Krull was using some of the wood from the old one, so he could feel that something he had made with Pris would still live on.

Krull and Sveinn sat down as Sveinn poured his beer "For you my liege".

Krull nodded his thanks deep in thought, *"What happened to you, my little one? Are you still alive somewhere?"* Krull drank a long sip.

Sveinn refilled Krull's mug, "Krull do you really not want another woman?"

Krull looked at Sveinn, he shrugged, "I've spent so many years as a widower, raising Tuli who has grown to become a beautiful woman. I just have become accustomed to being single in this life and frankly Rúna was so perfect a soulmate for me, I just cannot think seriously about others."

Rob nodded, holding an empathic smile.

Sveinn put his hand on Krull's shoulder "But sire, I have seen you enjoy speaking with and in the company of other women, why not open your old heart?"

Krull shook his head, "For me? No…"

Sveinn shrugged, "Some seem to think it is almost their responsibility to become your new mate."

Krull laughed, "Well, I am alright. Tuli comes to check on me, but since she got pregnant and had the baby, I have been checking more on her."

Rob spoke up "We know Krull, you seem to fight loneliness in your house, that is why you keep busy fixing up things, hunting, fishing or some days just watching the ocean waves crash against the rocks isn't it?"

Krull looked away.

Sveinn continued "My liege, you are our leader, we have waited decades for you to come around, but we all hope you can be happy again."

Krull smiled, "Don't worry about me, Drenor often comes over and to pass time drinking and talking, it is enough."

Krull grabbed a pretzel that a woman had brought him a day earlier. "This was a gift by one of those ladies."

Sveinn pointed to him "See, I am speaking the truth."

Krull broke apart his pretzel "My main joy now is my pride in Tuli, as you know she has married Peter Wolfsbane, a fine man; he is a good hunter like myself."

Sveinn and Rob nodded knowing that Krull had taught Peter carpentry, and eventually when Krull was confident that Peter was a good man, he gave his permission for Peter to court Tuli. They had married shortly after, Krull and others of the village had built their home, which was next door.

Sveinn looked at Krull in his eyes, "My friend, are you alright? We are here to listen if you want to share anything."

Krull looked up then down to the left and to the right, they were still waiting.

Finally, Krull took another sip of his beer and he looked at Sveinn then Rob directly "I awaken many nights screaming. At times I find myself anxious that something might happen to Tuli. I occasionally have nightmares of the attack all those years ago. Only all my family, even Tuli, are slaughtered by that Swabian chieftain and his men with Ubel laughing as their bodies fall…. The dreams… the shaking, they've never left me."

Sveinn waved his finger in the air "Sire, you are not at fault for that, you must not blame yourself."

Krull looked at him, beat his chest as he raised his voice, "I still blame myself for everything, all those who were killed, my wife Rúna and Pris kidnapped, Pris… maybe killed."

Krull looked from the ceiling, back to them. "I was their leader, it was my responsibility to keep them safe, I failed."

Rob shook his head, "No, no one could have predicted or prevented that from happening, and you were wounded at the end of that battle."

Krull shrugged, "I should have known Ubel would betray us, I should have ended him on that deer hunt."

Rob and Sveinn glanced at each other, then Rob started to say "You could not have…."

Krull nodded his head violently, "Damn right I should have known!"

Krull bit his lip, "Tuli is also still dealing with it. Yesterday she told me she had a dream recently, that she saw an adult Pris happily greeting them in her dream. Tuli must be seeing Pris' ghost welcoming Tuli's next future baby."

Sveinn said, "It is possible that Tulii might be right. She sees things like her grandmother Fiona."

Krull took another large gulp of mead "It was only after Tuli had given birth to her baby girl that I finally felt some real joy again, as a grandfather."

Rob patted Krull on his shoulder, Sveinn said, "Krull no matter what it was not your fault, and Tulli brought you a new future."

Krull nodded, but he had largely zoned out.

Krull said "What? Ah friends, I am sorry. All of his efforts to protect her had been in vain, My lessons had put her in harm's way. Fiona had once told me that it was not my fault."

Rob said "We all know that Rúna's death and Pris' kidnapping had also impacted Fiona terribly; she died shortly after."

Sveinn nodded, "It is important to accept what happened and move on."

Krull thought about all the things he had done. "For the longest time I had hoped to find Pris, but her trail was cold. Now all my hopes are aimed at Tuli and his granddaughter Fiona."

Rob and Sveinn said, "Well Krull, no matter what we are here for you." Sveinn burped as he said goodbye, Rob also drunk, helped Sveinn as they stumbled out as a tipsy

Krull walked them to the door. Krull waved at him, smiling "Come back again you beer animals."

The sun was shining, Krull closed his eyes, *"Oh Rúna, my soulmate, how I miss thee...."* Krull returned inside to his work and wiped away a few tears he suddenly found rolling down his face. Spike his dog came over so Krull played with him by throwing a stick across the room, he gave the dog some dried meat, then returned to his work.

Krull thought *"Come on old fool, get it together, must not cry."* He had lined up a couple of boards, had his nails out and was about to start hammering.

Chapter LXVI Reunion 129 BC

Spike came over smelling Krull then contentedly chewed on his stick. Spike's ears perked up, he stood up looking around and began to bark.

Then sounds of commotion hit Krull's ears. At first, he thought some villagers might be arguing, so deep in thought he was, but no it was not arguing, it was cheers. The cheers seemed to be increasing. Krull stood up off the floor, petted Spike and grabbing his scabbarded sword he went outside with his dog Spike following wondering what was happening. As he walked a few paces he continued to hear excited cheering and clapping, now someone was blowing a horn, people were coming out of their houses all equally curious about the sounds. Krull's excitement began to build, *"What was going on? Has the king decided to make a sneak visit? Our people don't really care so much for him, unlike his father Urix. This is odd, what's going on?"*

Suddenly Drenor, with his one eye patch who lived closer to the gate came racing around the home's corner with a huge smile on his face, waving his arms wildly he shouted, "Krull come to the gate it's a miracle you have to come! Where's your daughter Tuli?"

Krull had a curious look, "Tuli is in her house, what's going on?"

As he said this Tuli came outside beaming with excitement, "Papa! I saw it, today is the day!" Tuli exclaimed.

Before Krull could ask what was going on and before Drenor could answer him, a crowd of people brought Pris and her daughter Luciana around the corner.

Krull looked at Pris and Pris at Krull, they both stood in awe of each other for a moment, Pris spoke first "Papa!"

They rushed to each other, Krull's sudden surprise was so great an explosion of pure joy shot through his body, tears streamed down his face. Pris was followed by Luciana and they hugged for a long time to the sound of cheers and clapping.

From behind Krull they heard an excited voice "Sister!!" Tuli had rushed over and then she also embraced Pris, they looked at each other and at Krull.

Pris said to them, "Papa, Tuli, this is my daughter Luciana." Hans, Rob Sveinn and Drenor all gave a huge cheer as Krull gave Luciana a kiss, Lena and Karl arrived with smiling faces to give Pris and Luciana hugs as Krull welcomed Pris and Luciana into his home.

Sveinn, Rob, Drenor, Lena and Karl all of the crowd of villagers cheered, all had tears of joy as they congratulated the two ladies on their momentous journey. Then Krull raised his hands and called out, "My friends, I should like to see my daughter and granddaughter now."

The villagers nodded and returned to their homes. Krull led his family into his home where he motioned them to sit at his dining table. Pris came over and hugged Krull for a long time. Krull laughed, "I was not expecting company, Would you all like water, tea, beer or Glogg?"

Pris laughed, "Tea for Luciana, Glogg for the adults."

Krull nodded and prepared their drinks. "Papa it's so good to see you, you are still pretty fit, though you now have gray hairs."

Krull gazed at her, laughed and shrugged, "After all that happened, are you not surprised that I am elderly?"

Pris laughed, "I thought of you constantly all these years."

Krull nodded "And I of you... You've sure grown, you were just a girl when you were taken. Now you're a lovely woman. I am so proud of you and seeing you alive again is something I had lost all hope of. Today is truly a happy one."

Krull handed her a drink and one for himself. "Now tell me, I cannot wait to learn about what has happened to you Pris."

At that moment, Drenor, his wife Saxa and their four children all arrived to join the gathering. Luciana and Saxa's children played with Spike as Pris told the adults everything over the next hour, in much more detail than Luciana knew.

Krull felt a mix of emotions from controlled rage about the confirmation of Ubel's betrayal, relief that Aelianus had been a kind master, to the shock about her whipping, of her rape, the assassination of Aelianus, he wondered about the ship they had escaped in and the battles she and Luciana had survived through on their trip home. Krull's face showed concern as he thought about the fate of his grandson Sarth though he also felt immense joy to see Pris and Luciana here.

Krull sat for a long time listening, his gaze turned distant and Pris touched his hand, "Papa are you ok?"

Krull's attention returned to his daughter "The gods have been kind in returning you to me, I am proud of you. You survived…. through all of that. Luciana is beautiful, she can have a good life here. We must pray for Sarth and hope for the best."

Pris nodded, "I do every day and night. Have you ever seen that traitor, Ubel? He betrayed us, he is the reason mother was murdered, Drenor lost his eye and my kidnapping."

Krull shook his head as he stood up, Pris went on, "I saw him in Rome, he was at a market and threatened Luciana and I, but then seemed concerned when I told him he could be crucified if he touched us."

Krull felt his blood boil, "I should have killed him on our hunt. As soon as I was able to walk again, I led a raid on the Swabians village in which our warriors tracked your kidnappers. You were already gone, they must have traded you before you got there, or perhaps Ubel took you and traded you to the Taurisci?"

Pris shrugged, "I don't know, I was blindfolded at first until they put me in a cage on a wagon."

Krull bit his lip, "In the raid of the Swabians village, we killed many guards. I killed the chieftain of the attack, but Ubel was not there. I have never seen him. If he is still alive, I hope the Gods will give him a painful death."

Krull looked at Pris and Luciana, "Well, onto happier thoughts. Until something changes, you both will be living with me. Tuli is right next door, and we will have to introduce you to her husband and their baby'"

Tuli said happily "It's ok. Hold on one moment", Tuli left briefly, then she returned with her baby in her arms with a tall and solid bearded brown-haired man behind her "This is my husband Peter Wolfsbane and our baby Fiona".

Pris and Luciana greeted Tuli and her baby followed by a smiling Krull. They all felt happier than they had in decades.

Pris, Tulli and Luciana spent the next few days straightening up Krull's home, giving it their lady's touch to Krull's amusement and mild consternation.

--------------The End of Story #1: Wolf & Eagle----------------

THANK YOU, DEAR READER!!

I hope you enjoyed reading this story. It is the 1st of a planned series that will cover the Cimbrian-Roman war. I tried to create an early lead up story that takes historical events and persons, I weaved them with fictional ones in a way with the desire to give insight, respect, and enjoyment of the human condition. Also being that it is a fictional story, I added a steam powered ship engine to Seawitch. Being a huge original series Star Wars fan, I wanted something similar to the Millennium Falcon. In real history the first steam engine was created in ancient Roman Greece around the year 100 AD, so I simply made the same event happen about 200 years earlier. In actual history, the Romans never thought the invention was valuable and did not do anything with it.

If you enjoyed reading this story, please leave a review on Amazon on this book's promotional page.

Every review made in Amazon adjusts the algorithm, making it easier for other readers to discover my book. Thank you in advance for taking a moment to share your thoughts of this story, your kind support of this book is greatly appreciated.

Acknowledgements

My deep thanks to those who helped beta read, edit and promote my book. Also, I gained a great understanding of the Cimbrian-Roman war and of writing fiction from YouTube videos. Thanks to my wife Naoko and my daughters Lucy and Lori for their endless encouragement and for listening to this story read via speechify over and over in our cars as I drove them to ballet practice. Thanks to my father, David Krug for editing, to my mother Mary for her endless support and encouragement.

Huge thanks to my dear friend Mari Matsui for the book cover's front and back and for the great character illustrations throughout the book, for all the adjustments and extra illustrative requests I made, you added so much artistic enhancement to this book, thank you.

Thanks to my brother Peter Krug for listening to my crazy plot ideas as well as thanks to friends Ryan Monteith, Jordi Vollom, Brad Dorsey, Parrish Handa, Allan Chan, Brian Rugg, Sean Emery, Erskine Fred, Annelies Gilbert, Valdez Bravo, Katsu Shibata, Kazu Hirose and countless other friends for their support, encouragement, and ideas they freely shared as my story took on form.

I would be skipping over a big influence of my life, if I do not mention my having lived in Japan for 10 years. I experienced how different it is to be a foreigner in such a spectacular country. I found that most Japanese people are some of the most hospitable people anywhere. Yet being a pale skinned amber haired American, I became familiar surviving in a different culture in which I could never truly be Japanese no matter how good my fluency is in the Japanese language. I love Japan, while I have American and other foreign friends who have decided to stay there for even longer periods, I made the choice to return home, for better or worse. I believe my experience of being a foreigner in that country may have added some influence on Pris' experience in Rome. That said, Japanese food is amazing, Japanese people are probably the kindest anywhere, it is a beautiful and very safe country. It is a fabulous place to visit. Someday I would like to visit Italy, to see some of the places I have imagined, have seen videos and films about.

Also growing up my friends and I played countless hours of AD&D (Advanced Dungeons & Dragons). These friends, Jason Redman, Paul & Ara Weller, Brian Dupont really gave me a love of imagining and story telling what it would be like for characters to survive through dangerous encounters as well as playing across a range of personality types. I believed that as a dyslexic, it would be impossible for me to write a 500+ page story, and I plan to add at least a couple sequels to this story. Yet, I have a dream, I finally realized it and thank God my wife has not disowned me as I have chased after this dream.

Here is a list of online video and writing support sources that I used to do research and in writing this novel:

- YouTube videos by Abbie Emmons

  o HOW TO DO LOVE TRIANGLES

- How to REWRITE A NOVEL

- THE SECRET TO IRRESISTIBLE INTERNAL CONFLICT

- How To SHOW and Not TELL Internal Conflict

- How to Find Your Character's MISBELIEF (or Fatal Flaw)

- Youtube video by Diane Callahan

- 7 Lessons Writers Can Learn from Harry Potter

- Youtube video by Sebastian Ioan

- Ancient Steam Engines

- Youtube videos by Kings and Generals

- Cimbrian War 113–101 BC - Roman - Germanic Wars DOCUMENTARY

- Youtube video by Mimir's Brunner

- The Cimbrian War Part 1, Disaster and Migration

- Youtube video by Gillian Perkins

- How to Self-Publish Your First Book: Step-by-step tutorial for beginners

- Youtube videos by Brandon Sanderson

- o Brandon Sanderson Lecture 11: Three Rules for Fight Scenes (3/7)

- o Sanderson 2012.11 - Fight Scenes & Romances

- o Lecture #9: Characters — Brandon Sanderson on Writing Science Fiction and Fantasy

- Illustrations were gathered from Flickr, Unsplash and Pixabay.

- o In character illustrations my dear friend Ms Mari Matsui kindly used Adobe Illustrator to make adjusted copies that I found to give readers a basic frame to image characters. Some images of Rome from the named sources that depict how Rome probably once looked. Thank you so much Mari-san!

- Illustrations from https://sites.psu.edu/successoftheromans/

- Autocrit: Great editing program. Very effective at story enhancements.
- Speechify: Super helpful for me to listen to what I wrote while I drove and to gain perspective as a listener.

Image sources

---

[1] Roman Arch, Copyright free:

https://www.flickr.com/photos/psulibscollections/5832829634/in/photostream/

[2] Ancient Rome Copyright Free:
https://www.flickr.com/photos/psulibscollections/5833544816/in/photostream/

[3] Image of Ancient Rome, Copyright Free:
https://www.flickr.com/photos/psulibscollections/5832221541

[4] NOTE: While the defeat of the Greek army at Scarpheia by the Romans was a complete route, I was unable to find any actual information about the battle, and so the battle as it is described is this author's imagination.

Made in the USA
Columbia, SC
27 November 2023

26795911R00331